We'll Meet Again

Also by Elise Darcy

The Living Apart Together Series

Living Apart Together

It Takes 2 to Tango

Dear John

Love on the Rooftop

Standalone books

Lola & The Man

A Mallorcan Affair

The Villa in Sicily

We'll Meet Again

A Novel

ELISE DARCY

Penny Lane Press

ISBN 978-1-913147-05-1

"It is so important to keep going, keep smiling and keep hoping." Dame Vera Lynn

1

Autumn 2015

Cassie was sitting at the kitchen table scrolling through her Facebook page, keeping an eye on the time. Her late shift was starting in thirty minutes. She was about to put her phone away when she noticed a text from a cousin asking if she'd heard any further news about their grandmother.

Cassie blinked in surprise. She stared at the message. Had something happened to her beloved grandmother? Her sister hadn't been in contact to let her know, but then that wasn't surprising. They weren't close. Cassie hadn't spoken to her sister in years. Perhaps if she lived around the corner or in the next town, or even the same country, it might encourage them to keep in touch. A continent separated them.

Cassie scrolled through her sister's Facebook page showing photos of her husband and their two children, a girl and boy eight and ten years old, outside their apartment building in Toronto. She couldn't believe how grown up they looked. There was also a photo of their youngest, her little nephew she'd never met. There were still photographs up of their wedding day ten years ago. All her sister ever wanted was the white wedding, be a stay-at-home mum, and raise children. Sometimes she wondered if there wasn't such an age-gap between them or if she too had been blessed with a family, shared experiences of motherhood might have brought them closer.

Cassie frowned. The only mention of her grandmother was that she felt poorly last week. 'Are you kidding me?' Cassie said to the empty room. 'You couldn't get in touch and let me know?' She raced over to the phone and called her sister in Canada. There was no answer. She'd forgotten about the time difference. Her sister's husband would be at work and she would be doing the school run. Cassie rang her mobile, hoping she still had the same number, nervous about making that call.

She'd last spoken to her sister when their mother passed away five years ago, the year Cassie turned forty. It wasn't how she envisaged spending her fortieth flying home to attend her mother's funeral. She stared at the photos online of her sister's children while she waited on the phone. Had it really been that long since she'd seen them?

Cassie was about to ring off when she heard a woman's voice at the end of the phone. At first, she didn't recognise her. 'Oh, sorry. Wrong number.'

'Cassie?'

'Emma?'

There was a pause on the end of the line. 'Look, I'm kinda in a rush, Cassie, so I haven't got time to talk—'

'We haven't spoken in almost five years and you can't spare a few moments to talk to me?' Cassie frowned. She was being unreasonable. Did she expect her sister to drop everything?

'School run?' Cassie asked, wondering if that was the reason, although she had an idea that even if she had time, she wouldn't want to stay on the phone. Apart from being related, they had nothing in common. Their lives couldn't be more different. She imagined after dropping the two older children off at school, her sister would meet her friends in the park, perhaps followed by some lunch. It was the life Emma always wanted and a world away from her older sister who had a twelve-hour shift ahead of her, on her feet all day working as an occupational therapist in a busy London hospital.

'Cassie, I've got back-to-back meetings arranged today.'

'Yes, I can imagine.' Cassie didn't mean to sound sarcastic. Perhaps she had an appointment at the salon for some beauty treatments?

Cassie glanced at the clock on the kitchen wall; if she didn't speed it up a bit, she'd be late for her shift. 'Look, the reason I phoned…'

'Cassie, this really will have to wait. I'm at work.'

'Work? You've got a job?'

'Yes. There is such a thing as *working mothers*.'

Cassie shook her head. She made it sound quite noble of her to raise children *and* go to work as though she deserved a medal for something most people, without children, did every day. It still surprised Cassie that her sister had a job. She wondered what had precipitated such a change in her circumstances.

'You haven't split up from Don, have you?' Cassie blurted before she could stop herself.

'Of course not. Whatever gave you that idea?'

The fact that you're at work; something she would never have even contemplated unless there was a bloody good reason.

Cassie remembered the time and cut to the chase. 'Our cousin messaged me on Facebook about Grandma. I'm worried that she's not well or something's happened…'

'Well, if you were around—'

Cassie knew what she was referring to. She recalled that conversation like it was yesterday, her sister's accusatory tone when she said, 'I was there when Mum got ill. Dad was hopeless, he couldn't cope with it. She needed help to go through her illness. Where were *you*?'

'I live in England,' Cassie had reminded her. 'What was I supposed to do from this distance?' Cassie recalled feeling as though she was making excuses. Emma needed her big sister around to support her emotionally through losing their mother and Cassie wasn't there for her. She left her to do everything, even the funeral arrangements. It didn't help their already strained relationship when all Cassie did was turn up at the last minute to attend the funeral. And she realised who she had to thank for that. Cassie looked up as her husband walked through the door. She frowned at him.

He frowned in return. 'Oh, I didn't expect you to be here. Doesn't your shift start in ten minutes?'

'Crap!' Cassie looked at him wide-eyed and said to her sister, 'Look, is Grandma okay? I'm worried. Did something happen?'

'She had a fall.'

'Why didn't you let me know?'

'Don't blame me because you rarely get in touch.' Her sister's voice softened. 'It was really sudden. It happened the day before yesterday and we took her into hospital.'

'How long?'

'What do you mean *how long?*' There was a pause. 'Oh, it's

nothing like that. They're just keeping her in for observation because she had a slight concussion.'

Cassie's heart stopped pounding in her a chest.

'I'd rather be by her bedside, but I've got a meeting. As soon as it wraps up, I'm going back to the hospital. She enjoys having visitors. It would have been helpful if it wasn't all down to me…'

Cassie got the jibe loud and clear.

Emma said, 'I was going to phone. . .'

'Yeah – right!'

'Okay, I wasn't going to phone. I assumed you wouldn't have put yourself out to come back to see her if you didn't do it for mum.'

'That's not fair. It wasn't like that.'

'Oh, really? So how was it *exactly*? Nothing would have stopped me making it home to see her before she died – no matter where in the world I lived.'

Cassie gave her husband a black look as he walked past her into the kitchen.

He mouthed *what?*

She thought if it weren't for him, she would have dropped everything five years ago and flown home. Like a fool, she'd listened to him and put her husband first when he persuaded her not to go because it wasn't convenient for him.

He'd jacked in his old job in I.T. and decided on a change of career. Influenced by how much his wife enjoyed her clinical role in the NHS, and with a background in science which he'd studied at university, he'd applied for a place on an accelerated course to train to become a doctor. He said he needed her support, and wanted her at home, not flying back to Canada. It couldn't have come at the worst time for him.

Him, him, him. It was always about him. It was her mother for goodness' sake; why didn't she have it out with him when he made her choose? But more than that, why didn't she have a bit of backbone and put herself first for once in their relationship? She wouldn't make the same mistake with her grandmother.

Cassie was relieved she was all right, but what if she hadn't been okay? 'I want to see her. I'll come home.'

'Whatever,' Emma replied dismissively. 'I've got to go.'

Cassie replaced the handset. She could hear him in the kitchen, busy preparing a meal for one. He poked his head into the lounge and said again, 'I didn't expect you to be in when I got home from work. What's going on?'

'I'm thinking of . . .' Cassie rephrased. 'I'm going to see my grandmother in Canada.' A*nd you can't stop me this time,* Cassie wanted to add.

She expected some resistance. She was gearing up to receive a nice dollop of emotional blackmail. He would ask her to think about it first which gave him ample opportunity to wear her down and get her to change her mind.

He'd never been interested in going to see her relatives in Canada. It had always been so one-sided; all the holidays and special occasions, like birthdays and Christmas, they spent with his family in England. Over the years, she'd made excuses for him like it was work or he didn't enjoy long-haul flights.

Although there was that one holiday they went to Barbados, which was a longer flight than to Toronto. It was never *the right time* to visit her relatives.

Why was she still standing there staring at her husband as though she was waiting for him to give her permission? She said, 'I'm going, and that's final.'

He looked at her askance. 'Christ, Cassie, you say it as though I'm going to object or try to talk you out of it.'

Cassie looked at him. 'Well, aren't you?'

'Of course not – why would I?'

Because you've selfishly done that in the past, thought Cassie. Every. Single. Time. And I've been the biggest fool for letting you have your way.

'I think it's an excellent idea.'

'You do?' She was taken aback. 'What about you? I know you won't be able to drop everything—'

He was already shaking his head. 'No, you're right. I can't.'

She didn't think so. 'But you still don't mind me going on my own without you?' Cassie winced. Why was she still asking him?

'No, not at all. It's a splendid idea.'

Cassie stared at him. Since when did he *ever* encourage her to do something just for her when there would be nothing in it for him? The saying, *a leopard doesn't change its spots*, came to mind. What was going on? It made her suspicious that he wanted her out of the picture for some reason. She'd noticed over the last few weeks her husband had been avoiding her. At least it felt that way.

He worked as a doctor at the same hospital. They used to organise their shifts, so they had time together. Now it was the reverse. Often, she was already on her way to work when he arrived home. That's why her presence had taken him by surprise. They were like ships passing in the night.

She'd brought it up one day when she caught him as she was walking in the door and he was walking out. He blamed it on the new computer system that generated shift patterns. That excuse was fine, but as a doctor he had more say over his hours. She noticed he was working unsocial hours – lates, nights and weekends. Was he doing it on purpose just to avoid her?

'You had better get going,' he said, glancing at the clock on the wall. Cassie eyed him standing there with a colander in one hand and a fresh sprig of parsley in the other. Of the two of them, he was the one who did most of the cooking. Whereas Cassie wasn't one for spending ages in the kitchen – she was quite happy to pop something in the microwave – her husband had always enjoyed cooking from scratch with fresh ingredients.

He also relished shopping in small individual food stores, hunting down a herb he needed for a new recipe he wanted to try. Cassie didn't have the patience and would much rather visit the local supermarket and get the shopping over with all in one go.

She glanced from the chopping board to the pan heating on the stove and wondered what he was preparing. She missed his home cooking. It would have been nice if some leftovers from those tasty meals he made were put aside for her, but that never happened. Cassie had started to shop for her own groceries and often microwaved a ready meal when she got in from work.

Cassie put on her coat. 'I'll be off then.'

'Right.'

She watched him pluck two fresh leaves from the sprig of parsley. She added, 'When I get back, I'm going to search online and book my flight.'

'Fine.'

Fine? Was that it? Cassie stopped doing up the buttons on her coat and looked at him. In the past, when there was something she fancied doing and he did not, he would have worn her down until she changed her mind and came around to his way of thinking. She wasn't stupid. The fact that he was not doing that meant only one thing: he wanted her to go. But why? Surely, it wasn't because her grandmother was in hospital and, for the first time in their marriage, he was thinking about her?

The way she felt about Lars right now made him out to be hellish to live with, but apart from his selfish side, he did more than most husbands. He cooked and cleaned so she didn't have to lift a finger. Even though she was happy to share the household chores as they both worked full time, he wouldn't hear of it. She knew her version of cleaning was a quick wipe round, an even quicker hoover, and she was done. The same with the ironing; a quick rub over and she was finished. Bed making?

No hospital corners for her, which was kind of ironic as she worked in a hospital. Lars, on the other hand, liked to take his time and do everything thoroughly. Cassie spent her free time avoiding the gym even though she spent a fortune on membership, preferring to sit on the sofa reading a novel. She volunteered a few hours a week at a local hospice which reminded her that life was too precious to waste on extreme spring cleaning or hours spent ironing to get those creases just right.

Her eyes drifted to the ingredients sitting in neat little piles on the chopping board. When they first met, she thought he was doing this sort of thing to impress her. However, it didn't take long, and it got on her nerves.

Although she appreciated he loved cooking, why couldn't he buy a jar of cooking sauce just once instead of spending hours in the kitchen preparing everything from scratch? Maybe they'd have had more time in the evenings to watch a movie or play a board game or talk? Cassie frowned. That was a moot point now they hardly spent time at home together. This was the most she'd seen of her husband or spoken to him in weeks.

She lingered by the kitchen door. 'I'll book my flight then as soon as I get in from work.'

He barely looked up. 'Great.'

'I'll see you when I see you.'

'Yes, that sounds grand.'

Cassie narrowed her eyes. As usual, he hadn't listened to a word she'd just said. She felt like saying, *by the way, when I get back from Canada, I'm leaving you.* Just to see what his reaction would be. Perhaps he'd just nod his head and say, *that sounds grand.* She wouldn't say that in a million years, so why had the thought even crossed her mind? Cassie spent her commute to work on the crowded tube pondering that question.

2

Cassie paused with her tray and spotted her friend across the room in the busy hospital canteen. She walked over and placed her tray on the table.

Her friend looked up. 'Hey, why the long face, Cassie?'

'I'm working a double shift today, Dawn.'

Dawn, a nurse, commiserated. 'But you didn't answer my question. You love your job, even if you're on a double shift, so why the long face?'

Cassie stared at the hot meal on her tray. She'd got so tired of microwave meals at home that she'd started having her dinner at work. The food wasn't bad, and she'd tuck in, ravenous after hours on her feet, but today she'd lost her appetite. She pushed her plate away.

Dawn glanced at Cassie's plate. 'That's not good. Is everything all right?'

Cassie recalled the conversation she had with her husband before she left for her shift, and how he supported her decision to visit her grandmother in Canada.

It wasn't just that bothering her but the *ships passing in the night* issue to do with their shifts. Well *his* shifts.

Cassie looked across the table at her friend. 'It's our work patterns at the moment. I realise they have brought in this new computer system which allocates the shifts, but it's not like before when there was flexibility over when we wanted to work.'

Dawn nodded. 'Tell me about it. I suppose it's a fairer system. At least they spread the unsocial hours equally among the staff.'

Cassie frowned. 'That's just it. Lars keeps getting the late shifts and the nights. I don't understand it. There has to be something wrong with the system if—'

'There's nothing wrong with the system, Cassie.'

'What makes you so sure?'

Her friend paused.

'What is it? What are you not telling me?'

'Look, I've only worked on the same ward with your husband a few times, but I noticed he was swapping and volunteering to work additional hours when someone goes off sick.'

'Working *extra* hours?' Cassie stared at her blankly. Now she considered it, he spent an inordinate amount of time at work. She would understand if they needed the extra money, but they didn't. They weren't saving for anything, as far as she was aware. Nobody volunteers for those sorts of hours, week in and week out, without good reason.

Her friend continued, 'Whatever shifts they have given him, he's been changing them. That's what I noticed on the ward. So maybe he's doing that elsewhere in the hospital too.' She looked at Cassie. 'Surely, he's not working just lates and nights?'

Cassie shook her head. 'Well, no. But that's the other thing. When I'm on a late shift, he's on early.'

'Anyone would think he was trying to avoid you,' she joked. 'Either that or he's seeing—' her friend stopped.

'— someone,' Cassie concluded.

Dawn registered the look on her face. 'Cassie, I wasn't being serious. You know me and my sense of humour. How long have I known you? You've been married for years. That's the last thing I'd expect, which is why I said it as a joke. Ignore that last remark.'

Cassie wanted to ignore that remark. Affairs happened to other people. It happened in books. It happened on television. But not to ordinary people. Not to her.

They had worked hard and paid off their mortgage, which was an achievement considering they were only in their mid-forties. At last, things had become more manageable, comfortable even. The years of struggling with a mortgage in London on public sector pay was now over. They had savings and a cash home; an apartment for which they scrimped and saved to pay off and call their own.

Cassie was looking forward to retiring early. It would also mark the start of a new decade; in five years she'd turn fifty in the year 2020. She had already made some plans. They could rent the flat out and go travelling. Live somewhere cheap. Thailand came to mind for the winter months. She imagined sitting on a beautiful beach in the Far East, which was light-years away from dreary London and long shifts in the hospital.

Cassie had considered reducing her hours and going part time. She loved her job. Retiring from her profession as an occupational therapist seemed like an enormous leap. But there was more to life than work.

The reason they could both retire early was simple; they did not have the expense of raising children and they wouldn't have the complications of caring for grandchildren. Cassie's dream of retirement came with a tinge of regret for what might have been. As her mother used to say, everything comes at a price. For Cassie, that price was having a family.

Although she wanted children, her husband did not. He liked things the way they were – just the two of them. They didn't have that conversation when they first met. It wasn't a discussion you needed to have, was it? She assumed that marriage meant starting a family. Then she fell pregnant but lost the baby. She had a miscarriage. That's when he told her how he felt: he was so relieved. It wasn't the right time – for him.

That was the rocky patch in their marriage. While her friends were having children, she was struggling with the fact that she had to choose – him or a baby. She couldn't have both. In the back of her mind there had always been the hope that one day he would be ready.

'Cassie?'

Cassie had been sitting there staring at her cold meal, revisiting old wounds. 'Sorry, I was miles away.'

'Do you want to talk about it?'

She shook her head at her sympathetic friend who guessed there was more; but some things Cassie could never talk about even to Dawn.

He hadn't come right out and said, 'It's a baby or me,' but he might as well have. He'd confessed when she'd lost the baby that he didn't want it anyway.

When she looked back on it now, she wondered why she stayed with him after that. He wasn't going to change his mind. He said it so matter-of-factly that he didn't want children. What made it worse was the way he failed to take on board what she suffered losing a child.

Despite that, she'd stuck by him. She'd married him because she loved him and she believed in her marriage vows; marriage was for better or worse, through the good times and the bad. That was fine if you'd married the right person. Cassie tried not to think about the doubts that crept in back then. It was a bleak place where she didn't want to venture; the possibility she'd spent all these years married to the wrong man.

'Look, Cassie, his shifts – it's probably nothing. I bet if you speak to him, it will turn out that it's just been one of those things and you're reading too much into it. Everything will get back to normal – you'll see.'

Why didn't Cassie think it was just one of those things? Why did she have this feeling in the pit of her stomach that something wasn't right? 'What about these extra shifts?' She didn't know why she was asking Dawn. It was him she should be confronting.

Dawn reached for Cassie's hand and gave it a reassuring squeeze. 'You know what I think? He's working extra shifts and unsocial hours to save some money for your fiftieth.'

Cassie frowned. 'That's five years off yet.'

'Yes, but what if it is something big, like a really special surprise? He probably needs to start saving now.'

It had crossed Cassie's mind that he was in the throes of planning a surprise for her fiftieth. Perhaps it was extra-special to mark her big birthday and a double celebration for their retirement too. The problem was it didn't quite add up. They already had savings. It wasn't like years ago, at the start of their careers, when low incomes meant they needed to work overtime to make ends meet. Now, one of them could give up work and they'd still manage comfortably. They had more than enough money to afford an expensive cruise or a massive party.

There was another explanation; she would notice if he was withdrawing cash from their joint savings to pay for something. Perhaps that was it. She hadn't checked that account, but she imagined if he was planning a surprise, he didn't want to dip into those funds otherwise he'd have to explain where the money went. He was in a rock and a hard place; by working these extra shifts she was bound to become suspicious about what he was up to. Cassie said as much to Dawn.

'There you go. It's tough as a couple for one of you to surprise the other without giving the game away or raising suspicions that you're up to something behind your partner's back. It may be perfectly innocent, but you're bound to wonder what's going on. It's only natural.'

Cassie felt much better for talking to her friend. In fact, her appetite had returned. 'I think I'll grab a sandwich.'

Dawn watched Cassie take her tray and empty the contents in the bin before joining the lunch queue again. Dawn really hoped it was nothing, but she'd seen Lars on the ward speaking to a junior nurse. It was the nature of their job that they spoke with colleagues all the time, discussing patients. She spotted them outside in the corridor as she walked toward the ward. However, although she couldn't hear their conversation, something told her they were not talking about work.

It was the way they stood close together that caught her attention; the junior nurse with the blonde ponytail had her back against the wall. He was standing there in front of her, one hand on the wall, leaning in, talking in hushed voices. Any closer and they could have kissed.

She brushed that thought aside. It was only after what Cassie said that she was now reading into what was most likely an innocent encounter between two staff members about work. In which case was it worth even mentioning to Cassie? She was approaching the table with a pre-packaged sandwich.

'I feel so much better after our chat. I can't wait to find out what surprise he has in store.'

She looked at Cassie's smiling face and decided against telling her what she'd seen in the corridor. She hoped, for Cassie's sake, the surprise didn't have something to do with a young, fresh-faced nurse with the blonde ponytail.

3

Cassie took off her coat and hung it by the front door. She left her handbag on the sofa as she walked through the lounge. She was aiming straight for the kitchen to make herself a cup of tea. It was the end of another working week, and this was her usual routine after a long shift at the hospital.

She opened the door and came to an abrupt halt. Standing in the kitchen was her husband. A few weeks ago, this wouldn't have surprised her. Apart from the odd time they worked alternate shifts, she would arrive home to find Lars preparing the evening meal. But that had become a thing of the past – until today.

It shocked her to see him. She looked him up and down. He was wearing an apron. 'Are you cooking dinner?'

He waved a spatula at her. 'What does it look like?'

She spotted a saucepan on the hob. 'Aren't you leaving for your next shift at work?'

'Nope.'

'You mean we're having dinner together?'

'Yep.'

Cassie didn't know what to say.

'Would you like a cup of tea? I've put the kettle on,' he said offhand as he stirred the contents of the saucepan. He turned around when she didn't reply. 'What's the matter?'

'You didn't mention having supper together this evening.'

'Oh, didn't I?' He got out a packet of pasta from one of the kitchen cupboards.

'I assumed you were on a late shift.'

'Why did you assume that?'

Because you're never around when I'm home, Cassie felt like saying.

'Why don't you put your feet up in the lounge? You look exhausted.'

She blinked just to make sure she wasn't imagining all this. After a long shift, she wouldn't be surprised if her mind *was* playing tricks on her.

'I'll bring you in a cup of tea.' He shooed her out of the kitchen.

Cassie slipped off her shoes and sat down on the sofa. She put her feet up. From her vantage point on the couch, she could see him walking back and forward from the hob to the cupboards. She spied him laying the table and thought she heard a cork popping. Was he opening a bottle of wine? She was straining her neck to see what he was up to, when he walked out of the room. 'Here.' He passed her a mug of tea.

'Thank you.'

'You're welcome.'

She watched him return to the kitchen. *What was all this in aid of?* As she sat there sipping her tea, Cassie recalled the conversation she had with Dawn in the hospital canteen the other day. How prophetic if after worrying that something wasn't right –

Cassie had been building up to confronting him – it turned out he had a surprise in store after all. Was this what the meal was about? Had he been working all these unsocial shifts to set aside the money to surprise her with something? Did Lars have to plan it well in advance? Her big birthday, coinciding with retirement, was still some way off. So why was he telling her now?

Although it would be nice to discover what he was planning, after the past few weeks clocking into work and then returning to an empty flat, Cassie just wanted her husband back; the man who would cook her dinner, make her a cuppa when she arrived home from work dead on her feet, and massage said feet later in the evening when sitting on the sofa together.

Theirs was a comfortable, easy-going relationship. She missed that. She missed *them,* the life they had together before things changed. Despite Dawn convincing her she was reading way too much into his shift patterns, she couldn't shake an uneasy notion that something was going on that had nothing to do with a big birthday or their future retirement plans. *So ask him!*

He poked his head around the door. 'Dinner in five.'

Cassie got up from the sofa and walked into the kitchen. There were two glasses and a bottle of wine on the table. She sat down as he placed an enormous oval dish on the dinner table. 'Tuna pasta bake!' she exclaimed in surprise.

'Your favourite.'

She watched him pour the wine. Cassie picked up her glass and smiled at him across the table. 'What shall we drink to?' Before he replied, she said, 'The two of us?'

He hesitated.

She lowered her glass. 'What is it?'

'Let's eat.' He picked up his knife and fork.

That uneasy feeling was back again. This time she could not ignore it. 'But—'

'We'll talk afterwards, Cassie. Let's enjoy the meal.'

She put her glass on the table and was about to say no, she would not eat until they'd talked about the last few weeks. She needed to find out what was going on. She didn't care if it meant she'd spoil his surprise – if that's what this was all about – she just wanted to know why he'd been avoiding her.

She glanced at her plate and reconsidered. He'd gone to all this trouble to cook her favourite meal; the last thing she wanted was to spoil their first evening together in ages. What if this was leading up to the surprise he had in store for her? She could be about to ruin everything he'd planned just because she wouldn't do as he asked.

She picked up her knife and fork. Cassie studied him thoughtfully as they sat there eating their meal. They'd first met at a mutual friend's dinner party. It wasn't the sort of thing she'd normally go to, but her friend had twisted her arm. Cassie thought she'd be the odd one out, but it turned out her friend had an ulterior motive; she wasn't the only singleton there that evening.

All the other guests were couples. Neither of them expected they would hit it off with a perfect stranger. A short time later, Cassie moved in with him. Lars was tall, six foot two, slim built with blonde hair and piercing blue eyes. He blamed it on his Scandinavian genes. Lars' family originated from Sweden, although he had been born and brought up in England.

He had changed little in the years they'd been together, apart from the thinning hair. A year younger than Cassie, he still kept himself in shape by cycling to work.

She glanced at him across the table. She didn't know where he found the energy. After her shifts at the hospital, all she did was slump on the sofa with a book.

Lars loved sport and being outdoors. Cassie once expressed an interest in getting a bike. She imagined a gentle cycle ride on a Sunday afternoon together through Hyde Park and along the banks of the Serpentine. Afterwards they could stock the wicker basket on the front of her bike with warm croissants and the Sunday papers on the way home. When he accompanied Cassie to the shop and introduced her to the sleek racing bikes, like his own, and all the skin-tight cycling gear, Cassie pointed out an altogether different bicycle she had in mind.

He'd looked at it in disdain, shrugged his shoulders, and said, 'It's your choice.' That comment undermined her resolve to do something different and buy the bike there and then. She never went back and bought one. Probably because she knew she'd have no one to go out with for a Sunday bike ride.

Quiet and reserved, her husband's idea of the perfect evening was cooking a meal and watching television after going out for a run or a cycle ride on his own. She was an extrovert. On paper, they weren't a match made in heaven, but it worked. Although they had different interests, at the weekends they used to make time for each other, often dining out. Cassie would coax him out to a pub or bar in the heart of London.

Sometimes Cassie would persuade Lars to come clubbing if there was a venue with an eighties-themed night. He always looked uncomfortable surrounded by people like Cassie jumping up and down, arms thrown high in the air dancing to the New Romantics, reliving that special time in their lives; those teenage years when life was full of possibilities. She once mentioned how clubbing took her back to when she was young and carefree. He pointed out that was the advantage of not having children; they didn't have to grow up. They could go on holiday when the mood took them and indulge their hobbies outside of work, without feeling guilty about spending money on themselves instead of the kids. She knew what he was talking about; he spent a small fortune on his bikes and the canoeing holidays with his pals – another one of his passions.

Sometimes she wondered if their relationship worked so well because they led their own lives. It meant when they did things together, they always had plenty to talk about.

Cassie finished her meal and put her knife and fork down on her empty plate. She frowned at him across the table. The meal passed in silence. It was the first time she noticed they had nothing to say to one another. What made it worse was he'd spent the entire meal checking his phone. Now he looked as though he was sending a text.

Cassie pushed her plate to one side. 'Who are you texting?'

He put the phone down and looked up. 'There's something I need to tell you…'

4

There's something he needs to tell me. Cassie smiled. This was what she had been waiting for. He would reveal the secret he'd been keeping from her. Perhaps they would do something together they'd never done before, like take a cruise or even a trip to Canada to visit her family. It was what she'd wanted to do since they married. The next words out of his mouth stunned Cassie. 'I want to start a family.'

She looked at him as though he was stark raving mad. Cassie didn't know what to say. 'Ah, wait a minute, you're joking - right?' Her husband had always been a bit of a joker. Although given their history – Cassie losing their first child and then finding out he did not want children – it wasn't something she would expect him to joke about.

Lars sat there in silence.

'This isn't a joke, is it?'

He shook his head.

She stared at him across the table, at a loss what to say. He never wanted kids before. He was in his forties. Was this some sort of mid-life crises? With another big birthday on the horizon, was he having regrets over not becoming a father?

Although she never admitted it, she always felt her husband was too selfish to have children. This was the last thing she expected. What if she was too old to have a baby? Had he thought about that? The chances of conceiving in your forties were quite low. Would she need IVF to conceive at her age? That could cost thousands.

Her thoughts were racing until it came to an abrupt halt. Was that why he'd been working all hours; to save money for IVF treatment? Perhaps he didn't like to broach the subject with her, after all these years, because he was the one who decided against having children, and now he'd changed his mind. He must be conscious of the fact that time wasn't on their side.

Cassie looked at his downcast expression. 'Why didn't you tell me what was on your mind weeks ago?'

He stole a glance at her. 'Because it worried me how you'd take it.'

Cassie sighed. He was aware she'd always wanted a child. 'It will not be easy. I can't guarantee it's not too late for me to have a baby.'

'Oh, when I said I wanted children, I didn't mean with you.'

Cassie knitted her brow. 'You mean a surrogate?'

'What are you talking about?'

Cassie frowned. 'I don't know. What are *you* talking about?'

'Isn't it obvious?'

'Oh, I see. You're considering adoption.'

'Adoption? I don't want to adopt. Whatever gave you that idea?'

'But you just said—'

'Do I have to spell it out?' He breathed a weary sigh and gave her a condescending look.

Cassie didn't appreciate his tone or that look. 'Okay, spell it out, why don't you because I do not understand what—'

'I've met someone.'

'You've met someone? What are you talking about?' Now Cassie had lost the plot. Weren't they just discussing having a baby?

'We've sorted out a place. I'm moving out.'

'You're moving out?' She looked at him, unable to wrap her head around what he was saying. 'But I don't understand. One minute we were having a nice meal and chatting about—'

'Don't act all surprised. We haven't been together like that for weeks.' He threw his napkin down on the table. 'It's comical that you imagined I wanted us to have kids when we haven't even been sleeping together. To be honest, I felt you might have guessed by now what was going on.'

Cassie shuddered. This must be the mother of all practical jokes. Any minute now he would point at her, and say, 'You really fell for it this time. You should see the look on your face…'

Lars said no such thing. He remained deadly serious.

Cassie took a deep breath. 'Let me get this straight. You mean all this time you've been working different shifts because you were seeing someone else?'

'Good grief, Cassie, how can you be so dense?' Lars got up from the table.

She gave him a cold, hard stare. When he changed career and became a doctor, he'd developed this condescending attitude towards her. It was as though he looked down at her because she wasn't a doctor, wasn't in his league. She'd tried to ignore it hoping he'd snap out of it. He didn't. Ever since he qualified, she had noticed the change in him.

She sat there staring at him across the table, trying to get her head around all this, but she was having a hard time connecting the dots. It all seemed surreal.

He reached for her plate and picked it up. 'I'll pop these in the dishwasher.'

Cassie turned in her chair and watched him load the dishes as though nothing out of the ordinary had happened. She couldn't get over how flippant he was acting. It was obvious he felt this was no big deal, and that it was reasonable to cook your wife a meal, have dinner together, and then tell her you were leaving.

He walked back with something in his hands and placed it on the table.

She looked at the dessert; it was a homemade apple crumble. Her favourite. *What the hell?*

He took a seat. 'I thought we might sit down like two adults and talk through the practicalities.'

'The *what?*'

'You know, me leaving.'

She stared at the apple crumble. 'Over a last meal together.'

'That's right.'

Cassie wanted to pick up the dessert and throw it at him. Instead, she raised her eyes and asked, 'How long?'

'Pardon me?'

'How long have you been seeing someone else?' She didn't need to ask who she was. That was a foregone conclusion. He was a doctor. He worked in a hospital with an endless stream of young nurses. It was open season.

He didn't answer her question.

'How long have you been seeing her?'

It was the first time in the entire conversation he looked nervous. 'Let me see, it must be, oh I don't know…'

'I do. It started just before you changed your shifts to work nights and weekends, didn't it?'

'I suppose so.'

She rose from the table. 'All these weeks you've been seeing someone else, and you didn't tell me. That's… that's…' She couldn't put into words how she felt about that betrayal, apart from the obvious fact, 'We've still been sleeping together!'

'Oh, come on. Yes, we've shared a bed, but we haven't slept together in months.'

She opened her mouth to say something but couldn't argue with that. It was true.

He still hadn't finished. 'In fact, since I've been working nights, we've hardly shared a bed either.'

'And whose fault is that?' she threw back in anger, wanting to wipe that smug expression off his face.

'Okay, if you want to act like that then this conversation is over.'

Cassie was seething. She had every right to be angry, hurt and upset. It didn't help that, as usual, everything revolved around what he wanted. It was always about him. He didn't want children, so they didn't have them. He didn't want to go to Canada to see her family, so they didn't go. He didn't want to move out of London and buy a cottage with a garden, which Cassie had always wanted, so they stayed in their London flat. He didn't want to talk about it anymore, so that was the end of the conversation. Except he wasn't getting his way – not this time.

Cassie stood up and walked over to the kitchen door. 'This conversation is not finished.' She stood in the doorway. He had no escape. 'Why didn't you move out when you met this woman?' She folded her arms, waiting for him to tell her what she already knew; her husband had left her weeks ago, he just hadn't had the decency to tell her. And it was obvious why he hadn't moved out. It wasn't convenient. He was just hanging on here until they'd sorted out a place together. However, he didn't want any chance Cassie would kick him out in the meantime, so he just kept his distance, swopped his shifts and strung her along. He'd waited until the time was right – for him.

There she was, like the biggest fool, thinking he'd changed, putting her first when he encouraged her to book a flight to Canada to see her grandmother, and working unsocial shifts, saving up for a surprise for her.

She wished he hadn't brought up having children. He knew she'd always wanted a child. She assumed, after all these years, he'd reconsidered, and realised how selfish he'd been in their relationship. But not a bit of it. In fact, he was just as selfish and self-centred as ever, even at the end of their marriage. She eyed him coldly.

'I don't want to fight.' He stood up and thrust his keys to the apartment at her.

She stepped back in surprise, staring at the keys in her hand. Was he trying to pay her off by giving her the flat? Although she imagined he was only doing it for his benefit, to avoid further unpleasantness, she wasn't about to argue. At least it would be something to show for all the years they'd been married.

'I shall want my half.'

She raised her eyes. 'What?'

'We will have to get it on the market as soon as possible, unless you can buy me out.'

The flat had gone up in value since they first bought it. That didn't matter to Cassie. It was her home, the place she'd lived in for the last twenty years. He was aware she couldn't buy him out. She couldn't believe he would force her to leave. Just for a moment, when he handed her his keys, she imagined for once in their marriage, he was considering her needs for a change. The last thing she wanted was to lose her home as well as her husband. She threw the keys at him.

'Ow! What was that for?'

'What do you think?'

'Okay, I get it. You hadn't planned on moving. But you will have to find something else.' He shrugged. His whole demeanour said he couldn't care less. 'It's not as though you've got anything to worry about. Once we sell the flat and divide the proceeds, there will be more than enough to purchase another property.'

'Not in London. Not on my salary.'

'That's just it. I seem to recall you wanted a house.' He had it all figured out. 'You could move out of London and buy that place you have always wanted with a gard—'

'Are you serious?' She couldn't believe, after all these years, he had brought *that* up.

'What did I say?' He looked at her quizzically.

'You have no idea, do you? It's too late for a house with a garden, Lars. I wanted that when we were young, when I thought we would start a family.'

He changed the subject. 'I'm so glad we bought this flat though. It's turned out an excellent investment.'

'An investment?' She knew the Brits were obsessed with property values, but since when did they consider their home as an investment?

'The money will come in handy with a baby on the way.'

Cassie stopped and gaped at him. 'A baby on the way?' she intoned. 'Whatever do you mean?' For the first time since he told her he was leaving, he was tongue-tied.

She stared at him intently. She got the feeling he hadn't meant to say that. It just slipped out. 'You're seeing someone *and* she's pregnant?'

'It wasn't planned.'

I bet it wasn't, thought Cassie. What better way to trap a man, and a doctor at that, than by getting pregnant.

'It just kind of happened.' He shrugged. 'Now it has, I have surprised myself by coming round to the idea.'

'You're coming round to the idea?' Cassie was going through such a rollercoaster of emotions, she didn't know what to focus on first; her anger at the way he'd lied to her these past weeks or disgust at his behaviour. Or how upset she was that years ago, if she had fallen pregnant again, he might have come round to the notion of fatherhood instead of making it clear she better not bother trying for another child.

In hindsight, Cassie reflected, what kind of person makes you choose? And here he was telling his wife, the woman who gave up having children, he was starting to accept the idea of being a father.

'In fact, I'm looking forward to it. Not the nappy bit and the sleepless nights, but the thought there will be a little individual who looks up to me and calls me Dad, along with all the things I might do with him when he's older.'

'Him?'

'She had her three-month scan. We wanted to know so we can get the nursery ready. Exciting, isn't it?'

A moment later he was the other side of the front door to their basement flat, and Cassie had broken her favourite teapot. It was the first thing that came to hand when she had the impulse to throw something at him. She wished she'd reached for the apple crumble instead. Unfortunately, it was her teapot, and it didn't hit him but the wall when he ducked. That's when he took his cue to leave.

She heard him say through the letterbox. 'I've already had the flat valued by an estate agent. I'll instruct them, shall I?'

'Do what you want!' Cassie screamed at the door. 'You always do.'

'I'll take that as a yes, then.'

Her eyes drifted to the mess on the floor. She got a dustpan and began sweeping up the broken fragments. Five minutes later, she was sitting with her head in her hands, sobbing. The teapot, along with the matching cups and saucers, were the first things she'd bought when they'd set up home together before they married.

It was only an old teapot, but when they could afford new crockery for their updated kitchen, it had taken pride of place on a display shelf in the lounge. A pretty ornament, it had hardly been used. She had never made a pot of tea for the two of them. He was never a tea drinker. That silly thought made her cry even more.

5

Cassie was on an early shift. She'd applied copious amounts of concealer and foundation, but she wasn't fooling anyone, least of all her best friend. The puffy eyes gave it away that she'd been crying buckets.

Dawn caught up with her when she was leaving the ward for a coffee break. 'Are you all right, Cassie?'

Even though it was obvious she wasn't, Cassie shook her head anyway in answer to her question.

Dawn frowned. The pretty young nurse with the long, blonde ponytail came to mind. 'I'm guessing it turned out he *wasn't* saving for a surprise for your fiftieth?'

'Oh, it was a surprise all right,' Cassie replied, wishing she didn't sound so bitter.

As they walked along the hospital corridor towards the small staff café, Cassie told her all about what happened last night.

'Bastard!'

Cassie looked at Dawn as they took their cups of coffee to find a table. The café was filling up with staff on their morning break. Dawn said in a hushed voice as they sat down, 'I can't imagine what you're going through finding out that he's not only been unfaithful, but the other woman is pregnant.' She knew Cassie didn't have children. She cast a glance around the café. 'Do you know who he's seeing?'

Cassie followed her gaze. She realised what Dawn was thinking. The woman who ruined her life could be here, sitting at an adjacent table, chatting with her colleagues without a care in the world. Cassie shook her head. 'No, but I've got a pretty good idea. I bet he's besotted by a junior nurse. What a cliché – eh?'

Cassie frowned. If only she had known where supporting her husband to become a doctor would lead. She looked at Dawn and confided, 'I feel like getting away. I didn't want to come into work today in case I ran into him on a ward. I keep having sleepless nights, worried I might spot them together.' Cassie sighed. 'It's silly because I don't even know for sure if the woman works here.'

She caught Dawn biting her lower lip and avoiding her gaze. Cassie raised her eyebrows. 'You've seen something – haven't you.' Cassie leaned forward in her seat. 'Please tell me.'

The look on Dawn's face said she'd rather not. She sighed when she saw Cassie's pleading expression. 'I saw him chatting to a young, blonde-haired nurse.' She added, 'In our line of work that isn't unusual. We're talking to patients and colleagues all the time – you know how it is.'

'But something told you they weren't talking about work.' It wasn't a question. Cassie looked at her intently.

'You're right. It was their body language. He was standing a bit too close, almost—'

'Intimate?'

She nodded. 'I'm so sorry I didn't tell you. I just wanted to believe I was reading too much into it.'

They fell silent while they finished their coffee, both glancing at the clock on the wall. They didn't have long before they had to return to their respective wards.

Dawn set her empty coffee cup down on the table. 'What's this about you wanting to get away? Where will you go?'

Cassie shrugged. 'I have no idea, but I can't stay here.'

Dawn looked at her in surprise. 'But you're happy here. Why should you leave the job you love?'

Cassie glanced at her watch and stood up. She understood Dawn meant well. She was right: she didn't want to leave the hospital and find another job. Why should she? But the reality was Lars and his girlfriend would not jack in their jobs with a baby on the way.

Her friend followed her out of the café. 'Why don't you come round mine this evening? I'll get the kids to bed and then we can have pizza and chat some more – what do you think?'

She could tell that Dawn, a single parent, would not take no for an answer. Divorced herself a few years back, she was the prefect shoulder to cry on. She'd been through all this herself. But as much as Cassie would love to get away from the flat for a few hours, she had to decline. 'I've got a viewer this evening.'

'A viewer? Goodness, he didn't waste any time, did he?'

Cassie heaved a sigh. 'Tell me about it.'

She had been livid when she discovered he'd already instructed an estate agent. He couldn't complete the paperwork to instruct one without her signature, but he'd got around that by having it posted to her. Cassie signed the document and sent it by first class post to the agent. There was no point railing against the inevitable. What could she do about it? The flat had to be sold.

It was before her shift started, when she was about to turn off her mobile phone, that it rang. It was the estate agents. After checking she'd signed the contract to instruct them, and it was in the post, they booked a couple in for a viewing. They were sitting in the agent's office, very keen to be the first to see the flat.

Cassie spent the rest of her shift thinking about that appointment. She wasn't looking forward it.

6

Cassie heard the doorbell and felt a lump in her throat at the prospect of strangers nosing around her home. She had the impulse to ignore it. All she wanted to do was sit on the sofa reading her book and pretend this wasn't happening.

The doorbell chimed again. She recalled the estate agent telling her about the couple sitting in his office this morning, eager to arrange a viewing. It wasn't their fault they were turning up to a property about to meet a vendor who didn't want to sell.

If you were so dead set against selling, why did you sign the bloody contract? Cassie ignored that thought and listened to the voice of reason; she couldn't stop the inevitable. Her husband had left her. Unless the flat sold, she had no means to move on with her life and make a fresh start. As much as she wanted to ignore all this and pretend it wasn't happening, the practical side of her won out. Her job involved problem-solving, and this was an issue that had to be solved – and the quicker the better.

She put her book down and walked to the door. 'Here we go.' She took a deep breath and opened it.

The viewers, a couple in their early thirties, exchanged pleasantries and Cassie invited them inside. She noticed they had the property details to hand. The photos of their basement flat looked nice, although it made her wonder when Lars had had the estate agent around to take photographs. That was another perk of working different shifts; unbeknown to her, he had been setting the wheels in motion so he could get the apartment on the market as soon as it suited him.

She closed the front door and frowned at the young couple. She wasn't enthusiastic about showing them around. In hindsight, she wished she'd asked the estate agent to do it.

'This is the lounge,' Cassie said in a dead-pan voice. She was not inclined to tell them about the neighbourhood in West London. Shepherd's Bush was a lovely place to live with an eclectic mix of small individual shops and eateries. It's what first attracted her and Lars to this suburb of London.

She guessed the couple might already be familiar with the area. That's why they were here, eager for a chance to buy a well-maintained basement flat in a four-storey Victorian property. Best of all, it was located in a quiet tree-lined street. They rarely came on the market. And if they did, an investor would snap them up.

'It's wonderful. I just love it,' were the first words out of the woman's mouth.

Great. Cassie rolled her eyes. She wasn't surprised by her reaction, although she wondered how they afforded to buy in this location. She imagined they must work in the city. Nowadays, the salaries of public-sector workers wouldn't touch a place like this.

The couple walked through the lounge into the basement kitchen, then upstairs to the study on the landing and two double bedrooms. Space was what set it apart and why Cassie and her husband bought here. Spread over two floors, once inside, the flat felt like a house with the bonus of spacious rooms. Cassie was still frowning. Lars was right when he said it had proved an excellent investment. It upset her that, after all these years together, he could throw in the towel on their relationship and put their home on the market without batting an eyelid. Why was she surprised? With the end of their marriage it was just about the bottom line; all that concerned him was what he might get out of the flat so he could set up home with someone else.

She stood back watching the couple smiling at one another. 'You come across like two love-struck teenagers.' Cassie put her hand to her mouth in shock. She didn't know what came over her. What made it worse was the way she said it; the sarcasm, the bitterness in her voice was unmistakable. It was embarrassing. She shook her head. This wasn't working, showing viewers around her flat. It was rubbing her nose in it, meeting people just starting their journey together, knowing hers was over.

She was about to apologise when the woman said, 'Sorry, I guess we do come across like that which is pathetic at our age. We are almost forty.'

'Oh.' They looked younger. Maybe that's what falling in love does for you – keeps you young, thought Cassie. She wondered how much the odds were stacked against you finding Mr or Mrs Right as you got older.

As if reading her mind, the woman said, 'We were lucky to find each other again.'

'Again?' Cassie knitted her brow.

'Yes. I was crossing a busy London street when I bumped into him on the way to work.'

He smiled at her. 'Best thing that's ever happened to me, spilling my takeaway coffee down my shirt.'

She laughed. 'We hadn't seen each other since we were teenagers. I guess we're picking up where we left off.'

Cassie stared at them. 'How nice for you.' She did not want to hear this right now; why do some people's lives seem to fall into place so easily?

'So, why are you moving?'

Cassie sighed. And there it was, the reason she didn't want to show people around her home. Eventually, the question would pop up during the viewing. Whether it was just out of curiosity or potential buyers looking for a problem like horrible neighbours or barking dogs or a leaky roof; something that might put them off making an offer.

Cassie had already thought up several bullshit explanations like a job opportunity had come up in a different part of the country. That was the excuse she'd settled on. She opened her mouth, intending to say just that. However, when she looked at the couple standing in front of her, she didn't feel inclined to tell them a lie.

'My husband and I are splitting up. He's been having an affair and now he's moved out. His girlfriend is pregnant. She's probably a junior nurse by the way, half my age.' Cassie shrugged. 'So there you have it.' She could tell by their expressions, it was the last thing they expected to hear.

Flustered, neither of them knew what to say. It was the first time they were tongue-tied.

Cassie imagined she'd feel just as uncomfortable if she was in their shoes right now. The couple didn't know where to look as they hurried out the door. She liked them. They came across as nice, genuine people. The sort she'd like to sell to. However, she'd had enough of them oohing and aahing and making plans for the future centred on her home. Fifteen minutes later, the phone rang. She knew it would be the estate agents with an offer. The couple didn't even need a second viewing. It was everything they'd been looking for – and some. Cassie wasn't surprised in the least.

She sat on the end of the line listening to the estate agent. 'I'm duty-bound to put forward all offers, no matter how ridiculous. As far as I'm concerned, they're wasting everybody's time. I think they are rather naïve. Although they would love to live in the area, they don't have the incomes to afford it. We don't normally have their sort come into our estate agency.'

Cassie raised her eyebrows. 'Their sort?' She thought they were very pleasant. What on earth was he on about?

'What I mean to say is they are public sector workers.'

Cassie frowned. He said *public sector workers* as though it was a disease.

'He's a policeman and she's a social worker. They haven't got the incomes to afford to buy a property in your neighbourhood. They both have children from previous relationships. I believe she has a child that will live with them. There is an excellent school in the area. I can see why your flat would be perfect for them, but…' he trailed off.

Cassie understood. Nowadays their incomes meant they couldn't touch a place like this. She sighed. It was a shame. She really liked them. 'So, what is their silly offer?'

Cassie listened as her eyes roved around the kitchen, alighting on a small framed picture of her and Lars. Back then they were fresh-faced twenty-somethings, their happy smiling faces looking to the future.

She remembered that photo was taken by one of their

friends. They'd just got engaged. It was the day they put in an offer on this flat when people like them, a student and a newly qualified occupational therapist, could afford to live in this area. Cassie walked over with the cordless phone, picked up the photo and placed it face down on the worktop.

'I must apologise for wasting your time,' the estate agent was saying down the phone. 'I already told them that no one in their right mind will accept an offer that much below the asking price. It's ludicrous.'

'It's theirs.'

'Excuse me?' The estate agent paused before he said, 'Did you just accept their offer?'

Cassie sat down at the kitchen table. 'Yes, you can take it off the market and tell them the good news. Oh, and I'm throwing in all the furniture. They can have it fully furnished.' Cassie overheard a woman squealing with delight in the background. She smiled. They seemed like a sweet couple with luck on their side. Cassie recalled what they told her about meeting again after all those years apart. She gazed around her kitchen. Why shouldn't their luck continue?

Cassie wasn't completely selfless. This suited her. She didn't want to show any more viewers around. She had intended to leave it to the estate agents, but this was much better. Cassie liked that she had met the new owners. She knew she was being sentimental, but it pleased her no end that she would hand the keys over to a couple who would love the flat as much as she had. It was also great to think a family would live here. She didn't realise the woman had a child.

They probably couldn't believe their luck. Cassie was still smiling. She liked to think something good had come out of an awful situation. If it wasn't for them, she imagined it would have gone to an investor. She didn't want that.

Her husband wouldn't be happy with the offer one bit. Although he was desperate to sell and sever their ties, the problem he had was that the flat was in joint names. He needed her signature to proceed. Cassie decided she was only selling to the nice couple. She liked their story.

'Are you sure you want to accept this offer?'

'Absolutely.'

'I would have to check with your husband.'

'Go ahead.' Cassie grinned. He couldn't force her to sell to the highest bidder. He might be stuck with his ex-wife living in the flat forever or until he instructed a solicitor to get her out. That would cost money. With the expense of a baby on the way and the exorbitant price of renting in London, she imagined that was something he wished to avoid.

She had agreed to put the flat on the market to sell, but when Cassie was signing the paperwork she had already decided it would be on her terms. She'd just failed to tell him that. He was about to find out it wasn't only his wife who could have the rug pulled out from under her.

Cassie ended the call with the estate agent, leaving it to him to contact her husband and pass on the splendid news. She put her mobile phone on the kitchen table and smiled. She was expecting another call.

Five minutes later, her phone rang. She didn't pick it up straightaway. She sat there watching it ring and vibrate. Finally, she reached over and picked it up. 'Hello, Lars, what a surprise.'

'I've just got off the phone with the estate agents. What the hell are you thinking!?'

Cassie held the receiver away from her ear.

'Are you thick or something? That's way below market value! Are you out of your bloody mind?'

She nodded and smiled at his reaction. Some would use the phrase, *cutting off your nose to spite your face*, but she didn't care about the money. She'd lost everything, her husband, her home, the future she imagined together in retirement. What was a few thousand – give or take?

He'd notice it the most with his new commitments, but she didn't care about that either. That was *his* problem. Besides, Lars always fell on his feet. He'd work his way up to be a consultant. She imagined he wouldn't be short of a bob or two in the future. If she went to a solicitor, she'd probably get more than half the flat, much more.

She *had* supported him financially while he re-trained as a doctor. She reckoned she'd be entitled to a share of his pension too. Taking into consideration he would reach the dizzy heights of a consultant, it might not be an insubstantial sum. She could take him to the cleaners. But Cassie wasn't that way inclined. Her revenge was more straightforward and less involved; she gave their flat away instead.

'You stupid b—'

Cassie put the phone down and poured herself a glass of red wine to celebrate one minor victory in the car wreck that was now her life.

7

'You did *what*?' Dawn looked at her in horror when she told her the next day in the staff canteen. 'But you have given away tens of thousands of pounds. Can you afford that?'

'Nope.'

'You haven't signed on the dotted line – have you?'

Cassie thought of the nice couple and couldn't shatter their dream with a phone call. 'I can't go back on my word.'

'It's revenge, isn't it? Lars will stand to lose too.'

Cassie smiled.

'I never knew you had it in you. When I got divorced, I wished I'd had the guts to do something like that.'

Cassie looked at her friend. Her situation was different; Dawn had children to consider. She couldn't afford to do something rash. Cassie didn't have dependants. The tears rolled down her cheeks at the realisation she had nobody. No husband. No children. She was completely alone.

'Oh, Cassie. What did I say?'

'It's nothing you said.' She wiped her eyes dry with a tissue.

Dawn understood. 'When I was going through my divorce, I was an emotional wreck. I take my hat off to you the way you're handling things. You've been coping remarkably well. Too well.'

Cassie looked at her. 'What do you mean?'

'If you don't mind me saying, underneath this bravado, I bet you haven't been coping as well as you led people to believe.'

Cassie felt close to tears again. The least insignificant thing upset her. It wasn't surprising considering the circumstances. Dawn was right: she was making a show of holding it together. She turned up for work, got through her shifts and held her head up high when she saw him. At the hospital, she was the picture of professionalism and decorum. The problem was, she didn't know how long she could hold it together before—

Dawn interrupted her thoughts. 'Have you considered taking time off work? What about putting in for some annual leave?' She lowered her voice. 'Perhaps you could go to the doctors and get signed off with stress?'

Cassie didn't want to stay at home. Work was good. It kept her occupied and stopped her from collapsing in a heap, imagining her life was over. The problem was every day Cassie clocked into her job, she realised she might see him. That's what wasn't working for her. Taking annual leave or going off with stress was only a short-term solution. A week, a fortnight, a month later she'd be back to square one, having to face returning to her job and seeing him.

She took a deep breath. 'I need to get away.'

Cassie had spent yesterday evening searching the internet looking for another job. She told her friend.

'That's a bit drastic. Why don't you take a break somewhere and think it over first? What about booking that plane ticket to Canada to see your relations? How is your grandmother, by the way?'

'My grandmother?' How could she have forgotten her beloved grandmother? 'Dawn, I've just got to make a call.' Cassie walked out of the canteen swearing under her breath, 'Bloody Lars!' She wished he was here right now. She would give him a piece of her mind – professionalism and decorum be damned. She didn't care if the whole canteen heard her. This was his fault.

She stood in the corridor and switched on her mobile with a shaky hand, praying nothing untoward had happened in the last few days. Cassie was thinking of that concussion her sister had mentioned. She phoned Emma. Thank goodness, she answered straight away. 'Oh, it's you. I thought you were getting the next flight home?' Emma said with an edge to her voice.

Before Cassie responded, her sister added, 'Just as well you didn't.'

'Why?' Cassie's voice trembled.

'She's all better. They discharged her from hospital. She's home. No need for you to make the effort now.'

'That's not fair. I've had a few things going on.'

'Yeah – whatever. Don't suppose you'll bother coming.'

'Of course I will. I'm in the middle of something, but as soon as I've sorted out—'

The line went dead.

Cassie burst into tears. Now, more than any time in her life, she needed a mum or a sister to talk to. She still had her beloved grandmother – thank goodness. However, when she finally got around to that trip back home to see her, the last thing she wanted was to burden her grandmother with her problems.

There was Dad, but goodness knows where he'd be. Since retiring and losing their mother to cancer, he'd hit the road travelling around Canada, exploring his adopted country. Her father was British, but he'd lived in Canada since he was four years old. It was his dream to retire and buy an American RV or recreational vehicle. She was proud of him. He'd done it despite being alone. Although that wasn't strictly true. 'I hadn't reckoned on my travelling companion being a mutt called Albert,' he said of his dog fondly, last time they spoke.

Cassie smiled when she recalled her dad trying to make light of a sad turn of events. He'd just bought the RV and was fitting it out for their trip of a lifetime when her mother was diagnosed. Weeks later she was gone, and so was he, hitting the road and never looking back. Cassie was glad he left. It wouldn't do him any good sitting at home mourning her death. She missed him a lot. She missed them both.

She always kept in touch. Her dad was on Facebook too. When he had access to the internet, he'd message her or email. She looked at her phone and felt like calling him right now just to hear his voice. Cassie phoned his number.

She wasn't surprised it went straight to voicemail. It was likely he was on the road or somewhere remote with poor mobile reception. Cassie put her phone away. Perhaps it was just as well he wasn't contactable; she didn't want to worry him with her problems.

Cassie returned to the canteen. Her sandwich was still on her plate, half-eaten. 'I'm sorry I upped and left. I needed to make a call.'

'Is everything all right?' Dawn was staring at her concerned. 'Is your grandmother okay?'

Cassie breathed a sigh. 'Yes - thank heavens. With all that's been going on, I'd completely forgotten she was in hospital.' She grimaced. 'How bad is that?'

'Don't beat yourself up. It's understandable. I bet you feel you are walking around in a daze most of the time.'

Cassie nodded as she picked up the other half of her sandwich.

'Now, what were you saying about looking for another job?'

Before she got a word in, Dawn tried her best to talk her out of it. 'Your personal life has just been turned upside down, isn't that enough without things being up in the air with work too?'

Cassie listened while she finished her sandwich. 'I understand where you're coming from.' Cassie wiped her mouth with a paper napkin. 'I can't stay here. I see him almost every day.'

It wasn't just when she was in work that was the problem. There was the little café on the corner she passed each day where they used to go for coffee at the weekends. There was the flat. She was surrounded by things reminding her of the life they shared for so many years. 'I need to get away from everything.'

Her friend stared at her. 'You've applied for a new position already, haven't you?'

Cassie nodded. She'd trawled the internet and found opportunities for clinical staff around the country. She didn't want a job in a hospital as it would remind her of Lars. Then she saw an advert for a temporary position in a former stately home. It was now sheltered accommodation. The residents lived in apartments within the sprawling mansion. They also provided accommodation for their employees.

It was just what she needed, something far away from London, while she figured out what to do next. When the flat sold, she had a big decision to make; should she return to Canada and start over or stay in England?

Cassie knew she was being presumptuous, but as soon as she

filled in the online application, she'd got out two suitcases from her wardrobe, ready to pack up her belongings and leave. In her heart she realised once she closed the door on the flat, it would be for the last time. She wouldn't be back. She would drop her keys off at the estate agents and say farewell to married life.

'Where is the new job?'

'It's a place called Fletchling Hall in Sussex.' She told her friend she was drawn to the advert because the area was familiar. It was where it had all began; her life as a student occupational therapist in England. It was where she did one of her placements during her training. Back then it was a small cottage hospital; a throwback to the Second World War when the stately home was commandeered by the British Government. It became a convalescent home for soldiers after the war.

'It's the perfect location to escape my life in London.'

'Is it?'

Cassie looked at her friend. She was too insightful by half. As with all best-laid plans, there was a fly in the ointment. It didn't stop her applying for the position, although perhaps she'd rather it wasn't a place where she had a history.

Dawn sighed, realising Cassie had already made the decision to leave. 'Maybe it's not a bad thing to return somewhere familiar as you can't go home to Canada now. 'Is it a place with fond memories?'

'Yes and no.'

'Do you want to talk about it?'

'Not really. Besides, it's in the past – years ago.'

Dawn sighed. 'If they offer you the job, go for it. You know what they say: a change is as good as a rest.'

Cassie looked at her in surprise. 'You've changed your tune.

Now you sound as though you want me to go.'

'Not at all. For my own selfish reasons, I don't want you to leave. I will miss you. It's just I see how unhappy you are. Perhaps a change of scene, even though it's only temporary, will do you good. Put things into perspective. Make you realise he's not worth crying over.'

Cassie sipped her tea listening to her friend.

Dawn smiled knowingly. 'He'll soon change his tune when the baby is on the scene. Just you wait and see.'

'What do you mean?'

'Wait until reality sets in. It's hard work raising a child. The hardest work he'll ever encounter. I bet, in hindsight, he realises he had a splendid life with you. It will never surprise me if he comes crawling back to you, cap in hand, like the snake he is.'

'You think so?'

Dawn looked at her. 'Cassie, please don't tell me you'd even consider taking him back – promise me you won't.'

She couldn't make that promise. He was her husband. Could she forgive him? That was the question her friend should have asked. Cassie didn't know the answer to either of those questions. Besides, it was a moot point. He wanted to be a father – didn't he? He was with a woman half her age without middle-aged spread and a body that was giving in to gravity in all the wrong places. Why would he give all that up to come back to her?

'Don't do that.'

Cassie looked at her friend. 'Don't do what?'

'I know what's going through your mind. Don't put yourself down just because you're not twenty-something. You may be in your mid-forties, but you don't look a day over thirty-five.'

Cassie knew what she was up to.

'I'm not just saying that to make you feel better. Whether it's being Canadian, or something in your genes, you can still turn heads – and don't you forget it.' She pointed at Cassie. 'Don't you give up on yourself because of your lying, cheating husband who tossed you aside for a younger model. There's someone better out there waiting for you. You just have to go find him.'

Cassie sat there staring at Dawn. The couple buying her flat popped into her mind. She recalled what they said about how they met again by chance, bumping into each other crossing the road. It must have been serendipity. Her thoughts turned to a place she hadn't been in many, many years.

'What is it?' her friend asked.

'Oh, something came to mind I hadn't thought about in a very long time.'

'You mean *someone*?'

8

Cassie stood on the gravel, two suitcases by her feet. She watched the taxi that had dropped her off winding its way back down the drive until it reached the road that led into the village. Cassie turned around and looked up at the imposing Victorian Gothic house. After the euphoria of getting a new job away from London and the hospital where her husband worked, her elation gave way to doubt. Was she doing the right thing?

On paper, it was a perfect fit for her circumstances in every respect bar one; she knew this place. Fletchling Hall wasn't exactly the fresh start she was after. But it was only temporary, she kept reminding herself. Once the flat was sold, and their divorce finalised, she could move on with her life. Besides, it was too late to back out now; she'd accepted the position and resigned from her job in London. Cassie had also handed the estate agents her keys to the apartment. Now there was no going back. She'd packed all her possessions in two suitcases and walked out on her life.

She glanced at her cases. This is what she had to show for twenty years of marriage. She would receive some proceeds from the sale of the flat. At least that was something. It wouldn't compensate her for the years she'd put into a relationship that Lars had cast aside in a blink of an eye. No amount of money would. Cassie tried not to think about him. She turned her attention to the house and sighed. Where had the years gone? The last time she had stood on this drive outside the entrance to the grand old house, she had been a fresh-faced student in her late teens. She couldn't believe how many years had gone by and here she was starting again with no home, no husband, and no family of her own.

Cassie had the impulse to leave. She could walk to the village. It wasn't far. She'd passed through it on the way here in the taxi. There was a quaint pub, a small café, a church and a general store. There was also a bus stop. Perhaps she should catch the bus to the nearest town and sort out some accommodation in a hotel or bed-and-breakfast while she figured out what to do next.

Cassie was about to turn on her heel and leave when the front door opened. 'Ah, you must be Cassandra.' A lady nearing retirement age offered a friendly smile as she approached.

Before Cassie could object, she picked up a suitcase. 'Follow me.' She walked briskly up the stone steps to the double entrance doors, pausing for Cassie to catch up.

Cassie shrugged. Perhaps it was for the best. She shouldn't make any rash decisions. She could spend the night here and sleep on it. Maybe she'd feel differently in the morning. Cassie picked up the other suitcase and followed her up the steps to the front door where the lady was waiting for her.

'I go by the name of Cassie – if you don't mind.'

'Why would I mind? I'm Phyllis, by the way.'

They shook hands.

'Are you American?'

'No, I'm Canadian.'

'Oh, sorry, I just assumed—'

'It's all right. I get that a lot.'

'Ah. Well, let's not dawdle. Come inside.'

Cassie followed her into the large, imposing entrance hall of what was once a grand home. It had hardly changed since she was here last, although she didn't remember the thick pile carpet. She guessed that was fitted in recent years, but other than that the dark mahogany wood panelling and grand staircase was just as she remembered it.

'Welcome to the team,' said Phyllis.

Cassie was expecting a little welcoming committee with the rest of the staff turning out to meet the newest member of their team. Nobody else materialised.

'This is the grand hall, as you may have guessed. If walls could talk, I bet this marvellous stately home would have some tales to tell.' Phyllis fell silent for a moment.

Cassie fell silent too, thinking of the last time she was here as a young student occupational therapist doing her initial placement when Fletchling Hall was a cottage hospital. That wasn't the only reason this place was etched on her memory. It was here that she first set eyes on the boy she fell in love with.

'Let's start by showing you to your accommodation so you can get settled in.'

Cassie nodded, expecting Phyllis to walk up the grand staircase. Instead, she turned on her heel and walked back to the front door. Cassie followed her outside. Phyllis must have caught the bemused expression on her face. 'Ah, I forgot we have a leaky roof problem at the moment so the room in the house that came with the position is damp.'

'I don't mind a bit of damp.'

'No, I'm sorry that won't do.'

'What about a different room?' Or a different wing, thought Cassie, looking up at the not insubstantial house thinking there must be one spare habitable room, surely.

As if reading her mind, Phyllis added, 'There are plenty of rooms and vacant apartments, but they are not furnished. That's the problem.'

Cassie frowned. Now what was she going to do? She needed the accommodation provided by the job. Until she had the money from the flat, she couldn't afford to rent or buy a property in this part of the country.

'But don't you worry,' Phyllis was saying as she started down the drive. 'You are in luck. Our tenants have moved out of Gatekeepers Cottage.'

'A cottage?' Cassie halted. 'Look, I'm sorry but I won't be able to afford the rent.'

Phyllis smiled. 'The position comes with accommodation so we are honouring that. It's not your fault you can't live in the house. I imagine the other live-in staff will be quite envious when they find out. You don't mind the walk, do you? It's at the end of the drive, I'm afraid.'

'Not at all.' In fact, Cassie had been staring out the window as the taxi turned into the drive and spotted a sweet little single-story flint cottage.

She hoped that was the place. It had old-fashioned leaded windows, creeping Ivy and a little garden behind a low wall. Window boxes full of flowers and a vibrant pink rose bush, its vines creeping up the front of the cottage and round the top of the front door, added to its charm.

'So, what brought you to England?'

'I've lived here several years.' She got that a lot too. On hearing her accent, people seemed to jump to conclusions and assume she'd just arrived in England. They were surprised to discover she'd lived here practically all her adult life.

'I came to England with my father when I was seventeen. It was the first time I'd been abroad. I loved it here, so I stayed.' Cassie left out the other reason she'd chosen not to return to Canada. She did love England, but there was a young boy who'd stolen her heart. 'I got a place at university to do my occupational therapy degree. I've lived here ever since.'

That was the truncated version. She didn't want to get into the reasons her father had made the trip to England. It was the first time he'd set foot back in the country since he was four.

'Where is the rest of the staff?' Cassie asked. Apart from Phyllis, she hadn't seen another soul.

'They're making their rounds, visiting the residents at the moment. There's an afternoon break when they all gravitate to the kitchen for a cup of tea, so I'm sure you can meet them then. I'm afraid there is only a skeleton staff now. People have left, jumped ship to get fresh jobs before the place closes. Mind you, we haven't got many residents left…' she trailed off.

'It's closing?' Although she realised her contract was only temporary, she assumed that was just the norm with jobs nowadays; employers and employees testing the waters before a permanent contract was offered. Even though Cassie wasn't after a permanent position, she had thought if she liked her new job, she might have stayed on. It was disappointing to hear that was not an option. Still, Cassie wondered why they had to close.

She knew the stately home was converted into apartments.

The residents rented the lease-hold flats and lived as independently as possible in a sheltered housing environment. It was a beautiful place to live with extensive grounds, although it made her wonder if the rents was so expensive they didn't have enough takers. 'Aren't there enough residents to keep the place open?'

'No, that's not it at all,' replied Phyllis. 'There's no shortage of people who'd put their names down to move in here when a resident moves on to Rose Cottage.'

Cassie smiled at the euphemism. Only the English could come up with such a quaint turn of phrase for death.

'Oh sorry, what I meant was—'

'I know what it means, Phyllis. I remember when I first heard the expression it made me smile.'

'I bet it did.'

They exchanged pleasantries as they made their way toward the flint cottage at the end of the drive. Phyllis stopped at the little wooden gate set in a low wall. 'We haven't been taking any new residents for some time. The person who owns the property decided to sell up. I imagine it has got something to do with the cost of the repairs. The last residents have already got letters informing them of the owner's plans. I heard some property developers are buying Fletchling Hall. They want to turn the place into luxury apartments and build houses on the land.'

'Oh, that's a shame.'

Phyllis opened the gate. 'My sentiments exactly. It is a shame. Not just for the residents. This place has a history.' Phyllis paused, staring up the drive at the house.

Cassie knew a little about the stately home's history. Some might say, in a way, she was part of that history. Her thoughts turned to her father and their first trip back to England together.

She was so excited about going with him. Her mother and sister didn't accompany them. Emma was only six years old, so they had stayed behind in Canada.

Cassie and her father made the trip to England to try and find his mother, the English grandmother she had never met. She recalled her first visit when she stepped inside the stately home and thought of a young boy called Martin, her father, running up and down the corridors. It was a cottage hospital when they visited together. He still had vivid memories of this place when it was a family home, even though he was so very young when he was sent there, all on his own, during the Second World War.

He was billeted to stay with the family who owned Fletchling Hall. Her father recalled playing with a girl who was older than him. From what he'd said, he was quite attached to her. He should have returned to his family in London after the war, but that never happened. Her father never saw his English family again. However, after all those years searching for them, Cassie's Dad thought he had a lead. It was pure chance that he'd come across some pictures of the stately home someone had posted online; the place seemed familiar. Martin still had an old photo taken of him as a young child outside an imposing Victorian house. It turned out that house was Fletchling Hall.

For years he thought he must have had relatives who lived in a grand old house in England. When he came across the pictures online, he'd delved into the history of the hall and discovered working-class children from the East End of London had been billeted there during the war. It was towards the end of the war, when he was three years old, that he must have joined the last wave of children evacuated from London. In the only photo he had of himself from his childhood in England, he was standing on the steps of the hall. He had a box containing a gas mask, typical of children evacuees.

Cassie followed Phyllis' gaze. Had it been over twenty-five years since they had last set foot in that house, trying to piece together his past; the life of a three-year-old who had hardly been here at all when he was taken from the family who once owned the property and sent to Canada?

Cassie felt it was an episode in British history that was nothing to be proud of, transporting orphaned children to the other side of the world. The tragedy was many of them were not orphans; they had families waiting for them – mothers, fathers, and siblings. Her father always suspected he was one of those children. Maybe it's what he wanted to believe, that he still had living relatives in England. Unfortunately, nothing came of their trip. He was no closer to finding out the truth.

When Cassie realised the job was at the former stately home she'd visited with her father years ago, she'd had second thoughts about taking up the position. Now she was here, Cassie wasn't surprised the memories came flooding back. She recalled her father's disappointment had been palpable when he walked away from this place, having found nothing relating to his past, his history. On top of which he'd had to leave his eldest daughter behind when he returned to Canada.

That summer Cassie turned eighteen she had met someone. She thought she'd found *the one.* Despite their tender years, she expected they would stay together. It was not to be. That didn't stop her choosing to remain in England and build a life for herself.

It was the most peculiar of summers. During that six-week

stay in England, her father, a teacher, hadn't found what he was looking for, but Cassie had. She'd discovered the place where she felt she belonged – England. How much those feelings were wrapped up with the English boy she'd fallen for was anyone's guess, but despite their relationship falling apart, she couldn't leave. It was as though the moment she stepped foot on English soil, she'd come home.

Her father didn't feel the same way, which she guessed wasn't surprising. He'd lived in Canada practically all his life. Despite his English roots, he was Canadian through and through. Although it wasn't his choice to be shipped out there, he'd made a life for himself in his adopted country.

It was never his intention to return to England permanently or leave his eldest child there. She recalled reassuring her father he was doing the right thing letting her stay. It wasn't his choice to make, he was aware of that, but she wanted him to support her decision. She would have an amazing life here, and all her dreams would come true. That's what she'd told him. Little wonder she had yet to get online and tell him her news.

That was the other reason she'd had second thoughts about taking this job; how would she feel returning here all these years later with her dreams in tatters? She no longer had a home; that was being sold. She no longer had a husband. And any thoughts of early retirement and travel were not on the cards; she'd have to continue working to pay for a roof over her head on her own. Sometimes, lying awake in the early hours, she'd felt as though there was nothing to live for, no reason to carry on. Once, she'd even thought how nice, how easy it would be just to check into Rose Cottage instead.

'I know what you're thinking' said Phyllis turning around and catching the expression on Cassie's face as she opened the front door. 'It smells a little musty inside and it's a bit gloomy, but I'm sure a spring clean and a hoover will do it wonders.'

Her digs were the last thing on her mind right now. 'It's fine.'

Cassie followed her through the little hallway into the cosy lounge with an old-fashioned tiled fireplace with an inset electric fire, two brown leather sofas, and a small 1970s Formica table and chairs by a window. The flat-screen television surprised her. 'The last tenants left it behind.' Phyllis commented.

Cassie poked her head in the kitchen, which had light oak kitchen units and a cream tiled splashback. Although dated, it appeared clean. The white goods – a fridge, cooker and washing machine – seemed new.

'There are two bedrooms, one on the front and one on the back.' Phyllis opened both doors. 'Which one would you like?'

Cassie was going to opt for the double bed in the front bedroom until Phyllis opened the curtains in the single room to reveal a lovely view of the grounds and the house. Phyllis caught her smiling, so she walked into the small bedroom and put her suitcase down on the single bed.

Cassie followed her in with the other case.

'If one of the other staff leave soon, you're welcome to move into the house,' suggested Phyllis.

Cassie shook her head as she put her suitcase on the chair by the dressing table. 'Honestly, it's fine.' It was more than fine. She couldn't believe her luck. Why would she give up a rent-free cottage for a room in the house?

'Perhaps that's just as well,' mused Phyllis. 'I get the impression the remaining staff are holding out until the bitter end like myself. None of us want to leave.'

Cassie wasn't surprised. She stared out the window at the lush green lawn. Gigantic oak trees stood proud, lining the drive up to the house. Something struck her as odd until she realised what it was. There was no traffic noise, just the sound of birds chirping outside her bedroom window. It was a world away from her life in London.

'How about a tour of the house, Cassie? I bet you're dying to see the place. Most people are when they first arrive.'

Cassie forced a smile. She wasn't most people. 'I've been here before.'

'Really? When was that?'

Cassie hesitated. She fast-forwarded past the episode with her father; that was personal. 'When I was doing my occupational therapy degree, I did my placements here when it was a cottage hospital.'

'Crumbs, that's going back.'

'I know – tell me about it!'

'Mind you, I can talk. I qualified as a nurse when you didn't even need a degree back then. It was all on-the-job training.' She shook her head. 'Now that *is* going back.'

They exchanged a smile. Cassie guessed Phyllis was close to retirement age.

'I can still take you on a tour. I'm sure there are parts of the house you didn't venture in when you did your placements.'

'All right,' Cassie agreed. She was in two minds whether to mention the other reason she was familiar with this house; the connection with her father. Perhaps it was something she should mention. It occurred to her that Phyllis might know more about the history of the house.

Cassie frowned as she followed Phyllis back to the front door.

She couldn't bring herself to talk about it. If she didn't feel upset enough as it was over the breakdown of her marriage, it wouldn't help if she started talking about her father. It still made her sad at the thought he didn't find what he was looking for all those years ago. He'd made his pilgrimage back to England with high hopes of finding his English family. With the passage of time, the probability of discovering his biological parents alive and well diminished with each passing year.

In the following years, after his first visit back, he'd returned to England often. Cassie looked forward to those visits. Despite being settled and happy in her adopted country, it came at a price – not seeing family as often as she'd like. It didn't help that her husband discouraged her from using her annual leave to make trips back to see them.

Her father found it ironic that he had been transported years ago, uprooted from his homeland, his family, and left to fend for himself in a foreign land, and there was his eldest child doing the same, except hers was by choice. She realised he found it heart-wrenching every time he had to return to Canada and leave her behind. It was harder still that, despite his trips back to England, his search continued but to no avail. Then he stopped coming back altogether. It coincided with the birth of his first grandchild nine years ago. Cassie remembered what he'd said to her. 'If I don't stop chasing ghosts, I will miss what's right in front of me. I want to be a part of my grandchild's life.'

It was selfish of her to think it, but sometimes she felt he'd chosen her sister over her just because she had children. What would he have done if she'd had children too? But as her sister often reminded her, it was her choice to live thousands of miles away. He returned to England here and there to see her, but not as often as Cassie would have liked. He wanted to spend his vacations with his grandchildren while they were still young. Cassie understood. They wouldn't be young forever, and for someone like her father, family was everything.

When the grandchildren were older, he planned to retire and travel around Canada with Mum. She wouldn't fly, that's why she had never been to England. Then Mum died, and their plans to do things together went out the window. Cassie knew why it was still important to him to continue with his travel itinerary, making his way across Canada. He wanted to meet other people uprooted from their families, and the country of their birth, and sent to Canada by the British Government.

He planned to write a book, compiling their stories along with his own. That was the reason for his road trip, to connect with people like himself before they were gone and their stories died with them. She was proud of what he was doing. Cassie hoped he got a publisher. Their stories deserved to be heard.

'This is the staff kitchen. There are two fridges and a large Aga for cooking. You can store your groceries in these cupboards if you wish. The kitchen in the cottage is quite small.'

Cassie had been lost in thought as she followed Phyllis up the drive and back inside the house. She'd passed down the long corridor into the kitchen, barely taking in her surroundings. She'd been thinking about her father as a little boy playing in these corridors a lifetime ago. He would have been unaware that his life was about to change all because some government official rubber-stamped the transportation of little, vulnerable boys and girls like cattle. If she could, she'd start the search again for him, and see what she might unearth about the English family he'd left behind. But where exactly did she begin? If her father had no luck here almost thirty years ago, what did she hope to find all these years later? The pragmatic Cassie knew it was pointless. It was not what she came here for; to dredge up the past. A little voice in her head, or was it her heart, told her she at least had to try, even if the search would probably lead nowhere.

They were standing in the kitchen. Phyllis was showing her how to use the Aga when Cassie turned to her, and said, 'Phyllis, you mentioned this place has a history…?'

Phyllis smiled. 'Yes, it's got an interesting history. Would you like a cup of tea and I'll tell you all about it before we meet the residents?'

Cassie nodded. She sat down at the large wooden table in the centre of the kitchen while Phyllis put the kettle on and told her what she knew of the history of Fletchling Hall.

What she told her was all very interesting, but nothing Cassie didn't already know. 'What about the children billeted here during the war?' Cassie asked.

Phyllis put her mug down. 'Pardon me?'

'There were children evacuated from London to live here with the family during World War Two and then, for some reason, they were sent away before the war was over. I don't know why. It's not as though there wasn't enough room. They could have taken more. It makes no sense.'

'Are you sure? I don't recall reading about any children being billeted here.' Phyllis shook her head. 'Where did you find out—?'

They were interrupted by several people walking into the kitchen, chatting amongst themselves. They stopped talking when they caught sight of Phyllis sitting at the table with a woman they hadn't seen before.'

Phyllis glanced at her watch. 'Good heavens, is that the time?

It must be coffee break. Let me introduce you all to our new member of staff – Cassie.'

9

Cassie picked up her suitcases and put them on the bed. She opened the smaller of the two, the cabin-sized case, and got out her laptop. She'd unpack her clothes later. For now, she had a bit of free time before Phyllis came to call on her and take her to meet the residents she'd be working with. Cassie started her new job the next day. Today was all about familiarising herself with the staff, and the house. Although she was looking forward to meeting the residents, it was nice to have time to collect herself after her arrival. She fancied a walk in the grounds, but that would have to wait. There was something she needed to do first.

She placed the laptop on the dressing table and switched it on, thinking of her promise to friends in London to tell them how her new job was going. She hadn't started work yet so would catch up with them tomorrow evening.

Cassie sat there staring out the window while her laptop booted up, still grappling with mixed emotions about coming back here. She was already missing her colleagues she had worked with over the years; they had become good friends. In hindsight, she realised they would have been her support network, people to talk to, confide in, and a shoulder to cry on as she went through a divorce. Once again, the English phrase, *cutting off your nose to spite your face*, came to mind. By leaving her job to get away from Lars, she'd had to leave them behind too. That was the problem with living so far from relatives. Unlike other people who had family, parents and siblings close by; she relied on her friends for support.

Her laptop pinged to life. She shifted her gaze from the window. Although her colleagues and friends were just a phone call away, it wasn't the same as seeing them every day at work. It was easy to lose contact. Cassie was thinking of her family back in Canada – namely, her sister. She felt a pang of guilt for not attempting to stay in touch.

Cassie sat down on the wooden seat in front of the dressing table. When prompted, she typed in her password, anxiously wondering if the internet connection was any good. It was the one thing that had slipped her mind when they interviewed her for the post. She would be lost if she couldn't get online.

Cassie wasn't bothered about surfing the net or shopping. What concerned her was keeping in touch with Dad. She wasn't looking forward to telling him about the breakup of her marriage, but dying to tell him where she was sitting right this moment.

Cassie breathed a sigh of relief when *google* popped up. 'I'm connected!' It was fast too. The first thing she did was message him on Facebook. He wasn't online, otherwise he would have replied straightaway.

Cassie sent him an email instead. It began, *Hey, Dad, you'll never guess where I am…*

Cassie stopped typing and paused to re-read the sentence. Would he want to hear she was back at the grand stately home where his search for his long-lost family had gone cold? Not the best of memories. The next issue was how to explain why she'd left the job she loved, to come here.

Cassie sighed as she hit the delete button. All that remained on the screen were the words, *Hey, Dad…*

She sat there struggling to think what to write next. Cassie flexed her fingers above the keyboard, deciding that perhaps she wouldn't tell him she'd split up with Lars just yet. Not that Cassie would take him back, not by a long shot. It was the thought of telling her dad the circumstances of the breakup. What sort of person strings their wife along while carrying on with someone else? Despite being married for two decades, it made her question how well she knew him.

She still couldn't believe it had happened to her. Perhaps the reason she didn't want to tell Dad about her single status was not because there was a possibility her and Lars might get back together, but more to do with how embarrassed she felt. She recalled the first time he met her husband. It was a few days before the wedding when he had come over from Canada ready to give her away on the big day. He'd taken her to one side and surprised her with a question she had not expected, 'Are you sure you want to marry him?'

She remembered being dumbfounded and remarking, 'What sort of question is that? Are you saying you don't like him?'

His response took her by surprise. She was expecting him to say, *of course I like him, it's just nobody will be good enough for my daughter.* Instead, he brought up the boy she'd met on their first trip to England when she was a teenager. She remembered being cross with her father. Falling for a boy in her teens was years ago. What had that got to do with her wedding day? She was a mature woman in her twenties getting married; she'd made her choice.

She couldn't understand why he was bringing up a past boyfriend. In hindsight, she realised her father was just a concerned parent, worried about his daughter. The problem was he knew her too well. That boy wasn't just a teenage crush; despite her tender years, she knew he was, and always would be, the love of her life. She'd made the mistake of telling her dad. He had not forgotten.

Cassie bet that if she met the boy now, whom she thought she was madly in love with, they probably wouldn't like each other. If they'd stayed together, they might have grown to hate each other. That's what she'd told her father before she slapped a smile on her face and took his arm to walk down the aisle.

Cassie sighed. She was still sitting in front of the laptop and staring at those two words *Hey, Dad,* contemplating what to write next. Her thoughts turned to her perfect sister with the perfect marriage and the perfect children. Of course, they weren't perfect – nobody's life ever is. All the same, thinking of Emma only made her feel worse. If she told Dad about Lars, it would get back to Emma. Cassie wasn't in the mood to be judged by her little sister.

'I think I won't mention what's going on in my life at the moment.' She knew there would be plenty of time for that. She decided some things couldn't be said in an email or on Facebook. Perhaps when the dust had settled on her divorce, and she had sorted out what she wanted to do with her life, then that would be a better opportunity to let everybody know. Besides, she didn't want Dad getting on the phone to her. It was more than likely he'd try to call and find out how she was, and she bet he'd call her at an inopportune time like when she was at work.

Cassie nodded her head. She would email to ask him how his road trip was going; where he was, who he'd met, what stories he had written. She smiled. It was by far a better idea than telling him her news. She wanted something to take her mind off her situation. It didn't take her long to ping him off an email. She'd been following his exploits on Facebook. Cassie loved keeping track of her father's road trip.

She got up from her seat and walked over to the single bed. Secured in the zip pocket of her suitcase was a large plastic wallet. Inside was a neatly folded map of Canada. She took out the plastic wallet, retrieved the map and opened it out, spreading it over the bed. She'd also thought to pack the blu tack from the kitchen drawer.

Cassie suddenly came over tearful at the thought she'd never see that kitchen drawer in the flat ever again. 'Stupid woman, it's only a kitchen drawer.' She wiped away a tear with the sleeve of her jumper and got out the blu tack. 'Now, where shall I hang it?'

Her eyes roved around the room. Her bedroom was cosy with old-fashioned wallpaper in a chintzy delicate flower pattern that harked back to another era. Patterned curtains hung at the sash window. Cassie's attention was drawn to the house. Staring out the window, she wondered which bedroom her father had slept in when he was a little boy living at Fletchling Hall. Perhaps there was a nursery. Cassie pondered at how strange life was that she should return here after all these years to the last place her father lived, as a small boy, before he was sent away.

Cassie tore off some blu tack, scrunched it into a ball, and attached some to each corner of the map. She reached up and stuck the map on the wall above the dressing table. Each red dot on the map was where her father had visited. She'd even drawn a line from one dot to the next, marking his journey across Canada.

He'd set off from Toronto where he lived, and where Cassie

and her sister had grown up. He travelled through the regions of Quebec, visiting the capital Ottawa, then Montreal, Halifax and Quebec City before continuing on his journey through the province of Ontario. His plan was to travel to Vancouver and the Rocky Mountains on the other side of the country in British Columbia – a place he'd set his heart on visiting during his trip.

She stood there staring at the map, glancing at her computer now and then to see if he'd replied to her email. The last dot on the map marked his arrival in the Province of Alberta a fortnight ago, staying in Calgary in the foothills of the Rocky Mountains. Although he wanted to see Vancouver, she knew he didn't have a set route or a particular destination in mind. If it wasn't for social media, she doubted it would have been easy to make this trip. He was connecting with people online, some of whom agreed to meet him and share their stories.

She would have loved to accompany him on the trip, but her work commitments meant she could only join him for brief periods. So far, Cassie had never flown over to Canada to meet up with him. Perhaps it was for the best. He'd always said this was a journey he had to make himself. She worried about him being on the road travelling alone. Cassie smiled when she remembered his reply. 'I won't be lonely. I've got Albert.'

She turned around and picked up her handbag hanging on the back of the chair. Cassie opened her bag and found her purse. Slipped inside one compartment was a photo of her Dad and Albert. She stuck it near the dot on the map where they were last. She looked fondly at the picture of her dad, a tall, broad-shouldered man with a full head of pepper-grey hair, piercing blue eyes and a neatly cut beard. He was wearing pressed jeans and his trade-mark corduroy jacket he'd had for years.

Her gaze shifted to Albert, his faithful companion – an old Labrador cross. Cassie's smile faltered. Despite the way the British Government had rubber-stamped the removal of so many children from their homes, their families, and their country, her father was quite the royalist.

He didn't blame the royal family for a government policy of child migration which separated him, and many other children, from their families. The original plan was to evacuate children to the British countryside. As the possibility of invasion increased, countries that were part of the British Empire back then, Australia, Canada, New Zealand and South Africa, offered a haven for British children. The trouble was many of them never returned

As a teenager, she had little idea what many child migrants had been through. She might have felt differently about England if she'd known what some of those children suffered when they arrived on foreign soil.

Her father had been very fortunate. A chance encounter, soon after he'd arrived at a remote farmstead, meant he escaped the harsh realities of a childhood of servitude, more akin to slave labour. His childhood was far removed from the experiences of many child migrants to Canada. Her dad's story was not one of hardship and heartbreak that some of his peers suffered at the hands of those entrusted with their care. It was a cruel twist of fate that although sent away for their own safety, for some the reality was far from the safe harbour the British Government promised them.

She thought of her father travelling around Canada. He wished he'd done it years ago, but with work and family commitments, he couldn't just up sticks and travel. The six weeks he'd spent in England that summer in the late eighties was the exception. That was when an Australian friend, also a child migrant, brought to his attention the newly founded Child Migrants Trust in England which aimed to reunite child migrants in Australia with their British families.

He hoped that even though he was sent to Canada, they might help him trace his relatives. Some searches took weeks, others had taken many months. His was trickier. Martin was so young when he arrived in Canada he couldn't remember his last name. Official documents revealed that a bureaucrat gave him the name Smith – a common surname in Canada.

Cassie liked to think someone was still working on his case at the Child Migrants Trust. She knew he kept in touch with them, but unless some fresh information came to light, she couldn't imagine there would be any point pouring precious time and resources into the case of a little boy sent to Canada in 1945. She wouldn't dream of voicing that thought to her father, but as the years went by the chances of finding his parents, her English grandparents, slipped further away.

Her thoughts drifted to her father's trip as she stood there staring at the map. She imagined there would be tragic times ahead, hearing the heart-rending experiences of children sent to Canada, and other parts of the British Empire, supposedly for a better life. She knew the book her father was writing, telling their stories, would not make for easy reading.

Her father's story differed from some of the harrowing experiences she imagined would be within those pages. He'd been one of the lucky ones. It wasn't until her father spoke to other child migrants that he realised just how lucky he'd been. It shocked him to discover his experience was not the norm.

Although she couldn't wait to find out where he was, she wouldn't press him for details of the people he was meeting on his trip. She would wait to read his book. Not that she didn't want to know – far from it. At the moment she was not prepared for the heart-breaking stories of lost innocence she would discover in those pages.

She glanced at her laptop as an email popped up. *Hey, sweet-heart, great to hear from you…*

Cassie had barely put her bum on the chair when there was a knock on the cottage door. It was time to meet the residents.

'Coming…' she called out as she closed down her laptop. 'Sorry, Dad. I'll catch up later, I promise,' she whispered before answering the door.

10

Standing on the doorstep was a member of staff Phyllis had introduced her to in the kitchen. Phyllis wasn't joking when she said they had a skeleton staff. There were just four of them. Randall was a nurse who appeared to be in his thirties and sounded Australian. Jill was the health care assistant. She was a small thin woman with dyed blonde hair who, like Phyllis, was close to retirement age.

Olivia, who was standing outside her door, was a young, newly qualified physio in her early twenties. This was her first position. Apart from the cleaners who came in twice a week, a couple of young health care assistants who provided personal care for one of the residents, and a catering company that delivered the evening meals for the residents, that was it. The residents' breakfast and lunch were prepared by Jill. They could choose whether to eat together in the kitchen or have it in their apartments.

Olivia said, 'Phyllis is doing her rounds, so she asked one of us to show you around.' She swept her hair back from her face and tied it up in a ponytail with a hairband. She had a smooth complexion that didn't need a wisp of makeup, something Cassie envied at her age. Cassie had some fine lines under her green eyes and freckles she'd never liked; she covered them up with foundation. Although she highlighted her hair, she hadn't seen a wisp of grey yet. Her long mane of red hair fell to her shoulders in natural curls.

She had what her friends called big hair. What they didn't realise was the time it took with products and straighteners to tame it. Dawn once told her that if she was a cartoon character, her doppelganger was Princess Merida in the children's animated movie *Brave*.

Cassie had to check out the film to see for herself. They were right. If someone had drawn a cartoon character of her, Princess Merida would have been spot on, but for two things; she wasn't that slim, and the cartoon character was at least two decades younger. All the same, the thought of that cartoon still made Cassie smile.

She was still smiling as she stepped out of the cottage and closed the door. 'Phyllis could have given you my mobile number and saved you the walk down the drive.'

'Oh, I don't mind.' Olivia swept her hair off her shoulders. 'It gets me out of the house for a bit. Let's meet the residents.'

Cassie fell in step with Olivia as they walked briskly up to the house. She followed her along the hall and down a narrow flight of stairs she guessed used to be the servant's back stairs.

'Randall wanted to come and show you around, but I spared you.'

Cassie frowned wondering what she meant. When they reached the bottom, of the stairs, Olivia turned to her and explained, 'I nicknamed him Randy. He tries it on with all the new arrivals – if they're a certain age. I didn't mean someone

Phyllis' age. That would be weird. But didn't you notice him eyeing you up in the kitchen when Phyllis introduced you?'

Cassie nodded. In fact, he held her hand a little too long for comfort when he came over and shook it as he introduced himself.

'I know he's good looking,' continued Olivia. 'I mean he's like a poster boy for what you'd imagine a typical Australian surfer dude would look like with his blonde hair, bright blue eyes and that tanned physique.' Olivia's eyes glazed over as she stared off into space.

Cassie looked at her.

'Oh, he's not my type, not at all.'

Cassie hadn't even said anything.

'He tried it on with me when I arrived, asking me if I had a boyfriend. I told him I'm here to work. It's my first job. I don't want to screw it up by getting involved with another member of staff. I think that would be unprofessional. That's what I told him.'

'Fair enough,' said Cassie.

'Then he said I wasn't his type, anyway.'

'That's not very nice.'

Olivia brushed it off. 'I think he's such a good-looking guy he's not used to being rejected. I imagine I ruffled his feathers, if you know what I mean.'

Cassie nodded. She knew a good-looking guy once, a long time ago. Olivia reminded her of herself on that first visit here with her father. She had her heart set on being an occupational therapist. She didn't have time for boys. At least that's what she thought until she saw him. He was in his last year of 'A' Levels, a year younger than Cassie, doing work experience at Fletchling

Hall when it was a cottage hospital. The moment he set eyes on her, he followed her around like a lost puppy.

At first, Cassie rejected his advances. He said some mean things to her, she recalled. But she knew it wasn't out of spite or malice. She'd hurt his feelings, big time. He was only young – they both were. But the difference between Randall and the boy she once knew was that he wouldn't take no for an answer. What he didn't realise at the time was that she'd regretted saying no to him. Oh, how she wanted to take it back. She recalled that just looking at him made her knees weak and her stomach churn in the most peculiar fashion.

Only later did she realise that was the first time she'd fancied a boy, *really* fancied a boy. It was the stirring of something she'd never experienced before – genuine love. She was too young to know it at the time. She knew why she had rejected his advances to begin with. She didn't want a summer fling, for that's all it could be. She was only spending the summer in England before returning to Canada.

Then he told her about training to be an O.T. in England. She could apply to university. The idea had never entered her head to train for her qualification in England. She thought she had to do that in Canada and then come here to work. That summer changed her life. She found a boy and a country she loved.

Cassie sighed. At least it worked out staying in England. As for the boy, her first love—

'I heard he was dating someone in the village, but that didn't work out. He's single again and on the lookout, so to speak. Just warning you.'

'I'm sorry – what?' Cassie apologised for losing track of the conversation. She wasn't surprised her mind had wandered. Coming here had brought to the fore memories that were long-since buried; it was a time in her life when she was the happiest she'd ever been – all because of him.

'I was talking about Randall. He asked me how old I thought you were.'

Cassie's face went bright pink. Before she responded, Olivia said, 'I told him you look kind of in your thirties if you don't mind me saying.'

In my thirties? Cassie didn't mind her saying that at all.

'He kept pressing me, so I said, oh, I don't know, thirty-five, maybe?'

Thirty-five maybe? Cassie didn't mind that either. She'd love to turn back the clock ten years or perhaps twenty and have never married Lars.

Although flattered, like Olivia, she wasn't here to start a relationship. It had nothing to do with his age. Social norms and what society thought was acceptable didn't bother Cassie; love is love whatever your age, and whatever the age gap. You don't choose who you fall in love with. It was not that. It was the fact that she was in the throes of a divorce and at an emotionally low ebb. The last thing she imagined was walking into a new relationship. She didn't think she had it in her to start dating. Her life was complicated, trying to unravel a twenty-year marriage.

'I bet he asks you out.'

Cassie followed Olivia along the hall to meet the first resident. She sighed. Olivia glanced over her shoulder and laughed.

Cassie forced a smile. She'd come here to get away from her husband and sort her head out, not become involved with someone else. She didn't want to make the mistake of starting a relationship on the rebound. That wouldn't end well. Cassie decided that the only way to avoid things getting awkward was to stop Randall asking her out in the first place, thus avoiding any bad feeling when she said no.

They stopped outside the door to one of the apartments. Cassie turned to Olivia. 'It was very kind of you to say I was in my thirties—'

'I wasn't saying it just to be kind, Cassie.' She paused. 'You're older – aren't you.'

'Way older.'

'Really?'

'I've been working as an O.T. since I qualified straight out of university twenty-four years ago.'

'Oh. That's makes you…'

'In my mid-forties, not my thirties. If you could drop that into a conversation when you next speak to Randall, I'd really appreciate it.'

Olivia grinned. 'You're trying to avoid any awkwardness if you meet up in the kitchen on your break or something, and he asks you out.'

Cassie nodded.

'I can tell you now he's likely to get more turned on. I don't know whether he said it because I pissed him off, but he prefers older women.'

'Oh, jeez.'

'Sorry, but I don't think you will get off that easy. The age card will not work. Your best bet is to avoid him. It shouldn't be too difficult in a place this size. Anyway, back to work. I'm meant to be showing you around, not making small talk about randy Randall.'

Cassie laughed.

'Right, where was I? Oh yes, as you already know the reason there are so few staff working here now is that the place is due to close. It's such a shame.' Olivia echoed what Phyllis had said when Cassie first arrived. 'This place has got so much to offer. There are the beautiful grounds and the tennis court and bowling green—'

'They play tennis and bowls?' said Cassie in surprise.

'This is sheltered accommodation, not an old peoples' home. I guess people get confused about the difference. Not that I'm saying that's you,' she added. 'But mostly, the residents have always been active. When there were more of them, there used to be clubs, like the book club and the gardening club, cooking classes and outings. It was quite a community.' Olivia glanced over her should at Cassie. 'All that went by the board, along with the tennis and bowls, when the owner decided to sell.' She frowned. 'It's more profitable to let the property go. Now there are few residents, all the clubs and activities have stopped. That sense of community has gone. We've nicknamed the last ones left, The Quartet.'

'The Quartet,' repeated Cassie.

'There are only four of them. They have their own apartments and are pretty spaced out. The apartments I mean, not the residents.' Olivia grinned.

Cassie smiled. The young physio's ready humour was infectious.

'It can be a bit of a pain. It means lots of walking.'

Cassie didn't mind walking up and down stairs in a grand stately home. It beat clinical hospital corridors any day.

'The remaining residents are mostly independent. To be

honest, there's not an awful lot for us to do.'

Cassie frowned. That wasn't what she wanted to hear. She would prefer to be busy to take her mind off her situation, not standing around ruminating over the mess her life was in now.

'As you are an occupational therapist, I guess if you want to introduce any activities you think would benefit the residents, I'm sure Phyllis won't object.'

Cassie brightened. 'That's a splendid idea. I'll meet them first, assess their needs, and take it from there.'

'Great. Now, I thought we'd start with the easy ones.'

'Easy ones?'

'This is Iris' apartment,' said Olivia, avoiding her gaze.

Cassie got the impression the physio was holding back.

'Iris is our newest resident. Unfortunately, she'd been here hardly any time at all when they announced the place is closing and she has to leave. She's moving out at the end of the month.'

'Where will they all go?'

'Alternative housing has been arranged for two residents. The other resident will move in with relatives. You'll meet him next.'

'Did you say three of them are leaving?'

'Yes.'

'Doesn't that leave someone?'

Olivia sighed. 'We'll get to her last. Now, let's meet Iris.' Olivia knocked loudly on the apartment door and waited.

A tall, slightly stooped woman answered the door. 'Hello, hello, how are we today, Olivia?'

Olivia smiled. 'I'm meant to ask you that question, Iris, not the other way around. I'm very well, thank you. You have a visitor.'

'Come in, come in. I'll make some tea.'

'They stepped into a sizeable entrance with high ceilings and four doors off.

'This is Cassie, our newest member of staff. She's an occupational therapist.'

Cassie shook hands with Iris.

Iris put on her glasses. 'You're a pretty lass. What beautiful hair. And your complexion…'

'Thank you.' Cassie was feeling a little overwhelmed by all the compliments this morning. 'My complexion is all Dior. I spend a fortune on foundation.'

'Don't we all.'

After her wobble yesterday over whether she was doing the right thing, Cassie was now looking forward to starting her new job. Despite having to do her best to avoid randy Randall, the other staff and the residents seemed delightful. Cassie was in no doubt that she would enjoy working here.

The three of them sat down together over a cup of tea and a rich tea biscuit. It turned out the residents had their own kitchens in their apartments even though they all paid for their meals to be prepared by Jill.

'I'll be back to see you this afternoon,' said Olivia, closing the door after they finished their tea.

Cassie stood in the hall outside her door. 'She's lovely.'

'I know. Iris had a hip replacement, so we've been doing her rehab and getting her moving. It won't be long and she'll be back doing walks in the grounds before she leaves.'

'I'm looking forward to working with her.'

Olivia's smile faltered. 'She's not going to need a lot of your input – to be honest.'

'Oh, I see.'

'Come on. Next, we will meet our only gentleman resident. I have to warn you, though, he's like an older version of Randall; got an eye for the ladies has this one.'

'Oh, okay.' Cassie followed Olivia down the corridor, wondering if he would be her patient.

'Sorry, it's a bit of a trek.' Olivia glanced over her shoulder at Cassie following her down the hallway. 'When the other residents left, we thought of moving the last four nearer each other to save time doing our rounds, but we reasoned it won't be for long. It seemed unfair to make them go through the upheaval of changing apartments when they are on the move again in less than six months.

Cassie's contract was only for six months, so she guessed that was the time frame for the residents to vacate.

'Not far now,' said Olivia as she turned down another corridor. 'Here we are.' She knocked on the door. 'Bertie? I know you're in there.' Olivia glanced at Cassie and lowered her voice, 'He tries to hide from me. He doesn't like physio, so I have to be bossy.' She raised her voice. 'Bertie, I'm not leaving until you answer the door.'

The door opened a crack. 'I'm busy.'

'No, you're not. Come on, open the door for us to come in. Look, I've brought you a visitor.'

Bertie's round, grumpy face lit up when he set eyes on Cassie. The door was flung open with such force it banged on the wall opposite. 'Hang on a minute, wait here. I'll just be two ticks.'

They both watched him shuffling his sizeable frame into the room at the end of the short hallway.

Olivia turned to Cassie. 'Well, that worked. I've never known him to invite me in without an argument. He's always coming up with some excuse or another to get out of physio. I must bring you along to all of my shifts. Normally, it takes an age just to get in the door.'

Cassie gleaned that Bertie wasn't one of her patients either.

He appeared again. 'Right, you can come in now.'

'What was that all about?' whispered Cassie.

'Let's put it this way, unlike Iris he's not the tidiest of people. No doubt he was opening the curtains and doing a quick whip-round for your benefit.'

'My benefit?'

'As I said, he's got an eye for the ladies.'

They both walked into his lounge. The curtains adorning a window overlooking the grounds had been opened in haste. Cassie could tell because they weren't hanging straight. There were some newspapers sticking out from under the sofa, and some plates, cups and saucers in a pile on the sideboard. They needed washing up. She watched him brush a seat with the newspaper in his hand. 'Here, take a seat…'

'It's Cassie,' she said, introducing herself.

'Are you my new physio?'

'I'm afraid not,' Cassie replied.

'Bertie, you're stuck with me,' Olivia chipped in.

'Oh, darn.'

Olivia and Cassie exchanged a smile over the sweet old man.

Olivia looked at his glum face as he lowered himself into an armchair. 'This might cheer you up, Bertie. As I'm taking Cassie on a grand tour this morning, it means I won't be doing your physio until later.'

He cheered up. 'Did you say a tour? Can I come?'

Olivia exchanged a glance with Cassie.

Cassie shrugged. 'It's okay with me.'

Bertie stood up. 'Where are we going?'

'Next we will see Evelyn.'

'Oh, not *Her Ladyship*.' Bertie slumped back in his chair. 'You can count me out of the tour in that case.'

'Now, Bertie, that's no way to talk about your neighbour down the hall.'

'Have you met her?' He slapped a hand to his forehead. 'Of course you've met her.' His eyes shifted to Cassie. 'But you haven't.' He picked up a newspaper. 'Good luck.'

Olivia rose from her seat. 'We will leave you in peace. But remember, I'm coming back this afternoon.'

He grumbled something under his breath and opened his paper.

As they stepped out of his apartment, Olivia said, 'Let's meet Her Ladyship.'

11

'Her Ladyship?'

'That was unprofessional of me, sorry. It's a nickname she's acquired. '

Cassie raised an eyebrow. 'How come?'

Olivia gave her a sideways glance. 'Come on, let me introduce you. Then you will understand.'

They had just started down the hall when they heard a commotion up ahead. Cassie and Olivia were approaching the door to Her Ladyship's apartment when it flew open and Jill came scurrying out like a frightened mouse. Cassie took a step back in surprise as a plate whizzed past Jill's head and landed on the thick-pile carpet in the hall.

'Christ alive!' exclaimed Jill, glancing back into the apartment. 'I swear she gets worse with each passing day.'

Cassie knelt and picked up the plate. It had landed on the soft carpet, and was not broken, but there was cereal scattered all over the carpet.

'And if you bring me that for breakfast one more time, I swear I'll skin you alive!' came a shrill voice from inside the apartment.

Jill burst into tears and took off down the hallway.

Cassie stared after Jill wide-eyed. She glanced at the plate in her hands and turned to Olivia. 'What was *that*?'

'That was Evelyn,' she said matter-of-factly. 'She is not a morning person.'

That was an understatement, thought Cassie.

'Mind you, she moans about lunch and dinner too.' Olivia observed, talking in a whisper. 'She complains about *everything*. Evelyn acts as though she owns the place and treats us like we're her staff.' She shook her head from side to side. 'I think she's a bit, you know…' Olivia tapped her temple. 'Do you want to meet your patient?'

Oh, boy. Cassie sighed. The saying, *if it's too good to be true, it probably is,* came to mind. So far, the job seemed a breeze, with nice staff and pleasant residents in the most beautiful setting.

'The last occupational therapist just walked out one day and never came back.'

'Really,' Cassie replied in a dead-pan voice, staring at the plate.

'Here, let me take that.' Olivia relieved Cassie of the plate and left it on a windowsill in the hall. 'Shall we?' Olivia took a deep breath and stepped inside the apartment. 'Evelyn, it's Olivia. The door was open, so I'm coming in.'

Cassie breathed a sigh and reluctantly followed her through the doorway.

'Evelyn,' she called out once more as she walked down the wide wood-panelled entrance hall inside the flat. 'I've brought you a visitor.'

'A visitor?'

'Ah, there you are,' said Olivia when a door flew open.

Cassie's first impression of Evelyn was not someone who

had lost her marbles. She expected to meet an old lady with an unkempt appearance. She imagined Phyllis had employed her to show Evelyn how to take better care of herself and to encourage her to engage in stimulating interests to keep her mind active.

'Where's my visitor?' demanded Evelyn.

What Cassie saw standing at the door, leaning heavily on a walking stick, was a short but large lady of advancing years dressed in a beautiful mauve dress, elegant cashmere shawl and polished patent shoes. She wore a string of pearls with a matching bracelet and earrings. Her short grey hair framed her round face in a bob and reminded Cassie of the hairstyles worn in the 1940s.

Cassie looked her up and down in surprise. Anyone would think Her Ladyship was going out for an evening at the theatre, followed by dinner in a posh restaurant. Perhaps Olivia was right and she wasn't quite with it. Despite her advancing years, her complexion appeared smooth and supple. Evelyn must have been beautiful when she was young. That was another observation. She didn't know what she was expecting, but with her soft features and homely appearance, Evelyn didn't look at all forbidding or scary or hoity-toity as Bertie intimated. Cassie was all too aware appearances can be deceptive.

Her thoughts turned to Lars and the way he had connived behind her back, staying on in the marital home when, unbeknown to Cassie, he had left her weeks ago. Or was it months? That was the shocking thing. Cassie had no idea how long his affair had been going on, all the while putting on a front that he was still the perfect husband. If Cassie was honest with herself, looking back, she had a feeling something wasn't right; they hadn't slept together in weeks.

Evelyn studied Cassie. She turned to Olivia. 'What's the meaning of this? I don't know that woman. Where's my visitor?'

'Ah, I can see where I've confused you, Evelyn. Sorry, I didn't mean it quite like that.'

'Then what did you mean, girl? Come on, spit it out.'

Cassie sensed Olivia's confident demeanour slipping. Evelyn might look like a sweet old lady, but she had a brusque way about her and a biting tongue which she had no qualms using.

Cassie stepped forward. 'I'm Cassie, the new occupational therapist. Nice to meet—'

Cassie got the door slammed in her face. She turned to Olivia, wide-eyed. 'Is she for real?'

Olivia nodded her head. 'I'm afraid so.' She sighed. 'Let's see the final resident. You'll find her much more agreeable. We'll come back here later. Perhaps Her Ladyship will be in a better mood.'

Somehow Cassie doubted that.

They walked out of her apartment and closed the door. 'I'm sorry about that, Cassie. I hope it hasn't put you off. That was probably my fault. I shouldn't have said she had a visitor.'

'I don't understand…?'

They turned down another long hallway as Olivia explained, 'Evelyn doesn't get any visitors.'

'What do you mean?'

'Like I said, no one comes to visit her.'

'She has no living relatives?'

'I don't think that's it. Who doesn't have some relatives somewhere? We're guessing there's been a family rift.'

'That's awful.' Cassie genuinely felt sorry for her if that were the case. She couldn't imagine anything worse than losing contact with your family. Cassie was thinking of her father. She must read and reply to his email the first chance she got. Even her sister came to mind. She would attempt to stay in touch with Emma from now on.

'The trouble is, you've got to ask yourself, with the way she carries on it's not surprising.'

Cassie had lost the thread of the conversation.

Olivia paused at the top of the grand central staircase. 'I mean, she's not the nicest of people. I wouldn't want to visit her if she was my relative.'

'I understand what you're getting at.' It made Cassie wonder. Apart from the staff, who did she see all day, every day? No one. It must be a lonely existence. Perhaps she'd be a nicer person if she reconnected with old friends and family.

'What are you thinking?' asked Olivia, catching Cassie's thoughtful expression.

'Oh, ways I could help her.'

'Good luck with that.' Olivia frowned. 'Sorry, that wasn't fair. I know you're an O.T and are aware she doesn't need help with the basic tasks of daily living, washing and dressing – that sort of thing. Phyllis is worried about her mental state. I guess she felt that although you've been employed to work with our next patient, it wouldn't hurt if you could think of ways of engaging with Evelyn, perhaps with some stimulating activities.'

Olivia realised O.T.'s don't sit and do basket-weaving with their patients and such like. That's not what her job was about. 'I guess if you can come up with anything to interest her beyond staring out the window all day that would be fantastic.'

Cassie nodded. She was all for helping the residents in any way she could.

'I imagine she's depressed, but she refuses to visit her G.P. Says she won't take pills. I know she reads, but her eyesight isn't what it once was. That's to be expected at eighty-seven.'

'Wow. She doesn't appear in her late eighties.'

'I know. It's quite sad though. Did you notice how dressed up she was?' Olivia started down the stairs to the entrance hallway.

Cassie followed. 'Yes, it wasn't what I was expecting.'

'She dresses up to the nines every day as though she's expecting a visitor.' They reached the bottom of the stairs. 'Then she spends most of the day sitting by the window waiting for someone to come.'

'Crumbs, that *is* sad.'

They paused in the main hall.

'Right, let's meet the final resident. You'll be spending most of your time with her. She's lovely, by the way.'

Cassie smiled in relief, thank goodness.

'She's been our longest resident. Everybody will be sad to see her leave.'

12

Cassie followed Olivia through the open doorway. This resident lived in another part of the house, quite a trek from the others. It allowed Cassie to see an unfamiliar part of the house. They'd walked down a long corridor on the ground floor to a different wing with lovely views out the windows across the grounds.

Cassie stepped into an apartment and walked into a large airy lounge with high ceilings and double doors at the end of the room. She stood by the French doors leading out on to a private patio overlooking the gardens. Cassie was not just struck by the beauty and tranquillity of Fletchling Hall – she watched butterflies flutter around a rosebush in the autumn sunshine – but by the utter silence, such a change from her life in London. She'd love to live somewhere like this, surrounded by beautiful grounds and not a car or road in sight.

But I do live here Cassie reflected, brushing aside the thought that her new position was only temporary. She smiled, recalling the little Gatekeepers Cottage at the end of the drive with the pretty garden, a world away from her flat back in London, which wouldn't be her flat for much longer. She was feeling less upset about that. Would she miss the constant hum of traffic or the police and ambulance sirens going off day and night living in a city? She didn't think so. Cassie wouldn't miss their neighbours in the flat above either. They were a pleasant couple and couldn't help the noise to-ing and fro-ing on the wooden flooring above her head. Her only concern tonight was how she would feel in a strange place, in a strange bed, without the familiar sound of city life outside her bedroom window. Would the silence, although a welcome change, disturb her? She turned her thoughts to the final resident, wondering where her patient was.

She hadn't had a chance to look at the medical notes or discuss her history with Phyllis. However, she was aware today was not about work but familiarising herself with her surroundings and finding her feet before she started the first shift tomorrow. There would be plenty of time to learn more about each resident.

Cassie glanced at Olivia sitting on the sofa texting on her phone. They were still waiting on Ruby. According to Olivia, she had lived here much longer than the others, which meant she must be quite elderly. It would take her some time to get up in the morning. Jill was here, doing her rounds, delivering breakfast and getting Ruby up and helping her dress.

As she gazed outside, Cassie could just imagine an elderly lady sitting on the patio wearing a sun hat. It must be lovely to throw those doors open on a beautiful summer's day and sit with a cup of tea and a novel.

Cassie spied some ceramic pots filled with geraniums, petunias, colourful fuchsias and pansies. Beyond the terrace was a rose garden. She could see a high red brick wall marking the boundary to the kitchen garden. She stared outside, wondering if the same gardener still worked here, tending the grounds and the vegetable garden since her student placement here twenty-five years ago. On her free afternoons, she remembered venturing into the grounds to explore.

It wasn't just the beautiful gardens that drew her outside. That's where she met her English boyfriend for a snog – as he called it. He would wait for her, and they would walk hand-in-hand to find a quiet corner to talk, but mainly kiss and cuddle.

They discovered a place where they would not be disturbed, a long greenhouse in the kitchen garden. The greenhouse itself wasn't very private. The garden where the greenhouse stood had a six-foot high red brick wall around the perimeter. It made the location very private, if the gardener didn't come to tend to his vegetables.

Cassie smiled when she remembered that one time he appeared. He popped into the greenhouse with a watering can and watered some plants. She recalled the surprised look on his weather-beaten face when he discovered there weren't just plants in his greenhouse, but two frisky teenagers who couldn't keep their hands off one another. Cassie had been mortified as her boyfriend chose that moment to put his hand up her jumper.

She sighed. What she wouldn't give to turn back the clock to those heady, carefree days of her youth. To do something outrageous and fun like snogging in a greenhouse. The things they used to get up to. He had a motorbike. She remembered riding pillion behind him, her arms wrapped around his waist, her head thrown back, eyes closed, the wind rushing past her head. Cassie hadn't thought about that in years. Oh, to be young and foolish, and in love, she mused as she stared outside.

Olivia walked over and joined her by the glass doors. 'Cassie, I'd like you to meet Ruby.'

Cassie heard a peculiar whirring sound. She turned around and saw a young woman in an electric wheelchair. Cassie opened her mouth to say something to Olivia.

Olivia caught her expression. 'I know what you're thinking. I'll explain later.'

Cassie recalled the assumption she'd made, that her patient would be of advancing years, not a woman in her thirties. What was she doing living here? This was residential accommodation comprising self-contained retirement apartments meant for independent people over a certain age, not someone with complex needs.

Olivia walked over and knelt beside the wheelchair. 'Ruby, this is Cassie. She's an occupational therapist. She will be working with you.'

Ruby's head lolled to one side as she tried to focus on Cassie. She managed a lop-sided grin as her arms fluttered uncontrollably.

Cassie said in alarm, 'Is she having a seizure?' She looked as though she was having an epileptic fit.

'No, nothing like that. Ruby is pleased to see you – that's all. Aren't you, Ruby?'

The young woman squealed. Her body shook in the chair.

Cassie came over and knelt the other side of the wheelchair, wishing someone had prepped her before she met her patient. This wasn't what she was expecting. 'Hello, Ruby, I'm pleased to meet you.'

Ruby rolled her head in Cassie's direction throwing her another lop-sided grin, blonde hair falling about her face as she did so.

Cassie wasn't in the habit of being condescending by talking about her patients when they were in the room, but she had to ask Olivia, 'How much does she understand of what's going on?'

Olivia turned to Ruby. 'Cassie and I need to have a little chat outside. Jill will be come back with your breakfast in a minute. Is it all right?'

Ruby frowned.

'You will have lots of time to get to know Cassie tomorrow.'

Her infectious grin returned.

Cassie and Olivia rose from either side of her wheelchair and walked out of the room. The first thing Olivia said when they stepped out of the apartment was, 'Phyllis hasn't talked to you about your patient yet, has she?'

Cassie shook her head. 'I assumed everyone here was, you know, like Bertie, Iris, and Evelyn.'

'Yes, I gathered that from the surprised look on your face when you turned around and saw Ruby. Sorry, I didn't realise Phyllis hadn't spoken to you about her. She's far from independent. Jill does personal care, gets her out of bed, washed, dressed and into her chair. Then she brings her breakfast. She can eat herself but tends to make a bit of a mess. Jill's always on hand, though, to help.'

Cassie looked at her for a long moment. 'I thought this was sheltered accommodation. Shouldn't she be somewhere more suitable for her condition?' And by condition, Cassie was talking about the fact that she wasn't old and she wasn't independent. 'I have to ask – what's she doing here?'

'That's a good question.' Olivia walked over to a window seat in the hall. Through the little panes of glass in the Georgian window, Cassie saw a large circular stone ornamental pond in an inner courtyard. She joined Olivia on the window seat. 'Ruby came here around thirteen years ago, in her mid-twenties. She was involved in a car accident.'

When Cassie first saw Ruby, she imagined two possibilities concerning her patient's condition. Either she was born like this; Cerebral Palsy came to mind. She had all the classic signs apart from one obvious thing – she was in her thirties. Children born with that condition rarely lived beyond their teens. Cassie had already guessed what had happened to her patient. RTA's they called them in the hospital where she used to work, short for *road traffic accidents*. Most people with broken limbs and internal injuries, who didn't die at the scene, would eventually walk out of the hospital and get on with their lives. They were the lucky ones. 'Head injury?'

Olivia nodded. 'Yes, I'm afraid so along with damage to the spinal cord. As you may have gleaned, Ruby is a paraplegic; she can't walk and doesn't have full control over her upper limbs either. That's where you come in, by exploring ways of aiding her to be as independent as her condition allows. Also, we've noticed she's been down lately. She's usually so happy-go-lucky. That's the first time she's smiled in quite some time.'

'Why do you think that is?'

'She's aware she's moving soon. Maybe that's why she's unhappy. But then who wouldn't be leaving a place like this?'

Cassie understood. She remembered how sad she was when she was a student and her placement finished here. She was gutted when the time came to leave. Although she'd had mixed emotions. When her boyfriend dumped her, she couldn't wait to go.

'Her speech can be quite slurred so it's difficult and time-consuming for Ruby to make herself understood.' Olivia continued, 'It just goes to show that no matter how bad we feel things are, there are people worse off.'

Cassie agreed. Which brought her back to her original question, 'So, what's she doing here? Surely, there are more suitable places?' What she was thinking about was a place with other patients like Ruby. She knew they existed. A care home where she would be among people her own age and there would be more going on. She would be able to participate in activities with other residents, enjoy trips out, and generally have more to do than stuck in a large, albeit beautiful apartment, in the bowels of a mansion, out of sight of people. She voiced her thoughts.

'Hmm, interesting you should put it like that.' Olivia shrugged. 'I don't know. You'd have to speak to her family and find out why she's here.'

She was about to say, *I'll do that,* when Olivia added, 'If you can trace them.'

Cassie raised her eyebrows. 'What do you mean?'

'I'm afraid Ruby and Evelyn have got more in common than just being your patients. They both have no visitors.'

'What – none at all?'

'Nope.'

'But there must be somebody, a relative, a friend, someone who pays for Ruby to be here.'

'Yes, but they never visit.'

'How awful just to leave her here and not return to see her – ever,' Cassie replied. 'What sort of person does that?' It was a rhetorical question.

'Precisely.'

They sat on the window seat across the hall and stared at the door to the plushest apartment in the house.

'Her flat takes up the entire wing, you know,' commented Olivia.

'It does?'

'Tomorrow, when you start your first shift, I'm sure Jill won't mind showing you around.'

Cassie voiced her thoughts. 'It must cost a small fortune to rent.'

'Oh, yes.'

Cassie narrowed her eyes. 'Sounds like a guilt trip – if you ask me.'

Olivia looked at Cassie. 'Yes, I never thought of it that way.'

'Do you know how it happened?'

'The car accident?'

'Yes.'

Olivia shook her head no.

Jill came down the hall carrying a tray. She'd been back to the kitchen to prepare Ruby's breakfast although it was now mid-morning. Cassie had glanced at her watch.

They both rose from their spot on the window seat. Olivia walked over and opened the door to the apartment. Jill walked inside, carrying a tray.

Olivia turned to Cassie. 'So, you've met all the residents now. You've seen a bit of the hall.' She glanced behind Cassie out the window. 'There are still the grounds to explore. You've got a free afternoon and it's such a lovely day.'

Cassie turned around and looked through the little panes of glass in the Georgian window. 'It is, isn't it?' She loved autumn; it was her favourite season. She thought she might just do that, go for a wander in the garden and hope she didn't bump into that gardener. She couldn't imagine he'd still be here.

Olivia looked at her watch. 'I've got to start work. Bertie is due for his morning physio. I'm sure he will be *so* pleased to see me,' she said sarcastically. 'But he's not getting out of it this time.'

Cassie smiled at her. She recognised herself in the young woman standing before her. Olivia might be young and newly qualified, but she took her job and the welfare of her patients very seriously. She didn't accept any ruck. Which was important in their line of work; you had to be firm. It was always in the patient's best interests otherwise they'd never get back on their feet and lead the quality of life they deserved.

She knew why Bertie tried to avoid Olivia. It was the nature of their work, making their patients do things they rarely felt like doing because they were tired or in pain. It meant they looked at you as the enemy, rather than the person who had their best interests at heart. Cassie sighed. Sometimes, with all the will in the world, there was just no helping some people. Cassie was thinking of Her Ladyship. She imagined she would have a battle on her hands to get her to do anything.

Olivia heard Cassie sigh and guessed what she was thinking. Meeting Bertie and Iris had given her the wrong impression. Evelyn and Ruby were more complex patients, albeit for different reasons. Olivia wondered what her experience was, clinically. The other therapist who upped and left didn't have a background in neurological disorders like Ruby's resulting from a head injury.

She had experience with mental health issues and dementia, which meant she should have made some progress with Evelyn, but despite her clinical expertise in that area she didn't get anywhere with Evelyn either. Olivia was aware there had been no formal diagnosis. Her Ladyship refused to see a G.P. She wasn't that far gone that she didn't know why they wanted her to have a visit from the local doctor. 'I expect Phyllis will fill you in more about your patients. She's got the paperwork in her office so you can review their medical notes before you start work.'

Cassie nodded. That was her intention.

'If you want to follow me, I'll take you back to the main entrance hall. This place is a bit of a maze. Until you find your way around you are liable to get lost. I still get lost and I've been here almost a year! These hallways look all the same to me.'

Although Cassie was familiar with the house from her student placement, it had been a long time since she was here last. The house was bigger than she remembered. She didn't realise there were wings of the house she'd never seen before.

They walked together, retracing their steps down the carpeted corridors, passing framed pictures hanging on the walls. Cassie glanced at them as they passed by. There were paintings from a bygone era of horses and hounds in the grounds with the stately home in the background.

Cassie was thinking of the residents she'd just met, especially Ruby. Although she wouldn't say this was the best place for their youngest resident. A modern residential facility would be more practical, with more staff, and more activities suited to her needs. The fact remained that this had been her home for a number of years. It was sad she had to leave. A shame they all had to go.

Cassie said as much.

Olivia sighed. 'I've read of some places which have gone into administration, leaving people's relatives scrabbling around to find them somewhere to live. Although plans for redevelopment are being submitted to the council for approval real soon, at least everyone has time to sort out alternative accommodation.'

'That's good, I suppose.'

'Yeah, I guess,' agreed Olivia. 'Evelyn will be a problem, though.'

'How so?'

'She's adamant she's not going anywhere.' Olivia stared at Cassie. '*I can't leave until he returns from the war* – those were her *exact* words.'

'The war?'

'See, I told you she's not all there.'

13

Cassie stepped outside. Although she couldn't wait to return to the cottage and read her Dad's email, she had a free afternoon and fancied a wander in the grounds in the sunshine. The problem was her first shift tomorrow was playing on her mind. There didn't seem to be enough work. If she was bored, Cassie realised she would have too much time to dwell on her soon-to-be ex-husband setting up home with someone else, who was years younger, with a baby on the way. Cassie frowned. Sometimes life just wasn't fair.

She stood on the circular gravel drive outside the house, taking in the handsome building before her, with its soothing terracotta red brick façade and original leaded windows. The little turrets and the odd gargoyle gave the mansion a distinctly gothic appearance.

This was the first time since her arrival she'd had a chance to appreciate the stunning architecture of the building and its setting. It was in the heart of the Sussex countryside, surrounded by green meadows, but close to the south coast. Despite its size, Fletchling Hall still felt like someone's home. She imagined a couple from a by-gone era stepping out of the grand house and straight into their chauffeur-driven car, like something out of a period drama.

As she stared up at the house, she saw Evelyn sitting at the window in her lounge two-stories up. Despite being a rude, cantankerous old woman, Cassie felt there was nothing wrong with Evelyn. She seemed lucid for a lady of her age. Perhaps after what Olivia said, she had to revise that first impression.

I can't leave until he returns from the war.

The war? What year did she think this was? Evelyn sat there waiting for a visitor who would never come.

Cassie thoughts turned to her other patient. Cassie imagined she would be a pleasure to work with. She liked Ruby. Despite her disabilities, her radiant smile and positive personality shone through. Shame the same couldn't be said for Evelyn.

Evelyn spotted her. She threw Cassie a sour look and closed the curtains even though it was the middle of the day. Her behaviour didn't surprise Cassie. Evelyn was a whole other ball game. Perhaps Her Ladyship should meet the youngest resident. Maybe it would make Evelyn think twice before she complained about her breakfast and threw her plate at Jill or closed her curtains on such a beautiful day. Or took an instant dislike to people, like the new O.T.

Cassie frowned. Didn't Olivia say the last therapist walked out? She wasn't surprised. Her gaze shifted to another window where she spotted Bertie waving. His jolly round face was pressed up against the windowpane. Cassie smiled when Olivia appeared at the window wagging a finger at Bertie, no doubt telling him off for straying from his physio.

Cassie gave him an enormous wave in return before her eyes shifted back to Evelyn's window. The curtains were still closed.

Cassie thought about the reason she'd gone into occupational therapy. It was her instinct to help people. It had been there from word dot. She always knew she'd train in some clinical capacity. A therapist was the perfect fit. However, with what was going on in her life, did she have it in her to win round a difficult old lady? That was before she tried therapy. Evelyn must be suffering from dementia or depression, or some form of mental illness that was bringing on these time-lapses.

Cassie didn't have a lot of experience in this clinical area. She hadn't come here for a challenge. After meeting Evelyn, she realised she would have to use all her resources just to win her over, providing she tackled the first hurdle which was getting in the door. Cassie breathed a sigh and turned from the house. What choice did she have? She couldn't return to London and her old life; that was gone.

Cassie walked around the side of the house into the pretty gardens. Determined to enjoy her afternoon walk in the sunshine, she continued straight ahead through a rose garden. The sweet-smelling fragrance barely registered as she strolled along the pathway. Cassie was still thinking about her patients. She'd need to spend some time mulling over Evelyn and Ruby's differing needs to draw up an individualised programme of therapy. The youngest residents' condition was more in tune with the work she was used to – neurological disorders and head injuries. She taught patients how to regain some independence through adapting their physical environment and suggesting physical aids. Evelyn was quite different. That probably explained why she felt out of her depth.

Cassie felt mean for thinking it, but she *was* eighty-seven; apart from reading a book and staring out the window, what was she going to occupy her with? Gardening came to mind. The trouble was Cassie found it difficult to picture Evelyn with a fork and trowel planting a flowerpot, let alone getting dirty digging in the garden. She was at a complete loss how to draw her out. There was one thing she could do; spend time getting to know her. There had to be something that might interest her other than spending all her time living in the past.

Cassie walked down a leafy path and spotted a signpost up ahead. On the post was a small sign, *The Kitchen Garden.* It pointed down a short cobbled lane to an arched wooden door with a large brass door handle. Cassie recognised that door. She'd been here before, years ago. It was set in a six-foot red brick wall that ran the perimeter of the kitchen garden.

Cassie shrugged. That way was as good as any and she turned down the path. The door was ajar. She pushed it open and stood there staring into the garden. It hadn't changed much since she was here last. Cassie imagined, just for a moment, she was eighteen again with her whole life ahead of her; she was on the cusp of realising the life she had always dreamed of here in England.

It was a dream come true when her father announced one day, out of the blue, that he was returning to England to find his English family. Cassie couldn't pinpoint when she found out her dad wasn't born in Canada. It was as though she'd always known. It was a topic of conversation that had often come up here and there. She knew her grandparents had adopted her father.

It was her beloved grandparents, whom she adored, who told her when she was little the story about a boy – her father – who travelled by boat from a faraway land called England to come and live with them in Canada. They left out the part, which she found out much later, about the British Government's policy of transporting children to populate the British Empire. They also didn't mention her father was not sent to live with them but started life in Canada on a remote farm in Ontario.

Martin wouldn't talk about those first few months in Canada. Although he was very young, she realised those experiences were still seared on his memory. She imagined from what she'd read about other British children sent abroad, he must have had an awful time when he arrived. Thank goodness her father's story had a happy ending – in Canada at least. She was aware his life would always be tinged with loss and grief over not finding his English family.

Cassie recalled the first time she had wandered the grounds and happened upon this doorway. She'd been here with her father. They'd walked down this path together. He remembered it from his childhood. The older girl he played with called it their secret garden. This was a doorway to a fairy garden, she'd told him. He believed her. He was just a little boy.

When he returned all those years later, he discovered the secret garden was in fact the kitchen garden. He'd laughed. The girl had made it out to be this wonderful, magical place that only they knew about. He didn't remember her name. Cassie guessed she might have been another evacuee, but was she his sister?

Cassie felt a tinge of sadness that they'd come here with such high hopes. They imagined this would be the first step in their journey to find the English relatives he'd left behind, but it was not to be. There was a researcher at the Child Migrants Trust who had contacted her father in Canada. They had unearthed a record of a child called Martin at a local orphanage in Sussex and traced his arrival there from Fletchling Hall.

The orphanage was long gone. Although the building still stood, it was now a private boarding school. The researcher had surmised that although he had started his journey as an evacuee to Fletchling Hall, before the end of the war, they sent him to the orphanage. Did that mean his parents had died during the London Blitz? He was no longer an evacuee if he had no home to go back to. Is that why her father was sent by boat to Canada because he was an orphan?

The Child Migrants Trust's answer was astonishing. Children sent to orphanages, and then shipped to start new lives abroad, were not necessarily orphans. Many parents tried to claim their children after the war but learned they'd been put into care and then adopted by British couples. Nothing could be further from the truth. They'd been lied to about their children's whereabouts, about their fate. And so had the children sent abroad, painting a rosy picture for them of what they might expect in their new adopted countries.

After the Child Migrants Trust told him there was a strong possibility he wasn't an orphan, he travelled to England to find his family. Cassie was only a teenager back then. She didn't grasp the enormity of what it meant for her father to return to England and not find them. Although she would have loved to meet them, and she wanted to help her dad find them, what had been at the forefront of her mind was her career and leaving home. Cassie wanted her independence. Her dream was to live in England.

Cassie was standing in the doorway, staring into the kitchen garden, reminiscing about a teenage boy she once knew. After all these years, she didn't know why he came to mind. It must be returning here, to the place they first met.

'Can I help you?'

Cassie jumped at the sound of a voice. She whirled around to find an old man standing behind her with a spade in his hand.

'Oh, I'm new here,' Cassie said. She didn't want any trouble if someone thought she was trespassing. 'I start work up at the house tomorrow. They said I could go for a walk in the grounds.'

'Right you are,' he replied.

She stared at the old man. He was the gardener from years ago, she was sure of it. Although he seemed old back then, Cassie guessed anyone over thirty seemed ancient to a teenager. She imagined the gardener was in his seventies now. He was past retirement age, but Cassie wasn't surprised he wanted to stay on at Fletchling Hall.

'May I pass, young lady?'

Young lady? That brought a smile to her lips. 'Oh, of course.' Cassie stepped through the doorway into the kitchen garden so he could get by.

The gardener picked up his spade and walked past Cassie.

Even though it was years ago, she felt her cheeks blush at the thought of the gardener happening upon her and her boyfriend in the greenhouse, in the middle of a heavy petting session; he wouldn't remember her or that embarrassing incident.

She stood there for a moment staring into the garden until she remembered she had something to ask him. 'Excuse me!' Cassie called out.

He couldn't have heard her for he didn't turn around. She took the same path straight through the centre of the garden, quickening her pace to catch up with him. She didn't have to worry about losing sight of the old man in here. The kitchen garden was laid out in a grid pattern with similar-sized rectangular plots, some for growing vegetables and others for beautiful displays of flowers and fauna.

She caught up with him digging over earth in one of the vegetable plots near the greenhouse. She came to a halt on the path the other side of the plot.

He glanced at her but didn't stop what he was doing.

'Excuse me,' Cassie said politely.

'Take a left out of the kitchen garden and follow the path through the rose garden. That's how you find your way back to the house.'

For a moment she didn't know what he was on about. 'Thank you, but I'm not lost.'

The gardener stopped what he was doing and looked at her.

She took that as her cue to ask him a question. She wanted to know how long he'd worked here. Was he here during the war when evacuee children came to stay at the house? It was possible, although he would only have been a young lad. Perhaps his father was the head gardener and he had accompanied him, from time to time, and eventually taken over his job. It wouldn't be unheard of back then.

She wanted to ask if he remembered a little boy, the youngest evacuee. 'I hope you don't mind me asking, but I was wondering how long you have—'

'I recognise you.' He pointed a finger at Cassie.

'Who – *me*?' she said in surprise.

'I was digging over this soil, wracking my brain over why you seem familiar. I've seen you somewhere before.'

Cassie shook her head. 'You have me confused with someone else.' At least she hoped he did. She hadn't been back here for decades. Surely, he didn't remember that episode—

'The greenhouse – that was it!'

'I don't know what you're talking about,' she said defensively, feigning ignorance.

The gardener chuckled. 'I think you do.'

'Nope, no idea.' She was too embarrassed to look him in the eye. 'You must have me confused with someone else.'

He put his elbows on the spade handle and leaned on it, eyeing her intently. 'I never forget a face, young lady, especially one as pretty as yours.'

Cassie blushed even more.

He glanced to his right at the greenhouse.

She followed his gaze. If she had any doubts he was still confusing her with someone else, the next question only confirmed he did recognise her.

'Where's your fella, the good-looking, dark-haired boy?'

Cassie rolled her eyes. Why did old people have such long memories? 'It didn't work out,' she said bluntly.

'That is a shame. I seem to recall he was besotted with you.'

She didn't want to talk about it.

'You should have given him a chance. I think he was a keeper.'

Cassie looked at him. Why did he assume it was *her* that ended it? What a cheek.

'Found yourself someone better – did yer?'

That was it. Cassie was out of here. 'Well, I must go.' Cassie started at a pace down the path before she said something quite rude. The irony was it was *him* who dumped her suddenly with no warning and left her devastated. To this day, she had no idea why. Then she met someone else who turned out a complete shit too.

The gardener had hit a sore point. How come her little sister found Mr Right when she was a teenager, and they got married and had kids? Why didn't her life follow such a straightforward path?

'Wasn't there something you wanted to ask me?' he called after her.

Cassie had forgotten all about the reason she'd caught up with him. She wished she hadn't bothered. It was very rude, but she ignored him. She didn't need the gardener to remind her what rotten luck she had with men.

14

Cassie threw the bedcovers to one side and sat up. She fumbled for her phone to check the time. 'Are you kidding me?' It was midnight and she was still awake. 'This is ridiculous.'

She'd set her alarm for seven o'clock in the morning. It wouldn't take her any time at all to get to work; her patients were a ten-minute amble up the scenic drive. It was a world away from the crowded London underground commute she was used to every day. It was so quiet here and there would be no traffic noise to wake her. She was worried she would sleep in and make a poor impression arriving late for her first day. Cassie felt like the new girl starting school wondering if she would fit in, even after meeting the other members of staff.

After exiting the kitchen garden in double-quick time yesterday afternoon, Cassie returned to the cottage to pack up her stuff and leave. Bumping into the gardener and dredging up her past at Fletchling Hall only confirmed what she'd been thinking; she'd made a bad decision returning here. She wanted a fresh start. This wasn't it.

She'd been making her way back to the house to inform Phyllis about her decision, and hand over the keys to

Gatekeepers Cottage, when Jill caught up with her. Phyllis wanted to see her. Cassie's first thought was she'd learned what happened when she'd attempted to meet Evelyn. She'd got a door slammed in her face. That wasn't her fault, but it wasn't an auspicious start to her new job.

Perhaps Phyllis had second thoughts about employing her. Cassie was told in her interview that everybody started on a month's probation. Maybe hers had come to a premature end already and they were letting her go. At first she hoped that was the case. That saved an uncomfortable conversation whereby she had to tell Phyllis she was leaving.

Cassie wasn't unduly concerned resigning from the position. She was convinced she could still get her job back in London. There was a huge shortage of nurses and allied health professionals. One of her friends would put her up until the flat sold. It wouldn't be long, and they would exchange contracts. She could have a fresh start.

It appeared she had nothing to worry about until she was on her way to see Phyllis and got a text from her good friend back in her old job. Dawn was keeping her abreast of what was going on at the hospital. Cassie imagined she was also putting out the feelers to see if she had changed her mind and wanted to return. How fortuitous. Cassie knew what she would to say to that.

Cassie sat in bed in the darkened room thinking about that text. She recalled all those kind remarks about having her back in a heartbeat when she left the hospital. Now they had advertised her position and already compiled a shortlist of possible applicants for the post. Dawn wished Cassie luck tomorrow when she started her new job.

Cassie knew there would be other jobs, but she'd have to

apply like everybody else. And that would take time. She was stuck here. After finding out she couldn't just walk back into her previous position, Cassie was a lot less blasé when she met up with Phyllis. In fact, she'd felt downright nervous.

It wasn't as though she'd be penniless if she lost this job. She had some savings to tide her over, but for how long? She needed to stay in employment if she wanted to apply for another mortgage when the flat sold or even get a rental. The property prices in England to buy or rent just seemed to go up, whereas in Canada…

For the first time, it crossed Cassie's mind to return to Toronto. Canada had a shortage of O.T.'s. The income over there would be much better too. The clinical professions, especially nurses and therapists, seemed much more valued in Canada. There was greater clinical responsibility, but the roles were well remunerated.

'But I don't feel Canadian,' Cassie said, sitting there in the darkness. She'd miss England.

Lucky for her she didn't have to think about a fresh job or where she would live just yet. After all that worry over why Phyllis had summoned her, all she wanted was to see if she would join the other staff in the kitchen at seven for an evening meal together. Phyllis liked to make it an occasion, welcoming new recruits to Fletchling Hall.

Randall had volunteered to cook the dinner. Cassie smiled when she thought of him trying to impress her. The meal was good and the company lively. They all had stories to tell, talking shop about the places they had worked and patients they'd met. It was enjoyable, especially listening to Randall and hearing about his experiences living and working in Australia. Not that Cassie was taking an interest in him personally. She'd made sure she didn't sit next to him at the dinner table and was at pains to avoid any awkwardness. The last thing she needed was a relationship right now.

She got the impression he thought they had something in common. Randall was working abroad just like Cassie. However, unlike him, she didn't feel a foreigner. This was her home. If anything, returning to Canada after all these years would resemble a move to a foreign country. That didn't stop her considering the possibility after her divorce. Canada had one thing England would never have – family.

Perhaps that's what was keeping her awake. Plan B, returning to London, had just gone up in a puff of smoke. This was it until she sold the flat and could sever all ties with Lars, and possibly England too. For now, Cassie decided she better make the best of it.

Cassie breathed a huge sigh. It was no use lying down as she was wide awake. She reached over and turned on the bedside lamp, swung her legs out of bed and walked over to the dressing table. Cassie had forgotten to shut down her laptop. She tapped a random key on the keyboard. The computer powered up; the screen appearing in seconds. Her father's email was still open where she'd left it before she got into bed. She'd already read it – twice. It was long. This didn't surprise her. She smiled. Her father was a writer.

She asked him once why he never became a full-time writer. He'd written several articles that were printed in educational journals. Surely, it wouldn't be a great leap to write a book and get that published too. His response was that very few writers earn a living from writing. The reality was most needed a day job.

That's why he trained to teach. He enjoyed his chosen profession and he was good at it; he finished his career as a college professor. It paid the bills and afforded his family a nice home and his children a comfortable upbringing in Toronto.

Did he regret his decision not to give writing a go, even if it meant he might have spent some years on the breadline before he got a breakthrough? His reply didn't surprise her. Having a family was everything to her dad. If that meant giving up a dream, then it was a small price to pay. If he could go back and do it all again, he wouldn't change a thing for all the writing accolades in the world. He counted himself lucky in life. He had it all; a family and a fulfilling career. And now he was doing something he had always dreamed of – writing a book.

Cassie fancied sitting down and re-reading that long email. She hadn't replied yet. She thought she'd wing him one off after the meal, but it was late, and she was tired. When she eventually returned to the cottage, the eventful day arriving here, and meeting the staff and residents, had caught up with her. She assumed when her head hit the pillow she'd be out like a light. No such luck.

Cassie glanced at her bed with the sheets and duvet in disarray. How was she going to get to sleep now? 'I know!' She was thinking about a nice mug of warm milk. It was worth a try.

Cassie walked out of the bedroom, down the short hallway past the lounge and into the kitchen. Jill had kindly delivered a small box of groceries to get her started comprising a loaf of bread, butter, jam, cereal, coffee, tea, sugar and milk so she could have breakfast in the morning before work.

Cassie took the milk out of the fridge, wondering why the bottle felt warm to the touch. The inside of the fridge didn't feel that cold either. Cassie rolled her eyes when she realised she hadn't switched it on, which meant…. 'Ugh!' The milk was off.

Through the window, she glanced up the garden at the house. There was milk in the kitchen for their coffee breaks. Jill said she could help herself. She didn't mean sneaking in for a milky drink at midnight, but who was to know?

Cassie slipped on some jogging bottoms and a sweatshirt over her pyjamas, took the torch from the kitchen drawer, and a jug from a cupboard. She stepped outside the cottage. It was colder than she expected. Cassie started up the drive. She hoped she didn't bump into anybody when she reached the house. Randall and Olivia lived in, but Phyllis and Jill lived in the village with their families.

There was a duty manager on call for emergencies, and two young health care assistants on a rota during the nights for Ruby. They might be sitting in the kitchen on a break, but she didn't mind that. They were used to the staff in and out, rustling up something to eat or drink. Cassie's thoughts turned to Randall, hoping she didn't bump into him, raiding the fridge for a midnight snack.

Although she brought the torch, it wasn't necessary. Solar-powered lights lit up the driveway leading up to the house. Cassie swung the torch left and right, lighting up the gardens. She walked briskly, feeling a little spooked by the darkness. It wasn't something she was used to in London.

Cassie stepped into the house and was relieved to find table lamps with low wattage bulbs left on in the hallway, illuminating the stairs and the corridor to the kitchen. It was a welcome change from the eerie blackness of her midnight walk up the drive.

Cassie felt the warmth of the Aga as she walked into the kitchen. She was alone. There were two mugs left on the table where she imagined the health care assistants had sat together earlier in the evening before their shift started.

She opened the tall larder fridge and made a mental note to buy an extra pint of milk when she went shopping to replace what she was about to use. She found a mug in one of the cupboards, poured some milk and zapped the mug in the microwave. Cassie stood there listening to the whirring sound of the microwave oven, hoping that some warm milk did the trick and sent her off to sleep. She couldn't afford to be tired on the first day of her new job.

She took the milk out of the microwave and was standing with the mug in both hands, gently blowing on the hot milk to cool it down, when she froze. *What was that?* She thought she heard something. She moved away from the counter towards the open doorway and poked her head outside in the corridor. 'Hello?'

Nobody answered.

Cassie heard the rustling sound again. 'Oh no, we've got rats,' she said to the empty room as she whirled around, almost spilling the milk, her eyes darting around the floor. She was looking for something black, furry and repulsive scampering across the floor.

There was nothing there.

Cassie remembered to breathe. She was just putting her mug to her lips, thinking it must have been her imagination, when she heard it again. She put her drink down on the table and followed the sound. It seemed to be coming from a tall cupboard. She looked about her and spotted a broom standing against the wall in the corner of the room. Cassie grabbed the broom handle and returned to the cupboard. She couldn't leave until she'd investigated what it was.

Cassie held on to the broom handle with one hand and leaned forward. She gingerly opened the cupboard door. It swung wide open. She held the broom at the ready in case something scurried out in her direction. What she intended to do with a broom if confronted by a rat, she had no idea. Shoo it away?

Nothing scurried out at her. In fact, when she opened the door, she discovered it wasn't a cupboard at all but a doorway to the cellar. There was a flight of stone steps leading down into darkness. She was about to close the door when she heard it again, rustling. It was coming from down there.

Just close the door, take your milk, and return to the cottage.

Curiosity got the better of her. She put the broom aside and brought out the torch from the pocket of her jogging bottoms. She shone the light down the stairs and caught sight of a light switch. Cassie flicked the switch. The stairs and room below were bathed in a bright pool of light. The moment the light went on the rustling ceased. She made her way down the flight of stairs.

There was a musty, damp smell. Before she stepped off the last stair, she peered into the room. It was large with whitewashed walls, low ceilings and an old black and white tiled floor. There was a sink on one side of the room which suggested that in years gone by, this was a scullery. She imagined the original kitchen was down here too. This was where the servants from yesteryear cooked the Lord and Lady of the hall their meals. She recognised rooms like this from her visits to National Trust properties of a similar age.

'Ugh!' She hadn't seen a rat but spotted a spider. 'Silly

woman,' she said under her breath. What did she think she'd find down here besides cobwebs and spiders?

Houses like this with old central heating systems, created all sorts of odd noises. Cassie guessed why she found that unnerving. She couldn't remember the last time she'd spent a night away from the flat. Holidays with her husband or romantic trips away with Lars had become a thing of the past. Little wonder her ears were super-sensitive to strange sounds emanating from unfamiliar surroundings. It was probably nothing.

Cassie turned on the stair, intending to make her way back up to the kitchen, when she heard it again. There was no mistaking it this time. It sounded like rustling paper.

Cassie stepped off the bottom stair. To her left, there was a small basement window that was ajar. It was high up, level with the gardens at the back of the house. Old storage boxes were piled haphazardly under the window. One box had fallen on its side, revealing scrunched newspaper inside. She watched a ball of paper move around the floor in the gentle breeze from the open window. It made a rustling sound on the cold tiled floor. Cassie walked over and picked it up. She was about to return it to the box when she was startled by balls of paper flying out the box followed by furry animals scurrying over each other in their haste to escape their warm, cosy hiding place.

Cassie stepped back in surprise. 'Cats!' She gaped at them as they scrambled up the boxes and squeezed through a gap in the window. The second to last one disturbed the catch as it struggled through and the window banged shut, leaving one scared cat, the smallest of the feral litter, pawing at the windowpane.

She walked over, intending to open the window for him to

join his mates outside. The cat mistook her intentions, hissed at her in fright and darted behind another box at the far end of the room.

'Hey!' she called out gently. 'I was only trying to help.' She guessed they were a litter of feral kittens that had been left by their mother once they were weaned. They must go out to scavenge for food and return here to the warm, dry basement, Cassie thought.

'Here pussy, pussy, pussy.' Cassie frowned. What did she think she was doing? The feral cat would hardly come when it was called. Besides, she'd never been around cats. She had no clue what to do. Cassie had grown up with dogs. She thought perhaps it would be wise to give the cat some space, prove she wasn't a threat.

Cassie backed away from the cat's hiding place. She had an idea and retraced her steps back up the stairs to the kitchen where she'd left her mug on the kitchen table. She picked it up. Her milk was now lukewarm. Cassie found a saucer in one of the kitchen cupboards, returned to the basement and set the saucer down on the floor. She knelt and poured some warm milk into the saucer. She was just getting up when she spotted something in one of the boxes. She reached inside and found a leather-bound book. 'What have we here?'

The cat hissed at the sound of Cassie's voice.

She backed away and walked over to the old butler sink on the other side of the room. Cassie sipped what remained of her mug of lukewarm milk and looked at the book in her hands. It was full of dust. She'd just caught sight of the cat appearing from behind the box when Cassie had the bright idea to blow the dust off the leather jacket. It made her sneeze.

The cat scampered back behind the box.

Cassie sighed. 'You can come out now. No more loud noises, I promise.' She was just opening the book when a tabby head emerged with long whiskers and pointy ears. The cat appeared from behind the boxes. It looked over toward the saucer.

'Go on then, it's there for the taking.'

The cat looked warily in her direction before creeping out from its hiding place.

'I'm not moving from my spot,' she whispered. She watched the cat creep over to the saucer and pause, eyeing her as if deciding whether she was friend or foe. Now she had a good look at the creature she guessed he or she was around six months old. Not fully grown but getting there. It had beautiful silver-grey tiger-like markings.

'You're very pretty,' Cassie commented as she watched it lapping up the milk. 'Perhaps I should get some tins of proper cat food,' Cassie mused. She shook her head. What am I thinking? She couldn't keep the cat. It's feral. Besides, she was sure they didn't allow pets here.

The cat finished its milk and looked up at Cassie.

She smiled. The cat had milky whiskers and a white beard on its chin. 'You look kinda funny.'

As if the cat understood what she said, it sat up and wiped a paw around its mouth several times.

'That's better,' remarked Cassie.

The cat looked at the empty saucer and meowed loudly.

Cassie glanced at her mug of milk. She'd only taken a few sips. She looked over at the cat. 'Do you want some more?'

The cat sniffed the saucer and meowed again, louder this time.

Cassie put a finger to her lips and glanced up at the ceiling. It was a stupid thought. Nobody would hear them from down here. Anyway, why was she so bothered? All she had to do was open the window and the cat would leave, joining its siblings to find another warm, dry basement or garage where they wouldn't be disturbed.

The cat backed away as Cassie draw closer with the mug of milk. She poured some more in the saucer while the cat hid behind the box again. From the corner of her eye, she spied the cat poking its head out, watching her.

'There you go, that's the last of my milk. It was my bedtime drink I'll have you know.'

The cat crept out from its hiding place once more when Cassie retreated to the other side of the room.

She watched the cat lapping up the milk. While her feral friend was distracted, she tiptoed over to the window to see if she could reach up and open it. It was quite high but Cassie was tall. She reached the catch without climbing on a box. Cassie pushed the window open and glanced at the cat still lapping up the milk. Either he would join his litter mates or they might all return. With that thought, Cassie debated whether she should close the window.

She left it open. If the whole litter returned, then so be it. They weren't doing any harm and only wanted a warm, safe place to call home just like everybody else.

The cat finished the milk and licked the saucer clean, then sat cleaning its face again.

'Goodbye, little cat.' Cassie glanced at the open window. 'It was nice meeting you.' She turned around and headed up the stairs with her empty mug. She couldn't be bothered to make herself another drink, so she rinsed the mug in the sink and headed back down the drive.

When she closed the front door to the cottage, she noticed she still had the old leather-bound book in her hands. 'Oh bother, what did I bring that back for?' Cassie walked over to the dressing table and placed it beside the laptop. Before she got back in bed, she moved the little photo of her dad and Albert to the spot on the map marked Vancouver.

She stood back, staring at the map, looking at the distance he had already travelled. Although he was seeing some amazing places – she imagined the scenery was stunning in that part of Canada – she knew his journey was bittersweet. He'd talked a little in his email about some wonderful people he'd met along the way; child migrants like himself who started life in England, only to grow up overseas. He hinted at some sad stories.

She would read all about them in his book, if they were happy for him to write their stories. In his recent email, her father mentioned a group of child migrants he'd met who got together every year. Her father had a circle of friends where he lived who had been child migrants too; it is how he first came up with the idea to travel the country and meet others like himself.

What distinguished this group in Vancouver from the others was that, for the first time, her father met two people who had found their families. Out of all the stories so far, she knew it was the happy ending he was looking for. It might not have happened for him, but he was delighted for them and grateful they shared their story.

Cassie yawned as she closed the laptop. Replying to his email would have to wait. She was about to get into bed and switch off the lamp, looking forward to snuggling down under the covers, when she caught sight of the book from the basement. She picked it up and turned it over in her hand. It looked like a diary. There was no title on the spine or on the front cover. Cassie was about to open it and peek inside when she caught sight of her alarm clock. 'Oh no! Is that the time?' It was one o'clock in the morning. She cast the notebook to one side, switched off the lamp and lay down under the duvet. It was cold, dark and very, very quiet. She checked the alarm clock was set before she drifted off to sleep.

15

The sound of her mobile phone woke her. She reached out and grabbed it off the bedside table, hoping it wasn't Lars.

'Cassie?'

She sighed in relief when she heard Olivia's voice. 'There's toast, and cereal if you want to join us for breakfast up at the house.'

Cassie was about to tell her Jill had bought some provisions when she remembered the milk was off and she'd forgotten to bring some back with her last night.

'It was Randall's idea,' Olivia continued.

'Ah.'

'But don't let that put you off. I promise I won't leave you two alone.'

Cassie laughed although she was serious when she said, 'Promise?'

'Absolutely.'

'Great. I'll just shower first. See you in half-an-hour.'

'Oh, all right, but we start work at nine.'

Cassie was aware of that as she ended the call. She was still lying under her warm duvet wondering why Olivia had reminded her. She reached out, her hand closing around the little alarm clock on the bedside table.

When she saw the time, she could hardly believe it. 'It's eight-thirty!' She sat up with a start. 'I set my alarm, I'm sure of it.' She frowned. Cassie checked three times she had set it before drifting off to sleep. Or was she already dreaming? After that eventful visit to the house late last night, Cassie had an idea she'd fallen asleep the moment her head hit the pillow.

She showered in a rush and dressed in black cords and a grey turtle-neck jumper which was aeons old but she loved to bits. Cassie chose a warm and comfortable outfit for a reason; although the residents' apartments were heated, the leaded windows were draughty and the corridors outside cold.

Cassie looked at her reflection in the long mirror in the hall. She was lucky that despite not being as skinny as she once was, and putting on a few more pounds around the middle and the top of her thighs, being tall meant she could carry the extra weight and still look good for her age.

Cassie tried to tame her tresses with a straightener, decided she didn't have time, and tied it up in a ponytail instead. Wisps of red hair hung in curls about her face. She struggled to tuck them behind her ears with no luck.

About to head out, Cassie remembered the old notebook and returned to the bedroom to fetch it. She had no use for it. Cassie thought she'd better put it back where she found it. She stepped out into the fresh autumnal morning. There was a low-lying mist hovering above the dewy grass. Once it cleared, Cassie guessed it would turn out a crisp, bright day.

She was enjoying her new commute to work, taking in the beautiful morning in the grounds of Fletchling Hall. It beat the packed tube any day. Faint rays of sunshine were breaking through the mist, and the chirrup of birdsong could be heard even though dawn was several hours ago. Cassie looked at her watch. 'Crumbs, I'm late!'

She picked up her pace, rushed into the house and almost careered into Randall and Olivia who were heading towards the grand staircase. They must have just finished breakfast. Cassie came to an abrupt halt. 'I've missed breakfast – haven't I.'

Randall gave her a pearly-white grin. 'Someone slept well.'

Cassie wasn't about to correct that misconception, although it was none of his business.

Olivia stepped in. 'This place is so quiet, unless you set your alarm clock…' she trailed off.

Or think you've set it. Cassie frowned.

'Don't worry.' Olivia added, 'It's happened to all of us. It's so peaceful here. It is a wonder we don't oversleep more often.'

'Speak for yourself,' said Randall good-naturedly.

Olivia raised her eyebrows. 'Do you know how many times I've banged on your door to get you up in the morning…?'

Cassie looked at Randall's expression and had an idea missing the alarm clock was a ruse, an excuse to have Olivia call on him. She turned to Olivia. 'What about the residents? Do they sleep in?' Cassie was wondering if she'd have time for breakfast if Evelyn got up later.

'Sometimes, although Evelyn is another story. She's always up at the crack of dawn.'

'Why? Can't she sleep?'

'No, it's not that. Jill says when she brings her breakfast she's already sitting by the window. It's the same every morning.'

I can't leave until he returns from the war. Cassie nodded, not surprised. She remembered what Olivia had told her yesterday.

Randall chipped in, 'So, she's ready and waiting for your arrival.'

Cassie rolled her eyes. There goes breakfast. She wouldn't mind skipping the first meal of the day, but she was famished. Cassie didn't know whether it was the midnight walk or the exercise hoofing it up the drive that had given her such an appetite.

Phyllis walked out of the kitchen and overheard them talking about Evelyn. 'I didn't see you at breakfast, Cassie.'

'Phyllis, I'm *so* sorry, but I'm late.'

Phyllis waved away her apology with a flick of her hand. 'I bet it must be quite a novelty not to be woken in the morning by traffic noise.' Her tone turned serious. 'Just don't make a habit of it.'

'Oh no, of course not. I will make sure I set my—'

Phyllis nudged her arm. 'Oh goodness, I'm only pulling your leg, Cassie. Go on in the kitchen and have breakfast. Evelyn can wait. She's not going anywhere.' Phyllis smiled. 'I see you have come prepared.'

'Pardon?'

Phyllis's gaze shifted to the notebook in her hands, mistaking it for something that belonged to her newest member of staff. 'It's always a good idea to jot things down while they're fresh in your mind.'

Cassie decided not to mention her trip down to the basement last night where she'd found this notebook. She intended to return it. 'Yes, I'll do that.'

'I know you're here for Ruby. I'm afraid Evelyn was an afterthought, but we're concerned about her mental state. Anything you could come up with to get her interested in something other than staring out that window all day would be marvellous.'

Cassie wished Phyllis hadn't saddled her with Her Ladyship. The job would be a breeze if she only had Ruby to consider.

Phyllis turned to go. 'Oh, one more thing, Cassie. I was rather hoping you might think up some activities for Bertie and Iris too.'

Cassie smiled. The other two residents were lovely. She'd enjoy working with them. She had plenty of time on her hands, and if she didn't, she'd still make time for them. 'Yes, of course, I'll think about what I can do.'

'Yes, why don't you. And write it down.'

Cassie glanced at the old notebook in her hands and held it up. 'Sure.'

Phyllis returned to her office, while Olivia went to see Bertie. Randall smiled at Cassie and then went on his rounds to give the residents their medication.

Cassie turned down the corridor to the kitchen and almost walked headlong into Jill coming out with a tea tray. She sidestepped out of the way. 'Good morning, Jill.'

'Hello, Cassie. I'm taking Ruby breakfast. If you're here for a bite to eat, you'll find a selection of cereals with bread and Jam in a cupboard, and there's milk in the fridge. Just help yourself.'

'Thank you for the groceries to get me started, by the way.' Cassie didn't mention the milk was off. It was her fault for not switching on the fridge. 'Olivia phoned to ask if I wanted to join you all this morning.'

'I know, but you'll be on your own for breakfast, I'm afraid.'

'Yes, I overslept.'

Jill smiled. 'It happens to the best of us.'

'I can't believe I live on top of my job and I'm late for work!'

'That's one reason I don't live in. It's so peaceful here. Sometimes I'm tempted though. I've got a sixteen-year-old at home, my daughter. Never mind the terrible twos, what about the terrible teens?' Jill shook her head. 'When she turned thirteen, we didn't know what hit us.'

It surprised Cassie she had a teenage daughter.

As if reading her mind, Jill commented, 'Having a child later in life came as a bit of a shock, I can tell you.'

'How many children have you got, Jill?'

'Just the one. I didn't think we'd be blessed with children, so it came as quite a surprise when I fell pregnant in my forties. We wouldn't change a thing. Perhaps less World War Three every time we ask her to do something.' Jill shrugged and smiled. 'So, who are you seeing first?'

'Evelyn.' Cassie noticed Jill's face drop the moment she mentioned her name.

'Rather you than me. Her Ladyship is not in a good mood this morning.'

Is she ever, thought Cassie? She didn't want to ask Jill if she'd had a cereal bowl thrown at her already. Standing in the kitchen doorway, she eyed Jill making her way down the corridor carrying Ruby's breakfast. She bet there was a reason Jill took Evelyn's breakfast up first; after calling on Evelyn, her day could only get better. Cassie was not looking forward to seeing Her Ladyship either.

16

Cassie stood in the deserted kitchen not looking forward to her first shift with Evelyn, reminding herself that she would not be here forever; just long enough to finish her temporary contract while she waited for the flat to sell. Then she could sever all ties with Lars, the lying, cheating—

Cassie whirled around, her thoughts interrupted; she thought she heard something in the kitchen. Cassie sighed when she realised it was nothing. Used to the background cacophony of traffic and people walking by her London flat, it was so quiet here her ears were attuned to the least little noise, like a creak of floorboards or strange gurgling sounds that came from the ancient pipework.

She walked over to the kitchen cupboards and found a box of cornflakes. There was a clean bowl and cutlery already laid out on the table for her. Cassie set the cornflakes down on the kitchen table. She turned around and opened the fridge. Inside was the large carton of fresh milk she'd helped herself to last night. When she closed the fridge door, she jumped back in surprise and almost spilt the milk. Sitting by the fridge was a silver and grey tabby cat. It meowed loudly.

'Now look what you made me do!'

Randall chose that moment to walk into the kitchen. 'Sorry, I didn't mean to startle you. Here let me help you clear up.'

'Oh, I wasn't talking to you, I was talking to—' When Cassie cast her gaze at the floor, the cat was nowhere to be seen.

Randall picked up the mug of coffee he'd forgotten and glanced over the table, following her gaze to the floor by her feet. There was nothing there. He had an idea what she was referring to. 'Yes, I've seen one or two myself. Horrible creatures. Ugh!'

Cassie looked at him quizzically. She wouldn't call them horrible, not at all.

'Never liked rats.' Randall walked out of the kitchen.

Cassie raised her eyebrows. Did he just say *rats?* Maybe she shouldn't have disturbed the feral cats. They would have come in handy as mousers. Oh well, too late now thought Cassie, sitting down at the breakfast table. She looked about her. There was no sign of the tabby or any rats. Now Randall had planted that idea in her mind, she'd be doing a sweep of the cottage before she went to sleep tonight. She was just about to pour some milk when she spotted something out of the corner of her eye. There, behind the door that was slightly ajar – the one that led down to the basement – was a silver and grey tabby tail.

'You can come out now. He's gone.'

Cassie did a double take when the cat stepped out from its hiding place. She sighed. 'I left the window open for you to join your mates, you know.' She looked at the carton of milk. 'I suppose you'll want it warm like last night.'

The cat meowed.

Cassie had a soft spot for animals even though she never had the circumstances working full time to own a pet. And by a pet, she meant dogs. She didn't know why it never occurred to her to get a cat. Cassie put some milk in a saucepan to heat on the Aga. A few minutes later she poured warm milk into a saucer and set it on the tiled floor for the cat.

'Talk about déjà vu.' Cassie was thinking about last night. She returned to the table and sat down to eat breakfast. By the time she'd finished her cereal, the cat was back again, sitting by her feet, looking up at her expectantly. Cassie picked up the milk carton. 'Seconds?'

The cat meowed.

'I'm not warming it up this time.' She got up from the table and poured more milk into the saucer before putting the carton back in the fridge. Cassie stood there watching the cat lapping up the milk. 'Now what am I going to do with you?' She couldn't leave the cat here. She bent down to pick up the empty dish just as Jill walked into the kitchen carrying a tea tray.

'Ruby has had her breakfast,' she was saying to Cassie, 'but you're going to see Evelyn first, aren't you?'

'Yes.' Cassie put the saucer in the sink. When she glanced down at the floor, the cat was gone. She wasn't surprised. The clever tabby, with the beautiful silver and grey markings, had stopped here for breakfast before disappearing out the window in the basement. Cassie imagined that would be the last she'd see of her feline friend.

'Cassie, is everything all right?' Jill caught her staring forlornly at the door to the basement. She turned to Jill. 'Um, yes. Fine.'

Jill put the tea tray down on the kitchen table. 'I know what this is about.'

'You do?' Cassie shot her a look, wondering if she had met the tabby cat too.

'I'm no stranger to that feeling of trepidation when I knock on her door each day. Perhaps if Evelyn came down to join Iris and Bertie for breakfast, it might cheer her up and start her day on a better note.'

Cassie nodded, although it wasn't Evelyn she'd been thinking about. She could grow quite fond of that cat. As for Evelyn, that was a different story.

'Do you want me to come with you before Iris and Bertie come down to breakfast?' offered Jill.

'Did I hear someone call my name?' Bertie's booming voice could be heard before he entered the kitchen.

'What are you doing down here so early?' commented Jill. She narrowed her eyes when she caught Bertie grinning at Cassie. 'You were hoping to see Cassie again, weren't you?'

'Guilty as charged.' He looked at Cassie. 'Have you had breakfast yet, young lady?'

Jill cut in. 'Cassie has already had breakfast, and she's now off to visit Evelyn.'

'Oh darn.' Bertie's face fell.

Cassie smiled at him. 'I'll pop along and say hello later, I promise.'

He brightened. 'I'll hold you to that.'

She imagined Bertie would be very happy when he discovered she would be spending more time with him than merely popping her head in to say hello. As she watched Bertie take a seat at the table, Cassie wished she could stay rather than visiting Her Ladyship. Cassie's smile evaporated. She could hazard a guess what sort of reception she was in for. She glanced at Jill preparing Bertie's breakfast and thought at least Evelyn had already eaten so she wouldn't get crockery thrown at her. *Don't count on it,* a little voice in her head said as she made her way upstairs.

Five minutes later, Cassie was standing outside the door to Evelyn's apartment, except this time she didn't have Olivia with her. Cassie took a deep breath and knocked on her door. She had a feeling this would not go well. Cassie got the reception she was expecting when Evelyn opened the door, discovered it was a member of staff, and went to slam it shut. Then something caught her eye. 'What's that?'

'What?' Cassie looked about her, expecting to find the tabby cat had followed her. Who wouldn't stop and stare at such a beautiful creature? What a perfect icebreaker. Cassie frowned at the deserted hallway; there was no cat. She turned back to Evelyn. 'I'm sorry, but I don't know what you're referring to?'

'Right there. What have you got in your hand?'

Cassie looked down. 'Oh, this?' She held up the notebook. She meant to put it in the bin or back in the boxes in the basement, but after what Phyllis had said about writing things down, she'd wiped over the old leather cover and decided to use up any blank pages. 'It's just a notebook.'

'Is it yours?'

Cassie hesitated. She wasn't in the habit of lying. 'No, I found it.'

'You *found* it?'

She looked at Evelyn. Cassie did not appreciate Evelyn's accusatory tone, as though she had done something wrong. Even so, she didn't feel inclined to recount her trip down to the basement in the early hours and tell her where she found it.

'I see.' Evelyn scrutinised her. 'Are you in the habit of taking other people's belongings, young lady?'

'Of course not. It was lying around gathering dust, so rather than chucking it out…' she trailed off.

'You thought you'd keep it.'

Once again, Cassie didn't appreciate what she was implying. 'I felt it might be useful.'

'How so?'

'I might write in it?'

'Is it a blank notebook then?'

'I don't know.'

They both looked at the notebook. Cassie realised she didn't need the cute, cuddly silver-grey tabby cat to break the ice. She already had the icebreaker right here in her hands. 'Why don't I come in and we could find out what's in these pages together? What do you say?' She gave Evelyn her sweetest let-me-in smile, hoping she hadn't just blown it. She could tell Her Ladyship was wavering. Evelyn wasn't stupid. She knew what Cassie's game was. All the same, the animated expression on her face as she stared at the notebook suggested it had piqued her interest.

'I can read it myself if you're too busy.' Cassie turned to go. Out of the corner of her eye, she spotted the door to Evelyn's apartment fly open.

'I suppose you could come in just for a little while.'

Cassie didn't need to be asked twice. She smiled as she followed her into the lounge. Whatever was in the pages of the notebook might be interesting or nothing at all, but at least it got her in the door. One small victory thought Cassie. It was the first time she'd been in Evelyn's apartment, if you didn't count getting the door slammed in her face yesterday when she was standing in her hallway.

'I'll make some tea,' said Evelyn.

'Don't go to any trouble on my account.'

Evelyn looked at her. 'Who said anything about making *you* a cup of tea?'

It was most unprofessional of her, but when Evelyn turned her back, Cassie stuck her tongue out at Her Ladyship. She really was a difficult, stubborn customer.

While Evelyn was busy preparing tea, Cassie sat down on one of the two brown leather sofas. Although they were old – they harked back to the seventies – the sofa was surprisingly comfortable. She sat there gazing around the room. The lounge was a decent size with high ceilings. There were two individual high-backed chairs in a light green velvet material, one positioned in front of the window. Cassie frowned at that chair. She had the impulse to move it, but thought the better of it. She didn't want Evelyn accusing her of touching her things and getting thrown out of her apartment.

The other chair was in an alcove beside an ornate marble fireplace. The open fire was no longer in use; there was a large vase of dried flowers in place of a grate. Cassie glanced at the sofa opposite and the faded Persian rug on the floor between the sofas. On the mahogany coffee table in front of the sofa was a novel. Cassie ran her finger over the top of the hard-backed cover and discovered a thin film of dust. It was just as she suspected. Evelyn hadn't opened the book in a while. She glanced at the chair by the window. Little wonder Phyllis wanted to get her interested in something, to get her head out of the past and into making the most of what time she had left.

Cassie's attention shifted to the other side of the room. There was an old-fashioned mahogany sideboard full of framed photographs. Were they photos of family, Cassie wondered? Was

Evelyn waiting for one of them to visit her? She turned to look out the window once more. Evelyn had the perfect view across the gardens, down the drive. Cassie could see the cottage and two tall stone pillars marking the entrance to the grounds of Fletchling Hall.

Evelyn returned with a small tea tray, placing it on the coffee table. She sat on the sofa opposite Cassie and poured herself a cup of tea from the teapot. She caught Cassie staring at her as she spooned in some sugar. 'If you want tea, you know where the staff kitchen is.'

Cassie bit her lip, stopping herself from replying *yes, your ladyship*. She was here to do a job whether she liked her patient or not. And she couldn't do anything for Evelyn if she was booted out of her apartment. She had a feeling it wouldn't take much to get on the wrong side of her.

Evelyn picked up a small jug from the tray and added a splash of milk to her tea. She glanced at Cassie. 'So, what's inside the notebook?'

Cassie opened the leather-bound book on her lap. She looked at it in surprise. 'It's a diary.'

Evelyn leaned forward in her seat. 'A dairy – you say.'

'Yes.' Cassie flicked through the pages full of writing 'It looks old.' She turned to the first page. 'There's a date!' Cassie read the entry in the top right-hand corner of the page. 'It says first of October nineteen forty-three.' She looked up. 'Hey, we're the first of October!' Cassie and Evelyn exchanged a smile at the coincidence.

That wasn't the only coincidence they were about to discover in the pages of the book. Cassie said, 'You will never believe this…'

Evelyn leaned forward in her seat. 'What is it?'

Cassie shook her head in wonderment at her find. 'Someone who lived at Fletchling Hall wrote this diary.' She looked at Evelyn. 'Do you want me to read it to you?'

'What a stupid question.'

Despite a wisp of a smile, Evelyn was back to her old cantankerous self. Cassie turned her attention to the notebook and started reading, 'My brothers have returned home…'

17

October 1, 1943

'They're here!' She waved from the window, bounced off the bed and ran out of her bedroom along the corridor. 'Mama! Papa! Johnny and Tim are back.'

'Rosie, what have I told you about running in the house?'

Rosie ignored Nanny as she passed her in the passageway.

'How old are you?' Nanny's indignant voice followed her down the hall.

She laughed. 'You know how old I am! I'm nearly fifteen.'

'That's no way for a young lady to behave.'

'Who said I want to be a lady?' Rosie ran down the grand staircase into the main foyer and almost careered into the housemaid who was carrying a pile of clean sheets up the stairs. 'They're here!' she told the maid excitedly.

'I know, miss. I will make up their rooms now, miss.'

'Mama! Papa!' Rosie cried out.

They walked out of the dining room, her father wiping his moustache with a napkin, her mother scolding her for not coming down for breakfast. 'Mama, I'm too excited to eat!'

Her mother looked at her. 'What on earth are you wearing?'

Rosie didn't have time to explain that these were her play clothes. They were her brother's brown trousers and plaid shirts from when they were her age. They were a bit big for her slender frame, but she enjoyed wearing them. She'd found them in a trunk in Johnny's bedroom.

Her mother had seen her in them before. Rosie realised what she was really asking; why hadn't she changed into one of her pretty frocks before coming downstairs? The maid had laid a dress out for her, along with shoes, socks and a braid to plait her hair. Rosie was about to change when she heard the car. She'd told Arthur to sound the horn when he turned into the drive so she wouldn't miss their arrival.

Unlike her mother, she didn't care what she was wearing. It was more important that she was there to greet them when they arrived home. She hoped they didn't have to return to the front. Right now, she didn't want to think about that. Rosie missed them. The house came alive when they were here.

She'd always loved having older brothers until the outbreak of the war. That's when she wished she was the eldest; they would have been too young to join up. As the men working in the household and on the estate joined up to do their bit for king and country, Tim aged eighteen and Johnny who'd just turned twenty signed up too.

Rosie was so excited she could hardly contain herself. Leave to return home was a rarity even among the officers. She ran to the front door, flung it open and belted down the steps, watching eagerly as the motor car came down the drive.

The shrill sound of the telephone had woken her an hour ago. She'd shot out of bed and ran along the hallway in time to hear her father say, 'they are at the train station, dear. Arthur will pick them up.'

Arthur was their driver. He lived-in and also looked after their shiny green motor car. Rosie bounced from one foot to the other as she watched the motor winding its way up the drive. As the car approached the house, she could see Johnny leaning out of the window waving his hat at her. The car door flew open before the vehicle had even come to a halt.

'Johnny!' Sitting in the front seat next to Arthur, he had barely stepped out of the vehicle when she ran into his arms.

'Hello old gal.' He hugged her, lifting her off the ground and swinging her round in a circle. He'd been doing that since she was little, along with playing rough and tumble, and cowboys and Indians. There were lots of other fun games that she could only have experienced growing up in a household with two older brothers who, much to her mother's dismay, but Rosie's delight, treated her like one of the boys.

'Tim!' He stepped out of the back of the car. She ran into his arms while Johnny went over to their parents standing side-by-side on the front steps.

'Good to see you, Son.' Their father swallowed hard and held out his hand.

Johnny shook his father's hand. 'Good to be back, sir.'

Tim and Rosie walked over, Tim's arm around Rosie's shoulders, her arm around his waist. He held out his hand and shook hands with his father.

Their mother dabbed her eyes with a cotton handkerchief as both sons walked up and kissed her on the cheek.

'What's that?' Rosie saw Arthur getting something out of the car.

Tim smiled at his brother. 'You know Johnny. First, it was a radio, now he's into photography. It's ridiculous, but he takes it everywhere. So, it had to come home with us on leave.'

'Are you saying I'm ridiculous?' Johnny said good-humouredly.

Rosie turned to her eldest brother. 'Will you take a picture of us?'

He looked at his little sister. 'What a splendid idea.' Johnny glanced at his father.

So did Rosie. 'Papa, please say yes.'

He smiled at Rosie. 'All right, why not.'

'I want all of you in the photo,' Johnny was saying, directing that comment at Tim.

Tim nudged his brother. 'That includes you, then.'

Johnny frowned. 'So, who is going to take the photo?'

Five sets of eyes turned to Arthur who was taking the camera stand from the boot of the car. Arthur was the only young man left on their staff. He'd signed up like everybody else, but his weak chest as a result of tuberculosis meant he was not fit for active duty.

Arthur caught them all looking his way.

'Right, I'll give Arthur a quick lesson and he can take a photo of all of us right here on the front steps.' Johnny handed him the camera and set up the tripod a few feet away.

Rosie clapped her hands in excitement.

Tim rolled his eyes at his brother.

Father held out his jaw and put one hand in his pocket, turning his good side to the camera.

Mama ran a hand down her hair, checking her short, neat hairstyle was still in place.

Johnny gave the young man a reassuring smile. 'Don't look so worried, Arthur. It's easy.'

Rosie stood in between her brothers with Mama next to Johnny and Papa next to Tim. Rosie looked at her brothers and suddenly had a thought. 'Wait!'

'What is it?' asked Johnny.

'We've forgotten somebody!'

Her brothers glanced at their little sister quizzically.

Rosie turned to run into the house.

'Rosie!' Mama's voice stopped her in her tracks. 'I don't think—'

'Why not!' Rosie threw back. She knew Mama would object. 'But he's part of the family now.' She looked at Papa. 'You told him he must think of Fletchling Hall as his home.'

'Rosie, he can't stay with us forever, you know that,' said Mama. 'We talked about this.'

Rosie looked at Papa with pleading eyes.

'Go and fetch him.' He turned to his wife. 'What's the harm?'

Rosie smiled at her father. She got the last word. 'We've welcomed him into our family, so it's only fitting that we should include him.' She gave her mother a sour look before she ran into the house.

Rosie knew Mama never wanted him in the nursery. All the other children – there were ten more – were housed in a separate wing of the house. Her parents had employed a local woman from the village to care for them. They were all school age, so she marched them down to the village school every morning and brought them back at the end of the day. They ate their meals separate from the family, played with each other, and kept themselves to themselves. There was even an area of the grounds marked out just for them to play outside. Mama didn't want *that sort* running amok.

Then along came their last evacuee. He was younger than all the others and to Rosie's surprise, and everyone else, Papa insisted he live with the family. It was the only ever time Rosie had heard her parents argue. Papa was the head of the household. No one ever questioned him until that day the little boy arrived, and Papa decided he should sleep in Johnny and Tim's nursery and for Nanny, their own Nanny who had brought up his children, to care for him.

Was it just his tender years or was there something about him that differed from the other children, and made Papa love him so? Did he remind Papa of Johnny and Tim when they were small? Whatever his reasons, Rosie ran up the stairs to the nursery recalling that day her brothers went off to war, thinking life would never be the same again.

Then along he came, the little boy who changed everything and brought their house alive again with laughter and fun. It was like having another brother, except this time she was the older sibling, his big sister; that's how she thought of herself. The only blot on the horizon was when the war was over and he would have to leave. But like her brothers returning to the front, she would not let anything spoil this day or stop her having her photograph taken with him.

Rosie was crossing the hall when she overheard Papa outside say, 'I'm not surprised she wants him in the photo. You know she's grown attached to the boy.'

'That's what I'm worried about. Perhaps he should join the others.'

'He's got a name, Mama,' said Rose crossly when she reappeared on the front steps. Mama always called him *the boy*. Rosie was holding his plump little hand. She knelt in front of him. Nanny had dressed him in a pair of blue woollen short trousers, long socks, a starched white shirt and a matching blue waistcoat. They were probably handed down from her brothers when they were little. Nanny never got rid of their clothes or toys.

Rosie smiled. 'These are my brothers Johnny and Tim. Remember I told you about them?'

He brushed his blonde hair away from his face and looked up at the two men standing there in uniform.

Johnny knelt beside him. 'Hello there, little fellow, my name's Johnny and this is Tim.'

Tim was standing beside Johnny with his hand on his brother's shoulder, smiling down at the little chap. 'What's your name?'

The little boy looked at Rosie and then turned to Johnny. 'My name is….' He stopped and looked up at Rosie. 'Rosie calls me Ted 'cause she likes Ted, so that's my name.'

Johnny fell about laughing. 'That's a lot of words for a little chap. Do you want to know a secret?'

His head bobbed up and down, big blue eyes staring at Johnny.

'You're not the only one with a nickname. You know Rosie isn't her proper name either. She doesn't like her first name, so ever since she was little we've called her Rosie. But her real name is—'

'Johnny!' she exclaimed crossly.

'All right, I won't tell. Perhaps someday she will tell you herself. Now, would you like to have your picture taken? All you have to do is stand here and hold Rosie's hand. What do you say? Can you do that for us?'

Once again, he bobbed his head up and down.

'Splendid.' Johnny ruffled his hair and stood up.

They all grouped together once more, Rosie in the middle either side of her brothers, her parents standing at either end. In front of Rosie, taking centre stage was a little boy smiling sweetly for the camera.

Arthur looked into the camera and took what was to be the last photograph of the family all together.

❖

Cassie stopped reading.

'Why have you stopped?' Evelyn demanded.

She stared at the notebook. 'Ted.' Her father's name was Martin, but he thought his middle name was Ted. He had a childhood memory of someone calling him by that name although he couldn't place where that came from.

Cassie sat there in stunned silence. That was her father – she was sure of it. She couldn't believe she'd found an old diary written by the girl her father remembered from his childhood, who he thought was his big sister. She wasn't, but they still treated him as one of the family.

Cassie's thoughts drifted to the tabby cat. She hoped he was still down in the basement. Later on, she would nip into the village and get some cat food and treats, perhaps some toys. Cassie felt like rewarding the cat. If it wasn't for her feline friend, she would never have found this notebook. She couldn't quite believe her luck.

'Ted.' Evelyn tutted. 'One should use their proper name – if you ask me.'

Cassie frowned at her. She'd had it on the tip of her tongue to tell Evelyn that Ted was her father, but Cassie clammed up. She wasn't about to have her father or Rosie and her family criticised. That family took in her dad and treated him well. She would not hear a bad word said against them – especially Rosie.

'If you're not going to continue reading…' Evelyn went to snatch the notebook out of her hands.

Cassie wasn't about to give it up. It was unprofessional of her, and childish of them both, but a tug of war ensued which resulted in the diary flying out of their hands and landing on the rug.

Cassie, younger and more agile, leapt out of her chair, leaving Evelyn struggling to get out of the seat. Cassie knelt to retrieve it and noticed a loose page that appeared to have come away from the notebook. When she picked it up, she discovered it wasn't a loose page at all. 'Oh, heavens!' Cassie exclaimed in surprise.

'What is it?'

Cassie stood up, holding the diary in one hand and a photo in the other. She stared at it wide-eyed. 'It's the photograph!'

18

'Let me see it,' Evelyn demanded.

She felt like walking out on her rude patient. Cassie was not convinced Evelyn had dementia. She was more likely depressed sitting at that window all day; it would explain her bad mood.

Cassie heaved a sigh and walked over to sit beside Evelyn. She handed her the photograph. 'It's the one I was reading about in the diary; the photo Arthur took of the family.'

Evelyn looked at Cassie before gingerly taking the old black-and-white picture out of her hand. 'So it is,' she replied.

They both sat there studying the print. *That's my father* Cassie was dying to say, but she didn't want to share her dad's story with a stranger. Perhaps if she got to know Evelyn, Cassie would feel different. She'd like to think they might become friends or at least act civil towards one another. Cassie cringed when she recalled them fighting over the diary. She hoped Evelyn didn't mention that to Phyllis. She'd be out of a job if she did.

Cassie shifted her focus from the little boy in the picture to the fifteen-year-old girl who called herself Rosie. The photo was black and white so she could only go by the description of the clothes in the diary to know that Ted was dressed in blue and

Rosie was wearing brown trousers and a plaid shirt. She was small and slim, her brother's clothes ill-fitting. Her hair which looked blonde was in a short, wavy bob cut just below her ears, a hairstyle common back then Cassie imagined.

Her two brothers standing either side of them were in uniform, both beaming at the camera. Cassie wondered which one was Johnny and which was Tim. One brother was looking at the little boy and smiling. Perhaps that was Johnny, the eldest who had knelt in front of her dad and asked him his name.

Cassie shifted her attention to Rosie's parents. They looked younger than she expected – in their early forties. Perhaps it was the way their fifteen-year-old daughter had described them or the times. Rosie's father appeared stern, standing there dressed in a tailored suit, holding a cane in one hand. He was staring off into the distance. Rosie's mother, wearing a flowing dress below the knee, looked sheepishly at the camera as though she felt shy having her picture taken.

Cassie turned from the photo to look at the diary in her hand. What if there were more photographs inside? She started flicking through the pages, when Evelyn said, 'That really won't do. Who does she think she is, disobeying her mother and not changing into a dress? She looks like a common street urchin, just like that evacuee. It is most unseemly.'

Cassie looked at her in surprise. 'It's that it?'

'What?'

'Is that all you have to say?'

Evelyn shrugged. 'What do you mean?'

Cassie didn't think she'd have to spell it out. 'We found a photograph of the family who lived here during the Second World War and all you have to say is a disparaging remark about what the girl is wearing?' Evelyn's comment about her dad, the evacuee, looking like a common street urchin also upset Cassie.

'Well, it's true.' Evelyn shrugged. 'She should have obeyed her mother. What was she doing dressing in boys' clothes? And as for that little boy, who does he think he is ingratiating himself where he doesn't belong?'

'Right, that's it.' Cassie slammed the notebook shut and snatched the photograph out of her hand.

Evelyn looked at her in surprise. 'That was rude.'

'It takes one to know one!' She got out of her seat and stormed out of the lounge.

'I'll tell Phyllis,' Evelyn called after her. 'Don't imagine I won't, young lady. I'll tell her all about the diary you stole and how rude you are. You won't have a job here before the week is out, I promise you.'

Cassie reached the end of the hall and flung open the door to the apartment. She didn't steal the diary, she found it. However, she knew there was no point arguing with the likes of Evelyn. Cassie stepped outside and slammed the door shut behind her.

'And don't be slamming my door either,' came Evelyn's shrill voice from inside the apartment.

Cassie pulled a face at Evelyn's door, biting her tongue before she said something else she'd regret.

'She has that effect on people.'

Cassie whirled around at the sound of Jill's voice. She was coming up the hall carrying a tea tray. It seemed every time she saw Jill she was back and forward with people's meals. Cassie's face went bright red.

'Don't worry. You're not the only one who has stood outside Evelyn's door biting your tongue.'

'I'm afraid I already said things I shouldn't have.' Cassie felt embarrassed.

'Oh, she has that effect on people too. Did she say she'd tell Phyllis?'

Cassie nodded, looking worried. Ordinarily, she wouldn't give two hoots what a patient told her superior; in the hospital, that was par for the course. Not that she was rude to her patients. Cassie had never been harsh or spoken out of turn to a patient, ever. It was the patients who were often rude to her and her colleagues, but Cassie always kept her cool no matter how difficult some of them were. This was the first time she had ever let someone get to her.

Jill must have caught the anxious look on Cassie's face. 'You won't lose your job, Cassie. Phyllis is no stranger to Evelyn's theatrics. If Phyllis believed everything she said, they'd be no one left here!'

Cassie managed a smile. That made sense.

'She does it all the time,' Jill continued, 'threatening to report us for the smallest thing; she treats us like we're her staff.' Jill said, echoing Olivia's words. 'I'm sure she thinks Phyllis is the head housekeeper or something.' Jill sighed. 'At first, I found it funny. I even felt sorry for Evelyn. Now it's just annoying.'

'Maybe she lived in a place like this once, and that's why she's getting confused with the past?' Cassie replied.

'Have you heard her plummy, upper-class accent? Sorry, I didn't mean to be sarcastic. I just get worked up about this part of my job, having to deal with the likes of her.' Jill knocked on the door. 'I expect I'll get another plate thrown at me before the day is out. Perhaps I should use paper plates,' Jill added as an afterthought.

'GO. AWAY!'

They exchanged a glance and eyed the door. Cassie said, 'Why do I feel you will not get away with paper plates.'

'I was only joking. She doesn't like our crockery from the local supermarket. Apparently, she has fine bone china.'

Cassie rolled her eyes. 'I bet she does.'

Jill knocked again.

There was a lengthy pause before Evelyn responded. 'You can come back in as long as you bring the diary with you.'

Jill looked at Cassie in surprise. 'That's never happened before. She's being reasonable. Looks like you made a friend.'

Cassie shook her head. 'I don't think I'd go so far as to say that. She just wants me to read her this.'

Jill looked at the old leather-bound book in her hand. 'What is it?'

'It's a diary written by a girl who used to live here.'

'What a brilliant idea, pretending to find a diary and making up a story. You therapists are so imaginative. You do such an interesting job.'

'Oh, I wasn't pretend—'

'Evelyn, it's Jill.' She opened the door and walked into the apartment. 'I've brought your lunch.'

'Where's Cassie?'

She heard Jill say, 'It's lunchtime, Evelyn. I'm sure Cassie will be back later.'

Cassie thought *don't count on it.* She stormed off down the hall, still angry at Evelyn for what she had said about her father ingratiating himself where he didn't belong. He was just a little boy. It wasn't his fault he'd been evacuated and forced to leave his family for the safety of the countryside. And it wasn't his fault Rosie's father had singled him out and let him live with Nanny and Rosie in the nursery. Cassie was glad her dad, who was so young at the time, had become part of their family.

She glanced at the diary as she walked down the corridor. Cassie frowned. What she wanted to know was if they loved her father so much, why did they send him away? She slowed. The answer could be in the pages of this book. She'd stopped by a window seat. It was her lunch break. She had an hour to spare.

Cassie had just sat down and opened the diary when she heard a commotion. 'And there goes her lunch,' she commented matter-of-factly glancing down the hallway and catching sight of a plate whizzing past Jill's head as she scuttled out the apartment. Cassie sat there watching all this, shaking her head from side to side. There was a simple solution; stop bringing Her Ladyship any meals. Make her go downstairs and sit with everyone else. She had a kitchen in her apartment; Evelyn could do her own meals.

After picking up the sandwich debris from the carpet, Jill made her way along the hall towards Cassie.

Cassie closed the diary. She hadn't read any further.

Jill stopped in front of her. 'Evelyn asked me to deliver a message. Frankly, I wasn't going to bother, but she made me promise. And a promise is a promise.' Jill sighed.

'Okay, what does she want?'

'She told me to tell you, I mean, *ask you* if you wouldn't mind continuing to read the diary to her.' Jill glanced over her shoulder and lowered her voice. 'You'll never guess what?'

Cassie wanted to ask her why she was whispering.

Jill stared wide-eyed at Cassie. 'Her Ladyship said, *please,*'

Cassie looked down the hall. Despite her disparaging

remarks, Evelyn wanted to know what happened to Rosie and her family as much as she did. Cassie sighed. 'All right.'

'Don't go now though.'

'Why not?'

'As you may have gathered, she didn't like the sandwiches. Perhaps give her some time to cool off. Besides, you are on your break. Are you joining us in the kitchen?'

Cassie intended to disappear to Gatekeepers Cottage and continue with more of the diary, but as she would be reading it to Evelyn that afternoon, she changed her plans. 'I want to pop to the village store. Will I have enough time in my lunch break?'

'The village is virtually on the doorstep. I expect you saw it on your way here in the taxi.'

'Ah, kind of.' Cassie hadn't been paying a lot of attention to her surroundings when she first arrived. What had been on her mind was…well… *everything*; the flat, her husband, her old job, her new role. She wasn't sitting back enjoying the scenery. 'I'll just walk into the village—'

'Oh, I don't think you'll have time in your break if you walk it. It takes ten minutes just to make it down the drive.'

'Yes, of course it does.' Cassie knew that. It was a lovely long approach to the hall, but it did go on.

'Do you drive?'

'Yes.'

'There's a car in the garage. We use it from time to time, to run errands. I wouldn't go any distance in it, but it's fine for short journeys. Sometimes Phyllis picks me up in it, and we both come into work together. You know we live in the village. I like to cycle, but in inclement weather that's another story.'

Cassie nodded.

'If you want to go anywhere further, it will be a bus ride or the taxi, I'm afraid.'

'I only want to go to the village store. Is the car free then?'

'Yes. Do you know where the old stable block is? They are now garages.'

Cassie wasn't sure.

'Just head around to the right, keep walking, and you'll come to the stable block. The car is in the garage on the left.'

'Great.' Cassie bounced off the window seat and left Jill behind carrying the tea tray. She suddenly halted and turned around. Jill was still walking down the corridor. 'Where are the car keys?'

'Car keys? Oh, it doesn't have car keys.'

Automatic transmission. Great. She presumed they just left the car open.

'If you get stuck, you could always borrow my bike. It is leaning against the garage door.'

'I'll be fine using the car.' Cassie glanced at her watch and stood up. She had less than an hour. Mind you, in the car she'd be in the village in minutes. She wished she'd asked about parking, but there might be a village green or parking outside the local shop.

Cassie glanced at the grey clouds out the window. She would stop at the cottage on the way and collect her coat. It was very tempting to forget the trip into the village and sit down and type her father up an email. He wouldn't believe where she was or what she had found on her first day back at the hall.

Cassie stood there a moment, fingering the diary. She was dying to know whether there was more in the notebook about her father and why he was sent away before the war ended.

Would it reveal what had happened to his family? It wouldn't be long and the afternoon shift would start. Then she would return to Evelyn and read the next instalment of Rosie's diary. Cassie wanted to find out more before she emailed her father.

She didn't think to ask if they insured her to drive the car. She presumed anyone who worked here was. She skipped down two flights of stairs, crossed the hall and stopped outside on the front steps. This was where Arthur took the family photograph. She looked down the drive imagining Rosie standing right here in this spot as the green car made its way up the drive bringing her brothers home from war. She bet the grounds had changed little from the 1940s.

Staring at the gardens, she frowned at the notion the place might be redeveloped. She wouldn't be surprised if they built houses on the grounds. The gardens and the long driveway would disappear, giving way to a modern estate.

It would be such a shame if that were the case. She understood the housing shortage in England. People needed homes. But why here? Why couldn't this historic house and parkland be saved for posterity? There was a history here like her father's and a family whose sons left for the war along with most of their young household. She bet some of them didn't return.

Cassie walked down the steps, recalling Rosie and her story. That's when Cassie had an idea. Would her father consider writing about the family they billeted him with in the war and include their story in his book? Cassie imagined her dad would say yes in a heartbeat. But first, he would need Rosie's actual name. How would she find that out?

Cassie slapped her hand to her forehead. The diary, of course! She threw a backward glance at the house, her inclination to run back inside and continue reading. But as Jill just said, a promise is a promise – even if it was one she had made to herself. Cassie pledged to go into the village and buy some cat food and treats for her new furry friend without whom she would never have happened upon an old diary; it might just hold the key to her father's past and help him find his long-lost family in England.

19

Cassie followed Jill's directions around the side of the hall and came to the garage. She opened the garage door and stepped back in surprise. 'Oh, that's not what I was expecting.'

She stared at the green motor car. 'A vintage car in vintage green.' Cassie laughed. She stopped when something dawned on her. 'It can't be!' She walked around the old motor taking a good look. 'I don't believe it. It's the car Arthur was driving!'

Cassie opened the car door. 'That's where Johnny sat.' She looked at the front seats. They were black and in good condition for a vehicle this age. Cassie walked around and got in the driver's seat. She glanced in the back where Rosie's brother, Tim, sat. Cassie turned to the front. She'd never driven a vehicle like this before. She reached down, searching for the ignition. 'So that's what Jill meant when she said I wouldn't need a key.' Cassie had seen some old movies, so she had an idea how to get the car started.

She got out and walked around the front of the car. There was a starter lever inserted through a hole in the front. Cassie stood there staring at the lever. She knew what she had to do; rotate it a few times to start the vehicle. She wasn't worried about getting the motor running or having a go driving it. What was bothering her was if she made it into the village, would she get it started again for the return journey? Cassie glanced at the bicycle belonging to Jill standing against the wall.

A few moments later Cassie was riding down the drive, the wind in her hair. She couldn't remember the last time she'd ridden a bike or felt this happy. The surroundings with rolling countryside in the distance and the backdrop of the hall had a lot to do with it. Cassie had forgotten how much she loved the great outdoors. She didn't realise how cooped up she'd been in their flat, in the hospital on the wards and stuck on the tube crowded with people. Even the London parks, teaming with tourists, weren't as peaceful as the countryside.

Cassie approached the end of the drive, enjoying the tranquillity of her surroundings. She swung out of the drive, straight on to the road. She was just smiling to herself, thinking how pleased she was that she'd taken up Jill's offer of using her bike, when a blaring car horn interrupted the peace. The car passed her at such closer quarters, it gave her no time to avoid a pothole. The front wheel of the bike buckled, she lost her balance and landed sideways on the soft grassy verge.

She was no worse for wear apart from a large, muddy brown stain down her trousers. 'Oh, that's great.' Cassie stood up and frowned at the brand new shiny Range Rover that had sped off. 'Thanks a bunch for not stopping!' She shouted. She was embarrassed more than anything. Fortunately, the village was up ahead. She passed an old lady standing at a bus stop as she wheeled the bicycle along the road.

The old lady noticed the buckled wheel. 'Are you all right, dear?'

'Some idiot knocked me off my bike.'

The old lady tutted. 'Drivers these days.' She glanced at the bicycle. 'Your wheel needs fixing.'

Cassie nodded. So much for popping into the village. She'd have to return to the hall.

'There's a bike repair shop next door to the village store.'

'Really?' Cassie couldn't believe her luck. Not that she was feeling particularly lucky now her day was ruined by some careless driver. She'd have to explain to Jill what happened to her bike. Cassie looked at the old lady. Or perhaps she didn't. If the bike shop could get it repaired while she was shopping…

'Did you say it was next to the village store?'

'Yes, keep going along this road and just around the bend is the village green. There's the post office, which doubles as a village store. The video rental shop is also a bike repair shop.'

'Video rental?' That made Cassie smile. Who rented videos these days when everything was online? So old-school.

'There's a nice tea shop and a new coffee shop across the road, although it's a bit modern for my taste. You get a lot of youngsters in there.'

Cassie recalled the shiny new Range Rover that had just run her off the road, probably driven by a young man or woman with more money than sense.

'Oh, there's my bus!' The old lady waved.

Cassie pulled the bike on to the pavement as the bus drew up at the bus stop. 'Thank you for telling me about the repair shop.'

The old lady smiled. 'They also sell bikes too, in case they cannot fix it and you need to buy a new one.'

Cassie watched her get on the bus. She glanced at the wheel, hoping the shop could fix it. The last thing she needed right now was the cost of replacing someone's bike. She had savings, but with the uncertainty over her future, she could do with keeping every penny for a rainy day. She imagined there would be a few of those on the horizon if her luck didn't pick up. Cassie brushed that thought aside and focused on the here and now. 'Right, let's find that repair shop.'

Cassie walked the bike around the corner into the village. She spotted the post office-come-shop and the repair place that doubled as a video rental store. It was very parochial. Cassie didn't see that as a bad thing. In fact, it was when she was considering early retirement from her job in the hospital that an idea popped into her head. She meant to broach it with Lars. She couldn't imagine spending the rest of her life in London. Cassie had been thinking about a move to the country.

'Be careful what you wish for,' Cassie remarked under her breath as she wheeled the bike across the green to the shop. She couldn't fail to see the irony. Nowhere in her plans did she imagine moving out of London on her own. However, deep down she knew Lars would never leave the city and live in a provincial place like this; he'd be forever criticising the locals and coming up with lame, tasteless jokes involving the word *inbreeding* – silly man.

Cassie stopped outside the shop and made a mental note not to think about her husband. In the window was a brand-new women's bicycle for sale in a pastel green colour. Although it was a town bike with high handlebars, a comfortable brown leather seat and a wicker basket on the front, it had thick-tread tyres so you could use it off-road too. It was a lovely. She spotted the price tag and gasped. Was that how much bikes cost these days?

'I hope this is reparable,' she said under her breath as she opened the door. A bell tinkled. She wheeled the bicycle into the shop. The old lady was right: it doubled as a video store. Along one wall were all the recent film releases along with some old movies she recognised from a few years back. On the left was a row of new and second-hand bikes for sale. At the end of the shop was a middle-aged man sitting watching a small television. He looked up as Cassie approached.

'Do you repair bikes? I had a little mishap this morning. The wheel has buckled.'

He came out from behind the counter. He was wearing over-alls, which Cassie thought was a good sign.

'Let's have a look – shall we?' He knelt down and ran a hand around the rim of the wheel. He heaved a sigh.

Cassie held her breath, hoping the sigh wasn't a bad sign.

He stood up. 'Yep, that's easily fixed.'

'It is? Oh, thank goodness.' Cassie was about to plead with him to do it right now when he went around the back of the counter and returned with a large metal toolbox.

Cassie didn't bother asking how much the repair would cost. It's not like she could shop around, but she asked, 'Is it all right if I pop back? I have some shopping to do.'

'Fine by me.'

'When will it be ready to collect?'

'Half-an-hour, forty minutes. Don't worry, it will be ready and waiting when you get back.'

Cassie wanted to give him a hug. She imagined many scenar-ios like they had a lot of jobs on, so it would be weeks before it was repaired, or they needed to get a spare part.

'Great. Thank you *so* much.' Cassie walked out of the shop and emerged ten minutes later from the village store next door with a shopping bag. The live-in staff at the hall ordered their groceries online and had it delivered from the large supermarket in the town five miles away, but Cassie rather liked the idea of supporting local businesses. An evening meal was provided for live-in staff, so all she had to think about was breakfast and lunch.

She didn't have to buy much for herself, just a pint of milk, a loaf of bread for toast in the morning, and some ham and cheese for sandwiches. Along with some apples and bananas, that would see her through the week. The rest of the shopping comprised cat food, cat treats and a toy. The lady on the check-out pointed out the cat collars too, but Cassie declined. She lingered over the soft cat beds and the litter trays. The cat doesn't belong to you, Cassie reminded herself. It's not your pet. Besides, the kitten probably won't even be there when you get back. You left the window open, remember.

Cassie stood outside the shop and looked at her watch. She still had about half an hour to kill; enough time to have a sandwich or a scone and a cup of tea. She passed the village tea shop which looked nice and cosy inside, but it was small. Although she imagined the two ladies serving customers were friendly, she wasn't in the mood for someone striking up a conversation when they heard her foreign accent. All she wanted was to sit and eat lunch in peaceful anonymity.

Cassie crossed the road and arrived outside the coffee shop. It was a large modern building which, like the other two shops, doubled as something else – in this case, it was a small art gallery. It looked nice inside with modern leather sofas and plenty of space between the tables and chairs where she could sit on her own without being disturbed.

Cassie walked into the bright, airy coffee shop. They made

sandwiches too. Even better. Cassie ordered a simple cheese and chutney sandwich with a pot of tea. After trying to wipe the mud stain off her trousers in the ladies toilet, she sat down at a table by the window overlooking the village green and waited for her lunch. That's when she spotted the blue shiny Range Rover parked on the grass verge.

Cassie looked at the spattering of people sitting having lunch. She saw two young women, one of them with a pre-school child, and frowned. She felt like going up to them and asking if that car belonged to them and would they like to apologise for running her off the road? She wasn't confrontational by nature. She didn't want to cause a scene. Instead, she turned in her seat and stared out the window.

She saw a man walk by the coffee shop carrying a takeaway cup. He glanced in the window. Their eyes locked for a moment. Cassie looked away, embarrassed.

'Cheese sandwich and tea?'

Cassie turned to look at the young waitress standing at her table. 'Oh yes, thank you.' She watched the waitress put the platter of sandwiches, crisps, and a side salad on the table along with a pot of tea, a small jug of milk and a cup and saucer. When the waitress had gone, she looked up to find the man she'd locked eyes with a moment ago still standing at the window.

Staring at her, he mouthed, *Cassie?*

20

Cassie watched him walk through the door into the coffee shop. So did the two women sitting at a table nearby. He was carrying a laptop and a takeaway coffee as he breezed past them, aiming straight for Cassie.

She still couldn't believe it was him. He'd changed. He wasn't that grungy teenager anymore with black hair that fell in his eyes, skinny ripped jeans and a faded led Zeppelin tee shirt. Today, he wore a suit, with a white shirt under a matching waistcoat. Her first impression, apart from the tailored suit, was that he'd aged well. His thick hair was cut short; she'd never seen him with short hair which explained why, during the brief moment their eyes locked, she didn't recognise him.

He was still as tall and slim as she remembered. He hadn't lost the toned body of his youth, but his black hair dusted with grey gave away the fact that he wasn't in his twenties or thirties. The women sitting at the next table eyeing the attractive man crossing the room probably imagined he was in his thirties. Cassie knew better. She stared at him as he approached her table. Something told her he hadn't pursued any of the clinical roles he'd been interested in when they'd first met at Fletchling Hall.

He stopped at her table. 'Cassie?'

'Ben?'

His face was a picture when he realised it wasn't a case of mistaken identity. 'May I join you?'

Cassie nodded. After all these years, here he was. Here *they* were.

'I can't believe it's you,' they both said in unison as soon as he'd taken a seat. They exchanged a shy smile, both aware of the fact that they'd once known each other, intimately. But that was a lifetime ago. Cassie was more self-conscious because unlike him, she wasn't as rake thin as in the past. Although she hadn't let herself go, and her job involved a lot of time on her feet, she had put on a few pounds over the years. However, she still had her long mane of red hair; that's what had turned his head when they first met.

Cassie didn't know why she was reflecting on the past. He was probably married with a family. Besides, she wasn't in the market for a relationship either. They were just old friends bumping into each other. Except they weren't old friends; he was her first real boyfriend who'd dumped her with no explanation and left her broken-hearted.

She pushed that thought to one side. It was years ago. She glanced at his laptop.

Ben broke the uncomfortable silence. 'How long has it been?'

Too long, Cassie felt like saying. 'A good few years,' she replied, trying to sound nonchalant, like she didn't know or care how long it had been since he broke her heart.

'Too long.' Ben shook his head. 'Twenty-six years, seven months, two weeks and—'

'Would you like anything to eat?' A young waitress appeared

at their table with a notepad and pencil to hand. She was staring at the handsome man who came in often for a takeaway coffee. This was the first time he'd ever stopped at a table.

Cassie was staring at him too. She could recall the exact day of the breakup. It surprised her that after all this time, he remembered.

'No, I'm fine thanks.'

When the waitress left, he said to Cassie, 'I was on my way to a meeting, so I can't stop for long.'

I wasn't asking you to, thought Cassie. Not that she wanted him to go either. There was another awkward silence, both lost in their own thoughts. It was Cassie who broke the silence this time. 'So, what do you do for a living?'

'I'm an architect.'

'An architect?' Cassie said in surprise. She never knew he was interested in designing things. 'What happened to working in the caring sector?'

'When we split up, I lost my enthusiasm.'

Whose fault was that? Cassie held her tongue.

'I needed to do something different. Besides, I promised my dad that one day I'd build him a house.'

'Did you build it?'

'No. I trained and became an architect only for him to tell me every plan I presented him with wouldn't do. Stubborn bastard. Anyway, enough about him. What brings you back here after all these years?'

'I could ask the same of you, Ben.'

'I never left.'

But you left me. She dismissed that thought. She was only a teenager. It's not like they were married. She'd moved on – hadn't she? 'I've got a job here.' Cassie didn't mind talking about work. It was only small talk, anyway.

'Really?' He held up his hand to forestall her going any further. 'Let me guess. Like me, you didn't go into the medical profession.'

Cassie opened her mouth to correct him.

'No, wait; what was that other thing you were interested in? It will come to me…' He clicked his fingers. 'That's it! Didn't you want to run a rescue centre rehousing homeless and abandoned stray dogs and cats?'

Cassie glanced at the carrier bag by her feet containing the cat food and treats. She'd forgotten all about that childish dream. 'Yes, I remember.' She was just surprised he had.

'You know, it gave me the idea of running my own business.'

Good for you thought Cassie. At least something came out of their short but intense teenage relationship.

He studied her. 'Am I right?'

'That's what I'd always dreamed of doing, but I wanted to be an O.T. too.'

'Oh, yes, I remember. So, you qualified?'

'Yep, graduated, got my qualification and worked in London for a good while before getting a position here.' Cassie had no intention of bringing up her divorce. Her personal life was none of his business.

'Where are you working?'

'Fletchling Hall.'

They both fell silent. She wondered what he was thinking. Did he recall the time they'd spent there together when they were inseparable?

'It's sheltered accommodation now. The position is only

temporary. The place is due to close. I suppose you know all about that.'

'What do you mean?'

'You live in the area. It must be local knowledge.'

'Oh, I see. Yes, it might be turned into luxury flats – so I've heard.'

'Shame they couldn't let the last remaining residents see out their final days in peace.'

Ben didn't comment about that. 'What will you do when it closes? Has your husband got a job around here?'

'Husband?'

He nodded at her ring.

'Oh,' Cassie glanced at her wedding ring. It hadn't occurred to her to take it off; after almost twenty-five years, she'd practically forgotten she was wearing it. Her eyes drifted to Ben's hands. There was no ring on his finger. Like hers, that meant nothing. Who knew what his personal circumstances were? She wasn't going to ask. Once they'd exchanged pleasantries, they would probably never see each other again unless she ran into him in the village.

It made her wonder if they were both in the same boat, still clinging to a past life that no longer existed. She guessed neither of them wanted to talk about it. They both attempted to change the subject, which didn't go unnoticed on either side.

'So, this is a move from London?'

'Yes.'

'Did you apply for a job here in particular?'

Cassie looked at him. It felt like a searching question. If he imagined she'd returned here looking for him… 'No, the role just came up. I'd forgotten all about this place until I arrived here.'

She hadn't. Not at all. That was an outright lie. She didn't add that she'd been thinking it was a mistake coming back here, dredging up memories of her father, and her first love. Cassie avoided eye-contact. He was still devilishly good-looking. Why couldn't he have put on some weight, have a beer belly, be going bald? In short, be unrecognisable from the boy she once loved?

She recalled what he told her soon after they'd met as teen-agers. That she was out of his league. That's how she felt right now about him. A handsome, sophisticated middle-aged man who was turning heads amongst the young ladies in the coffee shop.

She imagined the women were wondering what he was doing talking to her, sitting there in her skinny black chinos with the brown mud stain. She was also wearing a tee shirt under her polo neck and a blue jean jacket that she'd owned since the noughties. If she'd known she would run into her ex-boyfriend, she might have made more of an effort.

But it wasn't just his attire that had changed. The Ben she'd known would have turned up riding a motorbike and wearing a leather jacket, ripped jeans and biker boots. The man sitting at her table didn't behave like that crazy, adventurous boy who had shown her how to have a good time.

All this she had noted from his appearance, but talking to him, she was starting to glean something else. Although he didn't look his age – the years had been kind to him as they had Cassie – he had aged in other ways; she sensed he was cautious, sensible, had responsibilities. Even though he wasn't wearing a wedding ring, she wondered if he had children. Neither of them touched on that subject.

Cassie took a sip of her tea and discovered it was cold. She looked at her watch. 'Crumbs, is that the time? I only popped into the village on my lunch break.'

Ben rose from his chair as Cassie gathered up her shopping bag. 'I must go.'

'Can I give you a lift?'

Cassie looked at him. 'That's kind of you, but I'm collecting my bike from the repair shop across the road.' At least she hoped she was. Fingers crossed the nice man had fixed it. She was concerned how much it would cost her. Still, it would be a lot cheaper than buying Jill a new one.

She walked out of the coffee shop. Ben held the door open for her. She decided not to mention the little mishap on the way here, even though it wasn't her fault. She was still embarrassed about the whole episode falling off the bike into a ditch.

'I don't mind waiting. I can still give you a lift to the hall,' Ben continued.

Cassie looked at her watch. Time was getting on. Although it wouldn't take that long to cycle back, she was already late for her afternoon shift.

'It's no trouble, Cassie. I was just stopping to buy a takeaway cup of coffee. Funny thing is I didn't see you when I ordered.'

Cassie guessed she must have been busy in the loo trying to get the stain off her trousers.

'The bike will easily fit in the back of my car. I'm just over there.' He pointed. 'I'm the blue Range Rover.'

'The blue Range Rover,' Cassie repeated slowly. 'That one?' She pointed to the vehicle parked by the village green.

Ben nodded. 'That's the one. Now, if you get your bike, I'll bring my car over—'

'You know what? Don't bother. I'll cycle back.'

'But I thought you said you were late for work? What if there's a problem with your bike?' He looked at her. 'What is the problem with your bike, by the way?'

'To start with, it's not my bike. I just borrowed it to get into the village. Then I was cycling into town when some *idiot* ran me off the road.' Cassie stared at him.

Ben's eyes went wide when the penny dropped. 'Oh, that was you?'

'Yes, that was me. I suppose you didn't notice the nice muddy brown stain down my trousers.'

'You're not hurt, are you?'

'No, but that's beside the point. Your driving is appalling.'

'My driving? Now look here, if you hadn't come out of the drive into the road without stopping.'

'Oh, so it was my fault you ran me off the road?'

He didn't reply.

Cassie glared at him. What sort of person doesn't bother to stop and check she was all right? She turned on her heel and stalked across to the repair shop. The bike better be fixed otherwise her promise to Phyllis that she wouldn't be late again had just gone out the window. She knew who she had to thank for that.

21

'You're late!' Evelyn complained. 'And why is your face so red?'

Cassie sat down next to Evelyn with the notebook. 'I popped into the village at lunchtime on Jill's bike and lost track of time.'

Evelyn tutted.

Cassie frowned. She didn't elaborate about anything else. Jill's bike was back in the garage, propped up against the wall. She would be none the wiser that there was a little mishap on her way to the village that morning.

Cassie could have done with a lift, but she wasn't about to accept one from the person who ran her off the road and cost her fifty quid.

It proved an expensive trip and she hadn't had time to drop her groceries off at the cottage. Cassie left the shopping on the table in the staff kitchen. That bothered her somewhat. There were tins of cat food in the bag. What if someone looked inside? And she hadn't fed the cat, assuming it was still around and hadn't left through the open window.

Cassie gave Evelyn a sideways glance, waiting for her to say – *I will tell Phyllis you were late, young lady.*

'Would you like a glass of water?'

Cassie looked at her in surprise. It wasn't a cup of tea, but it was a step in the right direction, and she wasn't threatening to tell on her. 'Yes, thank you.' She held up the diary. 'I'll see where we got up to.' Cassie smiled to herself. This was a clinical intervention of sorts. Evelyn wasn't sitting staring out the window. That was the whole point, getting her interested and engaged with something. Right now, the diary which she'd fortuitously come across was it.

Cassie opened the old leather-bound book and found the page she'd been reading to Evelyn this morning.

Evelyn walked out of her kitchen, carrying a glass of water.

Cassie turned the page. 'Oh, no!'

That stopped Evelyn in her tracks. 'What is it?'

Cassie was flicking through the diary. 'There's a whole chunk of pages that are illegible. Water has damaged the diary. The ink has bled all over the pages.'

Evelyn sat down beside her and put the glass on the coffee table in front of them. She looked at the diary. 'Are there any that *are* legible?'

Cassie kept turning the pages. She carefully prized apart those that were stuck together, until she came to a page of writing she could read. She looked back at the ruined middle section of the notebook and sighed. 'I'm afraid it will jump forward in time.'

Evelyn sighed too. 'How far forward do you think?'

Cassie read the date on the entry. 'It's December nineteen forty-four. We've lost almost thirteen months.' She turned to Evelyn. 'Do you still want me to read it to you?'

'Of course.'

Cassie began to read. 'The Canadians arrived today…'

❖

'They're here!' her father called out from the next room.

'I don't care!' Rosie shouted back. She was sitting at the small desk in her cramped bedroom writing in her diary, *tomorrow is my—* when Papa rudely interrupted her flow. She put her pen down, got up from her desk and climbed on her bed, shut the curtains and returned to her desk.

Her father poked his head in her bedroom. 'Ah, there you are.'

'Where did you expect me to be?' Rosie shot back, annoyed with Papa for saying such a daft thing as though he couldn't find her in the cramped two-bedroomed cottage.

'Why is it so dark in here?' His eyes drifted to her bedroom window. 'Your curtains are closed. You've got a perfect view up the drive to see them arrive.'

'I'm not interested. I'm busy.'

Her father hovered in the doorway a moment before leaving her in peace.

She didn't understand why her father was happy about their arrival at the hall. What was so great about the Government requisitioning their home? When he first found out, he'd told her about doing their bit for the war effort. Rosie recalled her reply. 'But it's our home, Papa. People in the village don't have to give up their houses for the war effort.'

He reminded her that some people might lose their homes like the children who were evacuated during the war because of the bombing raids in London. That was the other sore point; not only did they have to move into Gatekeepers Cottage, but all the children had to leave.

'Bloody Canadians,' she'd said, swearing in front of Papa, something she'd never done before. She was sent to her room. Rosie heard them talking about her in the room next door, through the paper-thin walls. Mama said although it wasn't lady-like behaviour, and she wasn't condoning it, their daughter was experiencing things neither one of them faced at her age.

Rosie said, 'Bloody Canadians,' under her breath again. She sat there staring at her diary, unable to concentrate. The noise of one truck after another, thundering past Gatekeepers Cottage as they made their way up the drive, was getting on her nerves. One of them even hooted their horn.

Rosie slammed her pen down on the desk and marched out of her bedroom straight down the short hallway to the front door. Her parents were standing outside, waving at them. She stood on the doorstep, skinny arms folded over her flat chest, frowning at the line of cars, jeeps and trucks winding up the drive. Why did there have to be so many of them?

One truck was open at the back. A young Canadian sitting inside caught her eye. He smiled and waved at her. Rosie gave him a sour look, turned on her heel and stormed inside the cottage. The cheek of it. Who did he think he was waving at her like they were acquaintances?

Even though she was feeling very cross, she ran into her bedroom and jumped on her bed to open the curtains. Kneeling on her bed, she placed her elbows on the windowsill and cupped her chin in her hands as she watched the convoy pass by. She noticed the cheeky airman who'd waved at her hanging out of the back of the truck, inspecting the grounds of his new home. Rosie sighed. Nobody knew how long they would be here.

Her father said they drafted in the Canadians to look after

the home front while their British counterparts were busy fighting the Huns. He'd told her we should count ourselves lucky that they were here. But why do they have to be here, in her house? That's what she wanted to know.

She glared at the young Canadian. 'I hope you fall out!' She grabbed her curtains and pulled them shut. 'Stupid Government and STUPID WAR!' she shouted out aware that she sounded like a six-year-old, but nobody would hear her over the rumble of the vehicles.

Rosie turned around and sat down crossed-legged on her bed. She stared at the empty cot across the room. It was an old army camp bed her father found in the basement when Arthur was helping them bring things they'd need down to the cottage. They'd made do just like all those government posters advised. The posters were everywhere; she'd seen one in the post office and the bakers and butchers in the village. Now they had no staff Mama was making do by shopping herself, although a woman from the village came and cooked their meals with the list of ingredients she'd given Mama to buy.

Rosie got up from the bed and walked over to the cot. She was upset about losing their home, but Papa said it was only temporary. They'd get it back after the war. When would that be? She'd overheard some people in the village talking about how there was no end in sight, and the war might drag on for years.

She lay down on the cot and stared at the ceiling. When they got the house back would Ted return too? It was a stupid question to ask Papa. Ted would go back to his family at the end of the war, just like the other evacuee children. But what if his parents had died in the bombing raids in London?

Rosie didn't miss the big house half as much as she missed

that little boy. She didn't know where the other children went when they first moved out of the hall. Her parents learned some of them went to families in the village and the next town. But Ted was different. He wasn't just part of their household; he was like a member of their family. So, while all the other evacuees who lived in the separate wing left the hall, Ted came with them to Gatekeepers Cottage.

They had to share a room, but Rosie didn't give a jot about that. She had helped Papa put up the cot, and she and Mama found sheets and blankets and made up his bed. They'd brought a trunk of her brothers' old clothes and some toys from the nursery, as much as they could fit into the small room.

At first, she imagined they would send Ted away like the other children. Rosie got cross and tearful. She'd never had a younger sibling before; she felt fiercely protective of him as though his welfare was her responsibility. Writing about how she felt at the idea of losing him upset her.

Although it was Mama who had been dead set against an evacuee living in the nursery in the big house, Rosie overheard her speaking to Papa when the other children were leaving. 'Rosie needs him more than ever now. Perhaps we all do.'

Papa decided that Ted was staying with them. Some evacuees were living with other families in the village who barely had room to accommodate their own children and yet they still took them in. Papa thought if their neighbours could do it, there was no reason not to bring Ted to live with them in the cottage. It meant Rosie had to share her bedroom. She didn't even have to think about it. She told her father she was doing her bit for the war effort even though it wasn't a sacrifice, not at all. She'd have slept on the floor if it meant Ted was allowed to stay.

The little boy had come with them to the cottage at the end of the drive and life carried on with a semblance of normality. Then they arrived, not the Canadians, but two government officials who came and took him away. It was the worst day of Rosie's life.

He'd clung to her leg. Papa had to prize them apart. Father tried bribing the officials. When that didn't work, he stepped outside with the two men and Ted. Rosie overheard him standing on the doorstep, talking in low voices. She'd stood with Mama in the hallway whispering under her breath, 'Please don't let them take him away.'

When Papa opened the front door, he stood there, head hung low. Rosie had run outside as the black car took off. She saw his little round face pressed up against the back window, tears rolling down his rosy, red cheeks as the car turned out of the driveway. She often replayed that episode in her mind wishing if only there was something they could have done differently. But no amount of wishing would bring him back; Ted was gone.

Rosie wiped the tears from her face and sat up. She could still smell Ted on his pillow. She stood up and plumped up the pillow, rearranging the blanket and neatly tucking in the corners. Nobody was allowed to touch the cot. It was staying where it was for Ted's return. That's what Rosie told her parents.

She opened the notebook on her desk. As for the other evacuees, it's not that she didn't care; she didn't know them. Although she knew people in the village had taken some of them in, there were rumours that others might have been sent to an orphanage; she'd overheard Mama and Papa talking. Is that where they'd sent Ted? Rosie picked up her pen and started to write to take her mind off that horrible day.

Today it's my birthday. She always hated having her birthday the day before Christmas. All she wanted for her birthday this year was to wake up this morning and for all this to have been a terrible dream or at the very least that the Canadians didn't come, so they might have their home back and Ted could return. But the Canadians did come on Christmas Eve and they would spend Christmas in her house.

Rosie paused to cast her eye around her cluttered bedroom. There hadn't been a lot of time to shift their belongings from the big house. They only took a fraction of what they owned. Rosie and her parents had brought what they needed to the cottage. The rest of the furniture was covered with dust sheets. They had hastily packed other items into boxes and took them up to the attic or down to the basement.

Rosie was sitting there looking around her bedroom, which seemed to double as a storeroom, thinking of the trips back and forward in the car, up and down the drive from their home to the little cottage. Arthur had helped Papa on the many trips.

She sat there lost in thought. Since they'd moved in, Rosie couldn't shake the feeling they had forgotten something important. She was sitting at her desk, staring off into space, when it came to her. She jumped out of her chair, launched herself on the single bed and yanked open the curtains. She could see the Canadians still unloading up at the house. There might still be time. She had to find it before they did. Rosie bounced off her bed and ran out of her room. She was just undoing the latch to the front door when she heard Mama. 'Rosie, is that you?'

Rosie's shoulders sagged. She sighed and let go of the latch. 'Of course it's me, who else would it be?'

Since moving into the small cottage, and being cooped up here with Mama and Papa, she realised what freedom she had to come and go, and do as she pleased, living in such a big house in a separate wing – the nursery. Nanny was annoying, always asking her where she was going, what she was up to. She became even more protective since her brothers left home. Then along came Ted, and Nanny had a little boy to look after again; she said it took her back to when Johnny and Tim were young. Rosie didn't want to think about them as she sidled up to the lounge doorway, trying to conjure up an excuse to get outside.

'Where are you going, young lady?'

She rolled her eyes at Mama. She could not remember a time since she was little when she didn't want to spend more time with Mama and Papa. Now she was older she couldn't think of anything worse, except having to live at such close quarters with them too.

Papa took off his reading glasses and looked at her standing in the doorway. 'You haven't opened your presents.'

With the Canadians arriving, Rosie had forgotten about her birthday presents. She looked at the little pile on the rug in front of the fireplace. She didn't want to seem ungrateful. How could she tell them that after all that had happened this past fortnight, she didn't feel like celebrating her birthday? She was sixteen today.

Rosie looked at Mama and Papa sitting on two large easy chairs that came from the house. Somehow Arthur managed to load them into the cart which he'd then hitched up to the car. He insisted that the Lord and Lady should have furniture that was befitting. The little parlour in the cottage, like her bedroom, was cluttered with oversized chattels that came from the house.

Rosie had an idea. She looked at Mama. 'I'm just going to

change into something more fitting for the occasion.' Mama smiled as she knew she would. 'It would be wonderful if you wore a dress for your birthday. I can't remember the last time you wore a frock.'

Rosie looked down at her brown breeches, her brother's hand-me-downs. She felt comfortable in what she was wearing. For some reason, she didn't think it was seemly to walk out dressed up as though it was an ordinary day and there wasn't a war on. She'd seen the land girls out in the fields working on the farms in place of the young men who'd gone to war. When she turned sixteen, Rosie wanted to do her bit for the war effort, just like those girls.

She hadn't told her parents yet. They would be horrified if they knew that she planned to join the Women's Land Army. Perhaps she'd let them cling on to their old way of life just for another day. However, before she put on a dress, there was something she needed to do first. 'It might take me some time choosing what to wear.'

Papa replied, 'It's your birthday, take as much time as you need, darling. You know where we are when you're ready.'

Rosie smiled at Papa. She gave Mama a sideways glance. She might not pull the wool over her eyes as easily; the look on Mama's face said she knew she was up to something.

22

Rosie couldn't leave through the front door, but she needed to get out of the cottage to make it to the house before the Canadians settled in.

She closed her bedroom door, clambered on to her bed and opened the window. Lucky Gatekeepers Cottage had only one floor. She climbed out of the window and raced up the lawn towards the house. Although she skirted all the jeeps and trucks parked outside the hall, nobody would have spotted her anyway; they were all too busy unloading the vehicles or barking orders.

Rosie made her way around the side of the building to the staff entrance. She looked about her before stepping into the house. Quick as she could, she ran through the narrow passage which led to a back stairway the servants used. She could hear people moving about downstairs and men's voices echoing in the main hallway. Rosie darted down several corridors before she came to her brothers' bedrooms. That's where she'd find what she was looking for.

Rosie stopped outside Tim's door. She had the impulse to knock. It seemed odd just to walk right in. Rosie stepped into the room. The curtains were drawn. She opened them to let in some light. She stood there for a moment. Her heart sank. She forgot that the maid had been in to make up the bed with fresh linen for his return. It was the last job she did for the family before they had to let her go. The grate was cleaned out and a bucket of coal placed on the hearth together with some old newspapers to get the fire going. She'd rather it was messy like it was when her brothers were home; it made her feel their absence even more.

Rosie walked over to his desk. It was undisturbed and just the way he had left it last time he was home. On the small oak desk under the window were a pile of photos. She picked one up. It was the photograph Arthur had taken of them all, including Ted, on the steps of the hall before everything changed.

She slipped all the photographs in her pocket. This bedroom and Johnny's next door were the only rooms in the house that Mama and Papa hadn't ventured into when they were preparing to move into the cottage. She understood why, but she didn't think they'd mind if she took the photos.

Rosie had just stepped out of Tim's room when she heard something. It sounded as though someone was in the bedroom next door. Rosie stood stock still, listening. *Johnny!* It was a stupid thought. How could he be here? Even so, her heart ruled her head, and she ran to the door and flung it open. She stopped dead in the doorway and gave the young man in uniform a cold, hard stare. 'Who are you and what are you doing in my brother's bedroom?'

The young Canadian officer turned around. He'd been unpacking his army issue rucksack. 'Hey, I know you! I saw standing outside the cottage down the drive.'

Rosie could feel her face growing red. She was blushing. She recognised him too. He was the chap who had been sitting in the back of the truck when it passed by. Although she'd given him a filthy look when he'd waved at her, she couldn't take her eyes off him. He was even more handsome up close with short, cropped blonde hair, chocolate brown eyes and a smile that gave her butterflies in her tummy.

'Is that the new fashion in England these days?'

Rosie looked down at the hand-me-down trousers hitched up above her slender waist with a belt. She was wearing one of her brother's old shirts, the sleeves rolled up. She looked away, embarrassed. Now she wished she'd put on a dress before she ventured out of the cottage. She stole a glance at the handsome Canadian.

'You look cute.'

Cute? Nobody had ever called Rosie cute before. Her cheeks blushed bright pink again. This just made her cross. Why was she feeling embarrassed? 'What are you doing in here?' she asked again, not looking him in the eye this time. 'This is my brother's bedroom.'

He glanced around the room until his eyes settled on her again. 'I'm sorry we had to move into your home.'

'Not as sorry as we are,' scoffed Rosie, although she recalled her father's words about doing his bit for the war effort. Rosie still wanted to do her bit. 'I might join the land girls.' She had no idea why she told him that, but she knew what he would say: *you're too young* or some such nonsense. That's what her mother would say.

'I think everybody should do what they can. We are all in this together.'

Rosie looked at him, surprised by his response. 'I agree.' She was feeling a little better about the Canadians arriving. Maybe it wouldn't be so bad having them here after all. They stared at each other across the room.

'I could find another bedroom and tell my superior that this one is out of bounds. I noticed the furniture in here and the room next door have not been covered up. He looked at Rosie. 'Why is that? Did they run out of dust sheets?'

'No.'

'So, why—?'

Rosie cut him off. 'You can stay in this room. I just came in here to get something.'

'Thank you.' He glanced about him. 'What are you looking for?'

She looked over at Johnny's desk. It wasn't there. Rosie turned to the young officer, furious. 'How dare you touch my brother's things!'

'I don't know what you mean?'

Rosie stormed over to the desk. 'What have you done with it?'

He glanced at the desk. 'I have no idea what you're talking about. I swear I haven't touched a thing.'

'Then someone else has been in this room.'

'Possibly.'

She stared at him. 'Who?'

He shrugged. 'I couldn't say.'

'You mean you're refusing to tell me.'

'No, that's not it. It won't be one of the airmen. They are bunking down in the larger rooms downstairs, but the officers can choose a bedroom each. Perhaps someone else looked in here? It beats the hell out of me why they didn't want this room. It's got the most amazing view.

'I know,' Rosie said coldly. She stepped up to the long Georgian sash window and gazed down the driveway. When she was little, she'd sneak in here and sit on the deep window box watching her brothers outside playing soldiers with wooden swords. Rosie loved this room. Johnny had the perfect view across the gardens, down the drive. She could see Gatekeepers Cottage and two tall stone pillars marking the entrance to the grounds of Fletchling Hall.

'What's your name?'

Rosie turned around and was just debating whether to tell him, when she spotted an older man, also in uniform, walking past the open doorway. He backtracked, glanced in and gaped at them, the expression on his craggy features one of surprise.

'What's the meaning of this, Scott? Get that girl out of your quarters.' He looked at Rosie and shouted at her, 'Out!'

Rosie glanced at the young Canadian called Scott and almost burst into tears; no one had spoken to her that way before. Who does he think he is? This was *her* house. And it was *her* birthday, which upset her even more. This was the first time she wouldn't be spending her birthday in the house she grew up in.

Rosie ran out of the room past the horrible man who had shouted at her. He turned on his heel and walked into Tim's bedroom next door, slamming the door shut.

'Hey - wait!' Scott raced to the door and called after her, 'You didn't tell me what it was you were looking for.'

She ran down the corridor without looking back, forgetting she should use the servants' stairs. On autopilot, she ran down the main staircase and was confronted by a sea of men piling into the hall with rucksacks and equipment. She stepped off the stairs and barged past them hearing young Canadians exclaiming,

'Who's that girl?' and 'Sorry, missy, didn't see you there,' and, 'Give us a kiss?'

Rosie burst out of the front door and belted down the front steps with tears in her eyes. She hit the gravel drive running and weaved in between the jeeps and trucks parked outside the house. Suddenly, she stopped and turned around. She looked up at her brother's window, and for a moment she thought it was Tim or Johnny standing at the window. That made her cry even harder. It wasn't Tim or Johnny; it was the Canadian called Scott. He waved. Rosie shoved her hands in her trouser pockets. 'I'm not waving at the likes of you!'

Now she wished Mama and Papa had moved to Scotland. Family friends asked them to come and stay until the war was over. They wouldn't hear of it. Papa wanted to keep an eye on the house. He'd heard what had happened to other stately homes that were requisitioned, leaving the owners with huge repair bills. Four years into the war and Papa assumed they had overlooked their home. Then they came.

'Bloody Canadians.' She cast her eyes down at the trucks and jeeps in front of her and the Canadians busy moving into her family home. Rosie glared at them. 'One of you stole my brother's radio,' she said under her breath, 'and I will find out who it was.'

She put both hands in her trouser pockets and stalked down the drive. Nearing the cottage, she darted to her right, walking purposefully around the side of the cottage. She'd left her window open for a reason.

Ten minutes later, she had changed into a party dress, run some water in the small sink in the corner of the room and wiped her face. She looked in the mirror and frowned at her reflection. This wasn't how she saw herself now. She wasn't that little girl anymore who lived in the hall without a care in the world. Too much had happened. Rosie stared in the mirror and thought *war changes you*. In a brief space of time, she had developed a maturity beyond her years. She longed for that carefree innocence, but it was gone. She didn't want to wear the dress because it reminded her of happier times when they were all together.

Rosie looked down at her dress. She was doing this for Mama, putting on a show, pretending things were like before. Life would never go back to the way things were, but just for one day, her birthday, they could all pretend.

Rosie sighed. 'Here we go. Let's get this over with.' She stepped out of her bedroom and appeared in the doorway to the parlour. Mama and Papa were still sitting on the chairs either side of the fireplace.

'Ah, there you are,' said Papa, smiling. He didn't mention how long she'd taken to choose her dress.

'What on earth were you doing? You have been gone a long time,' Mama remarked.

For a moment, Rosie imagined she knew about her trip up to the house.

Mama continued, 'I didn't think you had that many dresses.'

Rosie ignored that remark. 'I wanted to wear something special, but I couldn't decide. Does this look all right? If not, I will change.' She hated lying; it wasn't the done thing. But if they discovered she'd been standing in a bedroom with a young man unchaperoned. Rosie's face went bright red when she thought of being alone with the young Canadian called Scott. He was so good-looking.

'Rosie, are you running a temperature?' asked Papa looking at her with concern.

'No – why do you ask?'

'You look awfully flushed.'

'Do I?' Rosie said innocently, trying not to think about Scott. She caught her mother staring at her. 'I was changing in and out of my dresses in such a confined space it made me all hot and bothered.' Rosie tried to palm it off, although it was true; there was hardly any space to try on her clothes amongst all the clutter.

Mama looked at her hovering in the doorway. 'Don't dawdle, come in. You still haven't unwrapped your birthday presents.'

'I can't believe you bought me presents!' Rosie put on a show of acting excited even though that wasn't how she felt inside. However, she was surprised they had manged to buy her some gifts.

They had bought her some last year, and the year before, making things appear as normal as possible with the war on. However, she knew this year would be different. The young men who worked on the estate had gone off to war and she'd overheard conversations about money; something about a drop in income from her father's investments and rents from the land on the estate.

'Come over here and let me look at you,' said Papa.

Rosie walked into the room and did a twirl in her pretty dress.

Mama smiled. 'When the war is over, we will go to London for you to attend a coming-out ball.'

Rosie tried to keep her frown in check when she heard that. She didn't want to go to London to be presented to society. Next, they'd been finding her a suitable husband. She didn't care much for that either. Her thoughts drifted to the Canadian; perhaps she might be persuaded to change her mind if her husband looked like Scott and had a friendly smile and called her *cute*. Rosie sighed. Chance would be a fine thing. She'd been introduced to some of her parents' friends' sons around her age. None of them were like Scott.

Rosie unwrapped the two presents Mama handed her; one was some hosiery, and the other was a pearl necklace and matching bracelet. Last year, she would have been overjoyed to receive such grown-up gifts. But now these things didn't fill her with anything other than sadness that Tim, Johnny and little Ted were not here to celebrate her sixteenth birthday.

'Don't you like them?' asked Mama, exchanging a worried look with her husband.

'They're lovely, Mama, truly they are.' It surprised Rosie to get stockings. She'd overheard women in the village talking about how impossible it was to get hold of them. She stared at the pearl necklace. 'Oh, Mama, I couldn't possibly. These belonged to Grand-mama.' She tried to hand them back.

Mama closed her hand around Rosie's. 'If war teaches us anything, it's holding on tight to things that are most dear for we never know when we may lose them.' She squeezed Rosie's hand. They locked eyes in silent understanding. 'I wanted you to have them. It's what she would have wanted.'

'Oh, Mama!' Rosie flung her arms around her mother's neck. 'I do love you so.' She whispered in her ear. 'I just wish—'

'I know.'

They all glanced at the telegram on the mantle shelf.

'Come,' said Papa, 'open your last gift.'

The gift was sitting on the sideboard. It was a boxy shape wrapped in brown paper.

'What is it?' asked Rosie, intrigued. She tore open the paper to reveal the gift from Papa. She took a step back.

There was another long, heavy silence.

'I don't know if I did the right thing,' Papa began, 'but they would have wanted you to have it.'

Rosie launched herself at Papa and gave him a tremendous hug.

'Steady on,' said Papa, patting her arm, taken aback at the sudden display of affection.

Rosie returned to the radio. 'Where did you find it?'

'Before we left the house, I went upstairs to have a last glimpse in their rooms. I wanted a moment to—' He stared off into space and swallowed hard. He didn't finish that thought. Instead, he turned to Rosie and smiled. 'I expect some officers will move into their rooms.' Unlike Rosie, he didn't seem unhappy about it.

It was on the tip of her tongue to tell Papa he was spot on; Canadians had moved into their bedrooms.

'That's when I saw the radio in Johnny's room, on his desk. I know you loved sitting with them for hours listening to the wireless or watching them tinkering with their radio receivers, so I thought you'd want to have it. They were quite the radio enthusiasts, weren't they?'

There was another silence heavy with loss. Rosie stared at the radio. She was thinking of another young man, the Canadian. She'd practically accused him of stealing her brother's radio. 'Do you mind awfully if I take my presents to my room and have some time alone?'

Since the telegram arrived just before they moved into the cottage, it wasn't unusual for one or the other of them to disappear into another room and re-emerge later with red eyes. They didn't talk about it. Grief was a private matter, each to deal with on their own. Rosie knew that. It was how she'd been brought up. It was the same when Grand-mama and Grand-papa passed away. Nobody spoke of it. You just carried on; stiff upper lip and all that.

'Off you go then, Rosie.'

She gathered up her gifts, gave Mama and Papa another kiss on the cheek for being so thoughtful, and retreated to her room. When she placed the radio on her desk, she had the impulse to sit there and have a good cry, like she often did when something or someone reminded her they were never coming back. What stopped her was the thought she must return to the house and apologise to the Canadian. She didn't have to, but it was the right thing to do. And it had nothing to do with finding an excuse to see the good-looking young man again, she told herself as she climbed out of the window.

23

Cassie closed the diary. This time Evelyn wasn't pressing her to continue. She looked at Evelyn staring out the window and guessed why. She had lost someone too. She wouldn't be surprised if that episode in Rosie's life brought back some painful memories of her own. Cassie followed her gaze to the window and had a thought. She looked at the diary and glanced around the room. 'This was Johnny's bedroom.' She knew that by Rosie's description of the deep window seat and the perfect view straight down the driveway to Gatekeepers Cottage.

'Was it?' Evelyn said, sounding disinterested.

Cassie frowned. She was meant to be drawing her out and giving her an interest in the present, not sending her back into herself. Unless…

Cassie had an idea. Perhaps now was not the right time to broach it with her. 'Evelyn, are you all right?'

Evelyn turned her head. 'I'd like to be alone. You can go now.'

Cassie stood up. She had a question before she left. 'Evelyn, would you rather I didn't read the—'

Evelyn's head swivelled from the window; her hand grabbed

Cassie's wrist, 'Oh, you must come back with the diary. I want to know what happens next.'

Cassie smiled. 'Me too.' She needn't have worried that reading it to Evelyn was a bad idea. This boded well for Cassie's other plan. Evelyn retreating into the past had given her the idea. What if she could persuade Evelyn to write a diary like Rosie or a memory book to give to her family? The other residents might like to do one too.

She wouldn't expect them to write it. They could talk about their lives. Cassie would note down what they said. In her experience, older people loved to discuss the past. The only problem was would they want to talk to her? They hardly knew her and she worked here. Would that put them off?

Cassie stood up. 'I'll see you tomorrow morning, Evelyn.'

'I shall expect you here at nine o'clock sharp.'

Evelyn was back to treating her like staff. She was rather hoping they might get passed that. Cassie shrugged, thinking, give it time.

Leaving Evelyn's apartment, she paused outside her door to check the time. Cassie fancied grabbing a cup of coffee and unpacking her shopping before she resumed her afternoon shift. She was meant to see Ruby after her break.

Cassie walked along the corridor, thinking about the tins of cat food she'd bought in the village store. It would probably turn out a waste of money. She wouldn't be surprised if the cat had gone. As she strode down the grand central staircase, she discovered her feline friend sitting on the bottom stair.

Oh no. She hadn't expected the tabby to venture out of the kitchen. Cassie approached the cat saying, 'You can't be here. I will get into trouble if someone sees—'

The cat meowed – loudly.

Cassie winced. 'Okay, someone's not only going to see you, but they will hear you too. Pipe down.'

'MEEEOOW!'

Cassie stood on the bottom stair and looked at the cat. 'Oh, come on!' She'd grown up with dogs, but she'd never had a cat. They always puzzled her. Why would anyone want them as a pet? Cats could be contrary. They were a law unto themselves and often did the opposite of what you wanted them to.

Cassie frowned. She would rather the tabby stayed in the basement. It was her fault for giving it some milk. She didn't expect the cat to appear in the kitchen. It watched her take a carton of milk out of the fridge. How on earth did the cat know the milk came from a carton in the fridge?

The cat was getting more confident, venturing out from the kitchen. This wouldn't do at all, thought Cassie. She stared at the cat. 'You've been waiting for me, haven't you?' Cassie quickly added, 'Don't answer that!'

The cat stood up, stepped off the bottom stair and walked across the hall toward the corridor that led to the kitchen, then stopped and turned around.

'Are you checking I'm following you?'

The tabby meowed at her.

'You're after some milk, aren't you? Well, I can do one better than that.' Despite worrying that Phyllis would discover her feeding a stray cat, it pleased her that the food would not go to waste.

Cassie breathed a sigh of relief when she walked into the kitchen and nobody was around. Her bag of groceries she'd dumped on the table before shooting off to see Evelyn was still there. 'What have we got here?' Cassie said to the cat as she rifled through the shopping bag.

The cat jumped on to the table and ran up to the groceries, putting its head right in the bag.

'Hey,' Cassie said in surprise, although she smiled. 'Manners, please.' She gently picked up the tabby and put it down on the floor. 'We do not jump up on the table.'

A moment later, it was back again, this time sitting at the other end of the table.

Out of the corner of her eye, Cassie saw the cat stealthily creeping towards the bag. When she turned her head, the cat sat licking its fur pretending not to have moved an inch. Cassie smiled and reached in the bag for the cat food. When she found the tin, she looked up to find the cat sitting by the bag. She lifted the cat off the table. 'We can do this all day, you know. If you want something to eat, I suggest you behave yourself. You are not allowed on the table.'

When Cassie turned around with the food she had spooned into a dish, the cat was sitting on a chair, neck extended, a curious nose sniffing the air.

Cassie rolled her eyes. 'When I said you're not allowed up the table, I meant the chairs too.' She lifted the cat off the chair and put the little tabby down by the dish. 'Look, I've brought you some food. I guessed you're a young cat, so the helpful lady in the grocery store suggested this brand for kittens.' Cassie walked over and opened a kitchen window to let out the smell. 'I have a feeling she might have recommended that one because it's the expensive brand, but I don't mind.'

She sighed, recalling her eventful trip to the village. There was one thing spending an extra pound on two tins of gourmet cat food, but Cassie didn't have money to burn. Wasn't it just her luck to be nearly run over and have to spend fifty pounds on getting a bike repaired for the privilege.

Cassie eyed the cat. 'You better enjoy it because it cost me.'

The cat started purring. Cassie raised an eyebrow. Did they do that when they liked their food? She guessed so.

Cassie made herself a cup of coffee and sat down at the table, watching the tabby eating its dinner. She was feeling self-conscious talking to the cat but did it anyway. 'You and I have something in common, you know. We're all alone.' Her mind wandered to that encounter at lunchtime with Ben. Is it possible to grieve for a life that might have been? If he hadn't dumped her when they were teenagers, would they still be together? They might have had children. Perhaps she wouldn't be going through a divorce right now. Cassie sat there staring off into space, dreaming of a life that might have been, if only—

A loud meow interrupted her thoughts. The cat was back again, sitting on the chair beside hers. Cassie sighed. 'What did I tell you about jumping up the table?'

Not surprisingly, the cat paid her no heed.

Cassie reached out and gave her feline friend an affectionate scratch under the chin which it seemed to like. The tabby purred.

'Well, I can't sit here all day talking about regrets even though you are a good listener.' Cassie finished her cup of coffee and got up from the table. She was washing up her coffee cup, and the cat's bowl, when she had an idea. *A good listener.* Cassie turned around and stared at the pretty cat as she dried her coffee cup on a tea towel. Shame her feline friend couldn't accompany her on visits to Evelyn. She might not want to talk to the staff, but she might have a thing or two to say to a sweet moggy.

Cassie picked up the cat's bowl and put it back in her shopping bag. Inside the bag was another new dish. Cassie got it out of the bag. 'You will need some water, but we can't leave it lying around in the kitchen. Come on, let's fill this up and take it downstairs. If you are thirsty, you must go down to the basement.'

'Who are you talking to?'

Cassie froze, caught like a rabbit in headlights. Jill had walked into the room. Cassie looked at the bowl in her hand and hastily put it away in a cupboard. 'Oh, just muttering away to myself.'

Jill laughed. 'I'm guilty of that too. I'm glad I found you. I just wanted to let you know that Ruby has had her dinner, and an afternoon nap, so she's ready whenever you are.'

Cassie glanced at the chair next to her, and behind her, and even bent down to peer under the table.

'Have you lost something, Cassie?'

'Er no.' Just a silver, grey tabby who is quite the escape artist. Where had the cat got to?

Jill was about to walk out of the kitchen.

'Have you finished for the day, Jill?'

'No, I am nipping home. I'll be back later.'

'Nipping home? On your bike?'

'Yes. Is there something you need from the village?'

'No. Have a pleasant ride home.'

Jill threw her a curious look. 'Okay.'

Cassie hoped Jill noticed nothing amiss with her bike.

Alone again, Cassie searched for the cat, then filled the water bowl and took it down to the basement.

'Ah, there you are.' The cat was sitting on top of the boxes by the open window. 'Are you off then?' Cassie asked, knowing it would probably be for the best. She couldn't have a pet. Phyllis wouldn't allow it. Besides, she didn't know where she would end up after this temporary job finished. She might not be able to keep a pet or afford one.

The cat jumped down and brushed up against her legs. Cassie guessed the tabby wasn't leaving today. She put the bowl of water down on the floor. 'If you are going to stay for a bit longer, you could do with something to sleep on.' Cassie wished she'd bought one of the cat beds when she was in the shop, but unless she'd taken up Ben's offer of a lift back to the hall, she couldn't see how she would have manged to carry it back.

She looked about her and spotted an old blanket. 'How about this?' She pulled it off the top of some boxes and was about to arrange it in a cardboard box for the tabby to sleep on when she stopped. 'What's this?' The blanket had been covering a wooden box. The cat meowed and approached the box, jumped on the top, sniffing the edge. There was just enough room for the cat to stand on the top.

Cassie brushed some cobwebs away to reveal smooth mahogany wood and old black dials. 'It's an old radio.' She stared at it as something occurred to her. She recalled what she'd read to Evelyn before she came down to feed the cat. Rosie had been given her brother's radio. 'It can't be Johnny's, surely.' But it *was* near the spot where she found the diary.

'I've got the most brilliant idea,' she said to the moggie.

Cassie knelt down to inspect it more closely. 'I'll take it upstairs and clean it up. I'm sure there's some furniture polish somewhere. Then I'll give it to Evelyn. She's taking such an interest in Rosie's story. I'm sure she'd love it. We could tune it in together.'

The cat meowed.

'What is it?'

The cat jumped off the top of the radio and pawed at something on the floor.

Cassie picked up the wires under the cat's paw. The plug was missing. 'If I cleaned and polished the beautiful mahogany radio, it's still not going to work is it.'

The cat looked up at Cassie.

'I need to get it fixed first, but where?' There was nowhere in the village that sold electrical equipment which meant she'd have to go further afield. 'I'll search for a shop online when I've finished my shift.' She might have to send it away to be repaired. That would cost money. Cassie didn't want to think about the expense. She picked up the old radio, which was surprisingly heavy. Cassie decided against lugging it down the drive to the cottage until she knew if it could be fixed. Cassie glanced at her watch. It was time she went to see Ruby.

She carefully placed the radio in an empty box and left the cat drinking fresh water from the bowl. Cassie made her way upstairs to the kitchen, hoping she could remember where Ruby's apartment was. As luck would have it, Olivia appeared. 'Hi Cassie.'

'Would you mind showing me the way to Ruby's apartment again?'

'Not at all.'

Five minutes later, Cassie was standing outside her door.

'Just walk straight in,' said Olivia before she left. 'It's always unlocked.'

'Ruby, it's Cassie.' She turned around to shut the apartment door and found the tabby cat sitting in the open doorway. Cassie took a step back in surprise. 'What are you doing here?'

The cat stood up and sauntered inside as though it owned the place. 'No, wait! You can't come in here.' She chased after the cat down the inner hall and into the lounge. A young health care assistant who did the night shift was sitting in a chair scrolling through her phone, looking bored. She glanced up when Cassie walked into the room. 'Hi.'

Cassie's eyes darted around the room, but there was no sign of the cat.

'I'm standing in for Jill this afternoon.'

Cassie's eyes went wide. Had something happened on Jill's ride home at lunchtime? 'Is she all right?'

'Jill had to run some errands for Phyllis in the village. I guess it takes longer on a bike.'

Cassie breathed a sigh of relief as the young woman left the room. Ruby was sitting by the window. Cassie walked over, still keeping half an eye out for the cat. She knelt beside her wheelchair. 'Hello, Ruby.'

Cassie got a big grin in return and some slurred words which sounded like, 'I'm good, thank you.' Ruby was getting excited. Her hands started to flap. It made Cassie wonder how much control she had over her movements. She decided to do some exercises to find out.

'Today, we will start the therapy session by—'

'Meeeooow.' The tabby appeared from behind the long curtains.

'Oh, crumbs!' Cassie lunged, trying to grab the cat, but she wasn't quick enough. It jumped up and balanced on the armrest of the wheelchair.

Cassie looked up and saw Ruby lift her hand to gently stroke the cat.

The cat purred.

Cassie watched this with interest and thought what a perfect way to assess Ruby's fine motor skills.

Ruby said, 'Tab… bee… the…' She paused, her contorted facial expression trying to form the word *cat*. Cassie understood what she was trying to say – *tabby cat*.

Cassie looked at the cat purring away, leaning her face towards Ruby. *Tabb…bee…the*.

'Tabitha!' exclaimed Cassie. What a great name.

As soon as she said *Tabitha* the cat jumped to the other armrest nearest Cassie and meowed at her, as if to say, *that name meets with my approval*.

Ruby turned her head, following the cat.

Cassie made a mental note of Ruby's movements, continuing her assessment.

The cat tentatively put a paw on Ruby's lap, then another paw. She stretched her neck and nuzzled her head under Ruby's chin before settling down on her lap, curling into a ball and purring softly.

Ruby gently stroked Tabitha's head with a finger. She turned to look at Cassie, eyes bright, nodding and smiling.

Cassie had an idea. 'Would you like Tabitha to come with me next time?' She knew she didn't even have to ask that question. The expression on Ruby's face said it all. The real issue was, would the cat be willing to come?

Ruby looked at the cat on her lap. 'Tabeethe.'

Cassie knew she really ought to ask Phyllis.

Tabitha stood up and meowed, then nuzzled her head against Ruby's cheek. The cat seemed to understand it was time to leave.

When the health care assistant walked in, Tabitha did a disappearing act again. Cassie stepped out of the apartment to find the cat sitting on the window seat, preening herself. Cassie smiled at Tabitha. She'd heard about therapy dogs used in sessions for patients with head injuries, but never cats. Cassie walked over to the cat. 'I guess there's a first time for everything. I think you'd make a perfect therapy cat.'

Tabitha stopped preening herself and meowed at Cassie as if she understood every word.

Cassie smiled. 'Good, I'm glad you agree. How would you like to accompany me on my rounds?' Cassie didn't want to go behind Phyllis' back over this. She really ought to run it by her first, but Phyllis did suggest that if there were any activities she could think of for the other residents, she was welcome to call in on them. She looked at Tabitha. 'How about it? Shall we meet Bertie and Iris?'

The chances of bumping into Phyllis in this big old house were slim, and besides, if she did, Tabitha was adept at playing hide-and-seek.

Cassie walked down the hallway. She glanced over her shoulder. Tabitha was still sitting on the window seat. She wasn't surprised. Cats did everything in their own good time, and only if it suited them.

A few minutes later, after a brisk walk down several corridors and up a flight of stairs, Cassie stopped outside the door to Iris' apartment. She knocked on the door and looked down when she felt something brush her leg. 'Hello, there. I didn't think you were coming.'

Tabitha meowed as if to say, *of course I was coming.*

What if Iris didn't like cats? She looked at the young tabby and thought who could resist talking to such an adorable little cat? That's why she wanted her to come along. Would Bertie and Iris like to tell Tabitha their life stories? If they did, perhaps she could write them down in a notebook and find somewhere to get it bound into a memory book, a keepsake for their families.

Her thoughts turned to the diary. She wondered what had become of Rosie's family. Did she have descendants; were there children, grandchildren, even great-grandchildren who would love to read the diary about her life here during the Second World War? It was the first time this had occurred to Cassie. She'd like to meet Rosie if she was still alive and return the diary.

❖

An hour later, Cassie emerged from Iris' apartment with a notebook containing several pages of writing. She had found the unused notebook in a kitchen drawer for Cassie to use.

Cassie looked at Tabitha. 'Well, aren't you a clever cat?'

At first Iris had been reticent when Cassie suggested her idea for a memory book, but when Tabitha appeared everything changed. Iris had said, 'I had a cat just like you. Now, when was that?'

Talk about an ice-breaker thought Cassie. She walked along the hall towards Bertie's apartment and glanced at Tabitha. She wouldn't need the cute cat to break the ice with him; a ladies' man, he'd be over the moon she was stopping by and would sit with him for an hour or two. Evelyn, on the other hand, was probably not going to warm to the idea of a memory book immediately. Cassie looked at Tabitha. 'You have to promise you will come with me tomorrow morning to see Evelyn.'

24

'Oh no, it's nothing serious, is it?'

Phyllis sighed. 'Cassie, at their age everything is serious.'

'But I haven't finished reading the diary to her.' Cassie had just walked into the kitchen the next morning to be told Evelyn wasn't well.

'Cassie, you really will have to lighten up. She's got a stinking cold – that's all. But we don't want her to pass it on to you. Not only that, we wouldn't want Ruby to catch it with her weakened immune system. Then we will have something serious on our hands because it's liable to turn into pneumonia.'

Jill glanced at the notebook in Cassie's hand. 'Don't worry, Evelyn's one of those people who is not going anywhere. I swear she'll outlive us all, the stubborn—'

'Jill…' Phyllis warned.

Cassie breathed a sigh. 'What shall I do after breakfast?'

Phyllis shrugged. 'Why don't you pop into the village again? You seemed to enjoy it.'

'What makes you say that?'

'You were gone a long time. You must have found something of interest there.'

Cassie frowned. If you counted getting a bike fixed and running into an old flame, literally. The last thing she wanted was to run into *him* again.

Cassie wandered back to the cottage. Tabitha was curled up on the end of her bed, a ball of fur breathing softly as she snoozed. Cassie started at her. So much for sorting out that old blanket and a box for her bed down in the basement. Tabitha, being a cat, had other ideas. Unbeknown to Cassie, yesterday after her rounds, the cat had ventured out of the house and must have followed her at a discrete distance down the drive. When Cassie walked into the bedroom, she thought her eyes were deceiving her when she saw Tabitha sitting on her bed.

Several attempts last night to put her out of the room were met with resistance, from scratching, meowing and worst of all crying. On the last attempt, Cassie had flung open the door and let the cat into her bedroom. 'You little minx,' she'd said before climbing back into bed. Cassie now had a permanent roommate.

Her roommate woke up, stretched, and looked at Cassie as if to say, *weren't we meant to be going somewhere this morning?*

'I've got a free morning,' Cassie told Tabitha, wondering why she was telling the cat. Cassie didn't know what to do with herself. She'd already checked her emails – nothing from Dad. She'd looked at her phone several times; nothing from Lars or the solicitor or the estate agents.

She didn't expect to hear anything from her husband apart from through their divorce lawyer when the legal papers were ready. She supposed with the sale of the flat going through, no news was good news.

Cassie picked up the diary from the bedside table and glanced at the window. It was the same window Rosie had watched the trucks and jeeps full of Canadians making their way up the drive to the house. Cassie sighed. She'd promised Evelyn she wouldn't read any further, but she was dying to learn what happened next after Rosie was given the radio for her birthday.

'The radio!' Cassie left Tabitha snoozing on the bed and returned to the house. The kitchen was empty which meant she could scoot down to the basement and retrieve her second find from the bowels of Fletchling Hall. It was becoming a thing; first the diary, then the radio. It almost felt as though the house was giving up its secrets.

Back at the cottage, Cassie carefully lifted the radio out of the box and placed it on the dressing table. Tabitha was awake again, sitting on the end of the bed watching her.

'I'll go online and find a repair shop. Then I can surprise Evelyn.' She hoped it was Rosie's radio. The only way to find out if that was a possibility was by taking it to a repair shop where they might be able give her some idea of its age.

Tabitha jumped up on the dressing table. The cat was sniffing the radio again. Cassie couldn't help but smile. 'I imagine with Evelyn's interest in Rosie's story, she'd be over the moon to see the wireless.' Cassie stroked the cat. 'Now, remember, Tabitha, we made a deal. You could be my roommate if you promise to come with me to visit Evelyn.'

Tabitha turned to Cassie and *meowed.*

'I hope that means yes. I'd love Evelyn to open up and tell me her story, and you being there might do the trick. I have a feeling there's much more to her than meets the eye.'

Olivia suggested that perhaps Evelyn and her family have fallen out. That's why she has no visitors. Cassie knew she was taciturn and disagreeable at times, but there had to be more to it than that. Everyone falls out with their family occasionally; it's only natural. However, it was only a rumour. They had no idea why she had no visitors. Perhaps they were too afraid to ask.

It made her wonder herself. 'That's where you come in, Tabitha.' Cassie gave her a scratch under the chin. 'Who wouldn't want to tell you their secrets? Take me for instance; I can't stop talking to you. I'll let you into a secret. The reason I don't want to meet Ben again is that—'

A bang on the door interrupted Cassie. She stared wide-eyed at the cat. 'You've got to hide!'

Cassie did a double-take when Tabitha jumped off the dressing table and crawled under the bed. Her tail had just disappeared when Cassie walked up to the front door. It was Randall. 'I heard you had a free morning. Me too. Do you want a lift into the village? There's a nice café. We could have coffee or some lunch…'

Cassie looked at him. Was he asking her out on a date? She started to shake her head when something caught Randall's eye. From the doorway he could see down the hall into Cassie's bedroom. 'Hey, is that a valve radio?'

'A what?' Cassie made the mistake of turning around and leaving her door unattended. Randall took that as his cue to step inside. 'These are nice digs. I'm a little jealous,' he said good-naturedly as he looked around the cottage, poking his head in the lounge and the kitchen before walking into Cassie's bedroom where he'd spied the radio. 'Now that's a beauty.'

'You know something about old radios?' Cassie asked, joining him in front of the dressing table.

'Not really. My dad back in Australia is a radio enthusiast though, always on his ham radio.'

'His *what*?'

Randall knelt to take a closer look at it. 'Ham radio, that's amateur radio.'

Cassie looked at him blankly.

Randall smiled. 'Ah, you haven't got a clue what I'm talking about. To be honest, I never took much of an interest. The only thing I can recall was my father said it was an acronym, each letter was the surname of the three guys who started it, I guess.'

Cassie was lost already. She didn't understand what that had to do with the radio.

Randall must have caught her eyes glazing over. 'Sorry, that was a useless piece of information. Amateur radio – can't see the appeal myself either. Now this, I *can* see the appeal.' He knelt down in front of it, running a hand along the smooth mahogany. 'I do like the style of these old radios, or wireless as my grandparents used to call them.'

'Did they have one like this?'

'Oh, yes. They had it for years. Then someone bought them a DAB radio, that's a digital radio.'

Cassie knew what they were. She looked at the radio. 'Do you have any idea how old this one might be?'

'I would say around the nineteen forties.'

Cassie smiled.

'It's a shame we can't see if it works.' Randall held up the frayed wires. 'Where did you find it?'

Cassie glanced at the floor and spied two green eyes staring at her from beneath the bed. 'In the basement.'

'In the basement of the house?'

Cassie nodded.

'What were you doing down there?'

'I heard something when I was in the kitchen, so went down to investigate.'

'You're braver than I am. I wouldn't have gone down there if you paid me. Did I tell you I've seen rats?'

'Yes, Randall.' But what he didn't know, and Cassie would not divulge, was that there had been a family of feral cats down there, not rats. 'I want to get the radio fixed. I was about to go online and search for an electrical shop.'

'Ah.' Randal stood up. 'You won't be able to take this to just any electrical shop. It probably requires specialist parts and someone with the knowledge to fix one of these.'

'I hadn't thought of that.'

'It might be costly too. I guess you hadn't thought of that either.'

'Oh.' Cassie glanced at the wireless.

'If you get it working, a vintage radio like this will be worth a bob or two.'

'A bob or two?' Cassie looked at him askance and grinned. The very British saying sounded rather funny coming from an Australian.

He smiled, guessing what she was thinking. 'Yeah, I've stopped way too long in England. I was meant to be travelling around the world, but this country – this place – gets under your skin. I like it here.'

Cassie regarded him. 'I came to this country when I was seventeen – and never left. So, yep, I know exactly what you mean.' Cassie loved Fletchling Hall too. If she could find a way to stop them going ahead with the redevelopment of the house and grounds into a housing estate, then she'd do it – no question. She imagined the other staff felt the same.

Aware his gaze was lingering on her a little too long, Cassie decided it was time to change the subject. She was only being friendly and hoped he didn't read too much into it. She turned her attention back to the radio. 'I wasn't intending to sell it. I'm giving it to Evelyn.'

'Evelyn?' Randall looked at her in surprise. 'That old battle-axe. Whatever for?'

'I've been reading her a diary written by a girl who used to live here. The girl's brothers died in the war. She was given their radio. This may be it.'

'Seriously?'

'Yes, I'm pretty sure.' From what Cassie had read, it fitted the description and she'd found it in the basement near where she'd discovered the diary. 'Evelyn has taken such an interest in the story. I thought it would be a nice touch to have it repaired – if someone can get it working.'

Randall studied her a long moment. 'I would try searching online for a company that specialises in repairing old valve radios. That's what this is.'

Cassie had never heard of valve radios. This was news to her. She walked Randall to the door, surprised at how helpful he'd been.

He stepped out of the cottage and turned around. 'You really are a nice person, Cassie, do you know that?'

Cassie blushed. Before she arrived here, she couldn't remember the last time anybody had paid her a compliment. Lars didn't. She smiled at Randall, guessing he had an ulterior motive. 'I'm still not going to have coffee with you – or lunch.'

He grinned at her. 'I know. But I meant what I said and I hope whoever he is, realises what a lucky man he is.'

'I'm getting divorced,' she blurted. She hadn't meant to say that. Cassie sighed. 'There isn't anybody in my life.'

'There will be.'

'What do you mean?'

'Everybody in the world has a soulmate, the person we are meant to spend our lives with. That's what I believe. I'm still looking, but I will find her, and you will find him. Who knows, today might be your lucky day and you'll run into him.'

'I won't hold my breath,' Cassie said glumly as she watched Randall walk down the hallway. He closed the front door behind him. When she turned around, Tabitha was sitting on her bed staring at her as if to say, *what was that all about?*

Cassie shrugged her shoulders and sat on the edge of the bed with her laptop. She switched it on and watched Tabitha run over to where she was sitting. Cassie stroked her soft fur. 'Soulmates, honestly, is he thirteen?' She realised that wasn't a very kind thing to say; he was still in his twenties, he had time. She was forty-five and there were no fairy-tale endings on her horizon. It made her wonder where she'd be in five years when her next big birthday coincided with a new decade, 2020.

When the laptop booted up, Cassie went online searching for somebody who might fix the wireless. Would she even find a website that repaired old valve radios? She imagined some old bloke, like Randal's father, sitting in a shack at the bottom of the garden tinkering with…

'Oh, my goodness!' exclaimed Cassie, her negative train of thought stopped when a website popped up in the search engine. 'The Radio Shack. What a brilliant name!' She scanned the page, reading the information on the website. *I specialise in the repair and restoration of vintage radios…*

'Perfect.' Cassie glanced at Tabitha rubbing her chin on the side of the laptop. She continued reading, trying to ignore the cat. It sounded to Cassie like a one-man band, a small business that only repaired British valve radios from the 1940s and '50s. That was lucky.

Cassie read on. An estimate for repairs was free, which was excellent news. Unlike Jill's bike, Cassie would much rather know what she was getting herself into, financially. She frowned when the next bit highlighted the fact that it was only provisional. The website explained that once the radio was in working order, they may require a little extra time to restore it to its former glory. Hence the reason the final repair bill might differ from the estimate.

The guy worked from home in a small workshop. She imagined a shed at the bottom of the garden where an old guy had the perfect excuse to get away from his wife for several hours at a time. Cassie read with interest that she could bring the radio along herself for repair; it didn't have to be sent away, which would be more expense. And the best part was The Radio Shack was in the next village. She couldn't quite believe her luck. She smiled, looking forward to her visit. Now, how was she going to get it there?

25

There was a bus which stopped in the local village square and then went on to the next village. The radio was far too heavy to carry any distance. Cassie would need a lift to the bus stop, but she'd still have a problem at the other end once she got off the bus. The old vintage car was in the garage. However, after that episode with Jill's bike, she couldn't afford any more mishaps. Fixing a bicycle was one thing, but a car? Cassie shuddered at the thought.

She looked at Tabitha. 'I've got an idea.' It wasn't what she'd choose to do, but as her grandmother was fond of saying, *needs must.*

Cassie flew out of the bedroom and belted to the front door, hoping she could still catch him. She saw Randall ambling up the drive towards the house. 'Randall!' she called out. Cassie caught up with him.

He turned around and smiled. 'Changed your mind about going into the village with me?'

'Not exactly. Look, I know it's asking a huge favour, but can you give me a lift to the *next* village? You don't have to wait around.' In fact, she'd prefer that he didn't in case he got any ideas. This was not an excuse to have coffee or go for lunch together and it certainly wasn't a date. 'I will get the bus back. I want to take the radio to a repair shop.'

'You found one around here that fixes old valve radios?'

'The website says he looks at them for free and gives an estimate.'

'I'll get the car.' Randall glanced over Cassie's shoulder at the cottage. 'Do you need a hand carrying the radio out to the car?'

Cassie thought of Tabitha settling down for another nap on her bed. 'No, that's all right. I can manage.'

Randall had brought the car round to the front of the cottage by the time she walked back, gathered her coat and handbag, and the box containing the radio. He rescued her as she was trying to open the gate with her foot, relieving her of the heavy box. Cassie breathed a sigh of relief. 'Thank you.' The muscles in her arms ached as though she'd been lifting weights.

They set off out of the drive and along the road towards the village. 'So, what are the opening hours of the repair shop?' Randall shouted above the noise of the old car engine.

In her haste to get a lift, she'd forgotten that it might be prudent to phone first to check the person who ran The Radio Shack was in and let him know she was on her way. She had the address and the postcode. Cassie frowned at the vintage dashboard. No Sat Nav. 'Oh, dear. How will we find it?'

Randall reached in his pocket and got out his mobile. 'Google maps.'

Fifteen minutes later they arrived outside a modern detached property on the outskirts of a small village. Randall turned to Cassie. 'It doesn't look like a shop. Are you sure this is it?'

'I think so. The website said he works from home.'

Cassie got out of the car and reached for the radio on the back seat.

'Do you need help with that?'

'No, I'm fine.' She kneed the door shut.

'I'll wait just in case nobody is home.'

Although she didn't want him to hang around, she said, 'Good idea. I'll see if they're in, then you're free to go.'

'Are you sure you don't want to—'

'No, I'm happy to get the bus back.'

'What's your mobile number?'

'Why?'

Randall rolled his eyes. 'Don't worry, I will not do anything weird like ask you out on a date.'

'Oh, I didn't think—'

'Yeah, sure you didn't. I know Olivia's probably given you the low-down on me, making out I'm a lothario.'

Cassie didn't reply.

'I will send you a text, so if you get stuck out you can ring me, and I'll come back and pick you up. That's all.'

'Oh, yes, good idea.' Cassie reeled off her mobile number before carrying the radio to the front door and ringing the doorbell.

The house wasn't what she expected. Cassie imagined an old cottage or perhaps a small 1930s semi, even a bungalow. This place couldn't be more different; it was an ultra-modern detached home painted white with large grey framed windows and a matching front-door. It reminded her of the individual architect-designed properties she'd seen on the covers of magazines, all boxy shapes and Zen-like angles.

The house looked out of place in a street with cottages and

bungalows. Cassie imagined there might have been another property here at one time, and they knocked it down to build this. Fletchling Hall came to mind and the possibility a developer might come along and raze the beautiful old mansion to the ground.

Cassie tried to put that notion aside as she stood there, arms aching, hoping someone was in. Now she regretted not phoning ahead to make an appointment. She glanced over her shoulder at Randall waiting in the car, the engine turning over.

As she stood outside, she still had this picture in her mind of an old chap who ran The Radio Shack at the bottom of his garden. The garden belonging to a cosy ivy-clad cottage with a matronly, but friendly, wife who answered the door and ushered her inside, offering her a cup of tea and a digestive biscuit.

Cassie smiled. It was a nice idea, but somehow she doubted she'd be offered a cuppa or a biscuit. That perception of the owner of The Radio Shack had disappeared into thin air as soon as she turned up at this house.

She glanced at the box in her arms. Any minute she'd have to give in and put it down on the floor. She'd placed the radio in an empty cardboard box from the basement so she wouldn't trip over the exposed wiring, but it was bulky and awkward. Not to mention heavy. Cassie heaved a sigh of relief when she saw someone approaching through the frosted glass in the front door. She turned to Randall and managed to give him a thumbs-up just as the front opened.

26

It wasn't a matronly older woman who opened the door, but a petulant teenager with a sour look on her face. She looked at the box in Cassie's hands. 'If you're selling door-to-door, we're not interested.' She went to shut the door.

'Oh, I'm not selling.'

The teenager eyed her suspiciously. 'If you're a Jehovah's Witness – ditto.' She went to close the door again.

'I think I've come to the wrong house.' It occurred to Cassie that she may have copied down the address incorrectly. 'I was looking for The Radio Shack – sorry.' Cassie turned to go.

'Wait!' The teenager stepped forward. 'What's in the box?'

Cassie stared at her. She had a goth-like appearance that brought back memories of the eighties when Cassie was a teenager. The slip of a girl had long smooth black hair highlighted with a streak of purple. She was so petite, it was hard to gauge her age; she could have been anywhere from twelve to fifteen years old, although Cassie surmised, she was closer to fourteen or fifteen.

'Have you brought a radio?'

'Yes. I want an estimate for—'

Cassie was yanked inside by her sleeve, the door slammed shut behind her.

The girl turned around and eyed the box. 'Let me see.'

'Do you run The Radio Shack?' asked Cassie, finding that hard to believe.

'It's Grandpa, but he's out. I can give you an estimate.'

'You can?' Cassie couldn't hide the scepticism in her voice.

Dark brown defiant eyes narrowed. 'Do you want an estimate or not?'

'Sure.' Cassie did not expect a teenage girl to have the first clue about an old valve radio.

The girl whisked her mobile phone out of the back pocket of her ripped skinny jeans and glanced at it. Her eyes darted to the front door. 'Let's take this up to my room.' She slipped the phone back in her pocket.

Cassie followed her through the house; the interior walls were painted white offset by warm honey coloured wooden flooring which flowed through the sizeable living space. She glanced in the room on her left and right as she passed by. One room was a large airy lounge with cream leather sofas, glass coffee tables and a massive wall-mounted curved flat screen television. The room on the other side of the hall, a dining room, had faux-leather chairs set around a cream table. Modern artwork adorned the walls in both rooms. There were other rooms downstairs, but they were behind closed doors. Cassie imagined a study and perhaps a cloakroom, even a snug. It put her tiny flat in London into perspective, although Lars had been right; it had proved an excellent investment – assuming one sold it at current market value and didn't give it away.

Casting her gaze around this house as she followed the girl, Cassie tried to avoid feeling a pang of regret over that. If she'd sold the flat to someone else, the money might have afforded her a nice place of her own. She shook her head, knowing she still wouldn't go back on her decision. There were other cheaper areas of the country she could afford to move to.

But I like it here in Sussex. Cassie didn't want to think about uprooting again. She had a job and a cosy little cottage to live in, and had settled in to her new, albeit temporary, way of life quicker than expected. Perhaps that was the problem with returning somewhere familiar. She had slotted in too well. It would make it harder when the inevitable happened and she had to leave.

Cassie shook her head, trying to dispel any thoughts of leaving. Instead she focused on her surroundings as they headed up the open tread stairs. She thought The Radio Shack would be outside in a workshop. Cassie shrugged her shoulders and followed the girl into a bedroom. Her first impression was *wow.* The room was almost like a mini open-plan apartment with a large double bed, and a sitting area with a comfy sofa and wall-mounted television. There were stunning views from the floor-to-ceiling windows of the landscaped garden with decking areas and a perfectly manicured lawn.

Cassie recalled the teenage bedroom she shared with her little sister in Toronto where she grew up. They lived in a brownstone which was divided into two flats on the outskirts of the city. Her parents had a garden apartment, so at least they had a back yard. But it was nothing like this.

The girl must have caught Cassie staring out the window. 'It's Astro-turf.'

'Oh.'

'Yeah, I don't like it either.' She took the box out of Cassie's hands and placed it on her desk.

Cassie rubbed her aching arms. 'It looks like real grass.'

'Yes, but some people are not keen. Trouble with my father is that everything has to be perfect, down to the smallest detail. That's why there isn't any real grass. Too messy. Besides, he'd have to mow it and he hasn't got the time.'

Cassie turned away from the window and saw the girl lifting the radio out of the box and cradling it like a baby.

'It is a nice house, though.' Cassie had to concede. Whoever designed it had talent. Inside it was impressive, even though modern wasn't really her thing.

The girl put the radio down on her desk beside the box and sat down in her swivel chair. 'I preferred Grandpa's house.'

'Is that in the village?' Cassie asked, wondering if her Grandpa ran The Radio Shack from here.

The teenager pulled a face. 'Uh-uh, you're standing in it. Or the remains of it.'

'I don't understand.'

'The foundations. Dad knocked Grandpa's bungalow down and built this. He's an architect, so he does that sort of thing.'

'I see.' Cassie nodded, not surprised an older property once stood here. It was a shame to pull down a place just because it was old. 'Does your Grandpa mind that be built a modern home in its place?'

She shrugged as she sat down at her desk. 'I don't think it was up to him. He lives here too, so he hasn't got a choice.'

Cassie glanced out the window. She spotted some trellis with creeping ivy and spied the rooftop of a large shed at the bottom of the garden. The trellis was obviously put up as a screen. 'Is that The Radio Shack?'

'Yes. Grandpa's not in. I haven't got the key…' She trailed off. She sat there staring at the radio in silence for so long that Cassie eventually turned from the window, wondering what was wrong. She had a good idea. 'It's had it, hasn't it,' she said disappointingly.

'I don't know yet. I haven't had a look. It's just…'

'What is it?'

'This is amazing.'

That's when Cassie realised the girl was sitting there admiring it. She turned and glanced at Cassie. 'It's not every day we come across something that hasn't been touched since the 'forties. This wiring is the original. It's quite a rare find.'

'Really?'

'Oh, yes. These are collector's items. Did it belong to a relative? Grandpa says, in his experience, people often come across these in attics or basements when their relatives pass on.'

Cassie smiled. 'I found it in a basement where I work.'

'Where's that?'

'Fletchling Hall.'

'The old people's home on the outskirts of the next village?'

'It's not an old people's home, more like sheltered accommodation.'

'But it's still just old people that live there.'

'Not just old people.'

'You mean there are younger people who live there too? How come?'

Cassie changed the subject. It was unprofessional to talk about her patients. She wished she hadn't brought it up. 'I want to get the radio fixed for one of the residents.' Cassie noticed her staring. 'What?'

'It's just that some people might keep it for themselves or sell it. This is worth a lot of money.'

'Well, I'm not some people.'

She stared at Cassie for a long moment. 'Let me take a closer look. It means prizing off the back. Is that okay?'

Cassie replied, 'Whatever you need to do…'

While she took the back off the radio, she asked, 'Are you American?'

'Canadian.'

'What are you doing here in England?'

It was a familiar question Cassie encountered from strangers. No matter how many decades she'd lived in England, her accent told them she was a foreigner.

'I've lived here for quite a few years.'

'Are you married?'

Cassie didn't want to get into that. 'So, about the radio… Do you think your grandpa can fix it?'

The girl sat back in her chair. 'I won't lie. It requires some work. There are no guarantees, but I will… I mean my grandpa will try.'

'You said you could give me an estimate. Do you know how much he will charge?'

Cassie sucked in a breath when she mentioned a figure. 'That much?'

'That's his going rate. But as this is kind of special, I'm sure he will do his best to reduce his rates so you won't go elsewhere. It is quite rare and isn't every day someone brings us something like this.'

'Shall I write you a cheque now?' Cassie recalled the information on the website about estimates versus the final repair bill. 'I can pay the balance if the final bill is more.'

'No, that's fine. Let us have a further look at it and see what we can do. How can I contact you?'

Cassie gave her mobile number. 'Shouldn't I speak to your Grandpa to confirm?'

'No need. I'll be in touch if there's a problem. I do his books. I'm good at maths. My dad says I should be an accountant.'

'An accountant? That sounds so boring.' Cassie's eyes went wide. 'I shouldn't have said that. Sorry.'

For the first time since she met her, the teenager smiled, revealing a perfect set of teeth behind a brace. 'That's what I said. It's kinda dull.'

Cassie grinned. 'Dull is right. My name is Cassie, by the way.'

'I'm Devon.'

'Devon. What a pretty name. Not dull at all.'

She smiled again, but Cassie caught sadness in those large brown eyes. 'My mum wanted the name Devon.'

'It's really cool. What does your mum do?'

The expression on Devon's face told Cassie she had said something wrong. 'Sorry, it's none of my business.'

'It's okay. I live with my Dad and Grandpa now.' She stood up. 'I'll phone you when I know more about the radio.'

Cassie looked at her. 'Sure, that's great. I'll wait for a call.'

Devon showed her the way out. When Cassie walked out the door, Devon glanced outside. 'Where's your car?'

'I got a lift. I'm getting the bus back.'

'Hope you haven't missed it. There's only one bus and it comes along right about now.'

'I better dash.'

Devon stood at the front door watching the woman with the beautiful raven-red hair leg it down the drive. She turned around, closed the door and got her mobile phone out of her back pocket. Devon checked the time. Her dad was still at work. He worked all the time, so that wasn't a surprise.

Grandpa was at the dentist. Not his favourite place by any stretch, but he'd woken up with toothache and got an emergency appointment this morning. Lucky for Devon he was out when the interesting lady called Cassie knocked on the door with a rare 1940s valve radio. Devon couldn't believe her luck. And to think she'd almost slammed the door in her face.

Devon was on half-term holiday from school. She was in her final year of GCSE's. For her electronics assignment, she was meant to think up a project. Turns out Devon didn't have to think one up; it had been delivered right to her door on a plate, well more like a cardboard box.

She would have repaired the wireless whether she was doing a school project or not. She'd even fix it for free, but the Canadian lady didn't know that. Devon thought she'd use the money towards purchasing her very own vintage valve radio. She wondered if Cassie could be persuaded to let her buy this one. Devon hoped so, assuming she could get it working.

She had every confidence she could. Devon had been around old valve radios all her life; she'd sat with Grandpa in The Radio Shack watching him since she was little before she even started nursery school. Daddy was always busy working, so she made a beeline to Grandpa's workshop after school and became his little helper once her homework was finished. What she didn't know about old valve radios wasn't worth knowing.

Although Grandpa had let her help him, he wouldn't allow her to restore one herself because they were his clients' radios. He said he would buy a wireless just for her to repair. So far, that hadn't materialised. She realised why. They were far too expensive; he'd probably have to ask Daddy for the money. That would never happen. Her grandfather was stubborn and proud. Just like me, thought Devon. However, through a surprising turn of events, she'd ended up with one.

She knew she should take it down to The Radio Shack and leave it for Grandpa when he got back. Devon walked back up the stairs into her bedroom and stopped in front of the valve radio. 'If I can't get it working, then I *will* give it to Grandpa,' she told herself.

She could just imagine what her dad would say if he saw it on her desk. What is that thing doing in your room? You will never amount to anything, spending all your spare time tinkering with old radios. Honestly!

Devon rolled her eyes. Whenever he spoke to her, his sentences ended in a heavy sigh and the word, *honestly*! What was his problem? She was an individual. She didn't want to turn out like her dad – boring. In fact, she'd love to be like the Canadian, Cassie, with her wild hair, black jeans, loud, colourful jumpers and red army boots. She was cool.

Devon checked her phone. Grandpa and Dad both had an annoying habit of checking in with her as though she was a little child. She was nearly sixteen. It was embarrassing when she was with her friends. Now Devon was checking in with them. She wanted to know where they were because she had an errand to run. Devon needed to borrow some things from Grandpa's workshop at the bottom of the garden before he came back.

Unbeknown to Grandpa, she'd discovered he kept a spare key under the flowerpot outside the workshop.

She texted Grandpa. 'Hi Gramps, how did the dentist go? Had your appointment yet?'

She stood there eyeing the roof of The Radio Shack waiting for a reply. Gramps took an absolute age when he was writing texts. She really hoped Dad didn't walk in before Gramps texted back. 'How long does it take to write a text?' She sighed and caught herself saying, 'Honestly!' in exasperation.

He could be sitting in the dentist chair. Devon's phone pinged with a new message just as that thought crossed her mind. She looked at her phone. It wasn't Gramps. She read the text.

Hey, girl, what are you up to?

Devon smiled. It was Jodie. She texted her back. *Hey, yourself. Do you want to come round?*

See you in ten, Jodie replied. Devon frowned. She hoped Jodie got here before Dad returned home from work. It's not that he didn't like Jodie. He'd known Jodie practically all her life. Her father was a builder in construction and had worked on building projects for Devon's dad for years. His building company had even built their house. That was how Jodie and Devon first met; when Dad popped round their house about work, sometimes he'd bring Devon with him if Grandpa was busy. The first time she visited Jodie's house, Devon was three years old and Jodie was five. Despite the two-year age difference they had remained best friends ever since.

Unfortunately, because of the age gap that meant inevitably Jodie would pass her driving test a full two years before Devon. There was the rub; what Dad didn't appreciate was his only child riding in Jodie's clapped out old car, afraid they'd have an accident. Jodie didn't take offence. She'd assured him it had an up-to-date MOT and insurance.

He didn't need Jodie to tell him that. Her dad knew Jodie's parents; he had no doubt they maintained the car. For some irrational reason, he still didn't like it.

It's your dad being a typical helicopter parent – that's all. Jodie's words didn't make her feel any better. Devon wished she had more freedom like Jodie. She could just imagine there would be resistance when she learned to drive and wanted her own car. I had better start saving, thought Devon. Her Dad had the money, but she couldn't imagine he'd want her behind the wheel of a car. Devon smiled. He only ought to know I've already driven one. It was in an empty car park, not on the open road, but Jodie said as soon as she got her provisional licence, she'd take her out on the road. Not that either of them would tell her dad that plan.

Devon glanced at her desk. She couldn't wait to show Jodie the old wireless. Her phone vibrated, alerting her to another text. It was Gramps. He was just going in the see the dentist now.

Devon was smiling as she texted back *good luck* before putting her phone away. It was time to get those tools from The Radio Shack and set to work restoring the radio.

27

Cassie stood at the bus stop thinking about dropping off the radio. She was so keen to get it fixed that it was only in hindsight she felt it odd that the girl, Devon, asked her to bring the wireless up to her bedroom. Surely, if she didn't have a key to The Radio Shack, it made sense to leave it downstairs ready for her grandfather to take out to his workshop?

Cassie looked up and down the deserted street. She'd been standing at the bus stop ten minutes and there was still no sign of the bus. Unless she'd missed it. Cassie sighed and got out her phone. She scrolled through her texts, looking for Randall's number. Cassie didn't notice a car pass by and slow down further along the road.

She had just found Randall's number when the car reversed to a stop at the kerb by the bus stop.

'You, again!' Cassie blurted, instantly recognising the shiny blue Range Rover.

Ben wound his window down.

Cassie frowned. 'What do *you* want?'

'I take it you're waiting for a bus.'

'Yeah – what of it?'

'There is only one a day.'

'I know that.'

'You've missed it.'

'No, I haven't.'

'I think you have.'

'What makes you so sure?'

'You can set your watch by that bus.'

Cassie glared at him. If he imagined she would accept a lift in that car, he could think again. 'I'm texting my friend to come and pick me up.' She could tell by the expression on his face he hadn't expected that. 'I'm sure he will be along any minute.' Cassie put the emphasis on the word *he*.

Ben either hadn't listened or ignored what she'd just said. 'Will you have dinner with me?'

Cassie glared at him. Had he forgotten he'd nearly run her over and not even had the decency to stop?

'Lunch?'

She folded her arms.

'A cup of coffee? Look, I want a chance to apologise for the other day, running you off the road. That was inexcusable.'

Cassie eyed him. She didn't understand what it meant for your heart to skip a beat until that moment in the café when she heard his voice again for the first time in years. She'd felt a flutter in her chest as though she'd got heart arrhythmia.

And there it was again – that funny flutter.

For goodness' sake, get a grip thought Cassie, averting her gaze. You're not a love-struck teenager anymore. It was just a silly crush all those years ago, wasn't it? She looked at him warily. Or was it something else?

Cassie was thinking about what it felt like to fall in love. She stole a glance at him through the open car window. He was even more handsome than she remembered. Cassie frowned. She wanted him to go away and take that gorgeous lop-sided grin with him. 'You've said your peace. Apology accepted. Now can you go.' Cassie wasn't asking.

Ben leaned across the passenger seat. 'How about a cup of coffee? For old times' sake. Please?'

Cassie rolled her eyes. Knowing her luck, if she didn't say yes, she'd bump into him in the village or when she returned to The Radio Shack. It wasn't what Cassie was used to – small communities. 'All right, but if you really want to make it up to me, then a cup of coffee won't hack it.' Cassie had a better idea.

She guessed he was about to suggest lunch or dinner, so she stopped him in his tracks. 'Lunch won't do.'

He opened his mouth to say something.

Cassie was already shaking her head. 'Nope, not dinner either.'

Ben's ready smile slipped. 'What did you have in mind?'

Cassie stared at his car. She'd only been at Fletchling Hall a few days, but she already had cabin fever. Although she'd been down the road to the local village, without a vehicle she was stuck. Cassie was used to access to buses and the London underground at all times of the day and night. Public transport in rural areas was a joke.

'You want me to take you somewhere,' he said, reading her mind.

'This will sound like a weird question…'

Ben smiled. 'I'm a dad. I'm used to weird questions.' He grimaced. He hadn't meant to say that. It just came out. *Damn.*

He didn't want to put her off. Then again, they weren't teenagers anymore. For all he knew she might have children of her own, even grown-up children.

Ben sighed. Like most people their age, over time you accumulate baggage, be it the mental scars of a failed relationship or regrets about how your life might have turned out if only you could go back in time and change things. One drunken night cost him the love of his life. He hadn't forgotten. Ben stole a glance at his biggest regret. She was even more beautiful than he remembered.

He looked away. 'Sorry, I should have mentioned I had a child.'

Cassie shrugged trying to make out that it was no big deal, which it was. Her overriding emotion right now was one of regret. Regret for a life that could have been, and a child that might have been, if only they'd stayed together. *But it wasn't meant to be, just accept it.* 'It's not like we will start dating again,' Cassie quipped, unsure why she said that out loud.

They looked at each other and both cracked a smile at the absurdity of that idea. It had been a long time since they dated. They were virtual strangers – weren't they? Was it even possible to rekindle lost love after that many years? And would they even want to? Would Cassie? Those were Ben's thoughts as he stared at her through the open window.

They were both shaking their heads at such a ridiculous idea. Not that either of them would let on what they were thinking, that despite the years they were still attracted to each other.

Ben said, 'So, what is it you want to do?'

'I'd like to go to the public library.' Cassie could tell by the look on his face he thought it was an odd request.

Ben was disappointed. He imagined she'd suggest one of their old haunts. Taking a walk in the countryside; something he remembered she loved to do, along with packing some food in an old picnic hamper his mother used to have. Those were the days, thought Ben, before the reality of careers and mortgages and single-parenthood, and a recalcitrant father for whom he did nothing right.

'Ben?'

'Oh, right. Sure. The library it is then.' He'd drive her to Timbuktu as long as it meant he could see her again.

'Good.' Cassie intended to do some research on the local history of the area. She wanted to surprise her father by seeing what she might unearth about Fletchling hall around the time he was billeted there.

They had been down that route before on her first trip to England. She remembered their visit to the library and the old newspaper articles archived on microfiche. He'd sat and painstakingly gone through each paper, trying to locate any articles on the evacuees from London.

In hindsight, Cassie wondered if her father approached it from the wrong angle. Perhaps looking for news stories about the hall instead might shed some light on Rosie's family and, by association, the children living with them at the time.

Ben said, 'I'll find out the opening times and text you.' He hesitated. 'Can I have your mobile number?'

Cassie hesitated too. She didn't have to go to the library with Ben. She imagined Randall wouldn't mind driving her there. However, she had an ulterior motive; there was something else she wanted Ben to do for her. Before she gave him her number, she said, 'There is one more thing…' When she told him what it was, he gaped at her. After all these years, she remembered that promise he'd made her.

She saw his expression. 'You've still got it!' She really didn't expect that. It had been so many years. 'So, will you do it?'

'I could get it out of mothballs and see if it still works.'

Cassie grinned at him. She had another reason to smile when she saw the bus coming down the road.

Ben frowned when he saw Cassie holding out her hand. He turned around and saw the bus approaching through the rear window. *Damnation*. Of all the days, the bus had to be late today. He'd wanted to give her a lift.

'You better move your car. You're parked at a bus stop. Isn't that illegal?'

'Oh, crap!' Ben put the car into gear. 'I'll text you when I'm coming to pick you up.'

'Okay, but remember what you promised.'

How could he forget that promise? How could he forget her? When she left, it broke his heart. His father told him he'd get over it. He had to stand by the girl he'd knocked up. Trouble was he never got over Cassie. He had no one to blame but himself for getting blind drunk the night after Cassie left.

She'd applied to get on an occupational therapy degree, just like she said she would. She'd got on a course which meant she was staying in England, but he hadn't factored in she'd have to move to another part of the country. They intended to stay in touch. He could visit her in London. She would come down to Sussex in her vacations. They had a plan for how they could still be together even though they would live miles apart.

Then he blew it.

Missing her terribly, soon after she'd left he'd got drunk one night in the pub with his mates and met a girl. One thing led to another and he made the biggest mistake of his life. Cassie didn't have to find out, but could he live with himself for cheating on her? He wished it had been that simple; all he had to do was keep that indiscretion from Cassie, but the girl had fallen pregnant.

His father insisted he break it off with Cassie and face up to his responsibilities as a soon-to-be father. He was eighteen, still living at home, and totally unprepared for fatherhood. But if he didn't want to be kicked out, he had to do as he was told. It didn't help that Ben always suspected his father never liked Cassie.

Ben considered packing up his stuff and running away from home to live with Cassie in London, coming up with some bullshit about falling out with his parents – which was true, kind of. He'd get a job so they could live together. Why hadn't he thought of doing that in the first place before he got himself entangled with another girl? He regretted staying behind to finish sixth form.

Then the girl turned up at his house one day and never returned home. He guessed she'd been kicked out by her parents when she told them about the baby. A short time later, Ben left school, got a job and his parents helped with a deposit for a rental flat. With the second bedroom all set up for the new arrival, six months later the baby arrived, still born. She was inconsolable. They both were. Ben couldn't walk out on her. Besides, his first love was long gone.

At his father's behest, Ben wrote Cassie a letter soon after the girl came to live with them, afraid she'd turn up out of the blue, and discover what had happened. It was the hardest thing he'd ever done. To this day, he wished he'd been honest, but like the teenager he was, all his resentment, anger and frustration had built up and poured out on to that single sheet of paper in a diatribe of unrequited love, saying it was all her fault, and she should never have left to the do the stupid course. He blamed her for his predicament. He blamed her for his lousy choices in life. And he was dumping her with no explanation as to the circumstances of his decision.

It was only a matter of hours later that he regretted sending that letter. He'd tried to contact her, but in an age with no mobile phones, instant messaging or email, he was stuck trying to get in touch with her through a dormitory pay phone that was constantly engaged. He set about writing her another letter instead, taking all that back, but never sent it. What was he going to do – tell her the truth; he'd got a girl pregnant? How was that going to make things better? But he did send her a letter apologising for dumping her with no explanation and begging her to meet with him. He heard nothing back.

But that was years ago. Who knew that serendipity, running her off the road like that, would lead to them meeting again? Perhaps if she hadn't taken the bike into the repair shop, she wouldn't have been sitting in the coffee shop as he happened by.

Ben set off in his car towards home determined that, come what may, if there was any inkling he might be in for a second chance, he would not screw it up this time.

28

Ben's father took one look at it and said, 'She's back, isn't she?'

'Who's back?' a voice piped up behind them.

They both turned around.

Devon folded her arms when they both fell silent. They had arrived home at the same time. Her grandfather had just pulled on to the drive outside the house as her dad was putting his car away in the garage. She'd heard them both come in.

When she walked down the stairs, she'd stopped in surprise about halfway down and stared at her dad. What was he doing wheeling his Harley Davidson out of the house? Ever since she could remember, his shiny pride and joy had sat like a piece of artwork in their spacious, airy lounge behind the door. In fact, that's what she always thought it was – a piece of art. When she was little, Devon was often told off for putting teddies on the saddle. Once or twice, when daddy wasn't looking, she'd climbed up on to the seat and tried to reach for the handlebars.

Devon stood in the hall tapping her foot impatiently, but neither Gramps nor Dad answered her question. She watched her dad wheel the motorbike out of the house. Devon walked down the stairs and joined her grandfather at the front door. She looked at Gramps. 'What's he doing?'

He sighed. 'What do you think?'

Devon looked outside at her father sitting astride the motorbike on the drive. He was putting on a helmet. 'Does it work?'

'Yes, it works. He has it serviced every year.'

That was news to Devon. 'Why? He never uses it. Not until today.' She frowned. 'Why is he going out on that thing, anyway? Is there something wrong with his car?'

'Nope.'

'So…'

'Why is he going out on his Harley-Davidson?' Gramps voiced her question. He sighed as he turned to his granddaughter. 'Or are you asking why he keeps the damn thing in working order? Well, which is it?'

Devon frowned at Gramps. Why was he in such a foul mood? 'You know what? Forget it.' Devon marched back into the house. The sound of the motorbike roaring to life made her jump as she walked back up the stairs to her room. Her bedroom was a double aspect room. She ran over to the window and looked out on to the drive down below. Her dad was revving the engine. Gramps shrugged his shoulders before disappearing down the path and into the back garden.

She turned from the window thinking about what she'd overheard Gramps say, 'She's back, isn't she.' Devon wasn't stupid. Her dad had gone to meet someone on his Harley Davidson. He'd met other women in the past, but he'd never taken a date out on his motorbike before. What was so special about her?

Devon frowned. 'Stupid motorbike.'

'Hey, are you okay?' Jodie walked out of the bathroom. She could tell by the look on Devon's face that something was up.

'It's nothing,' she said glumly.

Jodie pulled her long blonde hair back away from her face and tied it in a ponytail. 'What the hell was all that racket outside? Scared the crap out of me when I was on the loo.'

Devon smiled at Jodie. Somehow, no matter the situation, she always cheered her up. 'That was my dad going out on his motorbike.'

'You mean to tell me all these years, that thing sitting in your lounge actually works?'

'It would appear so.'

'You have to ask him if we can take it out for a spin.'

Devon was already shaking her head.

'I'd be really careful.'

'I know you would, Jodie, but no one can touch that bike – not even me. There's no way he's going to let us take it out.'

She'd never really thought about it until now; why does it mean so much to him? Sometimes, when she was little, she'd walk past the bike after being told off for touching it and kick it when he wasn't looking; she felt like she was competing for his affections with a chunk of metal.

Devon knew it was a Harley Davidson, and was worth a bit of money, but she never imagined the bike still worked. Why didn't he go out on it once in a while or join a biker group? She didn't get it. 'It's really weird.'

'Is your dad having a mid-life crisis? He's that sort of age, isn't he?'

Devon shrugged.

Jodie glanced out the window at Devon's dad sitting on the motorbike. 'God, that's loud.' She turned to Devon. 'What's wrong with a sports car?'

'Daddy's already got one of those.' In fact, there were two in the triple garage, one in blue and one in red because he couldn't decide on the colour he liked best. Devon didn't want to tell Josie that. It was embarrassing. That was his reward for winning a big contract. She rolled her eyes. He worked hard for that contract, but that didn't excuse him being so frivolous.

She wouldn't dare tell Jodie that he bought two. She was all into saving the planet and believed people should do their bit, like Grandpa restoring old radios. Driving a gas-guzzling sports car – or two – was certainly not helping the environment.

Make do and mend was Jodie and her family's motto. They were a large family and with only one income, she imagined it was in part borne out of necessity. Devon agreed with their sentiments. Everyone should do their bit to protect the planet for future generations. She winced at the sound of her Dad's motorbike speeding off in the distance.

Jodie turned from the window. 'Who do you suppose he's taking for a ride on his bike? Do you think he's got a new—'

'Absolutely not!' Devon rounded on Jodie. 'If he did, I'd know about it.' Except, this time she didn't. Devon recalled what she'd overheard Gramps saying to her dad.

Jodie caught that expression on Devon's face. It was the same every time. 'I don't get it. Don't you want your dad to be happy?'

Devon wasn't listening. All that was on her mind was competition for her dad's affections; another person who would worm her way into their lives and take him away from her. She'd already lost her mum. She wasn't losing him too. She wasn't having it.

Jodie flopped down on Devon's bed and sighed. From what she'd gleaned, Devon had broken up every single relationship her father had got involved in since her mother died. Perhaps this time he'd learned his lesson and was trying to keep it under wraps. She saw that look of determination on Devon's face. She'd find out who she was and do her best to screw it up.

Jodie reached for her hand and gave it a squeeze. Sometimes she felt sorry for Devon growing up without a mum. Jodie couldn't imagine life without her mum. Hers was a very different household to Devon's. They didn't have a lot of money for one thing. They didn't live in a posh architecturally designed house. Jodie didn't have her own bedroom like Devon with her own walk-in closet and her own bathroom. She even had a large flat-screen television and a games console. There was an indoor pool in the basement that reminded Jodie of a spa. Not that she'd ever been to one, but she'd seen photos in magazines.

Jodie used to joke they could have a pool party like you see in American movies, except they wouldn't win a Miss Popularity contest at school. They had a small circle of friends, but nowhere near the numbers to have a decent party.

Jodie stared at her best friend. Unlike this house, her home was small and chaotic and overcrowded. She shared a bedroom with her nine-year-old sister. Her two brothers shared a room too. The youngest, who was almost four, had her own bedroom even though Jodie, the eldest girl, felt that it was unfair and she should have a bedroom to herself. But despite having a good moan about it when she was at Devon's house, she knew when she went to college she would miss her chaotic household with her siblings' arguments and tantrums, and she'd miss her Mum and Dad – her Mum especially. Devon's house was so quiet in comparison, which was nice for a few hours to get away from it all, but after a time she wanted to get back to normality.

Devon loved it over her house too. Jodie's squabbles and bickering with her siblings made her laugh. She enjoyed playing with little Isla, her baby sister. But above all Jodie knew Devon loved seeing her mum and dad arguing about trivial stuff or laughing about something silly.

'But if your dad met someone, that's what you'd have,' Jodie told her one day.

'No, I wouldn't.'

'Why not?'

'Because she wouldn't be my mum.'

'Look, no-one can ever replace your mum, but there might be someone who would come close.'

'No, there won't.'

Jodie came over and put her arms around her, kissing the top of her head. 'Would it really be a terrible thing if your Dad met someone? Have you ever considered that one day he might meet someone you like?'

Devon eyed Jodie. She didn't want this to turn into an argument, but Jodie didn't have the first clue what she was talking about. Her parents were still together and would probably remain so forever.

'He must be lonely. Have you thought about that?'

'He has me and Gramps.'

'That's not what I mean, and you know it.' She took Devon's hand. 'We have our families, but we're also on the lookout for someone special.'

One day, when Devon had been over at her house, Jodie had caught her brother, who was fifteen, staring at Devon. That didn't surprise her. What bothered Jodie was catching Devon glancing his way when he wasn't looking, eyeing him up. She didn't want her brother stealing her best friend. Jodie realised that was being a bit melodramatic. She wouldn't lose her, but it was inevitable things would change. She knew her brother wanted to ask her out.

Jodie hadn't told Devon that or her other piece of news; she'd met her special someone a fortnight ago. They'd started going out. It meant she'd be spending less and less time with her best mate, so she wanted to enjoy the time they had, just girls together, before Devon got a boyfriend too and both their priorities changed.

Devon heard Gramps walking up the stairs. She darted over to the wireless. What if he popped his head in and saw it?

Jodie's smile faded. She realised what was coming next…

'I want to continue fixing up the radio this afternoon.' She sat down at her desk with her back to Jodie. 'It's been almost a week since the woman turned up with it. I want to get it done.'

'Whatever.' Jodie flounced off the bed. She stopped at the bedroom door. 'Sometimes I think you care more about your stupid valve radios than me,' she blurted in frustration, disappointed they wouldn't be spending the afternoon together.

'Jodie that's not—' She was about to say *that's not true* when Jodie slammed the bedroom door shut and thundered down the wooden stairs. There was no point chasing after her. She heard her car starting on the drive. Devon turned back to the valve radio, wondering what had got into her.

'Is everything all right?'

Devon swung round in her chair to find Gramps standing at her bedroom door. She frowned at him. 'What do *you* want?'

Gramps hovered in the doorway. 'I'm sorry for being short with you. I didn't mean to snap. Come here, sweetheart, your silly Gramps wants to give you a hug.'

Devon was doing her best to hide the radio on her desk. 'Er, that's okay. I'm a bit busy right now.'

Gramps stepped into her room. 'Busy doing what?'

'I'm doing a project for school.' As soon as the words were out of her mouth, she realised her mistake. Gramps had always taken an interest in her schoolwork. While Dad was busy building his business as an architect, it was Gramps who got her ready for school when she was little. He also did the school run, which he'd been doing until recently when Jodie passed her driving test and got an old banger. And he was the one who helped her with her homework.

'That sounds interesting. Can I take a look?' Gramps stepped further into the room.

'I don't need any help,' Devon blurted. 'Really, I don't. I can do this on my own.'

Gramps held up his hands. 'I was only trying to be helpful.'

'I know. It's just I'm really busy. So, if you don't mind…'

He was about to go when he spied something on her desk. 'What's that?'

Devon leaned to her left, trying to keep the radio out of his line of vision. 'Gramps, I said I was busy.'

He looked at her. 'What are you up to?'

Devon rolled her eyes as Gramps walked towards her. There was no point struggling to hide it now. She stood up and stepped aside.

29

Gramps stopped in surprise when he saw it. He looked at Devon. 'Where did you find that?'

Devon heaved a sigh. 'I didn't find it. A woman stopped by with it last week after discovering The Radio Shack online. She didn't make an appointment.'

'What woman?'

'Oh, just some lady who works up at Fletchling Hall.'

Gramps sat down in the chair in front of the wireless. 'It's quite something.'

'I know.'

'When were you going to bring it down to the shack?'

Devon fell silent.

Gramps turned and looked at his granddaughter. He was a qualified radio engineer. It was his late wife, Devon's grandmother, who had encouraged him to turn his hobby, tinkering with old radios, into a job.

Ben never shared his interest, but Devon was another matter. She'd always loved the sound of those vintage radios. She could take one apart and put it back together by the time she was eight. That wasn't surprising. She'd spend hours in his workshop at the bottom of the garden, watching Grandpa, while Ben was busy working in his study.

Although he'd never come out and said it, Gramps was proud of his son. Through hard work and determination, he'd qualified as an architect, and gained a large client base, building a reputation in the industry as a talented designer. He'd even appeared on covers of magazines. But at what cost?

Gramps was still sitting there staring at Devon, trying not to dwell on her growing up without a mum and dad. Most of the time he felt like a single parent, ferrying her to school and back, buying her clothes, shopping, bathing and feeding her when she was little. He realised Ben had a business to run, but sometimes he thought his son used it as an excuse to avoid his daughter who was the spit of her mother.

Devon heaved a sigh, and admitted, 'Okay, I wasn't going to bring it down to the shack.' She looked at him when he didn't answer. 'You might as well take it now.'

Gramps turned in his chair to have another look at the beauty sitting on his granddaughter's desk. He was thinking about his business and how it had jogged along over the years. Then everything changed. When Devon started high school, she got her own laptop for schoolwork. In her spare time, she promoted Grandpa's business to enthusiasts online through social media. That's when his business took off. To his utter amazement, there was a whole new generation of youngsters like Devon who appreciated the warm sound of valve radios.

A surprising number were interested in attaining one or had a radio they'd inherited or found among a great-grandparent's things and wanted it restored. Thanks to Devon, he not only had an online presence through his website, but he was on *Twitter,*

Snapchat, Instagram, and *Facebook*. If he was honest, apart from Facebook, he didn't know what the others were. He just went along with it.

She managed his social media and now did his accounts. It meant with her schoolwork, she was spending less and less time in The Radio Shack enjoying what she loved most, which was helping him repair the radios. Little wonder she kept this one all to herself.

Grandpa had been having some thoughts about this. 'Devon, I am going to employ an accountant to do the books.'

Devon looked at him. Was this punishment for not telling him about the radio? 'Oh, right, so you don't think I'm good enough to help with the business now.'

'Devon, that's not it at all. You are an amazing young lady.'

Devon stared at her grandfather, surprised by his response. This was not at all what she had been expecting to hear when he found out she'd hoodwinked a customer and decided to repair their radio herself.

He continued, 'You go to school, get top grades, and manage my business. Not just my online presence, but all my accounts, which are getting ever more complicated because we are making quite a profit now.'

Devon wondered if she had misheard him. 'Did you say *we* are making a profit?'

Grandpa smiled at her and nodded. 'I don't know why I didn't think of this before. We should be business partners.'

'What does that mean?'

'It means you own half of The Radio Shack. It also means that although you've got schoolwork, you will have to pull your weight.'

Devon was about to argue that she already did a lot for the business when she caught him grinning at her. 'The fact is, Devon, I get all the fun, sitting in the shack doing what I love. But what are you getting out of it now? Your business acumen has paid off, but you're missing out on the grassroots – repairing radios. This proves my point.' He glanced at the old valve radio sitting on her desk.

'You're not mad at me then?'

'Whatever for? I'm mad at myself for not realising this sooner.' He missed spending time with her. The price of success was that he hardly ever saw her. Although he loved what he did, what he loved more, he realised, was sharing his hobby with someone – with his grandchild.

Gramps took her hands in his. 'We hardly spend any time together in The Radio Shack. I miss that, Devon. It was our thing. But since it's become really successful…' he trailed off.

Devon stood there staring at Gramps. She'd never thought about it that way before.

'We are earning enough money to hire an accountant and can hire someone to take care of the social media side of things too.' He had to get the go ahead from his business partner. 'What do you say, Devon? Is it a good idea?'

'You're asking *me*?' Devon said in surprise.

'Of course. We're business partners, remember.'

30

Business partners. Devon liked the sound of that. She was smiling at Gramps when she caught her father pass by her bedroom. He was still wearing his helmet, which suggested he'd nipped back into the house because he'd forgotten something. A moment later, he passed by carrying another helmet. This time he glanced in Devon's room and came to an abrupt halt. 'What's that?'

Both Gramps and Devon stared at him. They knew it was a rhetorical question.

Devon narrowed her eyes, feeling cross with her dad when she spotted the other helmet in his hand. Jodie was right: he *was* taking somebody out on the motorbike. Now she was cross with Gramps for getting her into trouble over the radio. If he hadn't come into her bedroom, she would have shut the door and Dad would be none the wiser.

Ben turned on his father. 'What have I told you about bringing that crap in the house?'

Devon gave her dad a black look. She hated him calling the beautiful valve radios *crap*. Devon recalled that time when she was younger, and she'd taken an old wireless from Grandpa's shack up to her bedroom. It had just been repaired and the sound it made was out of this world. She wanted to listen to it before they sent it back to the owners.

Dad went ballistic. She even remembered the argument that ensued. 'This is *my* house. If Grandpa wants you to bring this crap into the house, then he better get his own place.'

Dad reiterated that point again.

Devon knew why Gramps lived with them. She'd asked him one day, not long after she started school, when she found out none of her friends lived with their grandparents. It was because she didn't have a mum to care for her when Dad was working.

It wasn't just that. When she was little, Dad needed money to start his business and provide a home for them both. He'd told her that houses in these villages weren't cheap, so that's the reason they shared a house. Dad pulled down his parents' old bungalow and built an ultra-modern home on the land.

Devon's dad didn't like old houses at all; the only thing he left standing was his father's ramshackle shed, The Radio Shack, at the bottom of the garden. He called it an eyesore, and hated it with a passion, but he had to let Gramps keep something. Besides, he wasn't being altruistic. Devon wasn't stupid; she guessed her father wanted to make sure Gramps didn't run his radio repair business inside his home. He wanted it as far away from the house as possible.

Devon gave her grandfather a sideways glance. She did the books. She was aware how much his business was worth. He could buy a home of his own. This worried Devon. She wished they wouldn't argue. She didn't want Gramps to move out.

Gramps turned to Devon. 'Do you mind giving us a minute? Perhaps you could take the radio out to The Radio Shack.'

Devon stamped her foot. 'No.'

Ben raised his voice. 'Do I have to repeat myself? What have I told you, both of you, about bringing that sort of thing into the house?'

'It's not a *thing*,' spat Devon. 'It's a valve radio.'

Ben grimaced. As if he didn't know. 'I mean it, Devon.'

There was a short stand-off which ended when Gramps reached for the radio. Devon intervened. 'No – I'll do it.' She carefully picked up the wireless and glared at her dad as she left the room.

Ben sighed. He didn't have anything against valve radios, although he thought they were large, unattractive eyesores. What really bothered him was how much time she'd spent, over the years, in The Radio Shack fiddling around with those contraptions. He'd rather see her making new friends and doing things he imagined girls at her age do, like shopping and having her nails done.

Apart from her best friend, Jodie, he was acutely aware she didn't have any women in her life. There was no grandmother or aunties or cousins. He was an only child, as was his father, and Devon's mother had no relatives who had stayed in touch.

Ben caught Gramps staring at him. 'What?'

Gramps heard the back-door slam shut. When Devon was out of earshot, he said, 'I know what this is really about. You're worried about her.' Gramps worried too that she spent far too much time involved in his business rather than doing girly things. 'Let's face it, she lives with two blokes and has got no women role models in her life.'

'What can I do about that?' Ben sighed heavily. 'You have seen the way she plays up whenever I date someone. She will never accept a woman in my life – or hers. I get that now.'

'Is that why you've gone behind her back this time? That way she can't make you choose – can she.'

Ben looked at the spare helmet in his hands and fell silent.

Gramps lowered his voice. 'She has a right to be told about her mother.'

'Don't start, Dad. I know best. I'm her father.'

'Are you?'

'What's that supposed to mean?'

'Who really brought her up all these years, took her to school, helped her with homework and nursed her when she was sick?'

'I was busy building my business – you know that. Look at this place. Look what I've achieved. She never wants for a thing. Have you seen her state-of-the-art bedroom?' It was a rhetorical question. 'I put a lot of thought into the layout and design of her rooms knowing she'd be a teenager one day. And she will benefit more in the future. It's all going to come to her – the house, my business.'

'The future?' Gramps interrupted. 'What about *now*?'

'What do you mean? She gets everything she ever wants.'

'Does she?' He shook his head. 'You don't get it, do you? When she lost her mother, she lost you too.'

'I don't understand…?'

'The fact is you weren't around.' Gramps held up his hand. 'When was the last time you spent any time with Devon? When have you ever really given her the time of day?'

Ben frowned. 'How can you say that? I had responsibilities. I did all this for Devon, so I could take care of her financially.'

Gramps sighed. He'd heard it all before. 'There's more to raising a child than putting a roof over her head.' He found it ironic that Devon was so afraid of losing her father to another woman when she'd already lost him years ago to his career. But Gramps realised it wasn't just Devon, or his career, that was standing in the way of his son finding Mrs Right after all these years.

'Do you know why she spends so much time at The Radio Shack, Ben? It's not all about the radios. She loves spending time with her Gramps. You're worried about her. She's growing into a young woman. I'm worried too. She doesn't have a role model in her life. But that's not my fault, is it. There have been plenty of opportunities. No shortage or women who would beat a path to your architecturally designed door – given half the chance.'

Ben fell silent, hovering in the doorway.

Gramps shook his head. His son had always been such a good-looking boy, with many admirers, but he had a reputation for never making a commitment. 'I realise Devon plays up every time you date someone, but if she thinks she's getting her own way, and breaking up your relationships, she's very wrong.'

Ben shook his head. 'I don't know what you mean. She's my child. She comes first.'

Gramps was sick of the bullshit. 'That's as maybe, but you're the grown up. You have been using Devon as an excuse all these years to avoid making a commitment to someone else.'

Ben stood there staring at his father. His eyes dropped to the floor. He flitted from one date to another, blaming Devon for ruining his relationships. It was true she wanted him all to herself and felt threatened that someone would come and take her father away from her. But Ben had to concede he didn't fight for any of the women. One of them, his last girlfriend, said as much. 'If you really wanted this to work, you would fight for us instead of just giving in.' She was probably right.

There was one thing having a fling because he was lonely, but another thing altogether committing to spend the rest of his life with someone. Even the mother of his child. Ben closed his eyes, failing to block out the memory. The relationship with the young woman from his teenage years didn't last. Perhaps it was inevitable after the loss of the baby. Ben, single again, had moved back home, saved up enough money in a series of dead-end jobs and went to university to become an architect. It took several years of dedicated study, but he achieved the qualification he'd dreamed of by his late twenties.

Soon after, he met his new partner. She fell pregnant quickly and they welcomed their first child – a girl. Devon was the best thing that had happened to Ben. However, three years on from their first date, even though they were a family with a child, he still hadn't asked his partner to marry him. That's what they were rowing about when he lost control of the car and they ended up in a ditch. They'd been out on a dinner date together that ended in disaster.

He realised, in hindsight, she thought he'd finally pop the question. They hadn't been out on a proper date without a toddler in tow for an age. Instead of proposing, he'd told her he just got the business loan through to start his own business. That's what they were celebrating, which he'd hinted at on the way to their meal. She was expecting him to get down on bended knee. He'd produced a little card instead, which had the name of his new business printed in fancy gold lettering.

They'd finished their meal in silence, but the argument resumed on the way home. Thank God Devon was being babysat, so she wasn't in the car. He'd have never forgiven himself if something had happened to her too.

'And I'll tell you why you've never made a commitment…' Gramps was still having a go. 'Even if you won't admit it even to yourself, you're still holding a flame for that red-headed Canadian – aren't you.' He looked at the helmet in Ben's hand and said it again, 'She's back, isn't she?'

Ben changed the subject. 'You are lucky to have a grandchild and a girl at that, who actually takes an interest in your hobby. I never did.'

'It's not a hobby. I make money. Besides, the best work is a hobby you turn into a job. You had a hobby once. Perhaps you should have considered that as a job, and then you wouldn't be so petty and angry and unhappy.'

'Oh, so you think I'm petty and angry and unhappy because I became an architect?' Ben had other ideas why he was not content with his life, and it had nothing to do with work. Besides, how did his father think he could turn that hobby from years ago into a job? 'You know what? I'm not listening to any more of this.' He strode off down the hall.

Gramps remained where he was, sitting in Devon's chair, deep in thought. The last time they had argued like this was way back when Ben was a teenager and that girl had come into their lives. She was back again – he was sure of it. He sat there wracking his brain trying to remember her name.

Then it came to him. The Canadian's name was Cassie.

31

Cassie walked into Evelyn's apartment. She was sitting by the window. It reminded Cassie of when she first set eyes on Evelyn and discovered she spent most of her time sitting in that chair, looking out the window, as if she was expecting a visitor.

She turned her head when Cassie walked into the room.

Cassie smiled at her. 'Are you better?'

'What does it look like?' came back Evelyn's sharp retort. Cassie was used to that now. She liked to think Evelyn didn't mean to be rude. It was just her way.

Evelyn added, 'If I was still under the weather you wouldn't be here, now would you?'

Evelyn was back to her normal belligerent self, which suggested she was feeling better. It had been almost a week and she had just recovered from a chest infection. Cassie had spent more time with Ruby and used some sessions she would have spent with Evelyn visiting the other residents. Cassie had listened to their life stories and wrote them in a notebook. She wasn't sure how she would get them bound into a memory book. She hoped to find a company online who did that sort of thing.

Cassie looked at Evelyn. Perhaps now would be the perfect time to suggest the idea she'd put to the other residents. It wouldn't be long and she'd finish reading the diary. Wouldn't it be wonderful if Evelyn talked about her life? The sad part was, unlike the other residents, it appeared Evelyn had nobody to leave her notebook to; no relatives or friends who would be interested to hear her story. Not a single person came to visit her.

Cassie had grown attached to the residents. That didn't happen in her other job at the hospital. Here, at Fletching Hall, the staff and residents were like a family. Cassie's mind wandered to thoughts of the hall closing. It was such a shame. She tried not to dwell on that. She had grown fond of Her Ladyship too. Evelyn reminded her of her grandmother. She didn't suffer fools gladly either and, like Evelyn, on the surface she was quite stern. However beneath all that was a different person altogether – if you just got to know her. Cassie felt there was more to Evelyn than her public front.

Cassie was dying to broach the idea of the memory book. It would be the perfect follow up to the diary. Cassie was about to ask when she realised there was something she needed first. 'I'll be back in a minute.'

Evelyn turned from the window. 'You've only just arrived!'

'I won't be long, I promise. There's someone I'd like you to meet.' *If I can find her, thought Cassie.*

'Who?' Evelyn called out as Cassie strode to the door.

'You'll see.'

Cassie rushed down the hall. Olivia was walking out of Bertie's apartment a few doors down. 'Have you seen Tabitha?'

Olivia shook her head. 'She didn't join me for my session this morning. Try Iris, perhaps Tabitha is with her.'

'Thanks.' Cassie pondered at how quickly Tabitha had become part of the fabric of the house, doing her rounds, amusing the other residents, and keeping them company. She often joined her and her colleagues in the kitchen at coffee breaks and lunch time as though she was a member of staff. It was quite comical.

Cassie recalled how she arranged her breaks to avoid bumping into anybody in the kitchen when she was feeding Tabitha. She didn't have time to nip back and forward to the cottage to feed the cat. Being a young cat, she needed more than one meal a day. She realised she couldn't hide the tabby forever; someone was bound to discover her.

Tabitha appeared one break time when everybody arrived in the kitchen at the same time. She soon wormed her way into everybody's affections. That was her gift. It was the reason she wanted Tabitha to meet Evelyn. Who couldn't resist talking to a beautiful cat?

'Now, where are you?' She wasn't with Iris. Cassie bumped into Jill carrying Ruby's breakfast tray to the kitchen. The cat hadn't visited Ruby this morning either. 'That's odd. She normally does her rounds first thing.'

'Yes, I thought it was unusual too.'

Cassie walked into the kitchen. No sign of her there. She glanced at the basement door. Was she down there taking a nap on the old blanket in the up-turned box? She didn't usually sleep down there. Since getting to meet the residents and staff, Tabitha had no shortage of invitations to cosy on up at the end of someone's bed or in an armchair or someone's lap. Perhaps she'd wandered down to the cellar and somebody had shut the door, not realising she was down there?

Cassie walked over and was about to open the door when a short, shrill alarm sounded. At the same time Cassie's pager went off. The only time both things would happen simultaneously was when a resident had pulled an emergency cord or pressed the buzzer they wore on a necklace around their necks to sound the alarm. And chances are if that happened one of them had had a fall.

Cassie ran out of the kitchen and met Olivia running down the hall. 'Do we know who sounded the alarm?' Cassie shouted out. 'Which apartment is it coming from?'

'It's not Iris,' replied Olivia. 'I was with her when the alarm went off. I looked in on Bertie on the way here – he's fine.'

Jill appeared from the pantry where she'd been looking for some long-life milk. She still had the unopened carton in her hand. 'It's not Ruby – I know that much.'

They ran down to the main entrance where they met Randall, who'd just returned from collecting a prescription for Ruby from the chemist. He'd taken the car and gone with Phyllis, who also had some errands to run in the village. Phyllis said, 'What's going on? Who sounded the alarm?'

Cassie stared at Phyllis. Olivia had been with Iris when the alarm and their pagers went off. She'd looked in on Bertie. Jill confirmed it wasn't coming from the wing where Ruby lived. There was one resident not accounted for.

'Oh my God, it's Evelyn. I only left her a moment ago.' Cassie took off up the stairs, taking them two at a time, and belted down the corridor towards her apartment. Olivia, Jill and Randall followed, with Phyllis bringing up the rear, struggling to keep up.

Cassie didn't bother knocking. She dived into her apartment

and ran into the lounge, expecting to find Evelyn lying on the floor. She was already getting out her phone to call an ambulance.

As soon as Cassie spotted Evelyn, she came to such an abrupt halt that Olivia ran into her. 'Sorry!'

Jill and Randall were next, skidding to a stop in the doorway.

Phyllis brought up the rear. She couldn't see past Jill and Randall. 'What's going on in there?'

Cassie stared at Evelyn. She was still sitting in her chair, looking as right as rain. 'Evelyn, did you press your alarm?'

'Of course I did. What do you take me for – senile?'

Cassie pursed her lips. She'd rather not answer that. 'Are you feeling unwell?' She wasn't clutching her chest as though she might have a heart attack or pass out.

'What do you mean, am I feeling unwell? Of course not.'

'Then why did you sound your alarm?'

'Because of *that*!' she pointed her thin, gnarled finger at the window.

At first nobody understood what she was pointing at.

'I know you're still there,' said Evelyn, glaring at the curtains. 'You better come out.'

They all looked at Evelyn, thinking she's finally lost it. Then in the hushed silence, when everyone was wondering whether this *was* an emergency, out from behind the curtain appeared Tabitha. She meowed as if to say, *what are you all staring at?*

'There it is – see. I told you I saw something!'

There was a collective sigh of relief when they realised the emergency was over.

'What's going on?' Phyllis was saying, bouncing from one foot to the other trying to see past Randall's broad shoulders.

'It's only Tabitha.'

Jill and Olivia followed Randall out the door.

Phyllis looked over at Cassie. 'Is everything all right?'

'No,' piped up Evelyn even though the question wasn't directed at her. 'There's a blasted cat in my living room!'

Cassie walked over to Phyllis. 'It's fine.'

Phyllis stared at the cat sitting by the window licking her paw, acting all innocent as though the commotion had nothing to do with her. Phyllis couldn't deny she was a cat lover. She had three at home. The cat Cassie had found in the basement was a beautiful little creature. But the trouble with cats was they may look innocent enough, but boy did some of them have a mind of their own.

Phyllis narrowed her eyes as she stared at Tabitha; here was one such creature. She looked as though butter wouldn't melt, but beneath that stunning silver tabby coat and those long whiskers was a cat just waiting to cause trouble. She lowered her voice. 'A word of advice. Just watch yourself.'

'Oh, Evelyn's no trouble.'

'I'm not talking about Evelyn.'

Cassie turned around and looked at the cat. She had been searching for her everywhere. All this time she was snoozing behind the floor-to-ceiling curtains. 'You little minx,' Cassie said under her breath. She realised what had happened. When she'd arrived at Evelyn's apartment to start her shift, Tabitha had followed her, slipped inside and made herself nice and comfortable behind the curtains.

Cassie closed the door to the lounge. Now she had Tabitha where she wanted her, she wasn't going to let her escape. There was something she wanted her help with.

Cassie walked over to Evelyn.

Evelyn said, 'Are you getting rid of it?'

'I think you and Tabitha got off on the wrong foot.'

'Tabitha?'

Cassie nodded in the cat's direction. 'That's Tabitha.'

The cat wasn't all she'd brought with her as a surprise for Evelyn. In her hand was a new notebook.

Cassie sat down on the chair next to her. 'Evelyn, I had an idea. Because Rosie's story interested you, I wondered if you might like to write yours down.' Cassie held out the new notebook for her.

Evelyn didn't make a move to take it.

'You don't have to write it, if you don't want to.' Cassie picked up Tabitha and put the cute little cat on her lap. Tabitha purred. Splendid, thought Cassie, smiling. This will work. 'You could tell Tabitha about your life and I'll write it down for you.' Cassie opened the new notebook and held a biro at the ready.

Evelyn looked at the cat and then at Cassie. 'You want me to tell my life's story to a cat?'

Cassie's smile faltered. When she put it like that, it sounded—

'That's stupid.'

'I didn't mean it literally. It's just…'

'You thought if you introduced me to Tabitha, then a cutesy, purring little fluff-ball would encourage me to talk.'

Tabitha stopped purring.

Cassie smiled nervously.

Evelyn leaned forward in her chair. 'It may have worked on the other residents, but I can assure you I'm not like the other residents.'

And not a truer word was spoken, thought Cassie, eyeing her

rather formidable patient and, dare she think it, a good friend, even though the sentiment was probably not mutual. Cassie sighed. There was more to Evelyn than she would ever know. But the one thing she knew for certain was that she did not have dementia. Evelyn wasn't avoiding talking about her life's story because she was afraid she wouldn't remember certain details. She was afraid she would.

'Has it ever occurred to you, Cassie, that there's a reason some stories cannot be written?'

Cassie creased her brow. 'I don't understand…'

'Like yours, for instance. What are *you* doing here?'

'I'm working as an O.T. trying to help—'

Evelyn shook her head, stopping Cassie in her tracks. 'That's not what I'm asking.'

'Are you talking existentially?'

'You mean the bigger question: what are we all doing here?' Evelyn looked at her dismissively. 'Of course not. There isn't time for existential questions; they'll be plenty of time for that when we meet our maker. What I'm pointing out is that this is just a staging post, a pause in your journey. You haven't arrived at your destination yet.'

'And where's that?'

Evelyn shrugged. 'How do I know? That is for each man or woman to determine what path to follow and to what – or whom – they are looking for in order to make their story complete.'

Cassie thought of her father. She was beginning to understand. He was writing a book, but from what she'd gleaned from his emails, he was having trouble finishing it. Was it because it lacked something vital when he was telling his story – an ending?

'Ah, I see by the look on your face, now you understand.'

To finish his journey, and his book, what her father was looking for wouldn't be found in Canada no matter how many roads he travelled or how many personal stories of hardship, loss and courage he wrote about. Her father was looking for the family he'd left behind in England. She suddenly felt this enormous sadness that his story was still unwritten and might never be told. Cassie looked at the blank notebook in her hand.

Evelyn looked at it too. 'Take it away. And take that mangy cat with you.'

Cassie gently picked Tabitha up in her arms as she got out of her seat. 'Come on, Tabitha.' She stood for a moment looking down at Evelyn. Her Ladyship had turned in her seat and was staring out the window. Evelyn was waiting for her ending, but Cassie realised it wasn't a destination. Evelyn wasn't going anywhere. And there was a reason for that. Her gaze shifted to the window. She was waiting for someone, but whom?

Cassie walked out of the apartment cradling the cat in her arms and closed the door behind her. She looked at Tabitha. 'You're not mangy, you know that – right?'

Tabitha meowed.

Cassie smiled at her. 'One of these days, perhaps I'll tell you my story – when I know how it ends.' She glanced back at the door to Evelyn's apartment. 'I hope I'm here long enough to find out her story.' Something told Cassie it would be quite a tale.

32

Cassie sighed as she walked through the door into Evelyn's apartment. She'd arrived the next afternoon without the blank notebook or Tabitha. Evelyn made her feelings crystal clear regarding talking about her life and Cassie writing it down for posterity. They were back to just reading Rosie's diary.

Cassie discovered Evelyn was in a foul mood. Everything was wrong this morning; the temperature, the lighting in the lounge, even what she was wearing. It made Cassie wonder if she was coming down with something again. Either that or she was still annoyed about the cat in her apartment yesterday.

Cassie felt she better not tell her she'd been reading more of the diary. She couldn't wait to find out what happened when Rosie returned to see the Canadian to apologise for accusing him of stealing her brother's radio.

During the session with Evelyn, Cassie was almost caught out because she couldn't remember where she got up to when she'd last read to Evelyn. Cassie had finished a good proportion of the notebook and already knew a lot of Rosie's story, although she had yet to finish the diary. Things really got interesting when Rosie received the radio as a gift. It wasn't long before her parents had a visit from the Ministry of Defence. In her diary, Rosie said it was all very *hush hush.*

❖

When she saw the official-looking people turn up at the cottage, Rosie's first thought was that her father had bribed someone in government to bring little Ted back. But their visit wasn't about that.

They were recruiting radio enthusiasts for the war effort to work as VI's or voluntary interceptors. They got hold of her brothers' names through the RSGB, the Radio Society of Great Britain; an organisation of amateur radio enthusiasts. Rosie sidled into the room just as her father was telling them that the wireless would be no use to them now as her brothers died on the front.

'I can do it,' Rosie said. 'I want to be a radio interceptor.'

All three men in the room turned to the sixteen-year-old slip of a thing. She looked closer to thirteen. They dismissed her, but in a kind way, saying that they appreciated her wanting to volunteer, but she wasn't suitable.

Rosie answered back, 'Is it because I'm too young or because I'm a *girl*?' She expected them to say a bit of both. Instead, they surprised her by saying most of the lads they'd recruited were teenagers like her.

'So, it's because I'm a girl.'

They didn't beat about the bush. 'What girls have you met that know Morse code?'

Rosie's frown disappeared. 'Let me get this straight. You're saying that if a girl was familiar with Morse code you'd recruit them?'

They exchanged a glance and said to Rosie, 'Yes, why not.'

'In that case, I accept.'

The two government officials looked at her perplexed.

'I can assure you,' said Rosie, puffing out her chest and acting self-important, 'I am just as proficient in Morse code as the next man – or woman.'

'Um…' they both turned to look at Rosie's father with a question.

He said, 'I guess that's settled then. Gentleman, meet your new VI.'

Rosie grinned at her father before turning to the government officials. Over time, Rosie had sat with her brothers, watching them tinkering with their radio receivers. They had also taught her Morse code. That was the game-changer. Many of the RSGB members were just youngsters like her and her brothers, curious about what you could do with radio receivers. Now Rosie was about to find out.

Her dream of helping the war effort was about to transpire in the most unexpected way. Rosie couldn't believe her luck. She was to become one of Britain's voluntary interceptors. Around one and a half thousand radio amateurs were recruited. That's what the men from the Government told her. Their job was to intercept secret codes broadcast by the Nazis and their allies during the war.

❖

Cassie smiled when she read it out loud to Evelyn. 'I've never heard of VI's until I read about it in Rosie's journal. Isn't that amazing, Evelyn? To think she was only sixteen when she was recruited.'

Evelyn was back to her normal dismissive self. 'I suppose so.'

'It says here that voluntary interceptors worked for MI8, Military Intelligence Section 8. Everyone's heard of MI5 and MI6, but I've never heard of MI8.'

Evelyn shrugged her shoulders. 'Who cares. It was a long time ago.'

Cassie frowned at her. She felt Evelyn was enjoying Rosie's story, up until now. What had got into her? 'Well, I think it's really interesting,' she told Evelyn. 'I imagine most people are not aware there were young teenagers doing their bit to win the war.'

When she'd first read about the significance of the radio, Cassie was excited at the idea of giving Evelyn the very wireless used by Rosie. Now she suspected Evelyn would not appreciate it. She recalled her bright idea of asking Evelyn to write her life-story with a little encouragement from a beautiful cat. She'd assumed Evelyn would love Tabitha, but that episode hadn't gone to plan.

Evelyn heaved a sigh. 'Tell me what happened next then. You're here, so you might as well.'

Cassie stared at the diary. She wasn't looking forward to reading the next episode. She'd already read the part to Evelyn about Rosie slipping out of the cottage to visit the Canadian and apologise about accusing him of stealing the radio. It made for amusing reading because she'd put on a dress for her mother and hadn't bothered to change before she'd snuck back into the big house. When the Canadian saw her, at first, he didn't recognise her, and then he'd joked that she needn't have changed on his account.

She'd made sure he was put in the picture. She did not put on a dress in order to impress him.

That may not have been her intention but impress him she had. Rosie wrote it down in her diary. He said she was pretty. He called her a young lady. Turned out he was young himself. In uniform, they all looked older than their years. Scott was just eighteen.

Everybody seemed to grow up fast back then. It was the nature of war. And so began a covert friendship, which clearly developed into more than a friendship when Rosie wrote in her diary about their first kiss. 'I love him, but I haven't told my parents about him yet,' was one entry. 'I want to marry him and live in Canada,' was another entry.

Cassie sighed as she turned the page. Now for the awful part. Rosie's story was like so many others – a casualty of war. There were no happy endings; people parted, they died or went missing in action, never seen or heard from again. Cassie had read more of Rosie's story. She'd sat up the other night until the early hours. She didn't mind re-reading it to Evelyn, not at all. She was sad that Evelyn had yet to find out Rosie's story did not have a happy ending.

Cassie was about to continue when she was interrupted by an almighty noise outside on the driveway. It sounded like an old motorbike roaring up the gravel drive towards the house. The noise startled Evelyn. She wasn't the only one; Cassie almost dropped the diary.

Evelyn turned to Cassie. 'Help me up. It's him. He's returned.'

Cassie put the diary down and looked at her in surprise. 'What are you talking about?'

'I want to see. Help me to the window. Quickly!'

Cassie kept her mouth shut although it was on the tip of her tongue to tell Evelyn that if she imagined an old flame had come to visit her, he'd hardly be arriving on a motorbike, more like a wheelchair. Cassie humoured her. She rose from the sofa and helped Evelyn to her feet, passing her the two walking sticks she sometimes used. They walked the few steps to stand by the sash window. Evelyn put her glasses on.

As soon as Cassie looked out the window, she realised who it was. Ben was wearing a helmet so she couldn't see his face, but she knew it was him. She'd recognise his old Harley Davidson anywhere. She gaped at it. She'd assumed if he still had the old bike that it would have been rusting in the back of a garage.

The last thing she expected was for him to turn up a few days later with it in perfect working order, looking almost brand new. He must have really taken care of it over the years. Why was she surprised? When they first dated, she wasn't sure whom he loved the most, her or his motorbike. Perhaps that's why he'd never let his girlfriend have a go, even though he'd promised her he would someday.

She'd been joking at the bus stop when she said about making good on that promise. Cassie didn't think he'd remember what she was going on about. The last thing she expected was for him to take her at her word and turn up with the bike.

Evelyn turned from the window and returned to her chair.

Cassie continued to stare out the window. He looked devilishly handsome in blue jeans and a leather jacket. Was that the old leather jacket he used to wear as a teenager? It couldn't be, surely. Cassie glanced at the diary in her hand and frowned. She wouldn't deny she was pleased to see him again, but what made him think he could turn up here, at her workplace, and expect her to drop everything and go out with him? Cassie was not in the habit of skiving off work just to go for a joyride. However, she looked at the motorbike, looked at him, and was sorely tempted.

Cassie sighed as she turned from the window. Someone would tell him that she was busy. She was about to sit down again, and continue reading, when Evelyn said, 'You can go now,' dismissing her like she was the hired help.

Cassie glanced at her watch. 'We've got all afternoon.' She'd swapped her day around and saw Ruby in the morning. This was only the second time Cassie had seen Evelyn since she was unwell with a heavy cold. She thought if their session went over the allotted time it wouldn't matter. She could sit here all evening too if Evelyn wanted. After all, they had some catching up to do regarding reading Rosie's story. 'What about the diary, Evelyn?'

Evelyn turned to her. 'I said I want to be alone.'

Cassie stared at her. Were there tears in her eyes? She glanced at the window. The roar of the motorbike engine had ceased. All was quiet again, apart from the sound of birds chirping outside.

She didn't quite know how to tell Evelyn that whoever she was expecting to see would most likely never turn up. She'd been living here for ten years and they still hadn't come. Cassie found out Evelyn didn't have children, and was a widow, so who did she think would come?

'I'll be back in the morning.' She looked at the diary. There weren't too many pages left. When she was reading it alone, Cassie made a point of not finishing it. She wanted to savour Rosie's story and save the end to read with Evelyn. 'We can finish this tomorrow.'

Evelyn used her walking sticks to get up. For a moment, Cassie thought she would change her mind and ask her to stay for the rest of the afternoon. Perhaps she was off to make them both a cuppa. Evelyn did no such thing. She changed seats and sat in the chair facing the window waiting for someone who would never arrive.

Cassie heaved a sigh as she closed the door to the apartment. She jumped at the sound of her mobile phone ringing – a rare event these days. Since leaving her job at the hospital in London, although her friends kept in contact online, it wasn't as though she'd get a text or call asking her if she wanted to work an extra shift or go out for someone's birthday or just a drink after work. In fact, her mobile hadn't rung once since she'd arrived; nobody had phoned or texted to ask how she was coping in her new job.

It had made her feel sad and lonely that although she counted the people she'd worked with at the London hospital as friends, they were just work colleagues she'd seen every day. Now she was no longer around, she imagined they'd stay in touch less and less, especially as Cassie hadn't made the effort to call. There was a reason for that; she'd come here to get away from London and everything associated with her husband.

Perhaps if she'd stayed in contact with her school friends in Canada, then she would have some long-lasting friendships no matter where she was in the world. But she hadn't. The closest she had to a friend from her past, who'd known her from way back when, was ringing her right now.

Cassie answered her phone. 'Ben, I'm at work. What are you doing here?' She knew what he was doing, making good on that promise. Why did he think he could just turn up when he felt like it? *Because he wanted to see you.* Was that it? Cassie waited for his reply with bated breath.

'Ben – are you still there?'

'After the conversation about that promise I made, I didn't

know how long you'd be around…' He fell silent for a long moment. 'Sorry, I don't know what I was thinking, just turning up like this.' He paused again before telling her in a small voice, 'I wanted to see you.'

Cassie smiled. She was already making her way towards the main entrance hall. She now had an unexpected free afternoon. 'I take it you will make good on your promise this time?'

'Oh, absolutely.' He paused. 'So, can you come?'

Cassie was already at the front door. She could see Ben on his phone standing outside looking up at the hall. She hesitated. Cassie thought about her soon-to-be ex-husband. He let her down in the worst way imaginable, having an affair and leaving her. But he hadn't broken her heart; it wasn't his for the breaking.

Cassie stared at Ben. There was one person who could do that – who had already done it years ago – and he was standing right there waiting for her. She swore she would never let him break her heart again, although that was years ago. She'd moved on – hadn't she?

Cassie was hesitant about striking up a friendship again. She knew it wasn't as simple as that; for her it would always be something more – much more. She thought she had moved on from Ben, but seeing him stirred up those feelings again. It finally answered a question she had harboured for years; was she still in love with him?

She assumed those feelings would wane with the passage of time and she'd look back on that episode in her life as just an intense crush on a boy she was very attracted to. Love was different. Love happened when you grew in maturity, met someone, got married and bought a place together; all the things mature, responsible adults did. Love wasn't doing crazy, stupid things like riding around on motorbikes with the man of your dreams and taking a risk that you might get your heart broken again.

If that's what you really think, why are you still standing here? Any minute he will spot you. Her thoughts turn to the diary and a young girl who'd fallen in love. Cassie wasn't that much older than Rosie when she'd first met Ben. Rosie had lost her first love too. Except in wartime, there were no second chances.

It made Cassie wonder what Rosie would say if she was here now? Cassie bet she wished she'd had a second chance with the love of her life if only he'd come back to her like he promised. Cassie had almost read to the end of the diary. She knew what happened. Rosie never had that second chance; Scott was sent abroad with his regiment and never returned.

She imagined Rosie would say. 'You have a second chance. Ben kept his promise. Surely, that means something. He still loves you otherwise he wouldn't have come back.'

The voice in her head of a young girl in wartime, who'd suffered so much loss, willed her forward to take a chance on the boy she still loved.

❖

Evelyn sat at the window watching Cassie put on a helmet and climb on the motorbike. The good-looking young man climbed on behind her. They might not be in their teens or twenties, but at Evelyn's age everyone who hadn't had the misfortune of experiencing the war was young in her eyes. At least they had a future. They didn't know how lucky they were.

Evelyn smiled for the first time in a very long time as she watched the motorbike take off down the drive. It brought to mind a memory of a teenage girl sneaking out of the house to meet her chap, clandestinely. Sometimes they scooted off on his motorbike. Once he even let her sit up front and drive it herself. Her smile faded. That was a long time ago.

She knew what everyone was thinking; she either had dementia, or she was going doo-lally sitting at the window every single day waiting for him to return. But she couldn't help it. That's why she was still here. He'd made her a promise. No matter what obstacles they put in his path, he'd told her, 'We'll meet again.' She was still waiting, still hoping he would make good on that promise in this lifetime.

33

Cassie came to a stop and turned off the engine. She stood at the kerb, took off her helmet and caught the questioning look on Ben's face. He was sitting on the back of the bike, holding his helmet in his hands.

Cassie frowned. 'You said I could ride the bike wherever I wanted. This is where I wanted to go.'

Ben looked up at the old 1930s brick-built building. According to the plaque above the door, it was once a school. It was now the public library situated in the local town a few miles away. The fact that Cassie knew where the library was told him she'd been here before. He frowned. It wasn't quite what he had in mind when he came to pick her up.

She must have caught the look on his face. 'I told you I wanted to go to the library – remember.'

Ben nodded. He hoped she'd forgotten about the library and was taking them to some old haunts instead. Ben looked at her. 'So, what are we doing here?'

'Do you recall why I first came to England with my dad?'

'Of course I remember. He was sent by boat to live in Canada as a child. It's not something you forget in a hurry, finding out the British Government sent children abroad.' He'd read that some of them had families waiting for their return after the war. Later they were told they had been adopted by well-to-do couples in England, which was not the case. Ben couldn't imagine someone taking his daughter away from him

Cassie looked at him, surprised he remembered. It was common knowledge that children were evacuated from London during the Second World War to the safety of the countryside. Some were sent further afield, abroad to Commonwealth countries, which was a well-known fact too. However, it was in 1940, when a ship travelling from Liverpool to Canada sunk and many children lost their lives, that the British Government stopped the overseas evacuation scheme.

So how did her father end up in Canada after the war? That was perhaps a less familiar story. She wondered how many people had heard of the British Government's child migrant programme. It was the Child Migrant Trust who told Cassie's father about the government programme that ran from the 1920s to 1970. Children from deprived backgrounds, many in orphanages, were sent to former British colonies.

In post-war Britain the policy continued. Unfortunately, her father was sent to an orphanage from Fletchling Hall, and became one of those statistics, joining the thousands of children sent abroad as part of the Government's resettlement scheme. Cassie didn't want to think about the statistics. In the post-war period four thousand children were sent to Australia and Zimbabwe alone, that's without Canada and New Zealand. Tens of thousands of child migrants, some as young as her dad, were shipped over the course of the programme.

If that wasn't upsetting enough to discover children were

forcibly removed from the country of their birth and all that was familiar, it was the thoughts that some children might not have been orphans. Unbeknown to them, they left behind parents and siblings. Is that what had happened to her father? Had he been lied to and told his relatives were dead when it wasn't true? It's what he had come to England to find out.

Despite discovering the name of the orphanage where he was sent after leaving Fletchling hall, the trail went cold. There was a simple explanation for that; her father didn't remember his real surname or his date of birth. There was an online service to search the historical indexes through the General Register Office for England and Wales, but he couldn't order a copy of his birth certificate without one of the vital pieces of information. So, he was stuck in limbo, unable to trace his family.

Cassie breathed a sigh. 'My father is writing a book about his experiences. He's hoping to get it published.'

Ben climbed off the motorbike. 'Good for him.'

'It's called *The Lost Children.*'

Ben stared at Cassie and nodded his head. It sounded apt. He had read an article once in a newspaper about an Australian looking for his English family. What he suffered, what so many of them went through, being promised this wonderful life in a far-off land and then finding themselves virtual prisoners; little more than slave labour on remote farmsteads or orphanages in the middle of nowhere. Ben shook his head. 'It was appalling, and that's putting it mildly.'

Cassie nodded. 'It's been years since my dad visited, but as I'm back here, I thought I'd try to find out anything I can about the time he spent at Fletchling Hall. I'd love to unearth a clue to his past life in England. Do you know I found an old diary in the basement of the house?' Although it was a rhetorical question, he shook his head no.

'A young girl called Rosie wrote it. That's not her proper name, but a nickname. Anyway, it's really interesting because my father lived in with the family at Fletchling Hall, unlike the other evacuees who resided in a separate wing. He remembers a girl who looked after him, took him under her wing when her brothers went to war. I believe that girl was Rosie.' Cassie was thinking of the photo she'd found of her father with the family.

She smiled at the thought she could now put a name, or at least a nickname, to the girl in his memory. 'I can't wait to tell him. I wanted to visit the library to see if I might find out more. It can all go in his book, you see.'

Ben studied her thoughtfully. 'I hope your dad's experience growing up in Canada wasn't—' Ben stopped in his tracks. He didn't want to upset her. The word he was going to use was *brutal.*

'I know what you're getting at.' Cassie shook her head. 'He was one of the lucky ones.' She smiled. 'Did I ever tell you about my paternal grandparents? I suppose I should call them step-grandparents…'

Cassie told Ben about a lovely couple, missionaries, who were on the road spreading the word of God. They happened upon a farmstead in the middle of nowhere in the Canadian Rockies. It was there that they met a little British boy and fell in love with his cherubic face and sweet nature.

They'd lost their only child, a young boy, to dysentery. It wasn't their intention to replace him – nobody could replace their son – but when this little boy ran into the path of their caravan and broke his leg, they thought it was a sign from God.

The farmers were livid that they would have to house and

feed a child unable to work, so the young couple offered to take the English boy off their hands. It cost them every penny they had to release her father from a childhood of deprivation and hard labour. Once again, lady luck smiled on her father and brought him another family who would take care of him and treat him like their own.

'You love them – don't you?'

'Oh yes, they're the most wonderful couple you could ever hope to meet, although my grandfather is no longer with us.' Cassie thought about her Dad. 'I think his childhood influenced what he is doing now, hitting the road and driving around the country. He always loved the open road; that harks back to his childhood travelling with his adoptive parents.'

As they walked up the steps into the library, Cassie lowered her voice. 'When he lost my mum, I worried that he wouldn't cope. Then he came up with the idea for a book, a kind of expose of what happened to children like him. I should imagine he is finding it cathartic. At first, he was reluctant to leave his grandchildren. Family is everything to him. But he skypes the grandkids while travelling the country. Dad loves meeting people and writing their stories.' Cassie took a breath and looked at Ben, bemused. She couldn't quite read his expression. 'What?'

'Cassie, I'm still—'

'Can I help you?'

A stern-looking woman sitting behind a desk just inside the entrance to the library interrupted him.

Cassie wondered what Ben was about to say, but the moment was lost. She turned to the librarian. 'I was interested in seeing some archived newspapers about Fletchling Hall during the Second World War. My father was evacuated there.'

'Really?' Her face softened. 'Come, I'll see what we have.'

As they followed the lady through the library, Cassie turned to Ben with a question. She whispered, 'what did you intend to say before we arrived at the information desk?'

Ben glanced about him. The library was busy with people browsing the bookshelves, sitting at computers or reading newspapers. The atmosphere was hushed. It was so quiet he could hear someone turning the page of their newspaper across the room. He looked at Cassie. How could he declare he was still in love with her in the middle of an excruciatingly silent library? He could even hear the soles of his new shoes squeaking on the wooden floor. Ben shook his head. 'It's nothing.'

'Are you sure? It looked as though you were about to say something important.'

Ben frowned. It was important. He just hoped he got another chance. Ben was already thinking about whether he might persuade her to come out on another date with him. Although he had a notion she didn't think of this as a date, otherwise they wouldn't be in a public library right now. Perhaps he'd turn up on his motorbike again and take her out on a proper date next time.

Ben sat on a chair behind her, watching her scrolling through the microfiche. The office chair he was sitting on had wheels. Ben moved closer. And a little closer. And closer still, until he smelt her hair and a subtle fragrance – her perfume. Without thinking, he reached out and gently lifted her hair away from the nape of her neck.

Cassie swivelled round in her chair and looked at him. 'What are you doing?'

'Oh, er, nothing.' Ben flinched which sent his chair careering backwards along the smooth wooden floor. He knocked into someone. 'Shit! Sorry.'

'No harm done,' said the man sitting at another machine.

'Shh!' The stern librarian's voice carried from the front desk into their little anteroom.

Cassie and Ben looked at each other and slapped a hand over their mouths to curtail a laugh. It didn't work. The woman appeared at the door. 'Do I need to remind you this is a library!?'

They both burst out laughing.

'Honestly, you're like a pair of giggling teenagers. I will have to ask you to leave.'

Cassie gathered up her bag, her cheeks glowing bright red as they were escorted back through the library and shown the door.

'Heavens alive,' exclaimed Ben, 'I have no idea why I found that so funny?'

'Me neither!'

They stood outside the library doubled up with laughter. When their laughter subsided, Cassie said, 'I can't remember when I laughed so much over something so trivial.'

'When did life get so serious?' remarked Ben more to himself.

'Yes, I know what you mean…'

Ben was about to say something when Cassie turned around and picked up the helmet. That killed the moment. It was the end of the trip out. Ben breathed a sigh. 'I'll take you back then.'

Cassie put on her helmet.

He glanced at the library. 'I'm sorry I got us booted out of there. Did you find anything?'

Cassie shook her head, 'The diary told me a lot more than I'd have ever gleaned from a newspaper clipping with a brief story of the child evacuees to the village.'

'Oh, that's all right then.' He quickly backtracked, 'I don't mean that's all right that you found nothing more about your father's past. I was talking about getting us chucked out of the library.'

Cassie tightened the strap under her chin. 'What were you doing, anyway?'

Ben avoided her gaze. What he was doing was leaning in to kiss the nape of her neck. What on earth possessed him to do that? He knew the answer to that question. It was Cassie, the love of his life; he wanted to kiss the woman that, if he had another chance, he'd walk off into the sunset with.

'Ben?'

'Oh, there was a strand of hair on your coat – that's all.' Ben averted his gaze when he caught her expression; she didn't believe him.

'Are you sure you don't want to drive?' he asked.

It was nice of Ben to keep his promise and let her drive here, but she found the bike quite cumbersome and she really had to concentrate on the road. Cassie shook her head. They had just climbed on to the motorbike, when a flustered library assistant came running out of the library.

They both looked her way.

She stopped in front of them. Ben wondered if they might get an apology for being kicked out. He doubted it. She had something in her hands. 'Here, I almost forgot. There were individual photographs of the children billeted to the village. I believe they took them when they first arrived. You mentioned your father was the youngest. Is this him?'

She handed Cassie a photo she'd printed off the microfiche. It was of a young boy. He was dressed in short trousers, a shirt and a blazer that looked two-sizes too big, suggesting he may have had an older brother and was wearing hand-me-downs. But it wasn't his clothes that stood out…

'It's him, isn't it,' said the librarian, excitedly.

Cassie nodded. He looked different in the photo taken with Rosie and her family at Fletchling Hall. Apart from the clothes he was wearing, it took a moment for her to realise what it was. In the picture from the microfiche, her dad had something around his neck. Cassie pointed at it. 'What's that?'

Ben squinted in the sunshine. 'Looks like a name tag.'

'You're joking!' She turned to the librarian. 'Can you blow this photo up anymore?'

'I can't – no.'

Cassie's disappointment was palpable.

'The junior library assistant is in tomorrow. He's a whizz with our electronic gizmos.'

Despite being annoyed with the lady for cutting him off earlier when he was about to declare his feelings toward Cassie, he couldn't help but smile at the old-fashioned turn of phrase *electronic gizmos.*

Cassie jotted her number down on a scrap of plain paper torn out of the back of the diary. *Needs must.* Her grandmother's words came back to her as she did so. She handed her number to the librarian. 'As soon as he can read the writing on that tag, will you let me know?'

She nodded. 'Of course. Was your father a child migrant looking for his English birth family?'

Cassie looked at her in surprise. 'You know about that?'

'Not your father, specifically, but there have been other people inquiring at the library.'

'Really?

The librarian nodded. 'We have had people visit to search our archives to find out if relatives – brothers, sisters, sons, daughters – were billeted here and what happened to them.'

Now that was news to Cassie. What if her father's relatives had visited here? It had never occurred to her that while her father was looking for them, they might be searching for him. It was a nice thought, but it still didn't get him any closer to finding them. However, now she had a lead; a photo of her father with his original nametag he must have been sent away with.

'Is the young man who can enlarge that photo definitely back in work tomorrow?'

'Yes.' She held up the piece of paper Cassie had given her. 'I will phone you as soon as I hear anything.'

Cassie watched her walk back into the library. She turned to Ben. 'Oh, my goodness. I am so excited!' She jumped into his arms.

Ben was taken aback by her sudden embrace. So was Cassie. They parted awkwardly.

'Right – let's get going. You're still driving,' Cassie pointed out, patting the seat in front of her as she climbed on the bike.

Ben sat down in front of her. As he slipped on the helmet, he felt two hands moving around his waist. 'Tell me if I'm holding on too tight,' she said, her lips brushing his ear.

Ben looked down at her hands and smiled. 'Nope, everything's just fine.'

'Great, because I'd rather not fall off if you don't mind.'

'Don't worry. I'll get you back in one piece.' Ben kick-started the bike. The engine roared. Before he set off, he shouted above the noise of the engine, 'So, what's so special about the tag?' Ben wasn't aware that her father was given the surname *Smith*. The nametag must have gone missing, the records from the orphanage lost when he reached his destination in Canada. He was so very young it was little wonder he didn't remember his last name.

'It might just be the answer to everything!' If it was legible. Cassie didn't want to think about having her hopes dashed. Instead, she turned her attention to Ben. 'I saw you coming up the drive on your bike.'

'You did?' Another thing to smile about. She must have seen him from a window. That was his intention, to make an entrance.

Cassie hadn't meant to let on that she'd been watching him the whole time from the window when he'd arrived. 'I wasn't the only one. You could wake up the dead with this thing.'

'It's not a thing. If I remember, you thought I was pretty cool riding a motorbike.'

'That's a long time ago. You're not a teenager. Neither am I.'

'Yes, but it wasn't my idea to come out on the bike.' He grinned.

Cassie rolled her eyes. 'How was I to know you would remember that promise and still have this bike?'

Ben was still smiling. His heart had leapt when she'd mentioned that promise he'd made years ago about letting her have a go of his bike. She'd said it as a joke. She wasn't to know he'd kept that bike all these years because of some foolish notion that one day he would see her again. It was all he had left to remember her by. Before he set off, he had one question. 'Do you think I still look cool?'

'No!'

It wasn't the answer he was hoping for, but as she leaned

into his back, he could have sworn he felt her heart beating rapidly. 'Are you all right?'

'Of course. Why wouldn't I be?'

There it was again, her heart drumming in her chest like a locomotive. Was she nervous about riding pillion on the bike or was it something else; was she feeling anxious because she still had feelings for him? But how could that be when she'd married someone else, although she wasn't with her husband now? Ben heaved a sigh. He'd met someone else too, but that didn't change how he felt about her. Was there a possibility Cassie still held a torch for her first love?

He'd just released the foot brake when he felt her hot breath in his ear. 'Don't take me back just yet. Take me somewhere.'

He shouted over the noise of the engine, 'Where?'

'Someplace.'

Ben turned his head and felt her lips brush his cheek. 'Someplace?' That's what she used to say when they were teenagers. What she meant was some place they could be alone together.

'You know what I mean…' she breathed into his ear.

'Are you sure?'

Her lips kissing his ear answered his question.

As he set off, Ben's heart leaped in his chest.

34

Cassie took off her helmet. 'I don't understand…' She climbed off the bike and looked up at the hall. 'I imagined we were going someplace…' *private*, thought Cassie.

Cassie felt embarrassed. What made her think he wanted her kissing his ear? He must have been mortified and brought her straight home. She didn't know what got into her. They'd only just met again. After all these years, they were virtual strangers. What was she thinking? That they could rekindle their teenage love affair and pretend the last twenty-five years never happened.

She frowned at the bloody bike. That's what it was, turning up on his motorbike, sending her heart all aflutter, looking way too gorgeous for a man in his forties. Now she was back at the hall, she had a sudden moment of clarity. The last thing she needed was to get involved with someone. It was too soon, way too soon. She couldn't believe she'd even suggested he take her *someplace* – their secret code for being alone. Although she was taken aback he remembered what she meant after all these years. When he turned around to face her, she didn't know where to look. Cassie left the helmet on the seat of the motorbike and started towards the hall.

'Wait! Where are going?' He caught up with her.

'Inside. What does it look like?'

'But it was my turn to choose where we went?'

Cassie stared at him. 'I thought…'

Ben smiled that disarming smile of his reminding her of the teenager she fell in love with. 'We're not there yet.'

Cassie cocked her head to one side. 'Where's *there*?'

'Someplace…' He was still smiling.

'Someplace?'

He nodded.

Cassie hesitated. Something told her he didn't mind her lips brushing his ear after all.

Ben held out his hand.

Despite her better judgement, Cassie took his hand and smiled as he led the way. Her smiled faded when her husband came to mind. They never held hands. She remembered seeing older couples who'd probably been together years, still walking along hand-in-hand. How romantic that they should still feel that way about each other after so many years.

Romantic? Cassie released her hand from his. She wasn't ready to start a relationship, especially with Ben, who'd left her broken-hearted once before. She stopped.

Ben came to a halt too. 'What's the matter?'

'Where are we going?'

'You'll see – come on.' He took off again, leading the way.

Cassie still followed, trailing behind, wishing she hadn't suggested going anywhere else.

He walked into the gardens and led Cassie along the path that skirted the back of the hall. Cassie glanced through the windows into the passageway that led to Ruby's apartment. She was about to tell Ben about her other patient, not details because that would breach patient confidentiality, but just a titbit or two about the young lady who lived here, when Ben stopped. He turned to her. 'When you asked to go someplace, this came to mind.'

He stepped on to the small circular patio with a wooden garden bench beside an old-fashioned cast-iron lamp. What a streetlamp was doing in the garden of the former stately home was anyone's guess, but it was still there, along with the bench and the delightful views across open fields and farmland that stretched into the distance. Ben hoped she remembered this place and why he'd brought her here.

Cassie stood there staring at the bench.

'Don't you want to sit down?'

Cassie hesitated.

Ben wondered if he'd done the right thing. This was the spot where they'd had their first teenage kiss. He looked away, embarrassed. Her lips had brushed his ear when she was sitting behind him on the bike. Had he read too much into it? He realised she'd been reluctant to follow him here. Perhaps she'd asked, in the heat of the moment, to go someplace private where they could be alone and now regretted it.

'Sorry, I shouldn't have—'

'How could I have forgotten about this place?' Cassie interrupted. She gazed at the bench as though she'd bumped into a long-lost friend. Cassie sat down and looked up at Ben. She held out her hand. 'Don't you want to sit down?'

Ben joined her on the bench and took her hand in his once more. He looked up at the sky. 'It's been a fine day, so it might be spectacular. Are you okay waiting?'

Cassie smiled. 'Of course. Why wouldn't I be?'

'I thought you wouldn't want to do this with me.'

Cassie couldn't think of anyone she'd rather sit with to watch the sunset. She gave his hand a reassuring squeeze. The bench was old, the patio moss-covered and worn, and the streetlamp might not even work. But none of that mattered. Right now, Cassie was going to put aside all thoughts of relationships and broken hearts, and live in the moment. They were here together, sharing this occasion, and that's what mattered.

It made her think of Rosie and the Canadian. Had Rosie brought him here to sit and watch the sunset? Cassie hadn't finished the diary because she wasn't ready to leave Rosie and her world behind just yet. It felt akin to coming to the end of a good book, dying to learn how the story ends but not wanting to say farewell to the characters one grows so fond of.

Ben turned to her. He had so many questions. Were they on a proper date? Did this mean she might want to see him again? Would she mind if he kissed her right now? After they kissed, would she cuddle up to him with her head on his shoulder by the glow of the streetlamp, as they watched the sunset? He glanced at the lamp wondering if it still worked, before his gaze settled on Cassie. Would it be all those things, just like he remembered from years ago?

The light in the old streetlamp flicked on.

They both smiled. It was a sign. They drew closer, taking in the fine lines on each other's faces. Their lips parted, about to kiss, when a crack of thunder jolted them apart. They both looked up. Storm clouds were gathering.

Ben frowned. 'Seriously, of all the times, it has to rain right now?'

'Maybe it will blow over?'

A raindrop landed on Cassie's cheek, then another. 'Or not.'

Ben reached over and wiped the rain from her cheek.

'Cassie looked up. 'We will have to make a run for it.'

They sprinted across the lawn as the sprinkling of rain rapidly turned to a downpour.

'This way!' Cassie shouted as they rounded the side of the hall and arrived at some outbuildings. It was quicker to dive in there for cover than head for the main entrance to the house.

'Bloody hell. That came out of nowhere!' exclaimed Ben as he rushed inside. He turned around and pulled the large double doors shut. The wind and rain outside battered the doors. Ben felt deflated that his bright idea of watching the sunset, under the glow of the lamplight, in such a romantic setting had just been scuppered by the British weather. He wondered if they would get another opportunity.

He turned around to ask Cassie when he could see her again, but she was nowhere in sight. 'Cassie?'

'I'm in here.'

They were in a large brick outbuilding that was used as a garage. He looked at the green vintage car. The car door was open. Ben walked over and glanced inside. Cassie was sitting on the back-seat shivering. She wished they had made a run for the house instead. She was about to get out of the car when Ben joined her in the back seat. He put his arms around her and pulled her close.

'You're drenched too.'

'I know.'

The sound of the rain and wind subsided. 'Perhaps you should go back to the house, Cassie.' When he turned his head to face her, her lips were on his. She drew away, the look on her face unsure if she'd made a mistake. This wasn't what she intended. What happened to not starting a relationship and risking getting her heart broken again?

Ben didn't hesitate this time. His lips were on hers, the urgency of their first kiss in so long leaving them both in no doubt that they wanted something more.

They drew away, staring at each other. After all these years, was it possible they were still in love?

Cassie shivered with cold. She didn't want to spoil the moment. 'I need to get out of these wet things.'

Ben opened the car door and held out his hand for Cassie to climb out. They walked over and opened the barn doors. The sky was still black, but the downpour had subsided to a drizzle.

'Do you want to make a run for it?' Ben asked, looking over at the house. 'It isn't far.'

'I'm staying at Gatekeepers Cottage, not in the hall.'

'Is that the little flint cottage down the drive?'

'That's the one.'

'That's a bit of a walk.'

'Unless we hop on your motorbike?'

'A few minutes later, Cassie climbed off the motorbike outside Gatekeepers Cottage.' Her teeth were chattering, so were Ben's. He remained where he was, astride the bike.

Cassie hesitated. Should she ask him in?

Ben revved the engine and was about to set off when the engine died. 'Oh, crap!'

Cassie looked at the bike. 'What happened?'

He tried to kick-start the bike. 'I don't know. It's been working fine up to now.'

'How often do you take it out?'

Cassie looked at him in surprise when he replied. 'You mean to tell me that this was the first time you've ridden it since…?'

'I have it serviced once a year.'

Cassie rolled her eyes. 'Well, a fat lot of good that's been. One bit of nasty weather and it's stopped working. Perhaps you should have taken it for spin here and there. Why haven't you been using it?'

How could he tell her he was waiting for her to return? It would sound so stupid. Ben shrugged.

At that moment, the heavens opened again.

They both raced through the front gate to the door of the cottage. Cassie got the door open as fast as she could and they dived inside.

'There's an electric fire in the lounge, why don't you put that on while I get the kettle going. Do you mind if I nip into my bedroom and change?'

'Of course not. I'll switch on the fire to warm up the lounge.'

Neither made a move. They both lingered in the hall, staring at one another.

Cassie withdrew first before she did something she might regret, like kiss him again. Who knew where that would lead? Cassie hadn't forgotten how they had parted before. Although it was a long time ago, she knew she wasn't ready to take a chance on him again. 'I'd better go and change before I… I get pneumonia.'

'Yeah – good idea. I'll phone the local garage about my bike.

35

'I think you had better answer the door if the garage calls round for the bike – don't you?'

Cassie laughed as she handed him a steaming mug of coffee and took a seat the other side of the fireplace. The warming electric fire had all four bars switched on and Ben was sitting there wearing her long towelling pink bathrobe, his wet clothes in the tumble drier. Cassie had towel-dried her hair and changed out of her wet clothes into a pair of blue cord trousers and a cosy jumper.

Ben took the mug with one hand, while fiddling with the buttons on the bathrobe. He looked uncomfortable.

'Sorry, there was nothing else for you to wear while your clothes dry. If it makes you feel better, pink suits you.'

'Thanks – but I still won't make a habit of wearing this sort of thing.'

'Really – why not?'

He looked at her, wondering if she was coming on to him.

Cassie's face lit up. 'I'm joking.'

He smiled at her imagining what she looked like wearing this robe. And what she looked like not wearing it. He stopped undressing her with his eyes and turned away embarrassed. 'I'm glad my clothes won't take long to dry.'

'I can run you home after the garage collects your bike.'

Ben stopped sipping his coffee and looked at her askance. 'I assumed you didn't have a car.'

'Oh, I don't. We have use of the one in the garage.'

'What – that old green monstrosity? Crumbs, it's out of the ark.'

Cassie smiled. 'I know. That's why I cycled into town. I wasn't sure if I made it in the car, would it get me back?'

'Yes, that's the trouble with old cars…'

'And old motorbikes,' Cassie added. She smiled.

Ben returned her smile. The motorbike breaking down didn't upset him because it meant he could spend more time with Cassie. When they arrived back at the hall, he got the impression she was having second thoughts about seeing him – until he took her to their old haunt. It was all going so well, before the blasted British weather scuppered his bright idea.

'Give me a bicycle any old day,' Cassie added.

'As long as you don't get run off the road by some idiot.'

Cassie smiled at him. 'Apology accepted.'

'I hope the bike didn't cost you a lot to fix. Let me pay for it.'

'No, Ben, I wouldn't dream of it. Besides, it was partly my fault. If I hadn't been looking around at the views as I came out of the grounds, instead of watching the road, I wouldn't have ended up in a ditch.'

'I really am sorry, though. I wish there was some way I could repay you for the hassle of getting it fixed.'

'Don't be silly. It didn't cost much. There was no harm done, apart from my pride. After it was repaired, it was as good as new.

Jill didn't notice or if she had she didn't say anything.'

'So, you haven't got a bike of your own?'

'No. I'd like one. But with the divorce and all, I wouldn't want to fork out right now.'

Ben stared at her. An idea had just popped into his head.

'So, I can't tempt you to have a lift in the green car?' Cassie asked, wishing she hadn't mentioned her divorce. She didn't want to talk about her ex.

'No, that's kind of you to offer, but I'm sure the garage won't mind dropping me home.'

'Do you live far?' Cassie ventured.

'Not far.'

'That's good.'

The conversation stalled. Ben sensed that Cassie was holding back from something she wanted to ask. He realised what it was. She was waiting for an explanation about what happened years ago. He promised he'd wait for her while she did her degree and then just dumped her.

'I lied to you.'

Cassie had been sitting there staring into her coffee cup wishing she had put the dry cycle on longer, so he didn't have to leave so soon. She looked up. 'Pardon?'

'When I dumped you. I made a stupid mistake, but I wouldn't own up to it, not to you at any rate.'

Cassie turned from the fire to face him. 'What are you talking about?'

Ben realised at the time, he was damned if he did and damned if he didn't. If he'd told her he'd got a girl knocked up, and his father was telling him he had to do the decent thing and stand by her, would she have been empathetic? He doubted it, even though he was blind drunk at the time and not coping with Cassie leaving for London. He'd slept with a girl on the rebound. It was a stupid thing to do. But he couldn't take it back or the consequences.

Cassie stared at him as he told her all this. 'You got a girl pregnant?'

And that was the face he'd been dreading all those years ago if he'd had the balls to tell her in person.

'You never told me that. You said you wanted to end it and that it was all my fault. You wrote it in a letter rather than tell me personally.'

Ben sighed heavily. How could he forget? 'That was my dad persuading me I had to end it with you.'

'So, you're blaming all this on your dad?'

'Yes… no.' Ben shook his head. 'I thought you'd never forgive me if you found out I'd cheated on you, so I just dumped you. I screwed up and couldn't see any way of making it up to you.' He'd written to Cassie again, and tried calling, intending to tell her to hell with his final year of school, he was travelling to London to be with her. She never responded to his letter.

'What letter?' Cassie asked.

'You didn't get the letter?'

Cassie shook her head. 'I was living in a dorm with a load of other students, so it's not surprising mail was lost.'

'I should have come. I've regretted that this whole time.'

'Yes, you should.'

'Would you have forgiven me?'

Cassie shrugged. 'I don't know, Ben.' It sounded as though he'd made the biggest mistake of his life and regretted it ever since. 'What about the baby?'

'Stillborn.'

'Oh, Ben. I'm so sorry.'

'I couldn't just up and leave her after that. You understand – don't you?'

Cassie realised that one wrong decision in life can set you on a path from which it is difficult to turn back. Things get complicated and, before you know it, everything has changed. Cassie recalled her decision to leave for London all those years ago. If only she hadn't been so careerist. If only she'd waited a year for him to finish school so they could have gone to London together.

'Did you stay with her?' Cassie didn't know why she was asking him that. It didn't matter whether he stayed with her or went on to meet somebody else. His path was set. There was no way back, not to his first love at any rate. She hadn't got the letter. They didn't meet again. The rest was history.

'I was never in love with her like you, Cassie, or the woman I later met and had a child with.'

Cassie knew that. 'Are you getting a divorce?'

Ben shook his head. 'It's not like that…'

Cassie threw him a questioning look.

'We never married.'

'Oh.'

'We had a daughter, but when she was a toddler, I lost my partner, her mother, in a car accident.' Ben turned his head to stare at the fire.

Cassie sensed he didn't want to talk about it which was understandable. He told her that after the accident, he was left to raise the child on his own. He'd had several relationships since, but nothing serious.

Like Ben, Cassie did not wish to talk about Lars. He didn't even need to know the name of her ex. She didn't need to know the name of his. It was all water under the bridge now.

Cassie stared at him. She was not surprised his father persuaded him to write that letter telling her it was over. She understood the circumstances.

Cassie sighed. 'I remember he never liked me.'

'Who?'

'Your father.'

'It wasn't you, Cassie.'

'Ben, you don't have to make excuses. He didn't like me and that's that.'

A pained expression crossed his face. 'I was such an idiot, Cassie. I should never have listened to my father, but you're right, he was happy it was over between us. Perhaps if you'd been English…' he trailed off.

'What are you saying?'

'He doesn't much like Canadians. Don't ask me why.'

'You never wanted to find out what he had against us?'

'He tried to tell me once. It was soon after we split up. I was in a bad way over the split and he was worried about me. We'd had a hell of a row, but whatever the reason he had a chip on his shoulder, I didn't want to know. It was too late. I had ruined my life.' Ben stopped.

'Did you just say leaving me ruined your life?'

He swallowed. 'I don't blame him I blame myself for terrible decisions.'

'But you were so young – we both were.'

'If I could turn back the clock—' Ben shook his head. 'If it wasn't for…'

Cassie thought he was going to say if it wasn't for his partner.

'If it wasn't for becoming a father, I might have…' He looked away.

'Might have…? Cassie prompted.

'You know… done something stupid.'

Cassie stared at him. 'Oh.' She didn't know what to say. Perhaps she shouldn't say anything. All those years she'd imagined he never felt the same way about her when in fact it was the reverse.

Cassie changed the subject to lighten the mood. 'Well, I'm here now and… and *I'm* not going anywhere.' Not until the hall was sold, but she didn't want to think about that.

Ben's frown changed in an instant. He leaned forward in his chair. 'Neither am—' The sound of his mobile phone interrupted what he was about to say next. 'I better get that.'

'Work?' Cassie asked. She knew he was a self-employed architect running his own business. She imagined, apart from meeting clients, he would take calls out of hours working from home. It was getting on for six in the evening.

Ben reached for his phone. He'd left it on the mantel shelf. 'I'm working late, sweetheart, that's all.' He glanced at Cassie. 'I'm with a client.'

Cassie looked at him quizzically.

'Yes, a client.' He frowned. 'I'll be home soon, I promise.' Ben ended the call and turned to Cassie who was sitting with her arms folded across her chest.

'I can explain…'

Cassie said, 'I'd like to meet her.'

'Who?'

'Your daughter.'

Ben relaxed and sighed in relief. 'I didn't want you to think…'

Cassie grinned. She could just make out a teenage girl's voice on the line. 'I gathered you were speaking to your daughter.'

'Yes, sometimes I wonder who's the adult? I swear she keeps tabs on me.'

Cassie eyed him thoughtfully. 'Why did you call me a client?'

'It's complicated. Whenever I meet somebody, things go wrong when I introduce them to my teenage daughter.'

Cassie understood. Growing up in a single-parent household she'd had her daddy all to herself. She was probably afraid someone would take him away, even though it was obvious to Cassie that nobody could replace her in his affections. His daughter meant the world to him.

'I don't want her to find out about us just yet.'

Us. Cassie stood up. 'Have you finished with that mug?'

Ben sensed he'd said something wrong. 'What did I say?' He stared up at her, his expression betraying his fears that Cassie didn't feel the same way; there was no *us*. He had to find out. Ben reached for her hand. 'Cassie?'

She looked at her hand in his. Was she ready for this so soon after her marriage breakdown? She hadn't come here to get involved with someone. And yet here he was, the love of her life. She thought of Rosie

'Take a chance on me, Cassie. I won't let you down this time.'

'We would have to take things slow.'

'Absolutely.'

She squeezed his hand. He stood up, moving closer. They were about to kiss when the sound of a van turning into the driveway ruined the moment. They smiled at each other. 'Sounds like your ride,' said Cassie.

A van door slammed shut outside, followed by a knock on the cottage door.

'Will you answer that?'

'Sure.' Cassie made for the door. All was quiet in the kitchen, so she told Ben, 'The dry cycle has finished, by the way.'

'Thank God!' Ben rushed into the kitchen and took his clothes out of the drier. He crept past Cassie, hoping the guy from the garage didn't spot him wearing a ladies pink dressing gown. He whipped into her bedroom and closed the door to change.

'He'll be right out but yes if you could load up the motorbike in the meantime that would be great.' Cassie was aware Ben had already told the garage over the phone what had happened. She closed the front door and overheard his voice from the bedroom. 'Hey, who are you?'

Cassie's brow furrowed. Who was he talking to?

'Aren't you the cutest thing?'

Cassie's eyes went wide. *Tabitha!* She was about to dart into her bedroom and grab the cat when she heard him say, 'I'm afraid you're not the cutest thing in the cottage, you know.'

Cassie heard Tabitha meowing as if to say, *do tell…*

'I've missed her so much…'

Tabitha was at it again, extracting secrets out of poor, unsuspecting souls thought Cassie. Except this wasn't a secret. She knew what she meant to Ben, and what he meant to her.

'I love her.'

Cassie stared at the door, shocked. Did he really just say that? It wasn't until she heard those words that it finally sunk in; after all these years, not only had they met again, he was in love with her. She should have been ecstatic, but her heart was thumping in her chest, afraid it might all go wrong. *Take a chance on me, Cassie.* That's what he'd said a moment ago. What would Rosie do if she was in her shoes right now? For all those couples, like Rosie and Scott in the Second World War who never met their sweethearts again, she owed it to them to put her fears aside and take a chance on love. If Rosie and Scott's story told her anything, it was that happiness was fleeting, and if fate gave Cassie a second chance, then what had she got to lose?

My heart again. Cassie shook her head, dispelling that idea.

Ben opened the bedroom door, catching Cassie unawares. She was about to jump into his arms and kiss him, but the cutest cat in the world was cradled in his arms purring, enjoying the attention. Cassie frowned at her. 'Have you stolen my boyfriend?'

Ben looked at Cassie in surprise. *Did she just call me her boyfriend?* He grinned and held up the cat. 'Look what I found.'

Cassie gave Tabitha a scratch under the chin. How could she be cross with such a cute cat especially now she knew, thanks to Tabitha, how Ben really felt about her?

'You didn't tell me you had a cat.'

'It's a long story.'

'When we meet again, you can tell me all about it.' Ben put the cat down. 'How about…' He was tried to recall what his work commitments were. 'The day after tomorrow?'

She frowned.

'Too soon?'

Cassie wanted to see him again as soon as possible, but she reminded herself it was she who'd told him she wanted to take things slow. 'No, that's great. Saturday is perfect.' It was the weekend and meant they could spend the entire day together. She walked him to the door.

The mechanic from the local garage was sitting outside in his van, the motorbike loaded up on the back.

'So, I'll come and pick you up in my car.'

Cassie's glanced at the bike. 'Yes, good idea.'

'Is there anywhere particular you'd like to go at the weekend?'

'A picnic might be lovely and a walk in the countryside.' The forecast promised a dry, surprisingly warm, weekend for this time of year, perfect weather to get out in nature; it was something Cassie didn't get a lot of opportunity to do when she was living in London, apart from visiting the local parks. It still wasn't the same as having the countryside on your doorstep.

'It's a date.' Ben frowned. Should he have said that?

Cassie's smile reassured him it was indeed a date. 'As long as it doesn't rain!' She shook her head. 'The good old British weather. Shame about earlier.' It had stopped raining, but the sun had set; it was too late to return to the bench and watch the sunset together.

Ben no longer felt disappointed that didn't work out. There would be plenty of other opportunities. He hoped they had the rest of their lives to watch sunsets together.

Ben's heart was thumping in his chest, suddenly anxious it would all go wrong. He realised why. He was keeping something from her. Should he tell her now and risk losing her, or hope she never finds out?

'Ben, is everything okay?'

He forced a smile. 'Sure, yes, everything is perfect.' As long as he kept his mouth shut.

'She leaned in and kissed him. When she drew back, he lingered on the doorstep.

Cassie smiled. She knew what this was about; he didn't want

to leave. She understood. Cassie didn't want him to go.

Ben opened his mouth to say something and thought the better of it. She'd never find out.

Cassie glanced over his shoulder and saw the mechanic frowning. She'd forgotten he was still waiting. 'You better get going.'

Ben looked over his shoulder. 'Okay, you're right.' He looked at her. 'See you at the weekend.'

Cassie smiled. 'Yes, see you on Saturday. I'll have a picnic ready.'

'Great.' Ben lingered for a moment, searching her face before he left.

Cassie stood on the doorstep of the cottage and waved, watching the van pull out of the drive. Something brushed her leg and she looked down to find Tabitha sitting on the door mat. She meowed at Cassie.

'What is it?'

Cassie stood there for a moment thinking of Ben. She was sure there was something he wanted to say to her. She shrugged. It was probably nothing. 'Come on, Tabitha, let's go inside.' Cassie couldn't remember the last time she felt so happy. She picked Tabitha up and cradled her in her arms. 'I'll tell you all about the love of my life.'

36

'Haven't you got a spring in your step this morning,' Evelyn remarked.

'Whatever do you mean?' Cassie had breezed into her apartment feeling as though she was floating on air. Her face flushed with embarrassment when she caught Evelyn staring at her.

Evelyn smiled. She was thinking about the man who had turned up on the motorbike yesterday as she watched Cassie sit on the sofa, curling a strand of hair around her finger.

'So, how about we finish reading the notebook?' Cassie was avoiding her gaze as though she had something to hide or more to the point, someone.

Evelyn nodded. 'All right.'

'Great, let's get started.' Cassie was eager to change the subject. She opened the notebook. 'Ah, here we are.' She stole a glance at Evelyn, who was staring at her intently. It pleased Cassie that Evelyn was in better spirits. She could do without the awkward questions though.

Evelyn noticed her blushing. 'Is anything the matter? You sound quite peculiar this morning.'

'Peculiar? Me? No, not me. I'm just reading the diary.' Cassie held it up. 'See?' She was avoiding eye contact as though she had something to hide.

'I think I do.' Evelyn said, nodding her head.

Cassie didn't want to ask what she meant by that. 'Let's crack on. Now, where were we?'

'Rosie got the radio for her birthday and realised she'd falsely accused the Canadian of stealing it. Then she snuck out to visit him again,' Evelyn said in a deadpan voice.

'Your memory is as sharp as a pin this morning.'

'Why wouldn't it be?'

Cassie looked at her. *Because everyone thinks you have dementia.* She didn't say it. Cassie was just relieved Evelyn *did* remember where they had got to in the story. With all that had happened in the last twenty-four hours, all she had on her mind was Ben.

Cassie found the page. She continued to read about Rosie's clandestine meetings with the Canadian she'd fallen in love with but she was distracted with thoughts of Ben. Although they agreed to meet up at the weekend, would those plans change? Would he come again today? If they fixed the bike, there was a possibility he'd ride here on his motorbike looking as handsome as ever, wearing his leather jacket and jeans. What if he turned up in the middle of her shift? She couldn't wait to see him again.

Cassie's mobile rang. That was something she hadn't considered. Would he phone to tell her he'd changed his mind about the weekend and wanted to meet up sooner?

Cassie put the diary down. 'Oh, sorry, I must answer this. Do you mind?'

'Who am I to stand in the way of true love?'

'I don't know what you mean,' Cassie said defensively,

wondering how Evelyn guessed. 'I won't be long.' She slipped the phone out of her pocket, stood up and walked over to the window as she answered it. She almost expected him to be outside, waiting for her on his motorbike like yesterday. That wasn't possible. She'd have heard the bike coming up the drive.

She didn't bother checking the number. 'Hi! Have you decided you can't wait until the weekend?'

'Oh, um, hello. Is that Cassie?'

She heard a young girl's voice down the phone that she didn't recognise. Cassie turned from the window. 'Sorry, I thought you were someone else. Who am I speaking to?'

'It's me, Devon. Remember you dropped off the old valve radio at The Radio Shack a fortnight ago?'

'Oh, yes, of course.' Cassie glanced at Evelyn. 'How did it go? Did you manage to fix it?'

There was a hesitation at the end of the line. Cassie was expecting bad news.

'Yes, it's all repaired.'

'That's fantastic. When can I pick it up?'

Another silence, as though there was a problem.

'Can I bring it to you?'

'You will deliver it?' That suited Cassie. 'When can you come?'

'Now. Unless it's not a good time.'

The timing couldn't be better. 'Perfect,' she said. 'Call me when you arrive. I'll pop down and meet you.' She signed off and turned to Evelyn. 'Have I got a surprise for you!'

'I don't like surprises,' grumbled Evelyn.

'Ah, but you *do* like visitors.'

'I have a visitor?' That got Evelyn's attention.

'Yes, and she's bringing something with her.'

'It better not be that blasted cat,' mumbled Evelyn under her breath as Cassie picked up the diary and started to read while she waited for that call.

❖

Devon ended the call to the Canadian lady just as Gramps stepped into The Radio Shack carrying a cup of coffee. She'd made a point of making the call while he nipped up the garden to the house to make a drink. The last thing she wanted was for Gramps to overhear the lady on the phone. Despite the number of years the lady said she had lived in England, she still sounded *very* Canadian. Gramps didn't like Canadians much.

Devon noticed the expression on his face. Something was up. 'Is everything all right?'

'Er, yes.'

She caught him looking back at the house, frowning. There was something he wasn't telling her, but she didn't have time to find out. That would have to wait until later.

He set his mug down on the workbench. 'Did you get hold of the lady who owns the radio?'

'Uh-huh.' Devon put her mobile phone in her back pocket. 'I'm going to take it to her. She doesn't live far.'

'Why can't she come and collect it herself? We don't normally deliver.'

'She's tied up at work. Besides, it's no trouble. Jodie will give me a lift.' Lucky for her they had got over their falling out and made up soon after that stupid row. Jodie had observed her dad must be seeing someone. She'd hit a sore point. Devon knew her father must have met somebody, a fact she'd rather not be reminded of. It didn't help that Jodie suggested she should butt out; her dad deserved to find happiness. Jodie was right; he deserved to find some happiness. As for the other thing, *butting out*, that would not happen. He's my dad, thought Devon. Can't he buy a new car or another bike instead?

'Are you taking it today?'

Devon looked at her Grandpa and rolled her eyes. 'We can't keep it forever.' They both looked at the magnificent antique radio with the warm wood-cased exterior. Devon admitted, 'When I was on the phone to the lady, I almost told her it wasn't repairable so we could keep it. But I didn't,' she added quickly.

'It will be hard letting go.'

'Can we listen to the radio one more time before I take it?'

Gramps sat down at the workbench in front of the wireless. 'Yes, why not?' He plugged it in and tuned it to BBC Radio 2.

They both sat, eyes closed, listening to some classical music. The sound quality differed between vintage radios, depending on the type of speaker and technology inside, but this table-top wood-cased beauty, with its smooth, dulcet tones, was in a class of its own. Although they had to let it go, the soothing sound reminded them why they repaired these distinctive radios in the first place.

'It's amazing, isn't it, Gramps?'

'Yes, it's one of the best ones I've never had the good fortune to repair.'

They exchanged a smile at the joke. Devon had fixed it with no help from her grandfather. She reached over and turned the dial, switching it off. 'Well, I guess this is it.'

Gramps nodded. 'I guess so. Do you want some help loading it in Jodie's car?'

Although the wireless wasn't too large, she knew he would want to see it safely on its way. 'Yes, that would be great. Thanks.' They walked up the garden together with the radio in his arms. Jodie was already waiting in her car on the driveway. She got out and opened the door for Devon's granddad.

Jodie turned around to look at the house. 'Do you hear that?' she said to Devon as Gramps loaded the radio in her car.

Devon followed her gaze to the house. 'Is that live music?'

Jodie cocked her head to one side. 'Yeah, I thought so too. Weird – huh?'

'I'll say.' Devon looked at Gramps. 'What's going on in there?' Before he answered her question, Jodie and Devon were already walking towards the front door, drawn by the sound of someone playing a guitar. They walked into the hallway, still listening. Now someone was singing too.

Jodie smiled. 'Hey, that sounds like Kurt Cobain.'

'You realise he's dead – right?' Devon said, frowning.

'Yes, I know that. I'm just saying it sounds like *Nirvana.* I love that music.'

Devon smiled. She'd known Jodie long enough for that nineties grunge music to rub off. Devon liked it too.

They stopped just inside the lounge. Devon stared at her dad. She didn't know he could play the guitar.

Jodie whispered in her ear, 'Your dad is kind of cool.'

Devon rolled her eyes. 'Don't be ridiculous.' She stood there watching her dad, wondering how come she never knew he could play a musical instrument – let alone sing? And he was bloody good.

Ben hadn't spotted them standing in the doorway. He was sitting on a chair, his back to them, the guitar balanced on one knee, looking out the patio doors at the far end of the room as he played. Devon noticed he was also wearing jeans and a leather jacket. 'Okay, this is *really* weird,' she muttered. Since when did Dad wear jeans and a biker jacket? She was used to seeing him in a suit. He was always working.

Devon felt a hand on her shoulder. She turned around to find Gramps standing behind her. 'Come on, you two. You have a delivery to make.'

Before she left, she noticed her dad pause and scribble something down on a sheet of paper on the side table next to him. 'What's he doing?' whispered Devon.

Gramps sighed. 'Your father is writing a song.'

'He writes music too?' Devon whispered under her breath as she followed him back to the car.

Jodie got in the car and started the engine.

Devon was about to get in the car when she turned to Gramps. 'I don't understand. How come I never knew he could play a guitar and sing?'

'It was before your time, Devon.'

'Like when he was a teenager?'

Gramps nodded. 'Did he ever tell you how he met your mother?'

'Yes. She was backing vocals for some band that was playing at the local pub one evening. He walked in and… well, the rest is history.'

Gramps shook his head. 'Not quite. He was *in* the band. In fact, he wrote the songs. You could say he *was* the band.'

'My dad was in a band and wrote the songs?'

'Yep, said he would be the next…' Gramps furrowed his brow. 'Oh, I can't remember.'

Jodie, sitting in the front seat of the car with the window wound down, overheard. 'Not Kurt Cobain – by any chance?'

Grandpa pointed at Jodie, 'That's the one. Your dad almost got a recording contract.'

'What happened?'

'He stopped playing the guitar and gave up writing songs.'

'Was it when Mom died? Is that why he stopped?'

'No, it happened way before then. Although your mum and dad first met when she was backing vocals, it wasn't until…' he paused, 'later that they got together. By that time your dad had changed his mind about being a musician.'

'Why?'

'I guess his heart was no longer in it.'

'Why?'

'Oh, Devon,' Jodie interrupted, 'you sound like a six-year-old. *Why, why, why,'* she mimicked.

'Shut-up, Jodie.'

'Sorry,' muttered Jodie.

Devon cocked her head to one side and frowned at Gramps. 'Why do I get the feeling there's something you're not telling me.'

Gramps avoided her gaze. 'Ask your dad, Devon. It's not my place.'

'What does that mean?'

'Just what I said.' He opened the car door for Devon. 'Now, have a safe journey. It's not far, is it?'

Devon exchanged a glance with Jodie. They both knew she wasn't allowed near the hall. That was her dad's stupid rule for as long as she could remember. 'The lady is working at Fletchling Hall. That's where I'm taking the radio,' she said defiantly, waiting for Gramps reaction.

Gramps looked at her and then glanced at the house. 'Look, Devon, I really don't think you should go to—'

'Why?'

Jodie rolled her eyes at the *why* word again but didn't comment this time. Something told her this wasn't a joking matter.

'You'll have to ask your—'

'Fine, don't tell me.'

'It's not my—'

'Place, yeah – whatever!' Devon followed Gramps' gaze. Dad was still playing the guitar. 'Dad's kind of busy, so if he asks where I've gone, be sure to tell him.' Devon grinned and got in the car.

'Devon…'

'See you later.'

Jodie gave Gramps an apologetic look and put the car into gear. She glanced at Devon as she manoeuvred the car out of the driveway. 'Why do you think your dad doesn't want you to visit Fletchling Hall?'

Devon shrugged. 'I don't know, and I don't care.'

Jodie shook her head. 'Is that right?' She knew her best friend too well. The tone of Devon's voice said she cared a great deal.

'Maybe it's something to do with your his work. Didn't you mention he got the contract to draw up plans to convert the hall into luxury flats?'

Devon nodded. 'Yes, but what has that got to do with anything?'

'If he comes up with plans that the council approve then they will go ahead with selling the hall.'

'Yeah – so?'

'People live there. If he doesn't come up with suitable plans then…'

'They can stay – is that what you're getting at?'

Jodie nodded.

Devon couldn't care less. 'They're just a load of old people.'

'Those old people might lose their homes because of him,' Jodie remarked.

Devon remained quiet. She still thought they were just a bunch of old people who could go and live elsewhere. What did it matter? They were at the end of their lives anyhow.

Devon kept her thoughts to herself. 'I still don't understand what that's got to do with me and visiting the hall.'

'Your dad might be afraid someone will realise who you are, and you'll get stick over it.'

Devon glanced at Jodie.

'There you see, you hadn't thought of that, had you? I told you there's a simple explanation.'

Devon frowned. The problem with Jodie's *simple* explanation was that she'd been told not to go anywhere near the hall long before her dad got that contract.

Jodie drove the rest of the way in silence, sensing Devon didn't want to talk about it or anything right now. She was worried about her dad. Jodie wanted to tell her to quit worrying.

She glanced at Devon. She was already in a bad mood. Now was not the time to bring up the fact that her dad had fallen for someone else. It was obvious. He was in love. Love makes you feel different and do extraordinary things like getting a motorbike and a guitar out of mothballs for the woman you love or write songs. Or drive your friend to Fletchling hall to deliver a valve radio out of guilt; Jodie realised she wouldn't always drop everything for her best friend because her new boyfriend came first. She still hadn't told Devon about him. Now wasn't the right time.

She smiled at Devon glad she had come this time. She took one hand off the steering wheel and squeezed her best friend's hand. Devon was a worrier. Jodie knew she suffered from anxiety. Perhaps it was because she'd grown up without a mum. Maybe she'd have been like that anyway. Either way, all Jodie could do was offer her the reassurance that everything would be okay.

She felt Devon squeeze her hand in return as if to say, *thanks for being there for me.*

Jodie smiled as they turned up the drive to the hall. Her only concern was how Devon would react when she met the woman her dad had fallen for. Jodie wondered who she was.

37

Cassie spotted the old banger coming up the drive before her phone rang. 'Hi, Devon. I'll come down and meet you.'

On the sofa, Evelyn was frowning and muttering, 'I dislike surprises.'

'I'm just nipping downstairs. I'll be back in two ticks.'

Evelyn gave her a grumpy frown in response.

Cassie caught that frown and thought you'll change your tune when you see what the young lady has brought with her. *Change your tune?* Cassie smiled as she made her way downstairs.

If nothing else, the wireless would look nice on her sideboard, and would undoubtedly be a talking point. Perhaps it would encourage Evelyn to open up and chat about herself and her past? Cassie would like that to be the case, but she doubted it. All the other residents loved a good natter. Not Evelyn. Even Tabitha couldn't charm her into giving anything away.

The other residents had another nickname for Evelyn, it was *Lady Enigma.* Cassie was well aware they found her aloof and hard to get on with; she kept herself to herself. Cassie was hoping the wireless would bring Lady Enigma out of her shell and even make friends with the other residents.

She was just walking towards the front door when she felt something brush her leg. She looked down. 'Hey, there.'

Tabitha meowed at her as if to say, *Hey, yourself.*

Cassie smiled. 'Have you come to see the radio that we found in the basement?'

Tabitha meowed.

'Wait here and I'll fetch it.' Cassie walked to the front door and saw Devon standing on the front step awkwardly balancing the radio in one hand as she waved to another teenage girl sitting in the driver's seat of an old banger.

Cassie quickly opened the door and relieved Devon of the radio, afraid all that time spent getting it working would be lost if it slipped out of her hands.

'Oh, thanks. I was just waving to my friend, Jodie.'

Cassie also waved. 'Doesn't she want to come in?'

'Nah. She will come back in an hour and pick me up. If I finish setting it up before then, I'll wait outside.'

'Oh, okay.' Cassie heard the car take off down the drive as she ushered Devon into the hall. She noticed Devon gazing up at the grand staircase and the high ceilings, taking it all in. 'This is amazing!'

'Isn't it,' Cassie agreed. 'You've never been here before?'

'My dad won't allow it.'

Cassie thought that was odd. 'Why?'

Devon shrugged. 'I don't know.'

'You won't get into trouble being here, will you?'

'Probably. I really don't care. Besides, he's not going to find out.'

Cassie wondered what he had against sheltered accommodation.

Devon thought of what Jodie had said on the way here. She gave Cassie a sideways glance wishing she'd change the subject. Devon wasn't going to tell Cassie that her dad was the architect involved in drawing up the plans to turn this place into a gated community of luxury homes. From what she'd gleaned, and the conversations she'd overheard when he was on the phone, his work was almost complete. That's why she was confident he wouldn't make another visit and she'd run into him here. He'd leave it to somebody else to tell the residents and staff that the closure was imminent.

Devon paused in the middle of the hallway. She was still looking up at the grand staircase and the intricate coving. She sighed. Devon recalled the plans sitting on his drawing board. It was such a shame this beautiful old building would be demolished to make way for a luxury apartment block. Even the beautiful grounds she'd seen as they approached the house up the long driveway were being remodelled. He'd proposed large modern detached houses on the estate.

'Your father shouldn't tell you not to go somewhere without an explanation.'

Devon turned around and looked at Cassie. Although she agreed, she wished she hadn't mentioned it, afraid Cassie thought her visit here wasn't a good idea. 'Do you want me to go?'

'No way!' Cassie looked at the vintage radio. 'After all the work you've done restoring this, wouldn't you like to meet the person I'm giving it to?'

'Oh, yes.' Devon wanted to see the radio's new home.

Cassie had an idea. 'Perhaps you'd like to stay for a bit. I'll make some tea or squash. I'm sure I'll come up with a slice of cake, oh and the payment of course.' Once she had taken the wireless up to Evelyn, while Devon set it up and tuned it in, she'd have to disappear for a bit back to the cottage to find her cheque book.

Devon smiled at the Canadian lady. She was nice. She had kind eyes and the most beautiful mane of red hair she'd ever seen.

Cassie glanced toward the stairs and spotted Tabitha sitting on the bottom step. She'd forgotten all about the cat.

'Devon, while you're here I'd like to introduce you to Tabitha.'

'Who's Tabitha?'

'The newest member of staff.'

Devon frowned. 'I thought they wouldn't hire any more people because this place is closing soon.'

'Oh, you know about that?'

Devon nervously chewed her bottom lip. 'Everyone in the village does.' The last thing she wanted was to spoil the moment by mentioning her dad.

Cassie turned to the stairs. 'Tabitha is a little… different. She's one of a kind.'

'Huh?'

'Why don't you come and meet her? She's on her break from doing her rounds.'

'Is she a nurse?'

'No. I think of her as a therapist, like me.'

'Oh okay, like occupational therapy?'

'Not exactly.' Cassie pointed. 'There she is.'

Devon turned around. 'I don't see anyone.'

Cassie smiled. 'Look closer, on the bottom step, she's looking right at you.'

There on the bottom stair was a majestic-looking tabby cat. She meowed at Devon.

Devon turned to Cassie. 'Tabitha is a cat?'

'She's not just any cat. She's a therapy cat. At least she is now. Tabitha is helping me create memory books for the residents.'

Phyllis walked through the hallway on her way to the kitchen for her morning break. She spotted Devon and overheard the conversation. 'Indeed,' said Phyllis, pausing and looking fondly at the cat. She said to Devon, 'Ah, you're the clever young lady who repaired the radio Cassie found in the basement.'

Devon nodded.

Tabitha stood up and pounced off the bottom stair. She strolled over to Devon and did a circuit around her legs.

'Oh, you're *so* cute,' said Devon, watching her. She knelt, stroking Tabitha's gorgeous coat. 'Can I pick her up?'

'Be careful,' said Phyllis as Devon scooped her up. 'Watch yourself.'

'Why – does she scratch?'

'On the contrary, she's the most loving cat I've ever encountered. But she's a wily one. She has ways of making you talk!'

Cassie nodded, exchanging a knowing smile with Phyllis. The memory books were coming along brilliantly, thanks to Tabitha. The only person Tabitha still hadn't worked her charms on was Evelyn.

Devon looked at the most docile cat she'd ever met. She was quite happy in her arms, paws up in the air, a cute bundle of fur. Devon glanced at Phyllis. 'What do you mean *she has ways of making you talk*?'

Tabitha purred.

'There, you see, she's already worming her way into your affections.' Phyllis shook her head. 'Before long you'll be telling her your secrets.'

'I don't have any secrets.'

'I'm sure you do.'

'Why do you say that?' Devon answered back defensively.

'Because, my dear, everyone does.'

Devon blushed. She was thinking of her dad and his plans for the hall.

Phyllis turned to Cassie. 'It's lovely to see an old valve radio. My parents used to have one. I remember sitting around listening to it with my siblings when we were little. I'd love to hear one again. There's nothing quite like the sound of an old wireless.' She looked at Devon. 'I'll pop along to Evelyn's apartment soon. I'll rustle up some tea and cake, and we can all sit and listen to it.'

Cassie's face dropped. She wasn't sure how Evelyn would feel about people trooping into her flat to listen to the radio. On the other hand, perhaps it wasn't a bad idea to get Evelyn away from that window, sitting alone all day waiting for someone who would never come. Maybe Bertie and Iris could pop along one day, or even Ruby. Cassie bet she would love a change of scenery.

Phyllis headed off to the kitchen.

Devon was reluctant to put the cat down. She was so cute. 'Can I bring Tabitha with us?'

Cassie hesitated. Almost all the residents and staff alike had welcomed Tabitha, and word had soon spread of the new therapy cat. Still, there was one resident who didn't want the cat anywhere near her. Cassie said, 'We'll give it a go. You must put her down though. She's got a mind of her own. Let's see if Tabitha will follow.'

They walked up the stairs and along the hall. Devon glanced over her shoulder, pleased to find Tabitha in hot pursuit. This looked promising until they got to her door. 'Come on,' said Devon, when she spied the cat hanging back. 'I'm sure there's nothing to be afraid of.'

Cassie pursed her lips. Devon hadn't met Evelyn yet. She recalled the last time she tried to bring Tabitha with her. Evelyn had point-blank refused to speak to Cassie until the cat was out of her sight. 'I don't need therapy and I've got absolutely nothing to say to your cat, thank *you* very much.'

Tabitha clearly remembered that episode too. Cassie watched her jump on to the window seat across the hall and sit down.

'Come on, Tabitha,' said Cassie, 'let's give it another go, eh? She's not as bad as all that.'

It was a rather large book that Evelyn had hurtled across the room at Tabitha. *War and Peace* – if she remembered rightly. Cassie thought she better tell Devon what happened.

Devon stared at the door, wondering what she was about to meet. She walked over to Tabitha, scooping her up in her arms.

'What are you doing?'

Devon turned around, holding the purring cat. 'She will hardly throw a book at Tabitha if she's in my arms.'

Cassie wasn't so sure.

'Besides, she looks so harmless and sweet.'

Cradled like a baby, Devon held her up to her cheek and gave her a kiss. 'You are so cute. I'd love to show you to my dad. I've always wanted a pet.' She'd mentioned her dad before she realised what she was saying. Phyllis was right: she had ways of making you talk. Devon frowned at the cat, suddenly afraid Cassie might ask questions like what he did for a living.

Cassie turned to the door and took a deep breath. The wireless was heavy. Her arms ached. 'Let's do this.' She stepped into Evelyn's apartment, carrying the radio, closely followed by Devon holding the cat.

38

Evelyn was sitting in her chair looking out the window when Cassie walked in saying, 'It's only me,' hoping Evelyn didn't turn around.

Devon followed her in, still holding the cat in her arms. She realised Cassie was looking for somewhere to put the radio. 'Where's a plug?' commented Devon.

Evelyn turned in her chair. 'Who are you?'

Devon looked at the old lady sitting in an armchair by the window. She hadn't noticed her when she first walked into the room.

Cassie sighed. So much for a surprise. 'Evelyn, this is Devon, the clever young lady who repaired your radio.'

'*My* radio?'

Cassie smiled. 'Strictly speaking it's not your radio, but I thought you might like it.'

'What on earth for?'

Cassie hesitated. This wasn't going to plan, but then with Evelyn, nothing ever did. She should know that by now. She assumed Evelyn would be blown away by an unexpected gift, especially such a beautiful old wireless.

Evelyn was still staring at her, waiting for an explanation.

'You know we've been reading Rosie's story. It turns out I may have found her radio.'

'What are you talking about?'

'It was in the basement among some old boxes. Actually, it was Tabitha who found it.'

'Who?'

'Tabitha,' said Devon, holding up the cute cat.

Evelyn wriggled her nose in disdain. 'Just keep it away from—' She was about to say *me* when Devon ran over and held it in front of her face.

Evelyn reached out and moved Devon's outstretched arms. 'There is nothing wrong with my eyesight, young lady.'

'Oh.' Devon stepped back, still holding the cat. 'I thought old people had poor eyesight. My grandad keeps saying his eyesight isn't what it once was and you look a lot older than Gramps.'

Cassie resisted the urge to smile. She bet no one had ever talked to Evelyn like that before. Everybody spent so much time tiptoeing around the formidable Evelyn that it was quite amusing listening to Devon bringing her down a notch or two.

'My eyesight is perfectly fine, thank you,' said Evelyn as she put on her glasses to inspect the teenage girl with the big mouth. She was pretty in a delicate kind of way, with long black hair, dark eyes and very petite. Evelyn didn't much care for that streak of purple in her hair. Perhaps if she was wearing a dress instead of jeans and a tee-shirt, she might be quite pretty. Evelyn resisted the urge to smile. The outspoken teenage girl standing before her reminded Evelyn of someone she once knew – her younger self.

Cassie's arms were growing tired of holding the radio. 'So, now everyone's been introduced I still need to figure out where to put this.' She looked across at Evelyn fully expecting to be told, like her memory book idea and the cat, to take it away.

Evelyn waved her hand. 'Bring it here. I want to take a closer look.'

Cassie staggered over before she changed her mind.

Evelyn looked at it for a long moment.

'It's quite something, isn't it?' said Devon, still holding Tabitha in her arms.

Evelyn reached out her hand and ran trembling fingers along the smooth surface.

'You know what? I've got to put this down before I drop it.'

'Over there,' Evelyn motioned at the oak sideboard next to the piano on the far side of the room.

Cassie carefully placed the radio on top of the sideboard. There was a lamp on the sideboard and a plug on the wall. It was a double socket. She positioned the radio next to the lamp and picked up the lead. She looked over at Devon. 'Is it all right if I plug it in?'

'Sure, go ahead. I'll come over and tune it in.'

Devon turned around and dumped Tabitha on Evelyn's lap.

'Oh!' exclaimed Evelyn, looking down at the cat.

Tabitha stood on her lap, stock still as if unsure what to do next, then squatted down and curled herself into a little ball.

Devon glanced over her shoulder. 'Why don't you give her a stroke? She'll purr for you.'

Cassie plugged in the radio. She looked over at Evelyn and thought what a good idea, why didn't I just plonk Tabitha on her lap?

Evelyn lifted a tentative hand and started by patting the cat on the head. She ran her hand along Tabitha's smooth coat. Evelyn tried to resist a smile when the cat purred.

Cassie glanced over at Evelyn. 'Are you all right if I nip out to get my cheque book?'

'Of course, why wouldn't I be?'

Cassie left Evelyn sitting with Tabitha on her lap and Devon tuning in the radio. Devon had already told Cassie it sounded amazing. Growing up with a bog-standard wireless her father owned, and a digital radio she bought herself, Cassie didn't know what the fuss was all about. Cassie kept that thought to herself. She only wanted it repaired to give to Evelyn because she was convinced it had belonged to Rosie.

She threw Evelyn a backward glance before leaving the lounge, surprised she hadn't given the two of them their marching orders. Cassie left the door to the apartment wide open. It wouldn't take her long to return to the cottage and grab her cheque book.

A short time later, as Cassie approached the house, she heard a strange noise. Was that music? Cassie stepped into the entrance hallway. She stopped to listen. Down one of the ground-floor corridors, Bertie and Iris opened their doors. 'What's that sound?' they said in unison.

Phyllis and Olivia appeared at the top of the stairs. So did Randall. Phyllis said, 'She's got it working! Goodness, that takes me back.'

Although Cassie couldn't name the song if her life depended on it, she recognised post-war music. It sounded like jazz.

Randall looked at Phyllis. 'Where's it coming from?'

By the time Cassie arrived at Evelyn's apartment, she had

practically brought the entire household with her, apart from Ruby in the other wing with her carers. She bet Evelyn would not be happy to see them all. Although it crossed her mind that for someone who sat by a window all day, without a single visitor, wouldn't it be a lovely surprise to get nine all in one go, including herself, Devon and Tabitha of course.

As Phyllis, Randall, Olivia, Bertie and Iris stepped inside her apartment, there were gasps of delight at the sound coming from the valve radio.

'It isn't too loud – is it?' Devon was shouting above the music to Evelyn. 'You old people are hard of hearing, aren't you?'

Cassie walked in and smiled. 'I think you can turn it down a bit.'

Devon turned the music down as everyone gathered around the wireless. Iris and Bertie gingerly took a seat on Evelyn's sofa, looking warily at Her Ladyship seated opposite them.

Evelyn's eyes were closed, but she wasn't asleep; her head was bobbing up and down to the music. She hadn't even noticed everybody trooping into her lounge.

Cassie walked over and put an arm around Devon's shoulders, giving her a hug. 'I think you've just made everyone's day.'

Jill had made a detour to the kitchen at Phyllis' suggestion and walked in with a tea tray. There was a large pot of tea for a cuppa and a slice of cake all round.

Bertie couldn't resist breaking into song.

Evelyn's eyes shot open. She looked around her room in surprise. 'Oh, I didn't realise I had company.'

Cassie sidled over. 'Everybody wanted to see your radio. I hope you don't mind.'

Evelyn took the cup of tea Jill offered. 'Why would I mind?'

Cassie was taken aback. Did she just say, *why would I mind?* She rarely had a good word to say about anything or anyone, especially the staff and other residents.

Bertie singing was catching. Once everyone had finished their afternoon tea, there followed a spontaneous sing-along to songs they recognised and some they didn't.

Cassie looked around the room full of people enjoying the music from another era, the forties she guessed. She glanced at the piano. She could almost imagine Rosie sitting here with her parents and brothers listening to the radio or gathered around the piano, entertaining themselves with a tune and a song.

The music was interrupted by the one o'clock news. That was everyone's cue to leave.

Phyllis said, 'Gosh, that took me back.'

'Are you talking about when you were a child?' asked Devon.

'No, I was thinking about when we used to have more residents before the owner decided to sell and the plan was for this place to close. There were tea parties on the lawn and trips out, and lots of different activities for the residents. It's such a shame. We had a lovely community here not that long ago. Then everything changed.

Devon eyed her.

'We don't who owns the building and grounds,' continued Phyllis, 'but once they decided to sell, there were lots of interested parties. Unfortunately, developers could see the potential.' Phyllis sighed. 'I imagine all these interested parties had to do was find an architect to submit plans to the local council that would be approved for developing the site. Then a developer would buy the entire place, lock, stock and barrel.'

Devon stood there in silence staring at Phyllis. It was the first time she'd really thought about what it meant for the residents and staff to leave. She just thought they were a bunch of old people and couldn't put herself in their shoes. Now she'd visited the hall and met them, Devon felt differently.

Phyllis noticed Jill gathering up the empty cups and plates. 'Ah, let me give you a hand, Jill.' She glanced at Devon as she picked up a plate. 'You've made everyone's afternoon, young lady. Especially mine. You are most welcome to visit us again.'

Phyllis lowered her voice. 'Although I'm not sure Evelyn will always welcome the intrusion.' She looked over at Her Ladyship. Was that Tabitha sitting on her lap? Wonders would never cease, thought Phyllis.

Bertie and Iris were helped out of their seats by Cassie, reminding them the correct way to rise from their chair.

'Can we come again to listen to your radio?' they asked Evelyn.

Evelyn considered it for a moment. 'Yes, why not.'

'See, she's not so bad,' Bertie said as he walked out of her apartment.

When everyone was gone, Cassie turned to Devon and gave her the cheque she'd written out while she was drinking her tea.

Devon looked at it and frowned. 'There's been some mistake.'

'Oh, do you need more money?' Evelyn asked, reaching for her purse in the handbag by her chair.

'No,' said Devon. 'That's not it. This is more than we agreed.'

'I know. But you delivered it and spent time tuning the radio.' Cassie smiled. It wasn't just that. Devon had provided everyone in the house with an opportunity to get together and have a grand time. It was worth every penny.

'Thanks,' said Devon, pocketing the cheque.

Cassie glanced at her watch and turned to Evelyn. 'Unfortunately, we've run out of time.'

Evelyn's face dropped.

'We can finish reading the diary tomorrow.'

Evelyn's eyes shifted to Devon. 'Would you like to stay and read to me?'

Cassie started shaking her head. She couldn't imagine Devon would want to sit and read to Evelyn.

Devon looked at her watch. 'Okay. I've still got some time to kill before Jodie picks me up. It beats hanging around outside.'

Cassie walked over and picked up the diary. She handed it to Devon and gave her a quick rundown on who Rosie was and what she'd read so far. She flicked through the pages. 'Here, this is where we were up to.'

Devon took the notebook and sat down on the sofa opposite Evelyn.

Tabitha, who had somehow slept through the music and all the commotion in a room full of visitors, woke up, stretched and jumped off Evelyn's lap. She appeared on the arm of Devon's chair and peered at the diary, sniffing along the edge of the book until she almost lost her balance.

'Tabitha! Stop being so nosy!' Devon picked the cat up and put her on the floor. 'Okay, here goes….' Devon started to read.

Cassie walked over to the door and glanced back at Devon. Her attention shifted to Evelyn sitting there, eyes closed, listening to Rosie's story. Tabitha was back on Evelyn's lap, purring loudly. Cassie shook her head in amazement. If it wasn't for the feral litter she'd discovered in the cellar and one little cat in particular, she'd never have found the diary or the radio. She whispered, 'Thank you, Tabitha,' before closing the door.

39

Devon felt as though she'd just got into the story when she turned the page to discover it was all over. The next page was blank along with the rest of the diary. It made little sense. It wasn't as though Rosie had run out of space to write in the notebook. Devon frowned. The worst part was things were getting interesting. The Canadian Rosie was in love with had been sent abroad with his regiment. Her parents left Gatekeepers Cottage and Sussex to stay with relatives in Scotland. They intended to return when the Canadians had left and the war was over.

Devon stared at the blank page; there were so many unanswered questions; did they leave Sussex for Scotland and then return when the war was over? Whether the Canadian, Scott, returned to the hall as he promised was also a mystery. Or was it?

Devon closed the notebook and eyed Evelyn. 'So, what happened next?'

Evelyn had been sitting there staring out the window. She turned toward Devon. 'Why are you asking me?'

Devon shifted her gaze to the framed photographs on the piano. She returned her attention to the diary and took out the old black-and-white photo that she'd discovered loose in one of the pages. She'd been flicking through the pages earlier when Evelyn had gone to spend a penny.

'The girl in this photograph who is standing with the two young men in uniform, her brothers, along with her parents and little Ted outside the entrance to the hall…' Devon held up the photo to be sure Evelyn could see. 'That's the girl who wrote this diary – right?'

Evelyn nodded.

She pointed at the girl in the photograph. 'That's *you*.'

Evelyn sat up with a start. 'I don't know what you mean.'

Devon leaned forward in her chair. 'I think you do.' Devon's gaze returned to the piano. 'I saw the framed photos while I was tuning the radio.'

'You've been looking at my photographs?'

'If you didn't want anybody to see them, you shouldn't have left them out on display for all to see, now should you.'

A rare wisp of a smile graced Evelyn's lips. 'That's very true.'

'I saw the other photos on your piano of Rosie, some on her own, others with her family. It's you. You're Rosie. Your family lived here, owned this house. *You* wrote this diary.'

Evelyn turned to look out the window. All that time Cassie had been reading the notebook, she never guessed the truth. It had taken a curious teenager five minutes to figure it out.

'After you left MI8, did you continue working for the Government like a spy or something?' Devon, nearly sixteen herself, couldn't imagine signing the Official Secrets Act. She had no idea there were thousands of teenagers, up and down the country, working covertly for the British Government during the Second World War. Some deciphered codes before they even reached Bletchley Park. It was all so mysterious and exciting, and quite incredible to think most people would never have heard of this secret army of teenagers.

She had so many questions. Did her parents leave the hall for Scotland? Did she return after the war? What happened to the Canadian guy she fell in love with? But the first thing she wanted to know was, 'Why were you known as Rosie when your name is Evelyn?'

Devon was interrupted by her phone. She slipped it out of her pocket. 'Oh bother, Jodie's arrived already.'

Evelyn turned from the window. 'Are you leaving?'

Devon was already on her feet. 'I'm afraid so.'

'If you come back and visit me again, I'll tell you more of my story. Do we have a deal?'

Devon cast a gaze around Evelyn's apartment and nodded enthusiastically. 'I've always wanted to visit here.'

'Then why haven't you?'

'My dad won't allow it.'

Evelyn sighed. 'Sometimes, we have to follow our hearts, no matter what other people think.'

Devon looked at Evelyn and thought of Jodie's brother. She liked him – a lot. She caught him looking her way every time she was over Jodie's house. On the last visit, he was about to say something when Jodie yanked her in the bedroom and slammed the door in her brother's face. Devon realised what that was about; her best friend didn't want her brother coming between them. But he already had. It was the reason Devon insisted on going to her house every opportunity she got, hoping that her cute brother would ask her out. Perhaps I'll do the asking next time I see him, thought Devon.

'Is there a particular reason you wanted to visit the hall?'

Devon nodded. 'When I was little my granddad used to tell me stories about my great-granddad who used to work at Fletchling Hall.'

Evelyn looked at her. 'Your great-grandfather worked here? What was his name?'

'Arthur. I believe he was the family's chauffeur or something like that.'

'You are Arthur's great-granddaughter?'

'You knew him?'

'He was our driver. Arthur took that photo of me and my family outside the hall.' Evelyn slowly rose from her chair and walked over to the piano. She stood there a moment looking at the photos and reached over to pick one up. 'Come here, child.'

Devon walked over and joined her by the piano.

'This is a photo of the staff here at the hall just before the war broke out.' She pointed. 'That's your great-grandfather, Arthur.' Evelyn handed her the framed photo.

Devon stared at the photograph of the rather stern-looking young man with a moustache. 'He looks very serious.'

'I think everyone knew this would be the last time they would all be together. Everything was about to change. The men were going away to war. We had to let the staff go when the Canadians arrived.'

Devon nodded. 'Gramps told me great-granddad didn't go to war because he had TB as a child. He also told me about Arthur's life at the hall before the Canadians came. Gramps said he loved the family he worked for and the hall was his home.'

'I'm so sorry my father had to let him go. They couldn't afford to keep any staff.'

Devon nodded. 'It wasn't your family he blamed. Gramps said he hated the Canadians for taking it all away from him.' Devon just realised something. 'I think that's why Gramps doesn't like Canadians either because of what happened to his dad.'

'Oh, Devon, you can't blame the Canadians. They were just doing as they were told, like the rest of us. It was the war.'

'I know. I like Canadians. Well, I've only met one, and I like her. That's why I fixed up the radio myself. I didn't want to give the radio to Gramps. If he'd found out it was for a Canadian, he might have refused to repair it.'

Evelyn looked at the radio impressed that Devon had fixed it herself. 'Well, I'm glad you didn't tell him.'

'This was your brother's radio, wasn't it?'

Evelyn smiled and nodded. 'I suppose I have Tabitha to thank for finding the radio in the basement.'

Tabitha jumped up on the sideboard and meowed.

Devon walked over and stroked the cat. She looked at the radio. 'I have one question before I leave.'

Evelyn was about to say she wasn't telling her anything more until they met again.

'It's about the radio. There's a switch at the back. Neither me nor my grandfather could figure out what it was for.'

'Ah.' Evelyn joined Devon by the sideboard. 'This is a very fine radio, but it hides a secret.'

'It does?'

'Oh, yes. If you flick that switch…'

There was classical music playing on the radio. Devon had left it on in the background. Devon flicked the switch at the back. She heard static – and something else. She listened.

Devon turned to Evelyn. 'What is that?'

Evelyn rubbed her fingers together and reached for the knob. She turned it carefully. There was a crackle, then a voice, and another voice. They were listening in on someone's conversation. Evelyn grinned. 'Welcome to ham radio.'

'What's *ham* radio?'

'It's how it all began – amateur radio. It may look like an ordinary wireless, but it's also a receiver.'

'This was the actual radio you intercepted messages in the war?'

Evelyn smiled. 'It is.'

'Will you teach me Morse code?'

'As long as you come and visit me, I'll do whatever you want.'

Devon looked at the diary in her hand. She also had another idea. 'I'll keep you to that,' said Devon before she walked out of Evelyn's apartment.

40

Devon closed the door to Evelyn's apartment. Over the last month, she'd visited Evelyn as often as she could, sometimes taking the bus and walking up the drive, other times Jodie dropped her off in the car for an hour while she ran some errands for her mum in the village.

Each time she came to visit, she had to lie to her dad and Gramps about where she was going. It was stupid. She didn't know what the big deal was about coming here. Jodie kept trying to persuade her to ask her dad what the problem was, but Devon was afraid he'd ground her if he found out what she'd been up to. Although she did agree with Jodie; what was the harm visiting the hall?

Devon felt something brush her leg. 'Hey, I thought you were staying with Evelyn? That's what you normally do when I leave.'

Tabitha meowed.

'Yes I know you need to do your rounds and catch up with the other residents, but Evelyn is kind of special – don't you think?'

Once again, Tabitha meowed.

'Good, I'm glad we agree.' Devon looked up and down the long corridor. She returned her attention to the little cat sitting by her feet. 'Have you seen Cassie?'

It seemed that every time she had visited over the last fortnight, Cassie was either busy with another patient or she was out. Olivia, the physio, remarked that she reckoned Cassie had a boyfriend. Apparently, some secret admirer had bought her a bike so she could cycle into the village. They thought she was meeting someone for lunch every day.

Devon was disappointed she kept missing her. She looked at the cat. 'I wanted to tell her something. Do you know where she is?' She wondered what Jodie would say if she saw her talking to a cat. She did feel a bit silly.

Tabitha meowed, stood up, and walked down the hallway.

'Was it something I said?' Devon joked until something occurred to her. 'Am I supposed to follow you – is that it?'

Tabitha paused and turned around. She meowed at Devon.

'I swear it's as though you understand every word.' She followed the cat along the corridor and down the grand staircase.

Tabitha paused in the hall as though she was waiting for her to catch up.

'I'm coming.' Devon stepped off the bottom stair and followed Tabitha across the hall and down another long corridor. She slowed, unsure whether she should be venturing to another part of the house. Was she even allowed just to wander around?

The cat seemed to sense her hesitating. Tabitha turned around and ran up to Devon, circling her legs. Devon knelt down and stroked her. 'You are taking me to Cassie, aren't you?'

Tabitha meowed in her face.

Devon laughed. 'Okay, I think I've got the message. Let's go.'

She followed the cat down several corridors into a different wing of the house. There were large sash windows that looked out on to inner courtyard. 'That's a lovely little garden.'

Devon was so busy looking around her, taking in her surroundings, that she walked right past Tabitha. It was only when she heard the cat meowing that she realised. Devon turned around and spotted her walking through an open doorway. 'Okay, I guess this is it.'

Devon walked through the open door into an apartment similar to Evelyn's except this seemed much grander. Down a short hallway, she arrived at a door where Tabitha was sitting. 'There you are.' She picked Tabitha up in her arms and guessed this was the door to the lounge.

She was going to knock, but that seemed pointless. If Cassie didn't want someone to walk right in, she wouldn't have left the door to her apartment wide open. Devon thought that Cassie's job couldn't be half bad if an apartment like this came with it.

She opened the door. 'Hi Cassie—' Devon stopped short when she realised Cassie wasn't alone. 'Oh, sorry I didn't realise you had company.' Devon was kicking herself. Cassie was with a client, or patient, or whatever she called them in her line of work. This wasn't where Cassie lived in the hall. 'Sorry,' she said again. She felt like saying it was the cat's fault, but that would sound stupid and childish.

'It's all right, Devon, come in. Have you been to see Evelyn?'

'Yes.' Devon stepped into the room, still holding Tabitha. She stared at the disabled woman in the wheelchair. She looked younger than all the residents, much younger. 'I thought this was an old people's home. What's she doing here?' blurted Devon.

Cassie had thought the exact same thing when she was first

introduced to Ruby. 'She's one of my patients.' Cassie was aware she hadn't exactly answered Devon's question, but she didn't know either. 'Come closer, she likes to meet different people.'

Devon eyed her warily. 'What's wrong with her?'

The woman in the wheelchair seemed to be getting excited and trying to speak.

Devon backed away.

'Don't be afraid. She's just excited to see someone new. She had a brain injury.'

'You mean she used to be like you and me?'

Cassie nodded. 'You asked me once what an occupational therapist actually does. Years ago we may have sat and read books to people, introduced them to knitting, crocheted a pattern with them, done some basket-weaving. Perhaps we'd think up other activities like encouraging them to talk about themselves and create a memory book – that was an idea I thought up for the residents here.'

Devon had heard about that, Cassie visiting the residents and writing down their life stories for their descendants. She liked the idea a lot. She'd also heard about Cassie's attempts to encourage Evelyn to do the same. That's what she had wanted to speak to Cassie about for a while, but this was the first time she'd seen Cassie since her first visit here to deliver the radio.

Devon's mind had wandered while Cassie continued talking about her work. 'Unfortunately, it's very old school. I do that sort of thing with the other residents in my spare time. My job here is finding ways my patients can continue to live as independently as possible.' Cassie smiled at Devon. 'Why don't you say something to her?'

'I don't know what to say. We've got nothing in common.'

Devon kept staring at her long shiny blonde hair. She didn't know why, but she had the impulse to reach out and grab a handful and feel its silky, smooth texture running through her fingers.

'Ask her what her name is?'

Devon frowned. The lady couldn't stop moving her head. Her mouth was twisted in a hideous grin. She didn't look like she could speak. At Cassie's prompting, she asked her what her name was.

Using a mouthpiece to blow in, and one finger on the computer keyboard, the computer spoke her name, 'Ruby.

'That was my mother's name.'

Cassie smiled. 'There you see, you do have something in common after all.' Cassie was incredibly pleased with the bit of tech she'd thought of buying for Ruby. She'd found government funding available, and Randall had helped her to research and purchase it online. It was very new. The equipment had only been delivered the other day, but the look on Ruby's face when she realised she could communicate again was priceless.

When Cassie first met Ruby, and did her initial assessment after reading her medical notes, she realised why Ruby was not living at home. She needed twenty-four-hour care. Even if she had relatives, someone would need to cope with her needs and that wasn't always practical. This is where a home came in. But perhaps not quite like this one. Ruby was the only resident who would benefit the most from having to move from here when the hall closed. Ruby needed visitors and activities, stimulation and above all, friends.

The accident had robbed her of so much, but what she hadn't lost, Cassie soon realised, was her mental capacity. It was so sad that her physical disabilities profoundly inhibited Ruby communicating fully with those around her. She'd been shut away in this big old house. There was no doubt her apartment and surroundings were beautiful. However, what she needed were visitors, not just the staff here doing their jobs.

Evelyn was a prime example. Cassie had noticed the change in Her Ladyship since Devon started visiting her. It was remarkable, not just walking into a smiling Evelyn humming away to her valve radio, but the fact that a teenage girl would want to continue visiting a woman in her eighties. What could they possibly have in common? What did they talk about all afternoon? It stumped Cassie.

It must have something to do with the old valve radio. She smiled. She knew finding that wireless would be the start of good things; it had brought Devon and Evelyn together and the difference it had made for Evelyn's mood was incredible.

Ruby held out a finger and pointed at Devon.

Devon turned around and looked at Cassie.

'I think she wants to know your name.'

'Oh okay.' Devon turned around to face her. She spoke slowly. 'My name is Devon.'

The woman got even more excited this time, so excited she started tapping her computer so hard the keyboard became dislodged from her wheelchair and fell with a clatter to the floor.

Tabitha leapt out of Devon's arms and disappeared out the door.

Devon backed away. 'What is wrong with her?'

'I'm not sure. I'm sorry, Devon, but I think you better leave.' Cassie had never seen Ruby like this before. Was she having some sort of fit? 'Look, I will come and find you when I've seen to Ruby.' Cassie thought perhaps more than one visitor at a time was not such a great idea.

'I only wanted to ask you something.'

'Can't it wait?' asked Cassie, worried that if Ruby didn't calm down, she might topple out of her chair.

Devon stared at the woman. 'Do you need me to fetch somebody?'

'No, it's all right, Devon.' Cassie tried to remain calm, but she didn't know what the hell was going on. She got out her mobile phone while she was kneeling by Ruby's wheelchair and rang Phyllis's mobile number. 'Phyllis, it's Cassie. I'm with Ruby. I need medical assistance. You need to come quick.'

Cassie had no idea why she picked up the keyboard and slotted it back on Ruby's wheelchair, but as soon as she did, Ruby blew into the straw and frantically typed with one finger.

Cassie stared at Ruby and then slowly turned to the door. Devon had already left.

Out in the hall, Devon was standing there stock still listening to the tinny computer, coming from the apartment, saying her name over and over along with one other word – *daughter*. Her earliest childhood memory came to mind; running her fingers through something long, yellow and silky soft. Devon turned from the door and ran.

41

Cassie walked into Evelyn's apartment, smiling to herself.

Evelyn's sour mood soon wiped the smile off her face. 'What are you so happy about?' she spat.

Cassie was thinking about Ben. She'd spent another glorious weekend with him. She was aware he worked from home. Although she didn't mind getting a taxi or a bus over to his house and fitting around his schedule, he insisted on coming to pick her up. Cassie would have liked to see where he lived. In hindsight, it was probably for the best; he had yet to introduce her to his daughter.

The weather was no longer agreeable, so going for another picnic or using his motorbike, which the garage fixed, wasn't an option. That hadn't bothered Cassie. There were plenty of other things to do. She couldn't believe a month had gone by since their first proper date. It seemed like yesterday they went for a picnic; it had been the perfect day. They took a long walk in the open countryside, followed by a lunch comprising sandwiches, tea from a flask, and a slice of homemade cake Cassie baked herself in the cottage the evening before.

Why did every mundane thing like making a cheese sandwich

or baking a chocolate cake fill her with such joy? Cassie was in love – pure and simple. If anyone asked, she had to admit the last four weeks had been wonderful. Although they did nothing exciting or out of the ordinary, it was being together and revisiting old haunts that made their days special.

There were trips to the cinema and fish and chips on the beach on a trip to the Sussex coast. It was something they often did as teenagers, taking the bus to Camber Sands, a beautiful place with golden sand dunes. This time they went by car and spent time in Hastings; it was somewhere Cassie had always fancied seeing. After a stroll around the quaint sea-side town, on a whim they hit the amusement arcades on the seafront.

They got some curious looks from teenagers spotting a middle-aged couple having a whale of a time at the slot-machines. Cassie smiled when she thought about that weekend. There were other day trips where they browsed shops in a nearby town and sat in cafés just talking.

He still hadn't stayed the night at the cottage. Every time he dropped her home after another lovely day out, he'd kissed her goodnight and left, respecting her wish to take things slow. Then it happened. She blamed it on a place called Rye. With its steep, winding streets, and olde-worlde charm, Ben knew she would love the Sussex town. They strolled around the cobbled streets and narrow alleyways before having an evening meal together.

Ben had booked a table at the Mermaid Inn, one of England's oldest pubs, located in Mermaid Street, the most picturesque street in Rye. They dined until late. Then it started to hail. The publican asked them if they had far to drive, letting them know there was a lovely suite available. It wasn't Ben's intention to stay the night – or hers. They'd looked at each other across the table. They knew what this meant. It was the end of taking things slow.

She remembered what he'd said to her the following morning. 'You realise what this means – don't you?' He'd smiled at her. 'I think it's time the two women I love most in the world met each other.'

Although Cassie wouldn't deny she was a bit apprehensive, meeting his daughter, she understood; this time he knew Cassie was here to stay.

Cassie sat down next to Evelyn and thought about the hall closing. If only she didn't have to worry about finding another job. She didn't want another position. Cassie was happy here. She looked at Evelyn's sour expression and thought *well, most of the time*. She felt like remarking, *who got out of the bed on the wrong side this morning?*

Evelyn said, 'Have you seen Devon?'

'No, but I saw her on Friday.' Although it had been playing on her mind, Cassie didn't want to talk about that episode when Devon met Ruby. 'Didn't you see her this morning?'

Evelyn shook her head. 'She didn't come. That's most unlike her.'

'Oh.' Cassie looked at her. Devon was only fifteen. It wasn't surprising she might have forgotten or had something else more important to do, like schoolwork or going out with her friends. What did Evelyn expect would happen? It surprised Cassie her visits had lasted this long. Cassie tried to be diplomatic. 'Maybe something came up. I believe she's sitting her GCSE's this year, perhaps she had some exams to revise for.' It was now November and Cassie remembered having mock exams to sit before Christmas when she was at school.

Evelyn seemed to consider it for a moment. She said, 'Still, it's most unlike her.'

Cassie sighed. She obviously wasn't getting through to Evelyn. 'I have her mobile phone number. Do you want me to text her and check she's all right?' Cassie meant to do that, anyway. What if Devon overheard what Ruby said? Cassie didn't see how that could be the case because Devon had left. Even so, it was playing on her mind.

Evelyn watched Cassie get out her phone. 'I can do one better than that.' She reached for her handbag.

Cassie looked up as Evelyn handed her a piece of paper. 'What's this?'

'It's Devon's home address.'

Cassie threw her a questioning look.

Evelyn shrugged. 'I asked her for the address. It's her birthday soon and I wanted to send her a card.'

Cassie sent a text. There was no reply. She looked at the address. 'I know where Devon lives. I took the radio there to be repaired.' Cassie handed back the piece of paper. 'I'm on my shift, Evelyn. I can't just go out—'

'Why not?'

'I'm at work. I'm meant to be spending my time with you.'

Evelyn folded her arms and threw Cassie an indignant look. 'I can't sit here and wait to find out if this is it, she's not coming back. I need to know.'

Cassie stared at her pained expression.

'Please,' Evelyn said, taking Cassie by surprise. She never, ever said please.

Cassie tried calling Devon. She felt awkward just turning up out of the blue but, like Evelyn, she was worried about her. After several unsuccessful calls to her mobile, Cassie gave up trying to get hold of Devon and phoned for a taxi. It wasn't Evelyn that persuaded her to go. She had a few questions of her own that she would rather not put to Devon over the phone.

She climbed in the taxi and gave the driver the address of The Radio Shack. Last time she'd gone there, Randall gave her a lift in the vintage car. She wouldn't want to drive the car herself. Although it wasn't that far to the next village, she didn't want to waste the afternoon waiting around for public transport either.

Randall had somehow found out she was bunking off her shift. Cassie told Phyllis she was running an errand for Evelyn, which in a way was true. Randall got wind of it and offered her a lift in the car again. She could have cancelled the taxi. It wouldn't cost her a dime to catch a lift with Randall, but this time Cassie declined.

Cassie leaned back in her seat, staring at the lovely grounds of Fletching Hall as they sped down the drive. It was drizzling and cold, typical November weather. It didn't bother Cassie. She wound the window down a fraction and could smell the damp grass and feel the fresh breeze in her hair. The reason she refused Randall's offer this time had nothing to do with the thought he might come on to her or invite her out for coffee again; that would not happen now word spread that she was seeing someone.

It was what Randall said about the guy who called at the hall to collect her when she had the afternoon off the other day. He'd spotted Ben arriving. That didn't bother Cassie until Randall said something that took her by surprise.

'We were all a bit shocked, to be honest, when we found out you are going out with the guy who's responsible for turfing the residents out of their home and us out of a job.'

Cassie asked him what he was talking about.

'He's the guy, the architect, the one drawing up plans to turn this place into a housing development. Rumour has it the plans may involve knocking down the hall.'

Cassie told him, in no uncertain terms, that he must be mistaken. Surely, Ben would have said something. She worked here. This was her job and her home. She didn't have anywhere else to go until the flat in London sold. If he was the one submitting the plans, he would have told her. Cassie was convinced Randall had got it wrong. She didn't fancy sitting in the car with the possibility Randall would bring that up again.

Fifteen minutes later, she arrived in the village. The taxi passed the bus stop where she recalled Ben pulled over, when he noticed her standing there, and persuaded her to meet him again in order to apologise for knocking her off the bike. Cassie smiled. If she hadn't agreed to meet him again, she wouldn't have experienced the most wonderful four weeks of her life getting to know the man she still loved.

The taxi pulled up on the driveway outside the house. She sighed in relief when she spotted no other cars on the drive, although she eyed the double garage. The last time she'd called here Devon was at home alone, so she didn't meet her family. She wouldn't mind meeting them, but Cassie wanted to speak to Devon in private first. She recalled Devon had mentioned she was not allowed to visit the hall. Cassie didn't want to get her into trouble.

Cassie paid her fare and asked the taxi to return in half an hour. She was taking a chance that Devon was home. Cassie knocked on the door. It was a modern front door painted grey with two panes of frosted glass inlaid in the wooden door. Cassie spotted a faint outline through the frosted glass. It was someone small, wearing all black. Cassie knew it was Devon.

'Cassie?' Devon stood in the doorway with a glass of milk in one hand. 'What are you doing here? Has the radio stopped working?'

'The radio is still working perfectly.' Cassie sighed in relief. Devon appeared to be okay, but by the looks of things she wasn't on her way out to visit Evelyn. 'It's Evelyn. She was worried because you didn't turn up this morning. She thought perhaps you might come later today instead.

Devon was already shaking her head no. 'My friend's car broke down. I didn't have time to go by bus because I've got a mountain of schoolwork piling up. Sorry.'

'It's all right. You don't have to apologise.' Cassie was not surprised. In fact, she was relieved. 'Sorry to turn up unannounced. Evelyn wanted me to pop round and see you. She looks forward to your visits. They've been regular as clockwork, so she thought something had happened.'

There was an awkward silence. Cassie said, 'Can I come in? There's something I want to talk to you about.'

Devon looked at her warily and glanced back in the house. She turned to Cassie and opened the door wide. 'Okay, but my dad is working. When he's in his study, he doesn't like to be disturbed. Can we talk in the kitchen?'

'Whatever suits you.' Cassie stepped inside the house and followed Devon along a corridor past a lounge, a snug and a dining room into the most amazing kitchen she had ever seen. 'Wow! This is—'

'Amazing.' Devon rolled her eyes. 'That's pretty much everyone's reaction. My dad designed it.'

'Your dad is talented.'

'So they say,' quipped Devon.

Cassie stared around the room. The kitchen itself was similar to any other you might view in a catalogue or on display in a shop, but it was the room that made the kitchen unique; it was painted white with a high sloping ceiling, skylights, and patio doors that ran the length of one wall and looked out over the garden. The white kitchen cabinets, white-washed walls, and matching leather sofas near the patio doors, gave the room a feeling of space and light.

Cassie walked over to the patio doors and gazed at the landscaped garden with a neat, almost clinical layout, all squares and angles, wooden decking and a perfectly manicured lawn. 'Wow.' The garden looked even better from downstairs than when she'd first seen it from Devon's window.

'It's fake.'

Cassie turned around.

'The lawn. It's Astro-turf.' Devon sat down on a kitchen stool and finished her glass of milk.

'Oh, yes, I remember.' Devon had mentioned that on her first visit. That still didn't detract from the beautiful garden. Cassie peered through the patio doors and glimpsed a roof-top peeking out above a reed screen. She turned around. 'Is that The Radio Shack?'

Devon nodded. 'Yep. That's where we fix radios.'

'Can I see it?'

Devon put the carton of milk back in the free-standing American style refrigerator. 'Now is not a good time. Gramps is working in there at the moment.'

'Can't I just have a peek inside, see where he repairs them?'

Devon chewed her bottom lip. 'I've really got a lot of coursework to do so…'

'Right.' She gleaned Devon didn't want to introduce her to her grandfather. Cassie turned around and eyed Devon. 'May I ask you a personal question?'

Devon shrugged.

'You said you live with your father and grandfather . . .' Cassie hesitated.

'You want to know what happened to my mum.'

'Look, if you would rather not talk about it.'

'It's fine. It was a long time ago when I was still little. My mum and dad were driving home one evening, after a night out, and some idiot came out of nowhere. Daddy swerved to avoid the other car and they ended up in a ditch. Mummy… died.'

'I am so sorry. Did you go to her funeral?'

'I was too young.'

'Do you remember the funeral?'

'No. I told you, I was too young.'

'Of course, of course.' Cassie stared at Devon. There was no mistaking what Ruby typed on the keyboard. She was saying Devon was her daughter. Cassie re-read her medical notes. Ruby had a child, but she had a different surname to Devon. Cassie wanted to learn if Devon's parents were married at the time of the accident, but it wasn't something she could just come right out and ask.

Cassie stared around the beautiful kitchen. Someone covered the expense of Ruby's rental apartment and held legal power of attorney. The information on her medical notes listed her brother as next-of-kin, but he was long gone, dying of cancer in his forties. So, who paid for Ruby was a mystery – or was it?

42

'Devon, have you got any photographs of your mother?'

'Of course I have. Why?'

'Can I see one?'

Devon frowned. She hadn't forgotten what she'd overheard outside Ruby's apartment. That wasn't her mother. Her mother was dead.

Cassie noticed her hesitate. She asked, 'How did you learn your mother died in the car accident?'

'What sort of question is that?'

'Because you were too young to remember, I presume that's what you've been told.'

Devon looked at her for a long moment. 'Wait here. I can prove it.'

Cassie walked over and sat down on one of the plush cream leather sofas. She stared at the grey slate tiled floor wondering how Devon would take it if she found out she had been lied to all these years. Cassie suddenly had a moment of self-doubt. This was none of her business. She hardly knew Devon. What was she doing here interfering in their lives?

Cassie was just rising from the sofa, intending to leave, when

Devon appeared in the kitchen. She walked straight up to Cassie. 'Here.'

Cassie took the small-framed photograph of a cherub-faced toddler standing in a room with a young woman kneeling next to her. They were cheek to cheek, smiling for the camera. 'There, you see. That woman, Ruby, isn't the same person.'

Cassie stared at the photo.

Devon nervously chewed her bottom lip. 'What is it?'

Cassie turned to her. 'Devon, what I'm about to say next will be a lot to take in.' Cassie took a deep breath and continued, 'There's a photo of Ruby on file before her accident and . . .' Cassie held up the photograph Devon had given her and pointed at her mother.

Devon shook her head. 'No, you're mistaken. My mum died. That's what my dad told me.'

Cassie went quiet. 'What about your grandfather?'

'What about him?'

'Did he say the same thing?'

'Not in so many words. He won't talk about it.'

'When Ruby got excited, and you left, she said something over and over. *Daughter*.'

Devon shook her head. 'No. It isn't true.' She backed away from Cassie. 'Why would my dad lie to me?'

'I have no idea, Devon.' Cassie gazed at the picture and thought of another explanation. Perhaps she had it all wrong. 'I guess Ruby might just be her doppelganger.'

'With the same name!' exclaimed Devon.

They looked at each other. They both realised it was too much of a coincidence. Cassie handed Devon the framed photo.

Devon stood there staring at the young woman with the long,

silky blonde hair. She looked up. 'You said she had an accident; she hasn't always been like that – right?'

Cassie nodded.

'So, when was that? How long has she been disabled?'

'Almost fourteen years, I believe.' Cassie glanced at the photo. 'How old were you when you lost your mother?'

'Two.'

They stood staring at one another. Cassie opened her handbag. Inside was a small passport-sized photo of Ruby, stapled to her medical notes. It was a picture of her before the accident. The woman in Devon's picture frame was a dead ringer. She had no business removing the photo from her notes. She wasn't sure why she did it. But she was glad she did. Cassie handed Devon the little print.

Devon held the small photo up to the picture in the frame. She didn't say anything as she stalked out of the kitchen with both images in her hand. Cassie was not surprised. She followed Devon down the hall, passing the lounge, snug and dining room again on the way to the front door.

Across the hall from the snug was another door. Devon stopped in front of it. Cassie guessed that was her father's study where he was busy working, oblivious to the drama about to unfold when Devon opened that door.

'I'd better go.' Cassie strode straight past Devon, feeling guilty for just walking out and leaving a shit storm in her wake, but there wasn't anything more she could do. This was between Devon and her father now, and her grandfather, who'd also been complicit in hiding the truth. She had to keep reminding herself it wasn't her fault Devon found out. Fate had brought the teenager back to the hall and the discovery that, contrary to what she'd been told, her mother was very much alive. Little wonder Devon wasn't allowed anywhere near the hall.

Cassie glanced at her watch. The taxi would turn up any minute to take her back.

As she reached the front door, she glanced over her shoulder and saw Devon walk into her father's study, slamming the door shut.

Cassie stepped outside and closed the door. She looked at her watch again. 'Come on,' Cassie said under her breath hoping the taxi was early. She turned around at the sound of raised voices coming from inside the house. Cassie was standing there chewing a fingernail, willing the taxi to get a move on, when she heard Devon shouting, 'I told you already, she's not here. She left.'

As Ben approached the front door, he muttered, 'Who does she think she is butting into our family business? I want her name because she will not have a job when I've finished.'

Cassie was about to walk down the drive, and meet the taxi coming along the road, when the front door flew open behind her.

'Just who do you think you are coming here and—?'

Cassie turned around at the sound of a familiar voice.

Ben stared at her. 'Cassie?'

They both took a step back in surprise.

'Ben?

'What are you doing here?' they both said in unison.

Devon must have overheard them. She shoved past her dad and said to Cassie, 'You know my dad?'

Cassie's mouth dropped open.

So did Ben's. He looked at Devon. 'You know Cassie?'

Cassie winced wondering what his reaction would be.

'Yes. She's the lady who came here with the old valve radio that I repaired.'

'What are you talking about?'

'That's how I started visiting the hall after I fixed the wireless and gave it to the old lady.'

Ben held up his hand. His expression said he was baffled. 'I'm sorry – what?'

Cassie thought it was about time she stepped in. 'It all started when I discovered an old valve radio in the basement of Fletchling Hall. I found The Radio Shack online and brought it here to be repaired.'

'What that's got to do with—'

'It's how Devon came to be at the hall. She's been visiting a lady called Evelyn whom I gave the wireless to.'

'Wait, you've been going to the hall when I expressly told you not to go near that place?'

'Yeah!' Devon shouted. 'And now I understand why! You didn't want me to find out about my mother!'

Ben turned on Cassie. 'What the hell, Cassie? This is my family. You had no right to interfere.'

Cassie looked at him in complete surprise. 'Are you seriously going to blame all this on me? What sort of father lies to their child like that?'

'This is none of your business,' he said coldly. 'Please leave my property.'

Cassie stared at him in astonishment.

'I don't want her to leave,' said Devon.

'What's going on?'

Devon and Ben turned around at the sound of Gramps right behind them.

'This is nothing to do with you, Dad. Butt out.'

'Don't talk to me like—' Gramps spotted Cassie. 'I knew it! When he went out on his motorbike, wearing that old leather jacket and writing songs again, it could only be you.'

Devon looked from Cassie to her dad and back again. 'Gramps, what are you talking about?'

Cassie stared at Devon. *Crap!* Things were getting ever more complicated. 'Look, I better go.'

Gramps stepped forward. 'Don't leave on my account.'

'Dad, I told you to butt out, you don't understand what—'

Devon suddenly yelled, 'Is she my mother!?'

Everyone stopped in their tracks and turned to Devon.

Gramps glanced at Ben. 'What is going on?'

Devon turned to her grandfather. 'Did you know?'

'Know what?'

'About Ruby.'

Gramps rubbed his forehead as though a headache was coming on and then turned to his son. 'How did she find out?'

Ben threw Cassie a cold, hard stare. 'She's been visiting the hall.'

And that answered Devon's question. She stared at her grandfather, open-mouthed. They'd *both* lied to her.

Gramps caught the expression on Devon's face and went very quiet.

Devon wasn't the only one staring at Gramps. Ben said, 'You knew, didn't you, where she'd been going?'

'She wanted to fix the radio herself and hand-deliver—'

'Didn't you try to stop her?'

'Of course I did, but you know Devon, she wanted an explanation, a good reason why she couldn't go.'

'Well, what did you say?'

Gramps looked at Devon. 'I told her it wasn't my place. Besides, I really didn't see the harm…'

'You didn't see the harm?' Ben was lifting off.

'How was I to know she'd find out the truth?'

'You stupid—'

'Don't blame it on me that you made a big mistake. You should have told her.'

Devon's head was swivelling from one to the other. Her eyes finally settled on her father. 'Why, Daddy? Why did you tell me she was dead?'

Ben and Gramps went quiet.

Devon turned to Cassie.

Cassie breathed a sigh. 'I'm sorry, sweetheart, it's got nothing to do with me.'

'Actually…' Gramps was about to say something when Ben shot him a warning look. 'Don't! I mean it!'

Cassie stared at them. What was Gramps going to say?

Ben turned to Cassie. 'You shouldn't have got involved. Please leave.'

Cassie looked at him. What did that mean? Was this it?

Ben shut the front door in her face. As he turned to his daughter, he caught Gramps shocked expression that he had just sent the love of his life packing with no explanation. Ben ignored him and spoke softly to his daughter. 'I never told you how it happened, Devon.'

'Yes, you did. You said an idiot swerved into your path.'

Ben shook his head. 'I was the idiot, Devon.' Ben glanced at Gramps as the three of them made their way down the hall towards the snug.

'I'll put the kettle on and make some tea,' said Gramps. He hesitated in the doorway, watching the two of them sit down on the sofa in the room that overlooked the garden. His son was right: he should have stopped Devon visiting the hall. But what did Ben expect him to say? She wasn't a child anymore. She deserved an explanation and he couldn't give her one, not one that made any sense.

There were many occasions, over the years, that he'd had the conversation with Ben about telling her, especially as she got older. This was what he was afraid of. He'd warned him about it no end of times. The truth will out. It always does.

Gramps turned from the doorway, wondering if Ben would be honest with Devon over the circumstances of that accident all those years ago.

Ben took her delicate hands in his. He couldn't look her in the eye as he told her what had happened. 'We were driving home from a night out. It was your mother's birthday. In hindsight, I realised she thought I was going to finally propose.'

Ben took a deep breath before he continued. There was no point telling her half-truths. If he was going down this rabbit hole, he had to tell her all of it. 'She was aware they'd been someone else in my life before we got together. It was during that night out it must have dawned on her that I would never propose because… because I was still in love with another woman.'

He added quickly, 'I wasn't having an affair. It wasn't like that. But it didn't change the fact that I was in love with someone else – and your mother knew it.'

Devon recalled her dad's reaction when he saw Cassie

'It's Cassie – isn't it?'

Gramps appeared in the doorway wearing an apron and carrying a tea tray. He caught the tail end of the conversation. He looked at Ben. So, he'd told her. Gramps answered Devon's question. 'Cassie and your father go back a long way. They were teenage sweethearts.'

'Not for long,' Ben muttered shooting his father a dirty look.

Gramps slunk into the room without comment as Ben fixed his attention on Devon. 'Your mother and I, we were rowing over it, over Cassie. I wasn't concentrating. I… I drifted across the road. There was an oncoming car.' Ben winced. 'I'm *so* sorry, Devon. I couldn't bear visiting her knowing it was my fault.'

Gramps said, 'I could have taken Devon.'

Ben frowned at him. 'You're really not helping. I didn't want her growing up with a disabled mother. It shouldn't have been that way.'

'But I grew up with *no* mother – don't you get that?' Devon stood up and stormed out of the room.

Ben looked at his father. He held up a hand. 'Don't say it.'

The look on his father's face said *she had a point.*

'I suggest you go after her,' said Gramps matter-of-factly, pouring himself a cup of tea.

Ben rose from the sofa and rushed out of the room just in time to catch Devon racing out the front door. 'Devon, where are you going?' Ben legged it outside.

At the bottom of the drive, Cassie was getting in a taxi.

'I'm going to visit my mum!' Devon shouted at him as she ran down to the taxi.

Ben ran after her. 'Devon – wait!'

He saw Devon having a brief conversation with Cassie before climbing in the waiting taxi. It sped off before Ben reached it. Cassie turned around and glanced out the back window of the car.

'Just great.' Ben turned to the house and stormed back up the drive. 'It's all her fault. She shouldn't have stuck her nose where it didn't belong.'

'Ben?'

He ignored Gramps standing at the front door and shoved past him into the house.

Gramps followed him down the hall. 'Don't do anything you'll regret.'

'Leave me alone.'

'It's not her fault, Ben.'

He stepped into his study and turned around. 'Since when did you take Cassie's side?' Ben slammed the door in his face.

Gramps stood behind the door and heard him on the phone. 'Is that Fletchling Hall? I want to speak to the person in charge.'

Gramps sighed. It wasn't Cassie he was thinking about, and he wasn't taking sides; it was his son he was concerned about and the fall-out if Ben lost Cassie. Could he go through that again? Could Gramps? He recalled the last time, years ago, and how messed up his son was in the aftermath.

He heard Ben on the phone and realised he was about to do something he would bitterly regret. He was stubborn like his mother – God rest her soul.

Gramps shook his head as he turned from the door. He had a feeling in the pit of his stomach that Ben was about to make things a lot worse for himself – and Cassie – and there wasn't a damn thing he could do about it.

43

'I knew Dad was seeing someone. I wished I'd known it was you.'

Cassie hardly heard a word she said. She sat in the back of the taxi on the return journey to the hall, the scenery a blur; she was preoccupied with thoughts of Ben. Cassie was so upset over the way he had treated her. How was she to know Devon was his daughter and he had lied to her all these years?

'I'm sorry.'

Cassie wiped the tears from her eyes before she turned to Devon. She shook her head, wondering why she was apologising. 'You've got nothing to be sorry for. I'm the one who has come between you and your dad.'

'No, it's not true. It's his fault. He should have told me.'

'I agree.'

They sat there in silence for a few minutes.

Devon said, 'I am sorry though. I always came between my dad and his girlfriends in the past, but that was on purpose. This time I've really messed things up.'

'No, Devon, it's your father who has messed up.'

She stole a glance at Cassie. 'Do you think you can patch things up with my dad? I like you, Cassie.'

Cassie smiled warmly at the teenager. 'And I like you, Devon.' As for whether Ben had any chance with the way he had spoken to her and been so quick to blame her – that was a whole other ball game. How could they come back from this? The tears welled up again.

She turned her head, pretending to look out the window while the tears streamed down her face. She remembered that first day out together when they returned from a trip to the public library and his bike had broken down. They were soaked through in a downpour. After drying off in the cottage, she recalled when he left; he had stood on the doorstep for a long moment staring at her. At the time, she sensed there was something more he wanted to say.

Now she realised what it was; he'd lied when he told her his partner had died in a car accident. Perhaps he was having second thoughts about not telling the truth. Ben was aware she worked at the hall, the very place where Ruby, the mother of his child lived. How did he think he could keep something like that a secret? If only he had told her the truth – and Devon.

'Cassie – are you all right?'

Cassie composed herself before she turned to speak to Devon. She had her father's eyes. 'You remind me of someone I used to know a long time ago.'

'Who?'

'Your father. He was quite a rebel.'

'My dad, a rebel?' Devon scoffed. 'No way!'

'Yes.' Cassie smiled as a memory resurfaced. She shared it with Devon. 'He always wore ripped jeans, even when they went out of fashion. And he went nowhere without his leather jacket. He used to ride a motorbike when he was a teenager.'

Devon rolled her eyes. She knew about the bike.

'I wouldn't be surprised if there were a lot of girls in his sixth form that would have liked to go out with the cool guy. But he chose me, a Canadian, a year older than him, on work experience.'

Cassie's smile faltered. She still couldn't believe he'd done it again, broken her heart over something that was, once again, nothing to do with her. She caught the expression on Devon's face. She wasn't the only one in shock over Ben's revelation.

'Are you all right, Devon?' It was a silly question. Of course she wasn't; she'd just found out, after all these years, her mother was alive, albeit profoundly disabled, but Cassie didn't know what else to say. It would take Devon some time to come to terms with.

'I hope Dad doesn't do something stupid.'

Cassie frowned. He already had by blaming her for what happened today. The truth was bound to come out, whether it was Cassie's chance meeting with Devon and putting two and two together or something else. Even so she caught the anxious expression on Devon's face. 'What do you mean?'

Devon dropped her eyes from Cassie's gaze. Her dad wasn't the type to let things go. She didn't know what he would do, but he'd do something. That's what worried her. Devon tried to put that thought out of her mind. Instead, she focused on what *she* intended to do. It beat dwelling on her stupid dad and the years she'd missed out with her mum she could never get back.

'Cassie, do you like working at the hall?'

Cassie brightened. 'Yes, I do.' In the brief time she'd been there, it felt like home. She didn't want to think about the day she'd have to leave.

'Would you stay if the hall remained open?'

Cassie's face clouded over. 'That's not an option. My contract is only temporary because the hall *will* close.'

'But if it didn't close, would you stay?'

'Yes, I would.'

That's all Devon wanted to hear. She liked Cassie – a lot. She didn't want her to go, and she didn't want her mother to leave either. Devon turned to look out the window with one thing on her mind: she would put a stop to the sale of the hall. It would only get the go-ahead if her dad submitted plans which passed council approval. If developers couldn't build on the land, then who would buy the property?

Devon smiled to herself. Ever since she was small, she had him wrapped around her little finger. Now she had a trump card. All he had to do was stop the sale then she might consider talking to him again. For now, she wasn't only intending to give him the silent treatment, but also stay with her best friend.

She got out her mobile phone to ring Jodie. She was confident her parents, the most easy-going likeable couple she'd ever met, wouldn't object. Neither would Jodie. Devon frowned. There was one problem; unlike Devon's house with plenty of room – and spare bedrooms – she would have to share a room with Jodie and her little sister or sleep on the couch in the living room. Neither prospect appealed to Devon. She needed some time alone to digest what had happened.

As she stared out the window, her eyes alighted on the little flint cottage as the taxi turned into the drive of Fletchling Hall. 'Does anyone live there?' Devon asked.

Cassie nodded. 'That's my place, Gatekeepers Cottage, for as long as I work at the hall.'

'Really? How many bedrooms are there?'

'Two – why do you ask?'

Devon fell silent.

Cassie looked at her and had an idea what she was thinking. 'If you are planning to run away from home, I really can't be a party to—'

'Oh, please, Cassie. It would only be for a night or two. That'll teach them!' Devon regretted adding that. She quickly backtracked. 'What I mean to say is, I need some space and time on my own to process all this. Gramp's and Dad will be on my case, asking me how I am.'

'Hmm.' Cassie could see her point. Even so, she was very reluctant to agree.

'How old are you, Devon?'

'Sixteen.'

Cassie cocked her head to one side. 'I realise there are rumours Evelyn has dementia, but her mind is as sharp as a pin.'

Devon agreed, but right now she didn't see what that had to do with anything.

'Evelyn told me it's your sixteenth birthday soon. She took your address so she could send you a card. Now I know for a fact you can't leave home until you're sixteen without your parents' permission.'

Devon thought c*rap!* She had another idea. 'But I'm not leaving home. I'm just staying with a friend for a few days.'

That was just splitting hairs, thought Cassie. 'That's very kind of you to call me a friend, Devon.'

'But you are and I'm not just saying that to get you to let me stay in the cottage.'

Cassie still wasn't relenting. If Ben thought she'd been

interfering in their lives telling his daughter about Ruby, what would happen if he found out she'd encouraged Devon to move out too? She wasn't encouraging Devon at all, but she imagined that's what he'd feel if she let her stay.

Devon grinned when she had another idea. 'I'll just have to stay with my mum for a few days then. Ruby *is* my mum. Nobody can say anything about that!'

Cassie could. She had a lot of things to say about that, all of which she kept to herself. Devon's mum needed twenty-four-hour care. She had a live-in carer during the night. Devon hadn't stopped to consider the complexity of her condition or what that meant for her personal needs.

She would come to know in time, but now was not the right moment for Devon to stay with Ruby and discover what her mother's day-to-day existence was like. It would certainly upset her when the euphoria of finding her mother alive was replaced with the stark reality of her condition. She imagined Devon would go through a period of mourning for the person her mother once was before a car accident robbed them both of a future that might have been.

It occurred to Cassie that it was something Ben must have been at pains to spare his daughter from. When Cassie found out who Ruby was, her first reaction was how cruel of Ben to shut Ruby away and hide her from their child. Now she had an inkling why he did it.

After the accident, she imagined it would have been touch and go whether Ruby survived, and if she did – for how long? Perhaps it was easier to spare his daughter the heartbreak of knowing her mother had survived only to lose her. However well-intentioned, in hindsight Cassie bet Ben deeply regretted not telling Devon the truth from the outset, even though she was so very young; as time marched on, and Ruby not only survived but flourished despite her physical handicaps, Ben had set himself up for a massive fall when it eventually came out.

It upset Cassie that Ben blamed her. Although it wasn't her place to get involved, Ruby was her patient. So, like it or not, she *was* involved. And, as it happened, she was involved with Devon too.

She looked at Devon sitting beside her in the taxi. To find out your mother was alive after all these years, and come to terms with the fact that she was never going to be like other mums because of her physical handicaps, was quite a bombshell. Little wonder she wanted some space from the two people in her life, her father and grandfather, whom she'd trusted implicitly. They'd let her down – big time. Cassie put herself in Devon's shoes and thought, I would want some space too.

'Yes – all right.'

Devon shot her a look as they pulled up outside the hall. 'Are you saying I can stay with you?'

'Yes.'

Devon threw her arms around Cassie. 'You are the best!'

Cassie thought of Ben and imagined his reaction when he found out. This was not the way for Devon to go about getting her back in his good books. Cassie shrugged. Who said that's what she wanted? Right now, Cassie didn't know what it would take to get Ben back in *her* good books.

Devon gave Cassie a kiss on the cheek for being so amazing and squeezed her tight before releasing her from their embrace. Now she was even more determined that the hall remained open and Cassie keep her job, not because she was staying at the cottage, that would only be for a few days, but she was a wonderful friend. It was awful that Cassie and her dad had such a falling out. If her dad was going to be with somebody, then she wanted it to be Cassie. The problem was she had a lot more on her hands now than just saving the hall, now she wanted to save their relationship. How was she going to do that?

As Devon stepped out of the car, she looked up at the house and saw Evelyn sitting at the window in her apartment. Now she knew her story, she realised who she was hoping would return. Before all this blew up with her mother, it had been playing on Devon's mind how to stop the sale of the hall for Evelyn's sake. If they forced her to move out, Devon was convinced the person she was waiting for would never find Evelyn, and the chance they would meet again would be lost forever.

Devon realised how lucky she was. If the sale of the hall had already gone ahead, her mother would have been moved without her ever learning about her mum's existence. Now she had another reason to save the hall – for her mum, so she'd stay in her home. Devon couldn't wait to see Ruby again. She was excited about telling Jodie the incredible news; her mum was still alive, and she only lived a few minutes away.

It didn't matter that she was in a wheelchair and Ruby would never be able to live with her like Jodie lived with her mum. All that mattered was that she could talk to her and get to know her. If it wasn't for Cassie and the old valve radio, and Tabitha, that rascal of a cat causing mischief, Devon realised she might have gone through her whole life never having met her.

'Will you pop in and see Evelyn after you've seen your mum?'

Devon turned to face Cassie. 'Oh, yes. I've got something important to tell her.'

Cassie guessed what that was. 'You're going to tell her you met your mother, aren't you?'

Devon nodded. That wasn't all. She was going to tell Evelyn not to worry about moving. Devon smiled at Cassie. She wasn't just thinking about Evelyn. Cassie was here to stay too; she just didn't know it yet.

44

After Cassie accompanied Devon to her mum's apartment and introduced her to Jill, who had brought Ruby's lunch, she made her way upstairs to Evelyn's flat. She couldn't wait to tell Evelyn the good news that Devon would pop in to see her soon. She imagined Devon would visit her a lot more now she'd discovered her mother was living here. But what would happen when the hall was sold?

She was approaching Evelyn's apartment when she heard a car turn up outside. Cassie stopped in front of a window in the corridor and pulled the net curtain aside. She looked down on the gravel drive below and recognised the vehicle. It was Ben's. He stepped out of the car. Cassie sighed. She guessed what he was here for. To put a stop to all this and take Devon home.

Cassie stood there unable to decide whether she should run down the stairs and confront him about the secret he'd kept from Devon. He disappeared into the hall. She didn't know how long she'd been standing there but Ben soon reappeared outside on the gravel driveway, dragging his reluctant daughter behind him.

Cassie stood at the window, feeling helpless. She noticed Ben pulling Devon by the arm and trying to force her into the car. Cassie wondered if this was what Devon meant when she said he might do something stupid. This *was* stupid. Devon was sixteen – well, almost. She had a right to visit her mother if that's what she wanted.

Devon pulled away from his grasp, her arms flailing around, making big frustrated gestures as she spoke to her father.

Cassie couldn't hear a word from her vantage point upstairs, but she could tell it wasn't going well. They were arguing. Then Ben flung his arms in the air and shook his head. It was a standoff.

There followed a spell where neither of them was speaking. Then Ben held out his hands, appearing to plead with Devon. He shook his head up and down. Did that mean she could see her mother? Cassie got her answer when Devon ran over and put her arms around him, hugging him tightly.

Cassie exhaled. 'Thank goodness.' She didn't want them to part on bad terms. She saw Ben point to his watch. Devon shook her head *yes* as though a time had been agreed. She held up her mobile phone. The look on Ben's face said he wasn't happy with whatever arrangement Devon was making. He shrugged as if to say, *Oh, all right.*

Cassie caught her grinning as she turned and skipped back into the hall. Whatever that conversation was about, she bet Devon hadn't told him she was leaving home for a few days. She must have realised if she'd done that, he would have bundled her in the car, there and then, and taken her straight home. What Cassie guessed, when Devon held up her phone, was she said she'd call him when she was ready. That's probably when she was going to tell him not to bother coming to pick her up as she was staying with a friend. Let's hope Devon didn't tell him whom she was staying with, thought Cassie.

She stood at the window watching Ben. He looked up at the house. Cassie quickly let the curtain drop, although she could still see him. He seemed to hesitate. Cassie held her breath. Was he going to come in and apologise? Is that what she wanted? It would have to be one hell of an apology after the way he had treated her.

Ben turned around, climbed into his 4x4, and drove off at speed down the drive.

Cassie stared down the empty driveway. She had to admit that's what she hoped he would do, even if she didn't quite know what her reaction would be. At least it would have been nice to hear he regretted what he'd said to her in the heat of the moment.

She turned from the window. 'Come on, there isn't much time left to visit Evelyn before your shift with Ruby begins.' She had no idea why she was talking to herself. Perhaps to convince herself she had to get on with the rest of her day. It beat running back to her digs, falling on her bed in an emotional heap, and crying into her pillow. She would save that activity until later. Right now, she had to return to work.

Cassie took a deep breath, put her game-face on, and walked into Evelyn's apartment. 'Hello, Evelyn, you'll never guess who's coming to see you later.'

Evelyn was delighted to hear that Devon was back and she'd be visiting her very soon. When Cassie fell silent, Evelyn looked at her and noticed she wasn't her usual chirpy self. 'Cassie – what's wrong?'

That's all it took for Cassie to burst into tears and tell Evelyn what had happened; Devon had discovered her mother, Ruby, whom she believed dead, was alive and living here in the hall.

Evelyn sat there, shaking her head. 'And that is a bad thing?'

'It's Ben, her father. He and I… we knew each other years ago. When we met again, I thought it was… it could be….' A sob escaped her as Cassie sat down on the sofa next to Evelyn. 'I've ruined everything!'

Evelyn remembered the fellow she'd seen arrive on his motorbike to pick Cassie up one afternoon. 'That young man is a fool to let you go when he found you again, after all these years.'

Cassie wiped her damp eyes with a tissue.

'Ben,' repeated Evelyn. 'I'd wring his neck if I could *and* give him a piece of my mind. Perhaps not in that order.'

Cassie managed a smile. 'Thanks, but I really wouldn't bother.' Although she wasn't condoning his behaviour towards her, she had to admit, 'It was probably my fault. I shouldn't have interfered.'

Evelyn shook her head. 'Sometimes, we need people to walk into our lives and shake things up a bit and remind us what is important in life.'

She had undoubtedly shaken things up, but was it for the better? It was for Devon. And it looked as though her dad was back in her good books – at least for now. How he would react when Devon didn't come home tonight was anyone's guess. It hadn't been Cassie's intention to come between Ben and his daughter. She imagined he'd never forgive her for that.

Evelyn gave Cassie an affectionate pat on the hand. 'Ben doesn't know how lucky he is to have found the love of his life again. He'll regret it. It will not surprise me if he has a change of heart and comes back for you.'

Cassie wasn't so sure, but it was kind of her to say so. Evelyn was trying to cheer her up. Cassie leant over and hugged her. 'Thank you, Evelyn, you are a good friend.'

Before Evelyn responded to Cassie's sudden display of affection, the little St Christopher that Cassie wore on a silver chain around her neck slipped out of her blouse and dangled in front of Evelyn. 'Oh, sorry about that.' Cassie was about to slip it back.

'Is that a St. Christopher?'

'Yes.'

'May I?' Evelyn reached out and took it between thumb and forefinger. She turned it over. There was an E in swirly writing etched on the back. 'Where did you get this?'

'It was my father's. He gave it to me when I was seventeen. We came to England when I was a teenager to search for his birth family. He didn't find them, but I stayed here to do my degree. He gave me this to protect me on my travels. St. Christopher is the patron saint of travellers and children.'

'Did you say he was looking for his birth family?'

'Yes. He was born here but grew up in Canada. This was the only possession he had from his childhood in England. His mother may have given it to him, but he doesn't remember.'

Evelyn sat there staring at the St. Christopher in astonishment. She wasn't sure she believed what she as seeing.

'My father was only little, too young to remember much, but The Child Migrants Trust – that's the name of the organisation that's been trying to trace his family – found a record of where he was billeted in the war before he was sent away.'

'Sent away?'

Cassie nodded. 'Yes, to Canada. But before that, he was

evacuated from London and stayed here in this hall. That's why I was so interested in the diary. Do you remember the girl wrote about a little boy, she called him Ted?' Cassie paused, fingering the St. Christopher. 'The boy in Rosie's diary – I'm sure it's my father, Martin.'

Cassie caught Evelyn's surprised expression. 'What is it?' Cassie searched her face. She had never seen Evelyn lose her composure before. Was that a tear rolling down her face?

'Cassie, there's something I need to tell—'

The door to Evelyn's lounge burst open.

Cassie turned around. It was Jill. It wasn't like her to interrupt a session when she was with a patient. The look on her face said there was a problem. 'What is it?' Cassie's first thought was something had happened to Ruby.

'Phyllis wants to see you.'

'Okay. I'll pop along when I've fin—'

'I'm to tell you that you have to come right now.'

'Oh.' Cassie stood up and said to Evelyn. 'I'm sorry, but I have to go.'

'What's going on?'

'I'm not sure.'

Jill stepped into the room. 'I've got your lunch here, Evelyn. Would you like the radio on as usual while you eat?'

'Yes.' Evelyn cast a glance towards the door. 'She is coming back, isn't she?'

Jill didn't answer.

45

'I've been informed that there's been a serious breach of patient confidentiality. 'Tell me you didn't take the photo from a patient's file.'

Cassie's face went bright crimson. How on earth did she find out about that? 'Phyllis, I can explain…'

Phyllis held up her hand. 'Did you also let a minor in during your patient's therapy sessions?'

'Now hold on one minute. You met Devon. She repaired the valve radio I gave to Evelyn. They hit it off and she wished to revisit Evelyn. It's not like she gets many visitors. I thought – what's the harm?'

'I'm not talking about Evelyn.'

'Ah, look about that. It's not my fault Devon found out about Ruby.' Even when she was saying it, Cassie knew that wasn't entirely true. She added, 'Devon has a right to visit her mother.'

The look on Phyllis' face said she didn't want to hear it. 'Did you take the photo from Ruby's file or not?'

Cassie bit her lip. 'All I wanted to do was—'

Cassie didn't get a chance to finish that sentence. She stepped out of Phyllis' office and stalked out of the hall and down the drive. Storming into the cottage, she thrust her suitcase on the bed and started packing. *I've been informed…* That's what Phyllis had said. She didn't have to ask by whom. Ben. She knew what he'd done. He'd phoned the hall and got his own back. Now, thanks to him, she was out of a job. And a home.

Cassie slammed the lid of her suitcase shut. She was about to zip up the case when she remembered her laptop. She walked over to the dressing table and sat down in front of the computer; there was something she needed to do before she packed it away.

Ten minutes later, she was just collecting her last personal items from the bathroom, when there was a knock on the cottage door. It was Olivia.

'So it is true.' Olivia glanced at Cassie's suitcase in the hallway. 'You're leaving. I heard what happened. Jill said you found Ruby's family. I can't believe you've lost your job over it. That's *so* not fair.'

Cassie thought news travels fast. She didn't want to talk about what transpired with Devon's father.

'What are you going to do?'

Cassie had no idea. She wanted to say farewell to Evelyn, Ruby and the other residents, and the staff, but she knew that was out of the question. 'Will you say goodbye to everyone for me and wish them all the best?'

'Of course.' Oliva gave her a hug. 'I'll miss you.'

Cassie smiled at her. 'I will miss you too.' She stepped outside with Olivia and locked the cottage door. She stared at the keys in her hand.

'What is it?' asked Olivia.

Cassie looked up. 'Can you do me a favour?'

Olivia opened her mouth, keen to do anything for Cassie. She was going to miss her.

Cassie held up her hand. 'You don't have to say yes. I'd quite understand.'

Olivia frowned. 'What do you mean? I'm happy to help out – whatever you need.'

'I'd promised Devon she could stay here at the cottage for a few days. I assumed I wouldn't be leaving quite so soon, obviously. She was going to stay with me for a bit. Someone has to tell her it's not going to happen now.' Cassie didn't fancy texting or telling her over the phone. She had quite enough surprises for one day.

'I see.'

Olivia didn't ask any questions, but she did look at the keys in Cassie's hand. 'No problem, why don't you give me the keys.'

Cassie handed them over.

'By the way, I almost forgot. The other reason I came by, Cassie, was some guy arrived. He's waiting in the entrance foyer up at the hall. Says he needs to see you.'

Cassie had been packing when she thought she heard a car pass by the on its way up the drive.

'Who is it?'

'I don't know, but whoever he is, he's devilishly handsome.'

Cassie's heart skipped a beat. 'Ben.'

'Who?'

'Never mind.' Cassie walked to the front gate with her case and started up the drive. She didn't want to go back to the hall, but if Ben had returned to apologise and speak to Phyllis, then Cassie wouldn't want to leave just yet. Whether she could forgive him was another matter. All she'd done was told Devon the truth. How was she to know the repercussions?

Cassie walked up the drive still in a daze that this was it; she was leaving – unless Phyllis changed her mind. She came to an abrupt halt. That wasn't Ben's car.

'What is it?' asked Olivia.

Cassie rolled her eyes. 'Good grief, my day couldn't get any worse,' she said under her breath.

She turned on her heel, intending to hurry back down the driveway before she was seen, when Olivia said, 'See, I told you he's quite handsome.'

Cassie made the mistake of glancing over her shoulder.

He spotted her. 'Cassie!'

Olivia stared at him. 'Who is he?'

Cassie would rather not answer that question as she stood watching him rush towards her.

'Here, let me help you with that.'

Cassie noticed him eyeing Olivia and even throwing her a disarming smile as he reached for the case. Cassie couldn't believe it; he was in a relationship with a young woman who was expecting his child, and here he was flirting with her friend. Cassie thought it's true – a leopard doesn't change his spots. She felt sorry for the young nurse, wasting her life on someone like Lars.

Cassie pulled her suitcase out of his reach. She set it down on the driveway and glared at him. 'Well, where is it? Where do you want me to sign?' That's what she presumed her soon-to-be ex had turned up for.

Olivia looked from one to the other and realised who he was. Sensing the atmosphere, she said, 'I better get back to work.' She hesitated. 'You will keep in touch? It won't be the same without you.'

Cassie looked up at the hall. 'Of course I will.'

Olivia gave her one last hug.

Cassie's smile faded when she turned to Lars. She didn't know what cheesed her off the most, the fact that he'd made a special trip just to get her to sign on the dotted line or that one of her so-called friends from her old job had enlightened him of her whereabouts. She couldn't put the entire blame on whoever told him. Lars was a charmer; he could charm the stripes off a zebra.

'Do you want me to sign or what?'

Lars shook his head. 'I don't know what you mean?'

'The divorce papers. I presume that's what you're here for.'

Lars laughed.

'What's so funny,' Cassie retorted.

'Cassie, I'm not here about the divorce. I'm here to take you back.'

'Excuse me?'

'I've left her. It wasn't going to work. I see that now.'

Cassie gaped at him. Was he out of his mind? Did he think he could just waltz back in her life and they'd pick up where they left off as though him an affair, having a child…? 'What about the baby?'

'Oh, *that*.'

'Did you just say *that*?'

'Look, the whole baby thing… it was getting a bit much, you know?'

'A bit much? She hasn't even had it yet!' Cassie thought this was the easy part. Wait until the baby is on the scene.

'I made a big mistake, Cassie.'

You are not the only one, thought Cassie. She looked up at the hall. She wished she'd never come here. It wasn't the job, the residents, the staff or even what had happened with Devon; it was Ben. It had taken her a long time to recover from losing him. The years and her marriage had tempered that pain to a dull ache, but it was still there nonetheless, the knowledge that he was the love of her life and always would be.

Now what was she going to do? Return to her old life, to her husband? She looked at him and an unexpected notion crossed her mind – perhaps she was never meant to be that happy. Maybe this is reality, just getting by with someone like Lars so at least she wasn't alone.

Cassie shook her head, dismissing that idea in an instant. If coming here had taught her one thing, it was that after twenty-years of just getting by, she was not going back to that. She deserved more and she was capable of being on her own – right now, she preferred it. 'Look, my taxi will arrive any minute.'

'I've got the car. You don't need a taxi.'

Cassie's taxi wasn't arriving any minute. She still had thirty minutes to kill before it turned up. However, she didn't want to hang around any longer than she had too. She looked at Lars and said, 'All right. But I don't want you to get any ideas, I mean it.'

'Of course.' Lars picked up her suitcase and followed her up the drive, smiling to himself as Cassie phoned the company to cancel her taxi.

'Cassie – wait!'

Cassie was about to get in the car. She turned around at the sound of Olivia's voice and saw her running down the steps towards her. For a moment, Cassie thought Olivia was going to say that Phyllis had changed her mind, until she noticed what was in her hand.

'Evelyn was sad to hear you were leaving. She asked me to give you this. She called it a parting gift.'

Cassie shook her head. 'I can't take that.'

'But she wanted you to have it.'

Cassie reluctantly took the diary. She didn't want to take it with her. She felt it belonged in the house, like Tabitha and the radio, but if Evelyn insisted she keep it, then so be it. 'Thanks, Olivia.' She stood there for a moment, watching the young physio walk back inside. Her eyes drifted up to Evelyn's window. Her Ladyship was sitting there just as she expected she would be. Cassie held up the diary, mouthing *thank you.*

Evelyn waved back.

Lars put her suitcase in the boot and got in the car. As soon as Cassie sat down in the passenger seat beside him, he started the car and headed down the driveway. He glanced at her. 'So, where are we going?'

'I,' said Cassie emphasising that they weren't going anywhere together, 'am off to the airport.'

'The airport?' He was so surprised that he almost ran the car off the drive.

'Watch it!'

'Christ!' Lars steered the car back on to the drive, narrowly avoiding a blue 4x4 hurtling passed them in the other direction. Cassie didn't get a look at the other vehicle they'd nearly clipped. She'd leant down to retrieve her handbag from the footwell. It had fallen off her lap after Lars swerved.

'Idiot!' commented Lars at the other car even though it was his fault he'd swerved.

He glanced at Cassie. 'Why are we going to the airport?'

On the spur of the moment, before she packed her laptop away, Cassie had gone online to check whether she had any emails from Dad. She had been so excited a month ago, after that trip to the library where the librarian had unearthed the photo on microfiche of her dad and other evacuees; the photo was taken when they first arrived at the train station in Sussex. What set this photo apart was that they were wearing their name tags. Cassie remembered she couldn't wait for the other library assistant, a young man to come into work the following day and enlarge the photograph to see the nametag more clearly.

The library assistant was off work with the seasonal flu, so it was another week until she returned to the library. The disappointments didn't end there. Although the photograph would turn out a wonderful keepsake, and something she couldn't wait to show her father, the nametag was of no use; whatever was written on there was illegible.

The librarian even tried scanning it into the computer and blowing up the image, but that still didn't work. It must have been raining when they alighted from the train; his nametag was smudged. Cassie had emailed her father, to let him know where she was, and told him about the photo she'd found in her search for more clues about his biological parents.

She was still no closer to finding out the truth about their English relations. She had been keeping in touch by email. On the road, his mobile phone coverage was patchy at best, and she didn't have the money to keep making international calls on her mobile.

While checking her emails, Cassie debated whether to tell him the next bit of news; she'd been fired from her job. She then booked a last-minute plane ticket. She didn't know if they would have any availability, but there were spare seats on a flight that afternoon to Toronto. After twenty years, Cassie was finally returning to Canada.

'Canada? You're going home?' exclaimed Lars in surprise when Cassie told him.

'I want to see my family. It's been too long.' Cassie glanced at the diary in her hand. She thought of Rosie's family, especially her two brothers who never returned from the war. It wasn't just Rosie's story that left her with the inclination to return to Canada. It was the rest of them at the hall, making her feel a part of a large extended family. She realised, in hindsight, it was something that had been missing from her life all these years. She was heartbroken to leave Fletching Hall, but now there was no reason to stay.

46

Cassie walked up to the departures desk at Gatwick Airport after printing out her boarding pass at a kiosk in the terminal. She turned to Lars, and said for the third time, 'I can take it from here.'

Lars wasn't listening. He passed her suitcase to the young lady on the desk while Cassie handed over her passport and boarding pass.

Lars flashed a smile at the young woman when she looked up. He asked, 'Have you got a seat on this flight?'

'Yes, there is one seat left.'

Cassie looked at him. 'What are you doing?'

'I'm coming with you.'

'What?'

The young lady checked the time. 'The gate closes in forty-five minutes, would you like the last seat?'

'Yes.'

Cassie relaxed. He wasn't getting this flight because he wouldn't have brought—

Lars slapped his passport down on the counter and smiled at Cassie. 'You know I never leave home without it.'

Cassie rolled her eyes. She'd forgotten her husband's paranoia with identity theft. He wouldn't leave his passport at home even though Cassie pointed out once that it was safer in the sock drawer than carrying it around in his jacket pocket. She wished he had taken her advice and left it at home. Now what was she going to do? If she caused a scene in the middle of the airport, she was liable to get herself chucked off the flight. Was that his game, stopping her going to visit her family just like he had done in the past?

'Don't do this, Lars.'

'If we go together, it's a chance for us to catch up.'

A chance for us to catch up? Cassie couldn't believe he was serious. 'There is no *us,*' Cassie reiterated.

'Oh, I disagree. Look, I will leave her. I can't be dealing with all the baby stuff. It seemed a wonderful idea at the time, but I'm getting bored with it now, to be honest.'

Cassie stared at him, lost for words. For the first time in her life she didn't regret having children, not if it meant her child would have had an ass like Lars for a father.

'We can take the flat off the market and go back to the way things were.'

'The way things were?' Cassie couldn't think of anything worse. Her expression must have said it all. Lars looked at her. 'Women your age have a bigger chance of winning the lottery than meeting someone, you know.'

'Gee – thanks for pointing that out,' Cassie said sarcastically. She was pretty sure most women her age were aware of the statistics and didn't need reminding.

'You don't want to end up on your own – do you?'

'I'm not on my own.'

'What do you mean?'

Cassie frowned. She had no clue why she said that. It wasn't as though Ben was in the picture. Cassie took a moment to gaze around the crowded terminal.

Lars noticed. 'Are you expecting someone?'

An idea popped into her head of Ben rushing back to the hall, bumping into Olivia, finding out she'd left, and hightailing it to the airport to stop her leaving.

Lars was still waiting for an answer. 'Did you hear what I just said? Are you waiting for someone?'

'Of course not,' Cassie said, annoyed by the question, annoyed by Lars, but mostly annoyed with herself for having such a daft thought. This wasn't a rom com. Ben would not turn up, beg her forgiveness, and sweep her off her feet. Then they would live happily ever after, roll credits, end of movie reel. Cassie glared at the reality standing in front of her; her ex-husband come to whisk her away instead. Well, it wasn't happening.

Lars breathed an audible sigh of relief. For a moment he thought Cassie was taking this trip with someone else.

'Excuse me, sir.' The woman at the desk tried to attract his attention.

'What do *you* want?' Lars barked at her.

She pointed at the line behind him. 'Other people are waiting to drop off their luggage and collect their boarding passes, so if you wouldn't mind taking your passport and boarding—'

'I'll move when I'm good and ready!'

Cassie shook her head. He hadn't changed a bit. Why didn't she see that when they were together? Why did it take an affair to realise what she'd been married to? Cassie didn't know why she was still standing there. She turned on her heel and walked off.

'Cassie!' He was about to run after her when the young woman at the desk said, 'Sir – don't forget your passport and—'

'Give me that!' Lars said rudely, grabbing his passport and boarding pass out of her hand. When he turned around Cassie was nowhere in sight. For a split second he didn't know what to do. Then he relaxed. He realised where she would be. It was written in black and white on the boarding pass. Gate 12. She'd be making her way there now. He'd find her in the departure lounge.

He looked at his seat number and wondered where Cassie was sitting on the flight. It wouldn't be long and he'd find out. He grinned. 'Toronto here we come!' he said to himself, even though he wasn't that enthusiastic about visiting her family. He'd never wanted to do it before. Nothing had changed, apart from the fact that he'd taken a week's annual leave and told his girlfriend he needed a break to figure things out. That's when he'd bumped into Cassie's friend at work, Dawn, and persuaded her he had to see Cassie to get the divorce papers signed. That was a complete and utter lie of course.

What was that saying, thought Lars as he strolled to the departure gate; *you never knew you had a good thing until it's gone* – or words to that effect. Lars smiled. He wanted that *good thing* back. So, he'd had an affair. It happens. Get over it. He knew Cassie. She'd come round. He always got his own way, eventually. Even though he had not planned on a trip abroad, and he didn't want to go to Canada, this worked in his favour. He could spend the time with Cassie until she gave in. Whatever he wanted, she relented. That's why he knew he'd get her back.

His girlfriend, whom he hadn't got to know properly before

they moved in together, was a different kettle of fish. She ordered him about and insisted he do everything because he was the man of the house. Lars frowned. If he was honest, he was a little scared of her; she went off on one at the least little thing, although he imagined that was her raging hormones being pregnant.

She worshiped the ground he walked on while they were courting, but as soon as they moved in together and she got what she wanted, everything changed. He couldn't go out on his bike or arrange holidays with his mates. It was all about her. Lars wanted to pretend it hadn't happened and return to the way things were with Cassie.

Lars picked up a newspaper and a takeaway coffee as he walked through the airport terminal, confident he had nothing to worry about; it was all going to work out. He tucked the paper under his arm, showed his boarding pass and breezed into the departure lounge. It was busy, but that's what he expected. The long-haul flight was full and it wouldn't be long until they boarded. Cassie was here somewhere. It was annoying when he would much rather sit down and read the paper, but he would just have to do a walkabout first and find her.

❖

Cassie was in the back of a taxi when she got a text. *The gate is closing. Where the hell are you?*

'Where to, miss?'

Cassie looked up. 'Heathrow Airport, please.'

I'll tell someone you've got held up and are on your way.

Cassie smiled. She was on her way all right; off to another airport to catch a flight. It seemed a bit extreme, going forty miles out of her way to Heathrow to see if they had any seats to Toronto today, but if she'd changed her ticket to a later flight just to avoid Lars, knowing her luck she'd bump into him in Gatwick Airport again. Cassie wasn't risking it.

She'd had the presence of mind to leave her ticket to see if the airline could sell it on, although she doubted that would happen at such short notice. Catching another flight meant it would cost much more to get back home than she expected, but it was a small price to pay to get shot of Lars. There was no way she could force him not to get on that flight. That's when she realised what she had to do.

Cassie got another text from Lars. She grinned when she read it. *The gate has closed. They said all the passengers are accounted for. What did you do?*

What I did, thought Cassie as she texted him back, pleased that it appeared the airline had sold on her seat, was what I should have done years ago; put myself first. From now on she would not let any man dictate her life. Lars could still fly to Toronto if he wished, but luckily for her they had never visited her family together in the past. That meant he had no clue where they lived. There was no possibility he'd turn up even if he did take the flight.

Cassie finished writing her final text to Lars. She didn't expect to get a reply. She re-read it before she sent it. *I suggest you go back to your girlfriend, grow a pair, and face up to your responsibilities; otherwise you are the one who will end up alone!*

Cassie put her phone away. That was the last she'd hear of Lars, she hoped, apart from through her divorce lawyer and the estate agents selling the flat.

The taxi driver interrupted her thoughts. 'You're travelling light. Hope you don't mind me asking, miss, but you didn't forget your luggage – did you?' Cassie glanced at the small cabin bag on her lap. Fortunately, she hadn't checked in her laptop and Rosie's notebook. When she told the airline she would not be on the flight, she didn't have to worry about her luggage. It was international airline regulations if you don't board your flight, your baggage won't fly without you.

The trouble was Cassie didn't want to wait around in the airport to reclaim her suitcases. Sitting in the back of the taxi, she didn't feel upset about it. Like the flat, and Lars, she felt she was finally shedding her old life, and leaving behind all the things associated with it, even her clothes, to start anew.

47

Ben got out of the car and ran into the hall. 'Hello?' He frowned. 'Where is everybody?' He raced up the grand staircase calling out, 'Cassie!' There was no answer.

Ben's heart was pounding in his chest. Had she left already? Why would that surprise him? She'd lost her job – he was certain of it. 'What have I done?' His father warned him not to do something stupid. He didn't listen. He wished Devon had never shown him the photo of Ruby that Cassie brought with her. Ben shook his head. It wasn't Devon's fault. After slamming the door in Cassie's face, he'd got straight on the phone to Fletchling Hall. That's when he'd told the woman in charge about the photo and how his daughter, a minor, had visited a patient without his permission.

'Why did I lose my temper and do that?'

He wasn't just thinking about that phone call, but treating Cassie the way he had. He had no right to blame her. His father was right: the truth will out, but it had come about in the worst way imaginable, dragging Cassie, the love of his life, into it.

He desperately wished he could take it all back. Ben wanted to make things right. He needed to see her, although he had no clue what he would say. His behaviour towards her was inexcusable, but then to phone her job and get her fired into the bargain. Would she ever forgive him? It was that thought that was scaring Ben.

He legged it down a corridor at random and saw a door open. He ran inside. 'Cassie?'

Evelyn turned from the window. 'Who are you?'

'Have you seen Cassie?'

'She's gone.'

'Gone where?'

'How do I know?'

'When did she leave?'

Evelyn put on her glasses. 'I know you.' He was wearing chinos and a plain blue shirt rather than the leather jacket and jeans when he was here last, but she still recognised him. He was the chap with the motorbike. 'You're too late.'

'What do you mean?'

'She left a moment ago in a car.'

'Where did she go?'

'Home, I imagine.'

'What makes you say that?' Ben said with a start.

Evelyn had seen Cassie and a man arguing as they got in the car. They knew each other – of that she was certain. It was something about the way they argued as if they'd known each other a long time. 'If I had to hazard a guess, I'd say it was her husband who picked her up.' Evelyn knew Cassie was separated.

'Her husband?' Ben rushed to the window, recalling the car he had just passed that almost swerved into him.

'I'm not surprised he wants her back.'

'Who's saying she'd have him back!' Ben turned around and barked at her.

Evelyn was shocked when he rounded on her. Perhaps she shouldn't have spoken her mind.

'Sorry, I snapped at you.' Benn sighed heavily. 'I just need to see her.'

'You must have passed them on your way up the drive,' Evelyn said matter-of-factly even though the expression on his face said he realised that. Her face softened. The poor man looked bereft. Evelyn had an idea. 'If you're quick, you might catch up with them. Not that I'm suggesting you break the speed limit, although it might help if you put your foot down a bit.'

Ben stared at her.

'What are you standing there for? Go on. Go after her.'

Ben shot out of the room. A minute or so later, he flung himself at his car.

From her window, Evelyn watched him get in his car. He sped down the driveway after them. Unfortunately, Evelyn couldn't remember which direction they took. She watched Ben's car dawdling at the end of the drive.

'Do it,' said Evelyn. 'Pick a direction. What have you got to lose? You've got a fifty-fifty chance of picking the right one and then you might catch up with them.'

Ben looked left, then right, not sure which direction to take. What if he caught up with them and Cassie would not forgive him? Worse still, what if she *had* decided to return to her husband? He would look a complete fool.

Evelyn guessed what he was thinking. 'You're a bigger fool if you don't at least try. Perhaps you would still have a chance if you just caught up with her? Don't you agree?' she said to Tabitha who was sitting by her feet.

Tabitha meowed loudly.

Evelyn shook her head when Ben turned the car around and headed back up the drive.

❖

Ben took a deep breath and walked through the door.

'Dad, what are you doing here?'

Devon was kneeling by the woman in the wheelchair, showing her some photographs. He looked at his daughter curiously, wondering what she was doing. 'What are they?'

'Oh, nothing.' In her haste to put them away, she dropped one.

Ben walked over and picked it up. He recognised the girl in the photo. It was Devon's friend, Jodie. There was a boy in the photo too who had Jodie's blue eyes and blonde hair. He guessed that was Jodie's brother. He handed her the photograph. 'Are you showing Ruby your friends?'

Devon slipped the photo in her back pocket, feeling embarrassed that he walked in on them when she was showing her mum a photo of the boy she fancied. 'Sorry, Mum, I've got to go. Jodie is picking me up soon and I promised to pop in and see Evelyn before I leave.' Devon bent over and kissed her mum goodbye. 'I'll see you tomorrow.'

She glanced at her dad before she walked out. Her hand closed around the keys to Gatehouse cottage. She'd be staying there on her own, but Olivia was up at the hall and had given Devon the keys along with her mobile number in case she needed anything.

When Jodie picked her up, Devon intended to ask her if she wanted to stay over. There were two bedrooms at the cottage. Although Devon wanted some space from her dad and Gramps, she didn't fancy being alone, especially as Dad would go ballistic when he found out she wasn't coming home tonight. If Jodie was there, she could speak to her dad and make it sound as though she was staying over at Jodie's. He wouldn't storm round there and create a scene in front of her parents. Besides, she didn't think he'd see the harm if he thought she was at a friend's house. But staying in a cottage on her own would not happen – if he found out.

Devon glanced at the keys in her hand as she walked towards the door. She still didn't understand why Cassie had left in such a hurry. She got the impression Olivia knew more than she let on, but she wouldn't elaborate. All the physio said was she would catch her later and check she was okay. In the meantime, Olivia told her to let the cleaners in the cottage; it sounded as they would be preparing it to rent out again. Until they found new tenants, Devon had it to herself, although Olivia warned her to keep a low profile; she used the words, *stay under the radar.*

'I can do that,' Devon mused. She'd have to anyway if she didn't want her dad to find out. Devon still wanted to discover why Cassie left in such a hurry. It worried her. She threw a backward glance at her dad before she closed the door and wondered if it had something to do with him.

Ben watched Devon flounce out of the apartment. He caught her staring at him a long moment before she shut the door, as though something was on her mind.

Ben frowned. Did she know that Cassie had, most likely, lost her job and it was his fault? Ben doubted it. From what he had seen, his daughter liked Cassie. She wouldn't have held back sharing her opinion of him if she realised what he'd done. There was something bothering her though. He imagined she was still mad at him over Ruby. Even though he thought that was it, he decided to ask her as soon as he arrived home. Right now, there was something he needed to do.

Ben turned to Ruby, forcing himself to look at her. She still had that beautiful long blonde hair, and a ready smile. He thought, why does she appear pleased to see *me* – of all people?

He needed to clear his conscience. 'I bet you're wondering what I'm doing here…' Ben trailed off, shaking his head. 'What a stupid, stupid thing to say,' he berated himself under his breath. He dropped his eyes from her lolling head. Ben forced himself to continue. 'I want to apologise. I know it's too little, too late.'

Ben was doing his best to avoid eye contact, seeing first-hand what he'd done; she was brain-damaged in a wheelchair all because he drove recklessly while they were rowing about why he refused to marry her, because of the woman he still loved, because of Cassie. 'This is all my fault – the car accident.'

Ben turned to go when he was stopped in his tracks by the sound of a computerised voice. 'I blamed you for a long time…'

Ben slowly turned around. He heard the tapping on a computer keyboard, followed by a computerised voice again. 'I blamed myself.'

He stared at her. Understanding her after the accident when she came out of the medically induced coma was difficult. A speech and language therapist worked with her and that's how she communicated her wishes, but having a private conversation when he found it so difficult to decipher her slurred speech was next to impossible, until now.

'When I first saw you, I set my eyes on having you.'

Ben frowned. 'I don't understand…'

'I knew you were in night school training to be an architect – I thought you'd be a good catch. I'm sorry.'

'You're sorry?' Ben was taken aback. It was him who had come here to make a grovelling apology.

'I knew there had been somebody else. People in small communities talk. I was afraid you'd go back to her if she reappeared that's why I was desperate for you to put a ring on my finger.'

Ben gaped at her.

'This was all my fault. Perhaps I got what I deserved.'

Ben started to shake his head, about to say *it wasn't your fault.*

'Deep down I always knew you could never love me the way you did that other woman. That row in the car, it was more than about getting married, I just wanted you to forget her, but I knew that would never happen. We don't choose who we fall in love with. I fell in love with someone who was in love with someone else.'

Ben didn't know what to say. It was true, there was no point denying it.'

'I'm sorry, Ben.'

He stood there staring at her. He said in a small voice. 'Is that all you're sorry for?'

Ruby went quiet. Finally, she said, 'I was so happy when I fell pregnant with Devon. The two years before the accident were the happiest of my life.'

There was a long silence. Ben didn't know what to say.

'Do you know how hard it was for me to make that decision? To let her go?'

'Ruby, it didn't have to be that way.'

'If you'd been in my shoes, Ben, wouldn't you have wanted to protect her, give her a normal life?'

'But many children, for a variety of reasons, grow up with disabled parents.'

'And what of you, Ben? Looking after a disabled partner? What about your life?'

Ben knew what she was talking about, but that was beside the point. 'But she's your daughter, Ruby. She needed her mother, growing up.'

'Is that why you brought her to see me when she was still little, in the hope I'd change my mind?'

'Yes, I thought if you saw her…' he trailed off.

'You thought I'd change my mind. Have you told her the truth?'

Ben vehemently shook his head, no. 'How could I? She's just found her mother, I can't possibly tell her that it was your decision not to see her, that you cut your own daughter out of your life.'

There was another long silence. Ruby said, 'Thank you, Ben. I wish—'

Ben looked at her. She didn't have to finish that sentence; she wished she had stayed in Devon's life.

Ben sighed. 'We made a bit of a mess of things, didn't we?'

Ruby's head lolled from side-to-side. Ben guessed she agreed. She said nothing more. The tinny computer voice fell silent.

Ben stood there feeling uncomfortable. He glanced around her apartment. He'd rented the best one; an entire wing all to herself. He knew the hall would be sold, the house torn down. He realised what it meant; she'd have to move from a place she'd lived in for the last fourteen years. This was her home. He glanced at her computer keyboard hooked up to a clever little contraption. 'That's so clever,' he blurted.

'I know. It was Cassie's idea. She's my O.T.'

Ben looked at her. He'd never told her the name of the woman who'd come between them. 'Cassie got you this equipment?'

The robotic computer voice spoke again, 'Yes, she did.'

Ben inwardly groaned. He guessed Ruby hadn't heard the news about Cassie leaving either.

Ruby changed the subject. 'Devon told me about Jodie and her brother. She likes him.'

'She does?' It was the first time Ben heard about that.

'They'd make a nice couple.'

Ben shook his head. 'She's not into boys yet.'

'You are wrong.'

Ben frowned. She was probably right. He wished Devon told him about Jodie's brother. If it wasn't him, Ben knew it would be some other boy. Now he had to prepare himself for the trials and drama of teenage love. Cassie came to mind. Even now, in his forties, he still remembered the drama of being a teenager in love. Unfortunately, he'd brought all that angst back on himself for treating her appallingly and then getting her fired from her job. He didn't know if she got the sack, but he intended to find out. He couldn't imagine any other reason she'd just up sticks and leave. From what she'd told him, she loved it here.

That made Ben feel worse, because he realised if Cassie hadn't come into their lives and discovered the truth about Ruby, then that special relationship Devon could build with her mother would have been lost forever. That's why the last thing he'd do is jeopardise it by telling his daughter how it really came about that she didn't grow up knowing her mother

He acknowledged that it was down to Cassie too, that he was here, meeting Ruby again. He hadn't seen her for years, not just out of guilt over the accident, but he couldn't bring himself to see the woman who, despite trying to convince her not to cut Devon out of her life, had rejected their daughter all those years ago.

When he'd gone after Cassie and stopped at the end of the drive, indecisive about which way to turn, he knew he had to pick a direction. What was holding him back was remorse. He would have to find the courage to face Cassie, if he was going to have any hope of getting her back, just like he had to face Ruby.

Ben sighed. He came here to speak to Ruby and yet all he could think about was Cassie. He couldn't help himself. Ruby was right; they'd made a right mess of things. And yet although they were never destined to be together, they'd had a child, a beautiful, creative, fiery, independent girl who he was so proud of.

Ben looked at Ruby. Seeing her sitting in a wheelchair, blowing on a straw, and typing awkwardly with one finger, brought it home to him just how grave the accident was. But he saw something else; the old Ruby he once knew, with the infectious smile and carefree attitude, was still here, the mother of his child.

He'd always wanted Devon to know her mum. Although he didn't say it, a part of him felt when Ruby made her intentions clear, that she didn't want to see Devon she was punishing him for the accident. But that was all in the past now. Ruby was going to be so important in Devon's life from now on.

'Will you let me see her again?'

Ruby's question surprised him. Only then did it occur to him that after what Ruby had done, she felt she didn't deserve to see her daughter, and didn't deserve Ben's forgiveness.

'You know I will.' Neither of them could turn back the clock, but they could both make damn sure they made up for lost time. He was going to make sure Devon saw her mother as often as she liked. Him and Gramps weren't enough. In hindsight, he realised that Cassie coming into their lives, and consequently Devon finding her mother, couldn't have come at a better time. Now she was growing into a young woman, she needed her mum more than ever. The fact that Devon was already confiding in her mum about a boy told him that.

'I had better go.'

'I hope you find happiness, Ben.'

Ben looked at her in surprise. 'You think I'm unhappy?'

'You still have that look.'

'What are you talking about?'

'That haunted, faraway look. You tried to hide it when we were together, but….' She didn't have to say anymore. She realised what it was; even now, after all these years, he still missed the woman he loved. Ruby turned her wheelchair to face the window. 'Goodbye, Ben.'

Ben hovered there until he understood. This was goodbye. He'd said his piece. Ruby had said hers. Devon could come and visit. He wouldn't stop her this time. That's all she wanted to know. He wouldn't be visiting again. 'Goodbye, Ruby.'

Ben walked out the door wondering how to tell Ruby and Devon that it wouldn't be long, and she'd no longer be living here. He'd already made arrangements. She was going to an assisted living facility. He was sure Cassie would approve when he told her. The place had more activities, more people. Ruby wouldn't be shut away in the wing of a big old house such as this.

He glanced at her before he closed the door feeling guilty, not just about the accident, but something else. The one thing she wouldn't have in her new home was her daughter popping in and out regularly. He'd made her a promise that Devon could still see her, which she would, just not as often. Ruby's new home was almost a hundred miles away. It wasn't his fault the best place he could find was so far away. She had complex needs. It was not easy finding somewhere suitable.

That brought to mind the promise he'd made Devon. She made him swear to withdraw his plans for the house. It was blackmail – pure and simple. She wouldn't talk to him again if he didn't do as she asked. He knew his daughter. If he didn't follow through, the idea of Devon cutting him out of her life didn't bear thinking about. His plans he'd spent weeks drawing up went straight in the bin.

Devon mentioned another resident here, Evelyn. His daughter had clearly made other friends during her visits to the hall. Ben thrust his hands in his jacket pockets and grimaced as he walked down the corridor. The problem was there were other architects who would work on the behalf of the developer interested in acquiring the estate. They could also provide the council with what they wanted; sound plans to turn the house and grounds into a housing development that wouldn't be an eyesore and pass local planning scrutiny. What Devon didn't realise, and what he'd failed to tell her, was that bar some wealthy benefactor stepping in, buying up the place, and allowing the residents to stay, the sale was going ahead with or without his plans. All Devon had done was delay it a matter of weeks.

Ben returned to the entrance hallway and was just approaching the main door when one of the staff crossed the hall. 'Excuse me, I'm Ben. I wonder if you can tell me if Cassie still works here.' He was praying she hadn't been fired.

'Oh, I recognise you.'

For a moment he thought she knew about him and Cassie until she said, 'You're the architect.'

He was not surprised the staff remembered him. He'd been here in the past, on many occasions, to draw up the plans. They realised he was the person who would submit the proposals to the council which meant a developer stepping in and they would all lose their jobs.

He said, 'And you are…?'

She folded her arms. 'What do you want?'

Ben got the message loud and clear. That's why he'd been very reluctant when Cassie wanted to show him around the hall. What was he thinking when he turned up on his motorbike that one time to take Cassie out? It did not occur to him that someone would recognise him.

'I'm a friend of Cassie's.' He grimaced. That probably wasn't how Cassie would see it now. Ben tried not to think about that. He repeated the question, 'Does Cassie still work here.'

The young woman shook her head no.

Ben stared at her. It was just as he thought. *Damn!* 'Have you any idea where she might have gone?'

'Why should I tell you?'

'Please, I need to know.'

The young physio sighed. 'Cassie said she was going home.'

Ben swore under his breath. That's what the old woman in the other apartment said.

'When she told me, I got the impression that she wasn't talking about London, where she used to live.'

'Then where—' Ben stopped. He didn't need to ask the question. She was going home, home. His heart sank. Right now, she could be twenty-thousand feet in the air, getting further away every minute. She was returning to Canada.

48

Evelyn looked down at Tabitha, still nestled on her lap. 'I wish Cassie had come to see me before she left. It was important.'

Ben's visit reminded her why she wanted to speak to Cassie. She put her hand to her chest, searching for the little St. Christopher she used to wear. It was their parents who gave the necklaces to both her and her brothers. A single letter distinguished them; the first letter of their names was etched on the back. She'd given hers away years ago to a little boy who, it turned out, went on a long journey. He would always have a special place in her heart.

Evelyn sat there, reminiscing. Her brothers had just signed up to go to war. The house was eerily quiet without them. Then along he came, the little boy with the round, cherubic face and the brightest blue eyes. Suddenly she felt like she had a brother again. Except this time she was the big sister. Then the unthinkable happened, and along with losing their home, they lost him too. When the authorities found out they were moving to Scotland, which Evelyn was unaware of at the time, despite her parents' pleas that he could go with them, he was taken away. She didn't know where.

Evelyn assumed he was billeted with another family in the village and then returned to his family after the war. She knew in her heart, like her brothers, she would probably never see him again. Before he left, she took off her St. Christopher and put it around his neck.

Even now, after all these years, she remembered what she'd said to him. 'Wherever you are, he will always look after you, protect you. Keep you safe.'

She secretly hoped that one day she would see him again. She'd always wondered what happened to him; it was like losing another brother. Evelyn imagined that after the war he returned to his family in London and had few memories of his time as an evacuee. She thought of trying to find him once, but she never did. She knew why. He wasn't hers to find. She assumed he had a family, a home of his own.

Evelyn closed her eyes, recalling her shock when she saw the little St. Christopher again after all these years, given to Cassie by her father. It must be him. Who would have thought the woman who found her diary was the daughter of that little boy? 'God works in mysterious ways,' Evelyn said out loud.

Devon walked in. 'Hello, Evelyn. See, I promised I'd come. I never break a promise.' Devon hoped her dad didn't either.

Evelyn opened her eyes.

Devon walked up to Evelyn sitting in her usual spot in the chair by the window. She glanced outside and saw her dad climb in his shiny blue 4x4 and speed down the driveway. She hoped he was going straight home to shred his plans and phone the council to withdraw his contract. Devon turned from the window, smiling.

'What are you so happy about, young lady?'

Devon sat down on the chair next to her. She wasn't happy when she found out about Ruby and what her dad and Gramps had been keeping from her. But now things were working out; she had her mum, the cottage she could stay in for a bit, and the hall wouldn't be sold.

Her smile faltered when she thought of Cassie. Later, when Olivia popped in to see her, she'd get to the bottom of why Cassie left. It was on her mind why she didn't say goodbye. She really hoped it had nothing to do with Dad.

Devon perked up when she turned to Evelyn. She was dying to tell her that Ruby was her mum. But right now there was something more pressing she couldn't wait to tell Evelyn. She knew why Evelyn dressed up to the nines and sat looking out the window each day. She was waiting for him to return – the Canadian.

He'd made her a promise when he left; no matter what, someday they would meet again. That's why she sat at the window waiting, hoping he'd make good on that promise – if he was still alive. If he could find her. The only connection they had through the years was this house. That's why she would never leave.

Devon was still smiling. 'I've got something to tell you, Evelyn.'

Evelyn searched her face. 'What is it?'

'The house isn't being sold. You don't have to leave.'

Evelyn fell silent a moment. 'Is that a fact?'

'Yes, it is.' Devon frowned. Evelyn wasn't exactly jubilant. It wasn't the reaction she was expecting. She thought Evelyn would tell her it was just as well because they'd have a job making her go. *They'd have to carry me out and deposit me, and my possessions, on the lawn.*

I'd refuse to leave – simple as that. Knowing Evelyn, that's what Devon imagined she would say.

'Isn't it great? Now you're not going anywhere!'

Evelyn looked at her. 'How can you be so sure?'

'I just am.' She grinned at Evelyn. Perhaps her reaction was to be expected; it would take time for the good news to sink in. Devon bounced off the sofa. 'Let's put the radio on and celebrate.' She walked over to the sideboard saying to Evelyn, 'Now you've told me the rest of your story, what shall we talk about?'

Evelyn didn't have to think twice before she answered. 'I want to know all about Devon. Tell me *your* story.'

'There's not much to tell. I'm almost sixteen but compared to you, mine will be pretty boring.'

Evelyn looked at Devon as she turned on the radio. By her age, she had fallen in love, signed the Official Secrets Act, and already started what would turn out a long-lasting career working for the Government.

As for her personal life, when they came to take little Ted away, her parents were just as devastated as she was. That's when they made up their mind they were leaving for Scotland. Evelyn couldn't care less where they lived. The little boy wasn't the only one who had gone. The Canadian had left too and, like her brothers, she didn't feel she would ever see him again. Back then, in the thick of war, when she found out Scott was leaving she threw his promise back at him that he would return. Heartbroken, she left with her parents to live with relatives in Scotland until the war was over.

Two years later they returned to what was a shell of a place. The house had been stripped of everything; furniture, light fittings, anything that wasn't stuck to the floor and walls had been removed. It would take months, if not years, to put it right, and lots of money. Her parents were typical of that class who were property rich but cash poor. They lived off dwindling old money and depended on the income from the estate to run the household. But the tenant farmers were gone, along with the livestock, and her parents simply didn't have the money to restore the house. Her father had no choice but to sell his beloved estate that had been in their family for generations.

When they returned, she didn't want them to sell. Although she was attached to the place – it was her childhood home – that wasn't the reason; it was the thought the Canadian might return after the war like he promised. If they sold the house, how would he find her? Despite her heartfelt pleas, her parents had little choice. They sold the house and returned to Scotland.

It was around that time that Evelyn married an RAF pilot, a family friend, whom she'd met when her parents first moved in with friends in Scotland towards the end of the war. Her parents told her they were a splendid match. He was kind, charming, and a good sort. Although she liked him a lot, she knew she'd never love him in the way she loved the Canadian.

She told him one day, soon after they first met, that she couldn't marry him. Her heart belonged to someone else. Although he understood, he couldn't let her go. He told her it was highly unlikely she'd see the Canadian again. Evelyn had to decide to spend a lifetime alone or find happiness with someone else. The RAF officer loved her dearly and she was very fond of him, so fond in fact that she agreed to marry him.

But it was not meant to be. The day after they married, his unit was mobilised to return to Corfu. The wives and families were flying out to join them. He'd organised some leave for the two of them to spend their honeymoon on the Greek island. Evelyn never left England. Before she flew out to join her husband, his plane crash-landed on a military exercise. He died instantly. Evelyn never remarried. She had no shortage of potential suitors, but she declined them all. Instead, what she did was ahead of the times for a woman from her social background; Evelyn stayed in work.

She'd never told her husband or friends what she did in the war. She had signed the Official Secrets Act. Even though she was so very young, she understood the significance. Years later, it wasn't that she couldn't talk about it; it never came up. Her friends and family thought she went to work every day in a typing pool. Nothing could be further from the truth. With her background as one of the most outstanding teenage voluntary interceptors, her photographic memory, and her ability to process extensive amounts of information, GCHQ, the intelligence and security organisation based in Cheltenham recruited her. During World War Two the organisation was located initially at Bletchley Park.

She didn't work at Bletchley Park. It was during the last few months of the war they head hunted her to work at Arkley View, a large country house near the village of Arkley, which was requisitioned during the war years and used as the headquarters of the Radio Security Service. Evelyn remembered to this day the secret address of the voluntary interceptors at Arkely View in the London Borough of Barnet – PO Box 25 Barnet.

Although she would have chosen to remain with her family in Scotland, even at that young age she understood the importance of her work, and that of other VI's. They listened to enemy radio transmissions and recorded everything, which was then sent to Bletchley Park for decoding and interpretation. Although the information they gathered was forwarded to the code-breaking centre at Bletchley Park, some personnel, like Evelyn, were proving to be talented cryptographers, decoding cyphers ahead of Bletchley – not a fact that she imagined is well known.

Following the end of the war, that's when the opportunity arose for her to work at GCHQ. She didn't move straight away. Evelyn took a break and returned to her family in Scotland. That's when she met the RAF serviceman and married. She wanted children and to lead a different life. But it was not to be.

After she became a widow, she returned to her work as a cryptographer for GCHQ. She spent her working life there. Everyone outside of work still assumed she was a typist. They had no idea what she did or how it all started as a voluntary interceptor at Devon's age.

Evelyn watched Devon tune in the radio. She recalled what Devon uncovered whilst researching about interceptors online. Places like Arkely remained top secret until a historical researcher submitted a freedom of information request.

'Does that mean it's no longer top secret? Can I write it down in your diary?' Devon had asked her when Evelyn was telling her story.

Even though she'd retired from her job at GCHQ many years ago, she hadn't breathed a word about it to anyone. Devon was the first person she'd ever told. Evelyn knew she'd written it down in her diary about her first meeting with government officials who'd turned up at the cottage asking after her brothers. That's when they'd ended up recruiting her. She couldn't help it.

She was a teenage girl excited about helping the war effort, and she just had to tell someone. She couldn't even tell the Canadian, so she'd got it out of her system by writing it down instead.

Then the Canadian was sent away, and her parents left for Scotland. Although she'd gone with them, it wasn't long before she moved to Arkely View. In those few tumultuous weeks, leaving her parents and her childhood home for the first time, she didn't know what had happened to her diary and the radio.

She'd stop writing when she lost the love of her life. She'd thrown the diary out, or so she thought. She suspected her parents had packed up some of their stuff and stored it for safekeeping in the basement of the house before the move to Scotland. In the aftermath of the war, when the house was sold, the few personal possessions stored in the basement were left behind.

Evelyn smiled when she thought of her diary Cassie had found. If it wasn't for Tabitha, the diary and the radio would have remained boxed up and gathering dust forever. 'You're a clever cat, aren't you now.' Evelyn stroked the little tabby nestled comfortably on her lap.

Tabitha purred.

Evelyn thought of her old diary, the blank pages now filled with the rest of her story, written down by an inquisitive sixteen-year-old who reminded her of herself years ago.

She heard jazz playing on the radio. It took her back to another time, another era when she was Devon's age.

Devon ran over and sat down beside her. She said, 'I have to warn you my story will sound really boring.'

Evelyn had a feeling Devon's life would turn out anything but boring.

Devon took a deep breath. 'Okay, where do I start?'

'Let me see. I know. Why don't you start *in medias res*?'

Devon frowned. 'What does that mean?'

'It's a Latin phrase. It means starting your story *in the middle of things.* Then, like my story, we can go back to come forward.' Evelyn smiled. 'That's how all great stories begin.'

'You think my story will be great?' Although she was looking forward to telling Evelyn all about her mum, which Devon decided was the perfect place to start *in medias res,* she said, 'You might be in for a huge disappointment.'

Evelyn smiled at her. 'Oh, I doubt that.'

49

Cassie's idea to change airports worked out perfectly. Lady luck was on her side; she bagged another seat on a flight leaving from Heathrow later that afternoon. Fortunately, she changed her plans and didn't get on the aeroplane with Lars in tow; Cassie's bright idea to give him the slip when they arrived would have been foiled completely. Toronto airport had gone through a transformation since she'd been away. It seemed bigger, modern and more spacious. There was no chance to lose her husband in a crowd. Besides, there would be no point Lars coming; she'd bought a one-way ticket. Cassie didn't have any plans to return.

She set off towards the taxi rank and before long was seated in a car with her carry-on bag stowed in the boot.

'Where to?' asked the taxi driver.

Cassie gave the driver her sister's address. There was no reason to stop by her dad's place on the way because he was still on his fact-finding road trip across Canada.

'Did you have a nice vacation?' the driver asked conversationally.

For a moment, Cassie wondered why he thought she was returning from a vacation until she realised her Canadian accent gave her away. She was no longer a foreigner abroad. After all those years abroad, it was a bit of a novelty for a stranger to greet her without asking what she was doing in the country.

'I haven't been on holiday,' Cassie replied. 'I've returned from England where I've lived for many years.'

'So, what brings you home?'

Home. Where was that exactly? Cassie didn't know what to say. She still missed Fletchling Hall and the colleagues and residents she counted as friends. She knew what had brought her back to Canada. 'Family.'

The taxi driver nodded. 'Are your family in Toronto or all over?'

Cassie thought of her dad and smiled. 'All over, actually.'

'Well, I hope you see them all soon. I'm sure they will be thrilled you're back.'

Cassie hoped so. She was sitting in the car thinking about turning up at her sister's house, out of the blue, with no forewarning she was on her way. Returning to Canada had been a spur-of-the-moment thing. Now, seven hours later, Cassie wished she'd phoned her sister from Heathrow before she caught her flight, but there wasn't time. She was lucky to find an available seat on a plane taking off that afternoon. That she managed it again at Heathrow Airport after ditching Lars at Gatwick, told Cassie her decision to return to Canada was meant to be.

Now she wasn't so sure. She might need to find a hotel. Several scenarios were running through her mind. Did her sister still live at the same address? Cassie sent a Christmas card every year but never got one in return. It had been decades since she last stepped foot in Canada. Apart from the recent communication over her dear grandmother, they hadn't spoken in years.

That was another reason she wasn't sorry she'd returned. Perhaps Ben and Phyllis had done her a favour. After her grandmother had a fall and was taken into hospital, Cassie intended to take some leave from her job in London and fly back, as soon as she could, to see her. That was before Lars dropped the bombshell he was leaving her for someone else and they put their home on the market. It shouldn't have stopped her flying out to see family, but all Cassie could think about was getting her personal life sorted first.

She'd always envisaged she would return to Canada with her husband. And yet here she was. The divorce was still ongoing and her finances a mess. She had given up a permanent job for a temporary one and now she had no job, no reference, and no roof over her head. However, come what may, Cassie was still selling the flat. She didn't want to give Lars any reason to assume they would get back together.

So, what had changed? *Me* thought Cassie. She had no qualms about getting on a flight on her own and threw caution to the wind about the money; her savings were dwindling fast, but if she could get to Canada then she'd figure something out. Ironically, her grandmother would be quite proud of her. She'd always loved that Cassie had been adventurous, prepared to travel abroad to England with her dad and then stayed on to have her own adventure. Her grandmother once said, as missionaries on the road, travelling like gypsies was in their blood.

Cassie remembered that conversation when she was a teenager about to leave Canada for England. Her grandparents on her father's side, whom she loved dearly, were not blood relations. What did it matter? That was Cassie's attitude. Cassie always felt her and her sister were so lucky to have them as family.

Thinking of her sister, Cassie would not be surprised if they had moved to a new house to accommodate their growing family. The last she'd heard, they had three children. All her sister wanted was to get married and be a stay-at-home mum with a large family. That's why they clashed. When Cassie was in her twenties, the last thing on her mind was having babies. She preferred a career and the excitement of travel, living and working abroad; something her sister could never understand.

'This is the right address – isn't it?' The taxi driver turned in his seat to look at Cassie.

They'd arrived all too soon at their destination, her sister and brother-in-law's house in downtown Toronto. Now she was here, she didn't know how to go through with turning up unannounced. Throughout the journey from the airport, Cassie debated whether to phone her. It seemed stupid just to turn up at an address if she was no longer living there. Cassie called. It went straight through to an answerphone, but at least she knew they hadn't moved.

Cassie exited the car and opened an envelope containing Canadian dollars she'd bought from the airport before she caught her flight. The driver passed Cassie her travel bag and took the fare. She stood on the pavement outside the terrace row of brownstones watching the taxi take off down the street, hoping she wouldn't regret that she didn't ask the taxi driver to take her to a hotel. It was too late now. Cassie sighed and looked up at the house. Her sister lived on the first two floors of a converted brownstone in downtown Toronto, with another duplex apartment above. Although they would have liked a house, she recalled their apartment was spacious and had a garden.

Cassie walked up the stone steps to the front door, recalling her journey from the airport. She'd forgotten how dense the city was; it was the only way she could describe it. Perhaps it wouldn't appear so alien to someone from Singapore or Shanghai. London, however, with its open spaces and sprawling public parks, had a very different feel. The modern skyscrapers that dominated the skyline in Toronto towered over the city's small historic centre where her sister lived.

She imagined some tourists may be captivated on the journey from the airport. The city skyline looked so futuristic, like something out of the movie, *Bladerunner*. Cassie stared out the window at the sheer scale of those towering glass buildings, which seemed to have grown in number since her last visit, wondering how people lived in high-rises. She was missing England already.

Cassie could see someone approaching the front door through the frosted glass. She took a breath. The door opened. Cassie took a step back when a two-year-old yelled in her face.

'Jared – come on now, that's enough.' The little boy was being carried in the arms of a man Cassie recognised. It was her brother-in-law. 'Don?'

'Cassie? I don't believe it! Come in out of the cold.' He looked at his son. 'Sorry. Terrible twos. Come in. I've just got to change his diaper.'

She followed him into the hallway.

'Make yourself at home, Cassie. I'll be back in a minute.' He paused for a moment. 'I still can't believe you're here.'

Neither could Cassie. She walked into their lounge. There was no sign of her sister. Cassie guessed as it was a weekday, Don had a day off from work and her sister, who didn't appear to be home, was out shopping or having her nails done.

Cassie took a seat on the sofa and looked around the room. Their lounge was small and cosy, with white-washed walls, hardwood floors, comfy sofas, rugs and lots of scatter cushions, and toys strewn everywhere. There was a large framed studio photo of their three children over the mantel shelf. She recalled when little Jared came on the scene. She wasn't sure if he was planned. There was a gap between the other two, a girl and a boy aged eight and ten.

Cassie stared at the photo, taken when their youngest was a baby and felt a pang of regret that living so far away, she was never part of their lives. She always sent birthday cards and sent a card and present on the birth of their third child but had never met him until now.

Don appeared a few minutes later. 'I've put him down for a nap. Would you like a cup of coffee?'

Cassie smiled. 'Sure.' She followed him to the kitchen door and stood watching her brother-in-law make coffee.

'We had no idea you were coming, Cassie' he said, glancing at her as he switched on the coffee maker.

'I know. Sorry about that.'

'No need to apologise. You know you're always welcome.'

Cassie smiled. 'Thanks, Don.' She'd always got on well with her sister's husband. She wondered how Emma would feel about her older sister turning up out of the blue.

'So, how have you been? What brings you back to Canada? Are you moving home?'

Cassie sighed. There it was again, that word *home*. 'I don't know. Maybe. Things are up in the air at the moment.'

Her brother-in-law sensed she did not want to talk about it.

Cassie looked around the kitchen while Don poured two

mugs of coffee. It looked quite new with cream shaker-style units. 'This is nice.'

'You like it? I fitted it myself.'

Cassie wasn't surprised. He worked hard and was a doting father. Don also took care of jobs around the house. Her sister landed on her feet, marrying her childhood sweetheart. Thinking of her sister, Cassie heaved a sigh. 'So, when is she back?'

He glanced at the time. 'She finishes work in an hour.'

'Work?' blurted Cassie.

'Didn't she tell you about her job?'

Cassie gave him a look. Although she vaguely recalled Emma had mentioned something about being at work when she'd phoned her out of the blue about Grandma, Emma didn't stay on the phone long enough to have a proper conversation.

Don caught Cassie's expression. 'Oh, yeah, sorry.' As if he needed reminding that his wife and sister were not close. 'It's been about five years now.'

'Five years?'

'Uh-huh. We went through a bit of a rough patch. You heard I had an accident at work?'

Cassie nodded. Don was a firefighter. He'd fallen off a ladder and broken his leg. She didn't see what that had to do with—

'Break didn't heal as it should have. I was medically retired. Can't be a firefighter if you're unable to scale a ladder.'

'I'm so sorry. I had no idea.' From what she remembered, Don loved his job.

'Yeah well, shit happens. Anyway, my lump sum paid off the mortgage, but my pension wasn't enough to live on with a growing family so…'

'Emma went out to work.'

'Yeah, a bit of a role reversal.'

'You're a stay-at-home dad?'

'Can't you tell?' Don turned around holding two cups of coffee. He was wearing an apron with a big Donald Duck on the front. He glanced down at the apron. 'Not what you expected – right?'

Cassie shook her head. 'I'll say.' Her brother-in-law had also gained weight, which wasn't surprising at home all day with a toddler.

'I'm going to put the evening meal on soon. Will you stay for dinner, Cassie?'

Cassie didn't answer.

Don noticed. 'Are you okay?'

Cassie bit her lip. 'Look, I haven't booked a hotel room. Is there any chance you could put me up for the night…?'

'Why didn't you say so? Of course you can stay. There's the spare room. There's only a single bed, but as it's just you…?' He trailed off, letting the sentence hang.

'That's great.' Cassie imagined Don was probably wondering where Lars was, but she didn't want to get into that right now.

Don eyed her thoughtfully as he handed over a cup of coffee. 'I won't lie. Things haven't been easy since I left work. Your sister… well let's just say Emma has changed.'

'Changed?' As far as Cassie was aware, her sister was not inclined to have a career. Her focus was on getting married and having children. Cassie expected to turn up to a stay-at-home mum baking cakes and doing the school run, perhaps some charity work.

Cassie always felt her sister looked down on her and everyone else who didn't make it their life's work to stay at home and raise children. It made her wonder how her sister was coping with being forced out to work. 'What does she do for a living?' asked Cassie.

At that moment Cassie heard the front door. Standing in the kitchen doorway, she saw her sister breeze in wearing a smart black trouser suit and cream shirt. She was wearing heels, her long hair straightened so there wasn't a strand out of place. She put her briefcase down in the hall. Cassie stepped back into the kitchen out of sight and caught Don's expression which said, *see what I mean.*

Emma was too busy slipping off her heels. She hadn't noticed Cassie. 'Hi hun, I'm home! What a day. Where are the kids?'

'John and Eliza are at friends' houses for tea, remember?' Don called out from the kitchen, eyeing Cassie and winking. He couldn't wait to see the expression on Emma's face when she discovered her big sister was home from England.

Cassie was apprehensive and not sure what her sister's reaction would be. She took a deep breath and stepped out of the kitchen.

'Oh, yeah, I forgot they were out. These new shoes are killing—' She looked up and for a moment imagined she was seeing things. 'Cassie?'

Don grinned at his wife. 'We've got a visitor, by the way.'

50

'Oh, my goodness!' She ran down the hall into Cassie's arms. 'I thought you would never come back.' She stood on tiptoes to give her big sister a hug, squeezing her tight.

Cassie was shocked that she appeared so pleased to see her; she didn't know what to say. After their last conversation on the phone about their grandmother, which didn't go at all well, Cassie didn't expect this.

Emma whispered in her ear, 'I'm so glad you're here. I've been meaning to phone and apologise about talking to you the way I did when you called. It's just with one thing and another…' There was a cry from upstairs interrupting Emma.

Don raised his eyebrows. 'That nap didn't last long.' He scooted up the stairs while Emma released Cassie from her embrace and stood back to look at her. 'You look amazing.'

'Oh, don't be silly. I've got wrinkles and a few grey hairs, not to mention I'm carrying around a few extra pounds than I care to admit. You, on the other hand…' Cassie looked her up and down. She appeared every inch the professional office worker in her outfit. Her sister was also very slim. In fact, while her husband had put on weight over the years, her sister had slimmed down.

Don walked down the stairs carrying Jared in his arms.

'And who is this little fella?' she said to her son as he held out chubby arms for mummy.

Don seemed happy to give him up. 'I'll go check the dinner.'

'Have you been a good boy for Daddy today while Mummy was at work?' She bounced him up and down and kissed his cheek.

Cassie stared at them with a yearning she hadn't felt in a very long time.

Emma caught her staring. 'Do you want a hold?'

Before Cassie replied, Emma deposited him in her arms. For a moment Cassie thought he would cry, instead chubby fingers tightened around her necklace. He tried to put it in his mouth.

'Jared,' Emma warned, reaching for his hands.

Cassie smiled. 'It's all right, honestly.' She bounced him gently up and down as she followed Emma into the lounge, saying to him, 'I'm your auntie Cassie. Aren't you a good boy?'

Emma scoffed, 'Yeah – right! This is what he's like when we have visitors. Wait until you go later.'

'Ah, here's the thing…' began Cassie.

'Cassie's staying with us for a bit,' Don cut in, overhearing the conversation as he joined them in the lounge.

Cassie turned to her sister, wondering what she would say. 'It's only for one night while I sort out a hotel or bed and—'

'Don't be silly, Cassie. You must stay here with us. I don't want you to go to a hotel on your own.' Emma stopped. 'Did you travel on our own?' She glanced at Don who was standing behind Cassie shrugging his shoulders as if to say, *don't ask me!*

Cassie nodded. 'That's really kind of you to let me stay.'

'Nonsense. Your family.' Emma squeezed her arm. Sensing

she didn't want to talk about why she was here without Lars, Emma turned her attention to the state of their lounge. 'It's a bit of a mess in here, hun.'

Don handed Emma a cup of coffee. It was the first time his smile faltered. 'Being at home all day is hard work.'

'I know. You don't have to tell me. I was at home with the other two before I went out to work.' She slumped down on the sofa. 'Have you put the dinner on?'

'Yes.'

'Do you need to check it?'

Don was about to say no when he realised what Emma was really saying; she wanted some girl time with her sister. 'Oh, yes er right. I'll go check the dinner.' He glanced at Jared who was squirming in Cassie's arms, getting bored. 'I'll take him off your hands.'

Cassie reluctantly handed him over and picked up her coffee from the mantel shelf where she'd left it out of harm's way. She wasn't used to little ones around. She turned her attention to her sister. She'd never seen her looking so elegant and sophisticated. She'd grown up, matured over the years Cassie had been away.

Cassie looked down at her thick woolly jumper and baggy jeans. She'd just stepped off a flight, so it was understandable she dressed in a comfortable outfit for the journey. She felt frumpy and old compared to her glamorous thirty-something sister.

'So, Don tells me you've been working for the last five years. What is it you do?'

'Come, sit with me.' Emma patted the sofa seat next to her.

Cassie sat down beside her, overcome that her sister was genuinely pleased to see her.

'It was the best thing I ever did, Cassie, going out to work.

At first, I hated the idea.' That comment didn't surprise Cassie.

'I never thought I'd say this back then, but I love my job.'

'What do you do?'

'I'm a reporter for CBC.'

'CBC?'

'You know, the Canadian Broadcasting Company…'

Cassie raised her eyebrows. 'Oh, yes, I forgot.' She'd spent so many years in England she was used to Britain's equivalent – the BBC.

'I'm doing a journalism course at night school. At the moment, I'm a reporter for the service on radio but I'm hoping to break into television. I'm working my way up.'

Cassie was lost for words. She not only had a job, but she was aiming to work her way up the career ladder. This was not the little sister she knew once upon a time.

Her sister smiled. 'You seem surprised.'

'I thought you'd be—'

'Home baking cakes – and all that nonsense?'

All that nonsense? That wasn't quite how Cassie would have put it – not now, anyway. As she got older, and the probability of having children diminished with each passing year, she envied her sister and the life she had created. It wasn't like that in the beginning, when Cassie was young and carefree, but now her priorities had changed, and it was too late.

'I loved spending the early years with them, but honestly, Cassie, by the time Don had his accident I was climbing up the walls. It wasn't how I expected to feel – trapped. I wanted something for *me*. And this is it. I think I was mad at you all these years because you got the opportunities I craved but never had.'

'You mean going to England with Dad?'

'Yeah, I know I was too young at the time. But it wasn't just that. Then you trained and got your qualification, and went out to work, while I was stuck here with two kids under three. I know I'd made my bed. I thought it was what I wanted, but…'

'You needed something more.'

'Does that make me a terrible mother?'

Cassie looked at her sister in surprise. 'Of course not.'

'I'm so glad you're back. I'll get Don to make up the spare room. You will stay with us, won't you? The other two will be home soon. I can't wait for you to see them.'

Cassie was relieved. 'The thing is, I kind of invited myself. I didn't book a hotel or anything.'

'Well, that's settled. Stay as long as you like. How long *are* you staying?'

'I don't know.'

She eyed Cassie for a long moment. 'Wait. Are you thinking of moving back to Canada?'

'Maybe.'

Emma looked at her sister, wide-eyed. 'I thought you loved England. What's brought this about?'

Cassie stared at Emma and burst into tears. She was meant to be the strong, independent big sister and here she was crying in her younger sister's arms.

'Oh, Cassie. It's Lars, isn't it? You've broken up.' Emma didn't have to guess. The fact that Cassie had returned to Canada alone told her that her sister had gone through a big upheaval in her life. It made her wonder how the break-up had come about.

She bet Lars had cheated on her. From what little she'd seen of Cassie's husband – she'd only met him briefly at the wedding– her impression of Lars was that he was quite full of himself. She wagered Lars had gone off with someone else, because Cassie would never have left England otherwise.

Don chose that moment to step into the room to tell them dinner was almost ready. He quickly did an about-turn and sidled out.

Emma saw her husband walk in and do a quick exit. Now she regretted having words about the state of the lounge. For all his faults, and the difficulties in their marriage with raising children and him losing his job, they'd weathered the storms together and come out stronger, happier and more content as individuals and a couple.

Emma realised people met, married and had successful long-lasting relationships at different stages of their lives. For her and Don, theirs had lasted the distance because they were teenage sweethearts. She sat there with her arms around Cassie, wondering if things would have turned out differently for her sister if she stayed with the boy she'd found in England.

It was years ago, and Emma was only young, but she would never forget how she felt when she heard Cassie wouldn't be coming home at all because of a boy – that's what she thought at the time. She missed her teenage sister and was angry and betrayed that she left her for someone else. It was childish behaviour, but over the years she was unable to shake the belief that Cassie had abandoned her and her Canadian roots.

No matter how many times Cassie reached out through Christmas cards and messages on social media, Emma did her best to ignore her. Busy with raising a family, the years melted away until one day, she had that phone call from Cassie, contacting her about their grandmother in hospital. Emma regretted the way she spoke to Cassie and resolved to put things right. She would not go another ten years missing out on having a relationship with the sister she had adored.

Emma squeezed her tight, so pleased she was here, so glad to have her sister back, although wishing it wasn't under these circumstances. She smoothed her sister's beautiful red hair away from her face. 'Do you want to help me make up your room? Then, if you feel up to it, you can have dinner with us. John and Eliza are being dropped home later. If you'd rather turn in and meet the children tomorrow, I quite understand…'

Cassie wiped away her tears with a tissue and looked at her sister. 'I'm so sorry to turn up on you like this and dump you with all my problems.'

Emma was already shaking her head. 'You don't have to apologise, Cassie, really you don't. We're here for you.'

'I can't wait to meet the children. Although I'm not that hungry, I'd love to join you guys for dinner.'

'That's settled then.' Emma smiled and took her hand. 'Come on, let's go sort out that spare room.' She stood up and stepped on a toy. She picked it up and glanced around her lounge, strewn with toys and dirty finger marks up walls, thinking if only Cassie had had children, she would have something to focus on and, come-what-may, she wouldn't be alone.

Emma had an idea. 'Look, how about tomorrow we visit Grandma? I can't wait to see her face when you walk in. She will be in for the surprise of her life when she finds out you're back.'

Cassie's face lit up at the mention of their grandmother. 'Oh, bother, I haven't brought her anything back from England.'

Emma laughed. 'Yes, you have.'

Cassie looked at her bemused as they walked out of the lounge until she realised; their grandmother was never much into stuff. Like her father, all that mattered was family. She didn't have to bring a thing, just herself. Thinking of family, Cassie couldn't wait for John and Eliza to come home from their friends. She hoped she could stay awake long enough to say hello.

They were upstairs, putting on fresh pillowcases and a duvet cover, with Cassie looking longingly at the bed, when Emma read her mind. 'Why don't you get settled in, unpack your bag, and have a rest, then you can freshen up and come down to dinner.'

'Would you mind?'

'Not at all.' Emma gave her a hug and a kiss. 'See you soon.'

Cassie put her bag down on the chair by the small wooden dressing table and cast her gaze around the room. It was small, but cosy with a dormer window overlooking the front and the brownstones across the road. The walls, wooden floors, rugs and cushions on the easy chair, carried on the relaxed theme of the lounge. There was also a blue frieze with cars and aeroplanes running around the walls and a crate of toys in one corner. She guessed this wasn't the spare room, but Jared's bedroom. It was so kind of them to let her stay.

Cassie plumped the pillow and lay down. She made the mistake of closing her eyes and instantly fell into a deep sleep. She dreamed she was back at the hall surrounded by her friends. And it got better. She was with Ben. But they weren't middle-aged; they were young again, teenagers just starting out on their life's journey, riding off on his motorbike into the sunset towards a new and happy future together.

51

'I must be coming down with something. I can't remember the last time I was this sick.'

Cassie retched into the toilet bowl. They were meant to visit their grandmother today, but Cassie had woken up feeling ill. In fact she'd been feeling queasy and out of sorts for a while. She put it down to being in love again, before the worst happened and Ben dumped her again.

Emma was sitting on the edge of the bath. She passed her a tissue. She'd heard her sister in the bathroom early in the morning and had knocked on the door to see if she was all right. Cassie had unlocked the door and let her in.

'So, you've been under the weather. Headaches, funny tummy, things making you nauseous?'

Cassie wiped her mouth. 'Yes, sounds like I've got a virus.'

Her sister sat there regarding her for a long moment. 'You've got something all right, and it's not a virus.'

Cassie turned her head and glanced at Emma. 'What do you mean?'

'Now I know why you are looking amazing and positively blooming.'

Cassie retched again. When she finished and wiped her mouth once more, she turned to Emma. 'You call this amazing?' she scoffed.

'You're pregnant, aren't you? You can tell me.'

'Pregnant?' Cassie looked at her sister as if she were mad. 'Of course I'm not pregnant. It's a virus. Besides, do you recall how old I am?'

'It's not beyond the realm of possibility. My friend at work has recently had her first child, and she's forty-six, a year older than you. It's a trend, women having children later in life. It's becoming quite the norm. Nowadays, people are more surprised when I tell them I've already got kids aged eight and ten, and I'm only in my early thirties.'

'Emma, I am *not* pregnant!' Cassie was sick again.

Emma stood up. 'Wait here.'

'I'm not going anywhere,' Cassie said to the inside of the toilet bowl. She sat down in her PJ's on the cool tiled floor. Cassie was wiping her face with a cold flannel when her sister returned. 'Here.' She handed Cassie a small box.

'What's this?'

'It's a pregnancy test kit. I always keep a spare in case I miss my period.'

Cassie shook her head. 'It will be a waste of time. I don't need it. It's just a stomach bug. I'll be fine in a day or two.'

Her sister shrugged her shoulders. 'Suit yourself.' She walked out the door, leaving the box on the side.

Cassie stared at it.

Emma popped her head around the door again. 'Can I tell you something?'

Still feeling groggy, Cassie nodded. 'What is it?'

She slipped back into the bathroom and closed the door. 'When I was stuck at home with babies, and you were gallivanting off to England, I was jealous.'

Cassie didn't think Emma had any reason to be envious of her life. 'It wasn't nearly as exciting as it sounds. I was doing an O.T. course and looking for work, much the same thing I would have done here. It just happened that I stayed behind and did my degree in England.'

'Yes, but you had the freedom to find yourself.'

Cassie wasn't listening; her eyes kept roving to the pregnancy test.

Emma noticed. 'Oh, for goodness' sake, Cassie, take the test!'

At her sister's goading, she did it just to shut her up. She couldn't be pregnant.

'There, you see,' said Cassie when she came out of the bathroom. Her sister was waiting outside. She took the stick.

Cassie went to return to her bedroom.

'Cassie . . .'

She turned around. Across the hallway, Emma looked at her with a grave expression.

'What did I tell you? I've wasted a perfectly good pregnancy test.'

'Cassie, you may need to sit down.'

'Why?'

Her sister grabbed her hand and pulled her into the bedroom. She closed the door, turned around, and squealed, 'I'm going to be an auntie!'

'What?'

She hugged Cassie. 'Look,' she showed her the stick. 'You're pregnant.'

'What!? That's not possible.'

Her sister ignored Cassie's remark. She understood. Cassie was in shock. That's how she felt about her youngest. The difference was, Emma had not split up from her husband, unlike Cassie.

Emma didn't want to think about Lars. Instead she said, 'What did I tell you? Women in their forties are having children all the time!'

Cassie wasn't thinking about that. She was thinking about the fact that she hadn't slept with her husband for a long time.

Ben!

'When are you going to tell him?'

'Who?'

Her sister threw her a funny look. 'Lars – of course.' Emma knew her sister was thinking about the father. She hoped it wasn't true, that Cassie and her husband had split up.

Cassie stared at her. She didn't know what to say.

'You don't have to talk about it if you don't want to. Let's just celebrate. I can get the sitter in, and we can go out for a meal.'

Cassie frowned at the mention of food.

'Ah, maybe that is not such a good idea. We'll think of something. I'm so excited, and I'm not the one having a baby! I can't wait to tell Don the news.'

Cassie grasped her arm before she ran out the door and told the entire household.

The expression on Cassie's face brought Emma down to earth. She sat back down on the single bed next to Cassie and took her hand.

Cassie started to cry.

Emma put her arms around her. 'I thought you'd be happy? It's what you always wanted, isn't it?'

'Oh, Emma, it's all such a mess.'

She drew back and nodded. 'It's never the right time for a baby, I completely understand.'

'No – you don't.'

'It's Lars, isn't it?' She bet it was. 'Forget about him. We can do this together. You're not alone – you know that, right? It's probably come as a bit of a shock. You don't have to tell him if—'

'I haven't slept with Lars for months.'

Her sister stared at her. 'Then who is the—?'

That's when it all spilled out about Lars leaving her for a young nurse who was pregnant with his child and giving up her post in London to start a temporary job at Fletchling Hall. And meeting Ben again.

'Perhaps if we hadn't split up all those years ago, I'd have had children, a family just like you, Emma. But it wasn't to be.' Cassie wiped her face with the sleeve of her pyjamas. 'I was pregnant once, soon after I married Lars.' She'd never told Emma about that. 'But I…. I lost the baby, and then I found out he didn't want kids, anyway.'

'But now he's having a child by somebody else?'

'As am I – as it happens.' Cassie sighed. 'Lars came to Fletchling Hall, said he was leaving the other woman. He wants me back.'

Her sister laughed.

Cassie stared at her. 'What's so funny?'

'If he's got cold feet over the baby, he's hardly going to want you back – is he!'

Cassie hadn't considered that.

'I'm assuming you don't want him back.'

Cassie didn't even have to consider it. However much she couldn't envisage spending the rest of her life alone, Cassie wouldn't get back with Lars. She placed her hand on her tummy. *But I'm not alone.*

She recalled that episode at the airport when Lars was trying to persuade her to take him back, citing statistics that women her age are more than likely to end up on their own. Out of nowhere, she'd replied, 'I'm not alone,' with no clue why she said that. Now it made sense; deep down in her subconscious she already knew.

'What are you going to do?' Emma asked in a small voice.

Cassie looked at her sister and knew what she was asking. 'I'm keeping this baby.' She had no husband or partner, no job and no roof over her head. She would get some money from the proceeds of the sale of the flat in London, but it wouldn't support her and the baby, and provide a place to live. If there was any time not to have a baby, this was it. She voiced her thoughts. 'I want this baby so much, Emma. I just don't know how I'm going to support myself when the baby arrives.'

Emma put an arm around her shoulders. 'We will do this together. You can stay here as long as you like. I'm here for you.'

Cassie was taken aback. 'Why? I was never there for you when Mum died.'

Emma sighed. 'I was as much to blame for that, acting like a martyr coping with it all myself as though I was trying to be super mum.'

Cassie looked around the room. 'I can't stay here indefinitely. This is Jared's bedroom.'

'Yes, but he can sleep in with us and then he can share with John. Honestly, it's fine.'

'You know what? I will take you up on your offer to stay. I was fired from my last job.'

'Never!'

Cassie nodded.

'How? Why?' She eyed her sister. 'Did it have something to do with. . .?' She looked down at Cassie's tummy.

'No, it's complicated.'

'When you are ready, you can tell me all about it. Why don't you have a couple more hours in bed? It's Saturday. When you feel up to it, come down, and we will have some breakfast and tell Don the splendid news.'

'Will he be okay with this?'

Emma smiled at her sister. 'Do you even have to ask? You know Don. He'd love you to stay.'

Cassie felt the tears welling up again. 'Is this what it's like being pregnant, getting emotional all the time?'

'I'm afraid so. You better get used to it,' she joked.

Cassie lay down on the bed.

Emma paused at the bedroom door. 'Are you going to be okay?'

Cassie fingered the St. Christopher around her neck. 'Yes, I think so.'

Her sister quietly closed the door.

It had kept her safe on her journey through life, the little St. Christopher, just as it had kept her father safe. Cassie held up the pendant. She would give the St. Christopher to her child to keep it safe on its journey through life when she wasn't there. The necklace brought to mind Evelyn and her peculiar reaction when she saw the pendant. Cassie shrugged. It must have reminded her of something.

Cassie lay there staring at the ceiling. Although it didn't hurt to take her sister's advice and get some rest, even if she closed her eyes, Cassie doubted she would drift off to sleep. She cast her gaze around the room, looking for something to read. Then she remembered Rosie's diary. Cassie reached for her handbag. She decided to re-read her story – what there was of it.

She took the diary out of her bag and opened it on the first page. Cassie began to read.

An hour later, she had just dozed off when the notebook fell out of her hands and landed on the wooden floor with a thud. It woke her up. Cassie leaned over to pick it up. The book had landed open, face up. That's when she noticed something. 'That's odd.' Cassie picked it up and rolled over in bed. There used to be a lot of blank pages at the end of the diary.

Cassie flicked through the pages until she came to the last entry she'd read in Rosie's handwriting, but that was no longer the final page. 'I don't understand….'

Cassie sat up in bed and perused the next section that wasn't there before. It was all about Rosie's parents leaving Sussex and moving to Scotland. Rosie had stayed behind working for an organisation called MI8 that Cassie had never heard of. She went on to join MI6, and finally GCHQ following her marriage to the RAF pilot who died. She'd had a lengthy career working as a cartographer in the upper echelons of the British Government.

Cassie lowered the book. 'I don't get it. These pages weren't here before.' Cassie noted the handwriting was different. 'Who wrote this?'

She read the last entry. It was in the latter years of her life, after she retired, that Rosie thought about the Canadian and the promise he'd made to her. That's why she'd returned to Fletchling Hall hoping that somehow, they would meet again.

'She came back?' Cassie sat up in bed with a start. 'When was that?' The notebook didn't say. Cassie's thoughts turned to the last time she was at the hall, loading her suitcases in the back of Lars' car. She'd been about to leave when Olivia had run down the steps to deliver the diary before she left. Apparently, Evelyn got wind that Cassie was leaving and insisted she take it as a parting gift.

Cassie flicked through the pages again. She still didn't get it. There *had* to be a connection between Evelyn and Rosie. At the end of the diary, on the final page, was written *the life story of Evelyn Rosalind James.*

Cassie stared at the name, Evelyn Rosalind… *Rosie.*

'Rosie. Rosie! Oh, my word, Evelyn is Rosie!'

All those weeks Devon had been visiting Evelyn, she'd wondered what they'd been doing, what they had talked about. Cassie stared at the diary. Devon had been filling in the blank pages with the missing story of one Evelyn Rosalind James or Rosie as she was known when she was young.

And if she needed any further proof, that Evelyn was Rosie, Devon had written in the final page about Evelyn's memory of a little boy to whom she'd given her St. Christopher just before he was taken from her family. Evelyn had gone through life wondering what had become of that little boy she'd loved dearly.

Cassie looked down at the St. Christopher and turned it over in her hand. On the back was a single letter - E. Her dad always thought it was his mother who had given it to him. She recalled Evelyn had looked quite shocked when she'd taken a closer look.

Cassie couldn't believe it herself. 'This belonged to Evelyn. It was Evelyn who gave this to my father.' Cassie stared at the diary in astonishment. 'She knew my father.'

Cassie couldn't get off the bed and out the door quick enough. She rushed down the stairs and found her sister in the kitchen preparing breakfast. She held out the notebook. 'I've got to return to England.'

Emma turned around. 'What are you talking about? You've just got here.'

'We must get in touch with Dad. Have you any idea where he is?'

'The last time I heard from him, he was in—' she stopped. 'Wait – what's it got to do with Dad?'

'Oh boy, have I got something to tell him…'

52

After all these years Cassie had found someone in England who knew her father and she'd been right under her nose these past few weeks. 'Dad returned to England twice to search for his English birth parents.'

Emma remembered. 'Nothing ever came of it.'

'I've met someone who had a connection with Dad from the war. They're not family, but it's something.'

'Really?'

Cassie held up the diary. 'You've got to read this…'

Emma took the leather-bound journal and turned it over in her hands. 'This looks old. Where did you find it? What's it got to do with Dad?'

'I found it at Fletchling Hall.'

'The place where Daddy was evacuated in the war?'

Cassie nodded.

Emma was about to ask another question when Cassie pointed at the diary and smiled. 'Why don't you read it while I make a cup of tea?'

Emma sat down at the kitchen table and opened the journal. It didn't take long for her to put two and two together. 'The little boy that Rosie is writing about, the one she called Ted – it's Daddy.'

Cassie turned around with two mugs of tea in her hands. 'That's right.' She put them on the table and took a seat. 'Keep reading…'

She passed Emma a mug, but she was too engrossed in studying the diary to notice.

Cassie sipped her tea, watching her sister.

Emma continued to read Rosie's story. It wasn't long before she got to the part where Rosie had moved into Gatekeepers Cottage and the people arrived who took their father away.

'The St. Christopher!' Emma stopped reading and looked at her sister. 'Dad told me that his mother back in England gave it to him before he was evacuated from London.'

Cassie nodded. 'That's what he presumed, although he couldn't remember.'

Emma glanced at the pendant hanging around Cassie's neck. 'So, it was Rosie, the girl who wrote this diary, who presented it to him.'

'That's right.'

Emma's face clouded over. She stared at her sister. 'I've always been jealous that Daddy gave you his precious St. Christopher. You're his favourite.'

'Don't be daft,' Cassie said in a small voice although she knew it was true. Perhaps it was the fact that since she was little, she'd taken such an interest in his search for their English family.

In contrast, her sister had never been bothered about her English heritage. However, the expression on her face, as she read the diary, suggested to Cassie that her attitude had changed.

'Cassie, we have to get in touch with Dad and show him this.'

Emma had a thought. 'Didn't you say you found someone in England who knew him?'

Cassie was saving the best until last. 'Yes, I did.' Cassie felt like doing a drum roll. She grinned at her sister. 'You read about girl who wrote the diary…'

'Yes. Rosie.'

Cassie fingered the little St. Christopher. 'Would you believe she's living at Fletchling Hall? She was one of my patients.'

Emma's mouth dropped open. 'You're joking. Is that how you discovered this diary? Did she see the pendant one day and gave you her diary to read?'

Cassie looked at her sister. 'Um, not quite.' She smiled when she thought of Tabitha, the little kitten in the basement. Cassie missed the cat. She was about to tell her sister how she found the diary when Emma said, 'There's something I don't understand…'

Cassie looked at her curiously. 'What is it?'

'Daddy felt the pendant belonged to his mother – yes?'

'Yes.' Cassie wasn't looking forward to telling him that the pendant he wore when he arrived in Canada did not come from his mum.

'He believed his mother's name began with E because that letter is etched on the back.'

'Ah.' Cassie saw where she was leading. 'It's quite simple. Rosie was a nickname. This diary belongs to Evelyn.'

Emma looked at the diary. 'I can't believe you found Rosie, I mean Evelyn. Daddy needs to see her. I doubt she can shed any light on the whereabouts of our English relatives, but wouldn't it be amazing for him to at least meet someone from his past who knew him as a child back in England?'

Those were Cassie's sentiments exactly. Cassie walked over to the sink with the two empty mugs and washed them up.

'I'd so love to go with you this time and be part of all this.'

Cassie smiled. She wiped her hands dry on the dish cloth and turned around. 'Then come with me.' Cassie's smile faltered as she wondered if she even had the air fare left in her bank account to return to England.

Emma closed the diary. 'It's not that simple.'

'Why not? Take a vacation or a few days leave of absence. Tell your boss you've got to sort out a family affair.'

'I could take some holiday, but…' She sighed heavily.

'Don can mind the children while you're away,' Cassie suggested hopefully. When she'd rushed downstairs with the diary, she saw Don on his way out with the kids. Emma had told him to take them to the park so Cassie might have a lie down in peace.

Emma's face clouded over. 'To be perfectly honest, things haven't been great between us. You turning up like you did has been a welcome distraction.'

Cassie pulled out a chair and sat down next to her sister at the kitchen table. 'What are you talking about? You and Don have always been good together.'

'Yes, you're right, until recently. At first, he didn't mind being a stay-at-home dad. He didn't have a choice. Don assumed it would only be temporary – we both did. Then my career took off, and as he wasn't having much luck getting another job, it made sense to reverse roles. He was used to being the main breadwinner. Typical Alpha male…' She trailed off.

Cassie got the picture.

'Things have been strained. He didn't realise how hard it is being at home with children all day. We could do with having a break. We haven't had a vacation in years.' She stared at Evelyn's diary. 'To take a family of five away isn't cheap.' Although her wages were good, it wouldn't stretch to paying for a holiday, even if it was camping, let alone coming up with the cost for her to fly to England.

She looked across the table at Cassie. 'With my income and his pension, I must be honest, things are tight with three youngsters. I'd love to go, but if I had the money to take a vacation…' she trailed off. She could not justify spending it all on herself to accompany her father back to England, however much she wanted to.

Although Cassie was disappointed, she understood. Her priority was her children and Don. She glanced at the diary and told her, 'There are two photos inside.'

'There are photos of Dad?'

'I slipped them in the back, behind the sleeve.' Cassie took the diary and opened it to the last page. She found the pictures and showed them to Emma. There was one of their dad on the steps outside Fletchling Hall with Evelyn and her family, the other one standing on a station platform with a tag around his neck.

Tears rolled down Emma's cheeks. She looked at Cassie. 'He was so young.'

'I know.'

'I couldn't imagine sending John, Eliza or Jared away to strangers.'

Cassie stared at her sister and had an idea. 'You're a reporter – right?'

'Uh-huh.' Emma nodded.

'Does that mean you search for stories that your editorial team or boss might find interesting?

Emma's had a notion where Cassie was going with this. She glanced at the diary. 'Are you suggesting what I think you're suggesting…?'

'It's a story – isn't it? A Canadian – that's me – finds a long-lost diary in England that has a connection with her father and the time he lived with a family as an evacuee in the war.'

Emma's eyes went wide. She pointed at Cassie. 'You know what? I think you're on to something.'

'Perhaps if the CBC were interested, they might send you to England, all expenses paid, to look into it. You could interview Evelyn.'

Emma bounced out of her seat and raced around the table, giving Cassie a kiss on the cheek. 'You are amazing – you know that? Why didn't I think of it? Now, where's my phone?'

As she raced out of the kitchen to grab the cordless phone in the hall and ring her boss, Cassie shouted after her, 'Any chance your job would consider paying the airfare for Dad too? After all, they might like to interview him as well.' Cassie stood up and followed Emma into the hall. Her sister had already picked up the phone. 'How about an interview when they meet up for the first time in decades?'

Emma was staring at her. 'Did I tell you, you are amazing?'

'Yes – you did. Now, if you really want to add that extra personal touch to the story, you might suggest to your boss he pay to fly all of us – me, Don, the kids, even Grandma – to England too, to see where Dad was evacuated in the war before he arrived in Canada,' Cassie was joking of course.

Emma frowned. 'That might be pushing it.'

Even though she said it in jest, Cassie added, 'It's worth a try.'

'It would be a big ask.'

Cassie shrugged. 'You never know…'

Emma looked at the phone.

So did Cassie. 'Ah, you do realise it's Saturday. There won't be anyone in the office.'

Emma smiled. 'It's the news, Cassie. It doesn't stop at the weekend.'

Cassie laughed. 'Oh, right, of course. I'll leave you to make your phone call.'

Cassie retreated upstairs to shower and change. Even though today hadn't started in quite the way she expected, being sick in the bathroom and finding out some incredible news she was still coming to terms with – she was having a baby – Cassie still wanted to visit her grandmother. She had the two photos in her hand. She wanted to show Grandma the photograph of Dad with the family who took him in before he left for Canada and tell her about the young girl who gave him the St. Christopher.

She crossed her fingers that her sister's boss thought it was a newsworthy story.

Cassie hoped her family might all return to England together. She would pay for the flights herself, but her savings were dwindling and without the proceeds from the sale of the flat that wasn't possible. She doubted Emma would return with the promise of plane tickets. If she was lucky, she'd get sent to England herself to chase up the story. Cassie wouldn't mind if that were the case. Besides, it was only fair that this time she was the one who got to go with Dad.

Before she showered and changed, Cassie put the photos in her bag so she wouldn't forget them. She couldn't wait to see her grandmother and tell her the amazing story of Evelyn Rosalind James and the lost diary she had found at Fletchling Hall.

53

Cassie heard her sister's voice downstairs in the hallway. She was still on the phone. That sounded encouraging. At least her boss was interested enough to listen, if nothing else.

Cassie sat down on the bed, towel-drying her hair. Before she visited her grandmother, there was something she needed to do first. She put the towel to one side and combed her hair. Cassie switched on her laptop. She logged straight into Facebook, hoping her dad was online. She tried calling his mobile number, but that went to voice mail.

Cassie sent a brief email instead, tapping her fingers impatiently on the keyboard, waiting to see if Dad responded. He didn't. She asked him to get in contact with her or her sister – it was important. Although it was urgent, she didn't want to alarm him in case he imagined something had happened to one of them or the grandchildren – or Grandma. Cassie gave nothing away; she didn't want to tell him what she'd found out. She wanted to save the surprise until she saw him.

With one thing and another, she had kept the diary to herself. She was glad she had because it was only when Evelyn recognised the St. Christopher, and Devon finished writing her story, that Cassie understood Evelyn was Rosie, and her dad had a living link to his past; something he'd been searching for his entire life. She wasn't a relative, but Evelyn and her family had taken him in and treated him as one of their own. For that brief period, they became his family. In her heart Cassie realised time had run out to find his biological parents. Evelyn might be the only living connection, and the closest thing he had to family, back in England.

Whatever came of her sister's phone call, although Cassie would love them all to fly over together – she knew that's what her dad would have wanted – at least he could still return himself. He had savings, so he probably had the air fare. If not, between her and her sister they'd come up with the money for him to make that last trip back to England.

Cassie was on Facebook, checking for any messages from him, when she came across one from Devon. *Dad's a complete mess without you.* Cassie discovered Devon had messaged her several times saying her dad was sorry about what happened.

He misses you. I miss you. Evelyn misses you too, and so does my mum, and all the staff at Fletchling Hall. Tabitha misses you too, I'm sure.

Cassie felt tears in her eyes. 'I miss you all too,' she whispered.

The only good thing about all this is my dad shredded the plans like I told him too. He has also stopped working, which is so unlike him and quite worrying, but it means things have really ground to a halt with the idea to sell the hall. Please come back soon.

Cassie was staring at the screen, thinking of their unborn child, when her sister burst into the room with the diary. 'Have you heard from Dad?'

Cassie frowned. 'I sent an email and text but nothing so far.'

'I just tried phoning him but…'

Cassie nodded as they both said in unison, 'His phone goes straight to voicemail.' They exchanged a knowing smile. Dad always switched things off when he wasn't using them. It was something ingrained in his generation because of growing up in the post-war era and being the offspring of parents who experienced rationing and slogans like *waste not, want not.* He still didn't get the rationale that whether you were using them or not, the phone should remain switched on.

'So, what are we going to do?' asked Cassie. She desperately wanted to get hold of him. 'What did your boss say?'

Emma glanced at the old leather-bound diary in her hand. 'Yeah, it would be great if Dad met Evelyn again.'

Cassie was about to ask what does that mean, wondering if the CBC were interested in his story, when Emma said, 'What about the Canadian? '

Cassie knitted her brow.

'It's all in here. He was Rosie's, I mean Evelyn's first love. I was going over their story with my boss. They say you never forget your first love.'

Cassie frowned when Ben came to mind.

'Don't you see? Evelyn is waiting for him to return.'

Cassie recalled Evelyn sitting at the window every day waiting for a visitor. So that's who she was waiting for. It all made sense now. That's why she had returned to the hall, hoping that one day he would come back to her. Her sister was right. Poor Evelyn. Their story, like so many others, truly was a casualty of war. Cassie shook her head sadly. 'She can't possibly believe he's coming back. Not after all these years, surely.'

'But she does, Cassie. She wrote about it in the diary.'

'What do you mean?'

'The promise he made when they were teenage sweethearts, before he left Fletchling Hall. He promised they would meet again.'

'Oh, yes.' Cassie remembered reading that.

'What if we found him?'

'Who – the Canadian?'

'Yes. Wouldn't it make a brilliant story?'

'Was that your boss's idea?'

'No – it was mine, actually. But it seemed to seal the deal.'

'What deal?'

Emma clapped her hands together. 'Guess where I'm going…?'

'No way!' Cassie smiled at her sister. She guessed it would be a big break for her, being sent abroad to cover a news story. Emma would have the opportunity, like her big sister did years ago, to spend time with her father, just the two of them back in England. Cassie wasn't upset. Perhaps it was for the best. It wouldn't be easy if she returned to England for a brief spell, knowing she'd have to leave again.

Cassie was so happy for her. She looked excited. Emma had found her calling working for the CBC in Canada. Her sister was ambitious. She was acting like a reporter, looking for a news item worthy of broadcasting. Cassie sighed. It would make a grand story, an Englishwoman reunited with her Canadian lost love from the Second World War. There was one big problem. 'How will you find him?' Or perhaps two – was he still alive?

Emma's face lit up. 'Leave it with me. I have had a brilliant idea.' She shot out the door.

Cassie turned to the computer and re-read the messages

from Devon. She suddenly became homesick for her adopted country. She recalled the drive from Toronto airport, sitting in the back of the taxi. She hadn't expected it all to look so foreign. Although she put it down to the years she'd been away, she realised it was more than that.

She'd lived longer in England than Canada. She assumed she would return and pick up where she left off. What she was afraid of was just this scenario; she considered herself a foreigner in her native land. Perhaps deep down she'd always felt that way. That's why she'd jumped at the opportunity to travel with her father in the first place. The UK felt like home the moment she stepped off that plane, as though she belonged. She wanted her child to be born in England, to grow up there.

Cassie still couldn't believe she was pregnant. It was early days. She didn't wish to get her hopes up in case something happened. She would rather not know the chances of carrying a baby to full term at her age; the odds were probably not stacked in her favour. It made her realise how much she wanted this child.

Cassie was sitting there staring into space when, out of the corner of her eye, she noticed her computer screen flicker. She turned her head and saw a Facebook message pop up. 'Dad?' Cassie put her fingers on the keyboard and suddenly realised that when they met up, she wouldn't know where to begin. There was so much to tell him about Evelyn and Fletchling Hall and… the baby.

In that moment, Cassie decided she was returning home as soon as possible even though she had nowhere to stay and no job, and probably not the return air fare in her checking account. It was a ridiculous thought, but she realised if she boarded a flight and returned to England, everything would turn out all right in the end. She just needed to make sure Dad could come too.

Cassie didn't want to spoil the surprise about Evelyn, so she sent a cryptic message telling him she was here in Canada staying with Emma. She was returning to England, making the trip with Emma and wanted him to come with them. Was there any way he might ditch the campervan – Cassie assumed he was in the back of beyond somewhere, not within a few hours driving distance – and fly to Toronto airport? She sent the message and waited with bated breath. She'd added that she wouldn't ask him if it wasn't important. She knew why he was on the road; he was meeting people, gathering stories of other transported British children for his book. But this was about him, *his* story. She wanted to tell him about Rosie's diary face-to-face.

A message pinged on Facebook. 'Yes!' Cassie punched the air when she read he would leave the campervan with a friend and fly to Toronto. Cassie thought about Emma and finding the Canadian – Scott. It sounded as though her boss wouldn't fly her to England for the story unless she covered that angle. That wouldn't stop Dad going.

Cassie was about to log out – she wasn't sure how to pay for her air fare, but she had to tell Emma she was booking the flights – when another message popped up. It was Devon asking her again when she was coming home.

Cassie sat there chewing a fingernail. Would Devon be eager for her return if she found out about the baby? As for Ben, she appreciated what Devon said about her father not being in a good place, but it didn't mean he was pining over her and they would get back together. Besides, could she forgive him for the way he had treated her over Ruby? Cassie's thoughts turned to

Devon's mum. She hadn't meant to interfere, but whatever Ben's motives were for not telling Devon the truth about her mother, Cassie still felt it was the wrong call. Devon deserved to grow up with the opportunity to know her mum. Even if she forgave him for treating her the way he had, it would be difficult to get past what he had done to Ruby and Devon. Cassie was surprised that, by the sound of things, Devon had forgiven her father.

Cassie logged out. She felt guilty for not messaging Devon back. In hindsight, she realised it was too good to be true, meeting the love of her life again, after all those years, and rekindling their relationship. If only life were that simple. They were both bringing baggage to the table, and it had caught up with them.

Cassie rested her hand on her stomach. She would tell him at some point when she was ready. It didn't mean Ben had to be in their lives, but it wasn't a secret she was prepared to keep from him or the baby. Cassie was thinking of Ruby and Devon, and the fallout years later of keeping secrets.

Her thoughts drifted to Lars. She hoped he'd do the decent thing and go back to his girlfriend. He would have to make sacrifices by shelving his selfish streak and putting her needs above his own. If he did that, the irony was not lost on Cassie that someone else would reap the benefits of Lar's inevitable transformation from a self-centred, egotistical bore to an attentive father and family man. That didn't mean her child wouldn't grow up surrounded by family who loved him or her.

Emma interrupted Cassie's thoughts, poking her head around the bedroom door. 'Hey, Sis, are you coming down for something to eat? We haven't had any breakfast.' She caught the look on her sister's face. 'What's the matter?'

'Nothing.' Cassie did not want him back – transformation or not. Her problem was Ben. But then it always had been. She looked at her sister. 'Dad messaged me on Facebook. He's catching an internal flight to Toronto.'

'That's great news.' She could tell by Cassie's expression there was something still troubling her. She guessed what it was. 'Look, if it turns out I can't find the Canadian and my boss won't let me go, I want you to go with Dad.'

'Thanks, Emma.' That was on her mind, but it wasn't the only thing.

Emma caught her sister placing a protective hand over her stomach. She asked gently, 'The father – is he in the picture?'

Cassie shook her head.

'Would he like to be?'

Despite Devon messaging her to come back, after what had happened with Ruby, she couldn't imagine that Ben would want to see her again. Cassie heaved a sigh. 'I don't think so.'

In the best interests of her child, she knew what she had to do. 'Look, I've had some thoughts. You mentioned I could stay here as long as I like…'

Her sister's eyes went wide. 'You're staying?' She rushed into the room to give her sister a hug. 'I was so worried that if you visited England, you wouldn't come back. This is the best news!' She squeezed Cassie tight.

Cassie managed a smile. Despite what she really wanted, to return to England and stay, she no longer just had herself to consider. Her baby would need a support network, family. So would she. Cassie realised she wouldn't be returning to England for good. She wanted to travel there one final time, with her Dad, like she did when she was a teenager all those years ago. Except this time, she wouldn't be staying. Her dad would close a chapter in his life, and so would she before she started a new life in Canada. There would be no reason for her to remain in England.

Emma drew back and searched her face. 'It is the best news – isn't it?'

Cassie gave Emma a reassuring smile that she wasn't about to change her mind. She was trying not to think of the people she'd be leaving behind; Ben and Devon, Ruby and Evelyn, and the other residents and staff at Fletchling Hall. Oh, and their newest recruit who had caused quite a stir – Tabitha.

They were like family too, and the hall was her home. Except Fletchling Hall wouldn't be anyone's home soon, Cassie reminded herself; despite what Devon said, she couldn't stop the sale. All those people would leave for new lives in different places, just like her.

'Cassie?'

Cassie stopped musing about who she would leave behind. She wanted the baby to be born and raised in England, but had to be realistic; being a single parent, without a support network, how would she cope? Cassie stood up. 'How about that breakfast you promised me?'

'Great. Come on. Don and the children are back. He's in the kitchen, cooking some scrambled eggs.'

Cassie was pleased she didn't come over nauseous at the mention of breakfast. She was following her down the stairs when it struck her as odd that her sister had changed into a smart trouser suit. She seemed overdressed. 'Are you going to work today?' She assumed Emma didn't work at the weekend.

'Ah, about that.' Emma walked into the lounge and looked at her reflection in the mirror over the fireplace. She took a deep breath and turned around to face Cassie. 'They have asked me to see the chief executive of CBC.'

'The chief executive?' That sounded ominous, thought Cassie. 'Do you know what it's about?'

'I'm not sure. To be honest, I'm nervous. My boss told me it's nothing to worry about. She asked if I'd take along the diary.'

'Rosie's diary?'

Emma nodded. 'It might have something to do with the Canadian.'

54

Cassie looked at her watch and turned to her sister. 'We should start making our way to the gate?' She was anxious they would miss their flight.

'Let's just give it a few more minutes.'

'Mummy, I need a wee.'

'Me too.'

Cassie glanced at her niece and nephew who were standing either side of their mum.

Emma looked at her children. 'I asked you a moment ago if you wanted to go with Daddy and Jared to the toilet!'

'I could take them, if you want to wait here with the trolley?' offered Cassie. She was keeping an eye on the trolley piled high with their suitcases for the trip to England. The gate had opened, but they were still waiting on one of their party who hadn't turned up yet.

Emma frowned. 'No, they can wait until Don and Jared return.'

Cassie looked at the two children standing there crossing their legs and thought back to that moment they found out about the trip to England. Emma had returned from that meeting she'd been so nervous about with the big cheese of CBC.

Cassie recalled asking her how it went . . .

❖

'How did the meeting go – did he have something to say about the Canadian?'

'No. It was about Dad.'

'Dad? *Our* dad?'

'Yes.'

'Do they know each other?'

'No, nothing like that. But you'll never guess…'

Cassie stared at her sister, wondering what she would say.

'The chief exec – he's one of them.'

Cassie looked at her, bemused. 'One of *them*?'

'Like Dad. He came to Canada from England. They could have even been on the same boat.'

'You're joking.'

'Nope.' Emma grinned. She had something else she couldn't wait to tell Cassie. She got out her purse and squealed like a six-year-old. Emma was holding up a bank card.

Cassie looked at the card, then at her sister. 'What's that?'

'It's our ticket to take the entire family on an all-expenses-paid trip back to England.'

'What did you just say?'

'It's an expenses card.' Emma couldn't get the words out quick enough. 'It turned out that after I spoke to my boss on the phone, she passed the story to the editorial team and the chief exec got wind of it. Although they are interested in me finding the Canadian, Scott, it's Dad's story that piqued the chief exec's interest because he has been searching for his English family too.'

Cassie shook her head. 'What are the chances?'

'I know. He understands that Rosie, I mean Evelyn, is not family, but he said he would love to hear all about Dad meeting her again at Fletchling Hall, and for me to cover the story. He said it was important to him – personal.'

'I'll bet,' said Cassie. 'So, does that mean…'

'We're all going. Even Grandma – if she's up to it.'

Emma took Cassie's hand and they danced around the room.

Eliza and John ran into the room and halted when they saw their mum and auntie dancing. 'What's going on?' asked John.

Emma turned to her children. 'How would you guys like to see the country where Granddad came from when he was a little boy?'

'Do you mean England?' Eliza asked.

Don walked in the lounge with Jared in his arms. 'What's going on?'

'Daddy, Daddy, we're going to England?'

'Pardon?' He looked over at Emma, raising his eyebrows as the children chanted, 'We're going to England, we're going to England….'

❖

'I need a wee, I need a wee…' they chanted.

She looked at her sister. 'Are you sure you don't want me to take them?' Cassie was looking toward the toilets when she thought she spotted a familiar face. *Dad?* She didn't wish to raise her hand and wave at some random stranger until she was sure.

It had all been very last minute. As soon as Emma was given the go-ahead, and the expense card, they booked flights, packed their suitcases, and planned to leave. There was just one fly in the ointment; Dad still had to get to Toronto to catch the international flight with them to England. She'd messaged him the details and prayed that, all going well, he'd get an internal flight in time to meet them at the airport.

It is him! 'Dad!' Cassie shouted out. 'Over here!'

He didn't hear her. She was about to fetch him when he passed the toilets as Don and Jared walked out, practically bumping into them. She saw her dad's face light up at the sight of his grandchild. Cassie smiled. They did a swap, her brother-in-law passing Jared to granddad for lots of fuss and cuddles. Don took his suitcase.

Cassie rushed forward as they strode towards her. She wasn't sure he'd make it. To accommodate their large group, they had to fly that week or delay for an entire month. Neither Cassie nor Emma wanted to wait that long, so they booked the seats. The only problem was her dad was in another part of the country; would he get back in time? It was a chance they had to take. Evelyn wasn't getting any younger. What if they delayed their trip then something happened and her father never got the chance to see Evelyn again?

'Oh, Dad!' Tears rolled down Cassie's cheeks. It had been an age since she'd last seen him in person. They'd kept in touch on Facebook, by email and Skype, and often spoke on the phone, but it wasn't the same. 'It's been too long.'

He handed Jared over to Emma and gave his eldest daughter a hug. When he stood back, he said, 'My, don't you look well – positively blooming.'

Cassie exchanged a knowing smile with her sister while John and Eliza clamoured for Grandad's attention. He accompanied them both to the toilets. Thankfully, Emma said nothing about another grandchild on the way; she must have guessed Cassie would tell him in her own time. Right now, it was all about Dad and finding some closure.

Even though Cassie was convinced he would never find his English parents, he had a living link to his past back in England; after all these years that was quite something.

Cassie stood there holding her father's hand, overwhelmed to see him. He was just the same as she remembered, a little thinner, but tanned, and looking really well. Being on the road, travelling, suited him. He had the same half-moon glasses on his nose and peered over the top of them when you were talking.

Cassie smiled at him affectionately. He was wearing brown corduroy trousers, a white shirt, and blue jumper. Typical Dad – nothing matched. In his hand was an old leather briefcase, the one he used to take to college before he retired from his job as a lecturer at Toronto University. Cassie glanced at the briefcase and wondered if he had brought along the book he was working on.

Martin glanced at his watch. 'Now I'm here, shouldn't we make our way to the gate?'

'That's what I said,' remarked Cassie, glancing at her dad.

Don echoed their sentiments.

Emma sighed. 'Can't we give it just a few more minutes?'

Martin furrowed his brow and followed his youngest daughter's gaze around the airport terminal. He looked at Cassie, perplexed. 'Is there someone else coming with us?'

He knew Grandma wasn't coming. While preparations were being made to fly to England, Cassie had visited her grandmother. She only lived a short taxi-ride away in a flat in a brownstone like Emma's. It had overwhelmed Cassie to see her again.

She looked old and frail, which had taken Cassie aback. She'd always remembered her as a robust woman, but time is never on anybody's side. Cassie knew it was to be expected. The fall hadn't helped. Despite showing her the photographs, and telling her all about Evelyn and their imminent trip to England, she chose not to make the journey.

Cassie wasn't surprised. Always one for an adventure, she'd love to have come with them but her declining health meant she had to accept a journey abroad was out of the question. Cassie promised they would take more photos and tell her all about Dad's meeting with the lady from England who gave him his St. Christopher.

Cassie looked at her Dad. He was under the misapprehension they were just accompanying her back to England and all having a family holiday together. Cassie turned to Emma. 'Shall I tell him or you?'

'You found the diary.' Emma handed it over. 'I think you should tell him.'

Martin looked from one to the other. 'Tell me what?'

Cassie squeezed her Dad's hand. 'Here.' She gave him the little leather-bound diary.

'What's this?'

'It's for you.' Cassie fingered the little St. Christopher around her neck. 'When I was back in England, I met an interesting lady; her name was Evelyn…' They headed toward the gate as Cassie began her story.

Don put Jared on his shoulders and turned to his wife. 'We have to go now, honey.'

Emma prised her attention from the busy airport concourse to look at Don.

'Sorry it didn't work out, sweetheart.' He followed her gaze around the terminal one last time.

Emma frowned. 'I really thought—'

'I know. But it *was* a shot in the dark.' Don heaved a sigh and spoke his mind. 'I don't like to say it, but maybe he has passed on. Even if he was still alive, the chances he'd have been listening to your broadcast….'

Emma turned to him. 'It's just the thought of Evelyn sitting at that window and never seeing him again.'

Don put his arm around her shoulders. 'I know, but at least you tried.'

Over the last few days, before their flight, Emma had been busy broadcasting Rosie's story in instalments on CBC and posting it on social media, hoping that the Canadian from her diary would get in touch. That hadn't happened.

On her final broadcast, she told him she'd left a plane ticket at Toronto airport with the details of the flight. When he arrived, all he had to do was go to the check-in desk and collect it. However, there was one small detail; whoever claimed that seat had to answer a question before they joined them on the journey to England – what was Rosie's proper name?

She worried that he might not remember or not even know, but they hadn't asked Evelyn's permission to use her story, so it was the only way forward to stick to her nickname, Rosie. However, it looked as though that would be a moot point. Nobody had turned up to claim the ticket.

55

Cassie glanced at her sister and caught the look of disappointment on her face. They were in the departure lounge. The gate had closed and they were standing in a queue waiting to board their flight. She sidled up to her.

Emma held up her hand. 'Please don't say *at least I tried*.'

'Perhaps he—'

'Yeah, Don suggested that too.'

They fell silent as the queue moved forward.

They reached the desk, ready to show their passports and boarding passes, when they heard raised voices. Emma and Cassie glanced behind them. A woman who looked in her fifties was arguing with one of the airport staff.

'I know we're late and the gate closed five minutes ago. I used a wheelchair so my father wouldn't have far to walk, but it was hard work pushing him through the airport terminal. I asked a member of staff for help. They just said I had to leg it. Did they expect me to run pushing this? Anyway, we're here now. He needs to board that flight.'

Cassie looked at the older man in the wheelchair. 'Do you think…?'

Emma read her mind. 'Let's find out.'

'Ma'am, the plane is boarding.'

Don caught Emma's arm. 'Where are you going? You heard the woman; we're boarding.'

'Ma'am, I have to insist you stay in the queue.'

Emma turned to the young woman on the desk. 'That man over there, he's with our party. I know he's late, but you've got to let him through.'

Cassie whispered in her ear. 'Are you sure that's Scott?'

While the lady motioned at her colleague to let them through, Emma whispered back, 'I have no idea, but the guy needs to board – so stuff it.'

Cassie grinned at her sister as a member of the airport staff wheeled him towards them.

Other people in the queue had noticed the old man being barred at the gate. They clapped when he was allowed through.

Martin said, 'Is he…?'

'Possibly.' Cassie had filled him in on who they were hoping would turn up. She'd also told her dad about his connection with the woman from Fletchling Hall who wrote the diary, Evelyn.

Tears welled up when he realised she was still alive, the girl who had given him the St. Christopher. He truly believed it had kept him safe.

Although he didn't say it, Cassie imagined he was feeling mixed emotions about this discovery. He'd always felt the little pendant was from his mother; the only connection he had to the parents he'd left behind in England. Martin had also spoken of his earliest memory of a young woman who he thought may have been an older sister. Her dad remembered playing on a big lawn and running down a wide staircase. Now he realised those recollections were of people who had taken him in and their teenage daughter who loved him like a brother.

Cassie had spoken to her sister about this before they contacted him. Would he want to learn the truth? Those memories and that St. Christopher were nothing to do with his English relatives. They both came from the same direction; he would want to know.

Evelyn was still so very important. She wasn't a relation, but after reading the diary, there was no doubt in Cassie's mind that in the brief space of time he was with them, he had become as much a part of the fabric of their family as Evelyn and her brothers.

If those government officials hadn't taken him away, they would have done the right thing and tried to find his parents. If the search had drawn a blank, or his father and mother died in the blitz, Cassie had no doubt Evelyn and her parents would have become his new forever family if events hadn't conspired against them. Cassie was so excited. She couldn't wait for her father to meet Evelyn again.

'Is it Scott, the chap from Evelyn's past?' Martin asked Cassie as they watched him approach. They overheard the old man complaining, 'I really don't need to be wheeled around like a baby,' in a grouchy voice.

The woman pushing the wheelchair grimaced. 'I know, Dad, but how would you have walked all this way? As it is, we almost missed our flight.'

Cassie and Emma exchanged a look, thinking the same thing when they realised they were both catching the flight; they'd only left one plane ticket for the Canadian to travel with them. It couldn't be him after all. He was travelling with his daughter.

As they all moved aside to let the gentleman in the wheelchair board first, his daughter paused at the desk to hand over their passports and boarding passes. The old man glanced at the people queuing, and said, 'Which one of you is Emma, the CBC broadcaster?'

Emma looked at him in surprise and stepped forward.

'Scott?'

'Yes.'

Cassie glanced at her sister. Could it be him? 'Did you know Rosie?'

'Oh, yes. I haven't heard that name in a long while.' He wiped his eyes with a handkerchief.

Cassie noticed. 'Were those tears in his eyes?'

'Do you know Rosie's first name?'

Cassie turned to her sister. 'I don't think we need to—'

'Cassie,' warned Emma, 'I just wanted to ask – that's all.'

She sighed. She realised what her sister was doing. Checking it wasn't some random guy who wanted a free plane ticket to England. Cassie imagined a guy his age would hardly go through all the hassle of turning up at an airport to take an international flight if it wasn't for a good reason.

Emma folded her arms. 'Well?'

The woman on the desk trying to board the passengers said, 'Is there a problem?'

Cassie was about to say, 'No,' when her sister got there first. 'Maybe.'

Scott's daughter stepped in. 'Let me explain. I was visiting him the other day and he had the radio on as usual. His hearing isn't what it once was, so he doesn't listen to it much. It's just background noise, but he always insists I leave it on. There was a broadcast about a Canadian they were looking for, by the name of Scott, who met a girl called Rosie in England during the Second World War.'

Everyone was listening to her; even the three children were quiet.

'I knew he was stationed in England, but there were probably a good number of young Canadians by the name of Scott. Two days later, when they ran the broadcast again, I mentioned to him an interesting story on the radio; they were looking for a guy who met a young woman called Rosie whose family lived at Fletchling Hall in Sussex. For a minute there I thought he'd had a heart attack, he was so stunned. It turns out he was my father.'

'Okay,' said Emma, 'but you still haven't answered my question. What was her first name?'

'Her first name? I thought it was Rosie?' She looked at her father. 'Can you answer the lady's question?'

He looked from Cassie to Emma. 'Her name was Rosie.'

Cassie glanced at her sister and bet she was thinking the same; his daughter had told him what she'd heard on the radio. At his age, his memory wasn't what it once was, so although he believed he once knew a girl called Rosie, he was just confused.

As he stood up to board the plane, his daughter guessed what they concluded. 'Dad, you had better sit back down.'

'Aren't we boarding the flight?'

She shook her head. 'I don't think so.'

He looked at her in surprise. 'But we came all this way, and I want to see Rosie.'

Everyone stared at the confused old man. 'I know you do, Dad. Let's forget what was on the radio, eh?'

Cassie was helping him into the wheelchair, a reflex being an

O.T. used to working with older patients and those with disabilities. She was leaning over him when her pendant slipped out of her blouse and dangled in front of the old man's face.

'Oh, sorry.' She was about to slip it back when he said, 'Let me see that.'

Cassie knelt and held out the little pendant. 'Do you recognise it?'

He smiled. 'Yes. Rosie used to wear one. That's what she'd told me. I never saw it myself, but from what she described, it looked a lot like this one.'

'Really?' Cassie glanced at her sister. She was standing there, holding her breath. It was the thing they had taken a chance on when they added that little caveat if someone turned up claiming to be the Canadian. What if Evelyn had never told him her first name?

'Is there anything else you remember?'

'As I recall, she told me her two brothers had one each with the first letter of their names engraved on the back, but I never understood why she said hers had the letter E engraved on it.'

Cassie turned the St. Christopher round to reveal the letter etched on the back.

He held it between his thumb and forefinger, the look on his craggy features one of complete surprise. He stared up at Cassie. 'Is this…? Where did you get it?'

Cassie grinned as Emma exclaimed, 'You're him! You're the Canadian. You knew Rosie.'

'Yes, that's what I told you.'

Cassie said, 'Her first name was Evelyn, but she never mentioned that, did she?'

He shook his head. 'How did you come by this necklace?'

Before she answered his question, Cassie wanted to learn more. Their party had stepped to one side, allowing the remaining passengers to continue boarding the flight. Fortunately, it had allowed them some precious time to establish he was the man they'd been looking for.

Cassie glanced at her father before continuing. 'You mentioned she spoke about her necklace, but you never saw it?'

'That's right. Rosie told me she gave it away.'

'Did she?' Out of the corner of her eye, Cassie caught her father step forward.

'Did she ever mention a boy who used to live with the family, an evacuee?'

He started shaking his head, no, then a memory stirred. 'There was a little boy… yes. Now I remember. She spoke of him so fondly. I believe he was one of the evacuees from London who was billeted to the hall. I got the impression she was heartbroken he had to leave. At first, she blamed us, the Canadians. Now, what was his name…?'

Cassie's Dad was listening to all this. She could tell by his expression he was finding all this quite overwhelming. She glanced at her dad. 'His name was Martin, Marty. But Rosie called him—'

'Ted.' The old man nodded. 'Yes, that's right – Ted. He was a little blonde-haired fellow in short trousers. I saw a photograph. She loved that child like he was her brother. I often wondered what became of him.'

Cassie squeezed her dad's hand. He found his voice. 'Ahem, I'm Martin, the little boy.'

The older man furrowed his brow. 'That can't be. You're Canadian. He was British.'

'Excuse me,' interrupted one of the airport staff. 'I will have to ask you to board. The captain says he is closing the doors, so if you don't get on now, I'm afraid you *will* miss this flight.'

Cassie looked up and discovered the airport lounge was empty. Everyone had boarded.

Martin glanced at his plane ticket and looked at the Scott and his daughter. 'I'd love for you both to sit with me on the flight and I'll tell you how I came to be in Canada. What are your seat numbers?' He doubted he'd be lucky enough to have the seat next to them on the flight. When they told him, he didn't think so. However, he intended to have a word with a member of the cabin crew to see if some kind people would be prepared to change seats.

As Emma took the seat next to Cassie, leaving Don sitting with the children in three seats across the aisle, she caught the expression on her face. 'Are you all right?'

As soon as Cassie boarded the plane to return to England, she thought of Ben. After meeting him again and having the most wonderful time, even though it hadn't worked out, she had learnt something that deep down she'd known all along; she was never meant to be with Lars. She just wished it hadn't taken all these years to find that out. But as her grandmother often said, *better late than never.*

Cassie gave her sister a reassuring smile that she was okay. She glanced down the rows of seats and saw her father talking animatedly to Scott and his daughter, showing them Evelyn's diary. Cassie laid a gentle hand on her stomach and fingered the St. Christopher. Her grandmother was *so* right.

56

The taxi dropped them off at the pub in the village. With accommodation in a converted stable block, the pub offered breakfast and evening meals if they wished to dine in. They were lucky; almost all the rooms were free. There was a family room for Emma, Don and the kids, two singles for Cassie and her father, and a twin for Scott and his daughter who didn't mind sharing. Cassie collapsed on her bed and felt she could sleep for a week. It wasn't the journey. The flight and the trip by taxi to the village were pleasant with no hold-ups. Cassie guessed why she was tired; it was being pregnant.

Although they were all keen to go straight to the hall, by the time they arrived and checked in it was late. The visit would have to wait until the morning. Cassie needed to contact Phyllis and tell her there was a sizeable party on their way to see Evelyn.

In hindsight, she should have phoned before they flew out. It was an oversight, but she realised why she didn't. The last time they spoke, Phyllis called her unprofessional and fired her. She was worried that in the brief time she'd been gone something drastic had happened. The hall might have closed. She resisted the urge to contact Devon to find out.

'For goodness' sake, just ring the place,' Emma exclaimed in exasperation when Cassie knocked on her door to say goodnight and told her what was playing on her mind. Cassie could hear the children watching television and Don telling them to change into their pyjamas.

Cassie returned to her room, sat down on the bed and picked up her mobile. She could do without speaking to Phyllis. Although she didn't have Olivia's number, she had Randall's. Cassie continued to scroll through her contact list and came to the one person she could call – Devon. She would know if the hall was still open and if Evelyn was up to visitors.

Cassie stared at Devon's number. That was the other thing on her mind – Ben. She missed him terribly, but somehow, she had to move on. Coming back here wasn't helping. Cassie reminded herself why she returned. She was here for Dad and to help him find some closure with his past. Cassie sighed and rang Devon's number.

Devon answered in a sleepy voice. Cassie glanced at her watch and realised she'd lost track of time. It was eleven o'clock on a school night. 'I'm sorry I woke you up, Devon,' Cassie said hastily. 'I'll call back in the morning.'

'Cassie? No wait, don't hang up.'

Cassie stayed on the phone. 'The reason for my call is I wondered if the hall was still open.' Although Cassie knew she hadn't been gone any time at all, she still didn't know what might have happened in her absence. 'I would like to visit tomorrow.'

'You've come back?'

Cassie didn't want to get into that right now. 'Is the hall open? They haven't all left – have they?'

'Er, about that.' There was a pause.

'Yes?'

'I told my Dad that if he put in his plans, and they turned the hall into a housing development, then I'll never speak to him again.'

Cassie thought Devon would do something like that; hold her dad to ransom.

'Do you want to speak to Dad? I can wake him up.'

'No!'

'I'll tell him you called.'

'No.'

'Why not?'

Cassie sighed. 'We had a falling out, Devon, over your mother – remember?'

'You weren't to know Ruby's my mum or Ben is my dad.'

'I shouldn't have got involved, Devon. It wasn't my place.'

'If you hadn't, I would never have found her – don't you see?'

Cassie fell silent.

'He's sorry for the way he treated you.'

Cassie believed her, but she still couldn't get past what he'd done, keeping Devon from seeing her mother. Cassie wasn't just thinking of Devon, but Ruby too. She missed out on all those years watching her daughter grow up. It made her feel she didn't know Ben at all. When Cassie voiced her thoughts, Devon fell silent.

'Devon – are you still there?' Cassie hoped she hadn't said something wrong.

Devon was sitting on the end of the line, frowning. She didn't want to talk about what she'd found out. Although she'd got over it now, she was still coming to terms with the fact that it wasn't her dad that stopped her from seeing Ruby.

She'd heard them rowing one morning – her dad and Gramps. That wasn't unusual since she'd started visiting Ruby. She realised Gramps had fallen out with Dad over not telling her about her mum. It was the revelation of what her dad was still withholding that shocked her. She'd stormed in on them, tired of hearing their raised voices. That's when she confronted them both.

Dad stood there warning Gramps not to say anything, but he said it anyway, and that's how Devon found out what they'd all been hiding from her – her mother included.

'It wasn't your dad stopping you from seeing Ruby,' Gramps told her. 'He was only respecting your mother's wishes even though he tried so very hard to change her mind.'

Her dad tried to dissuade Ruby from that decision, adamant that she was wrong. He believed his daughter needed her mother regardless of Ruby's disabilities. At first, he took Devon to visit her as often as he could. Devon suspected that's why she still retained the memory of her silky, smooth hair. But the visits didn't last. Ben had little choice but to stop taking her. He couldn't bear to watch Ruby rejecting their daughter; not touching her or cuddling her. He'd had enough.

In the beginning, he chose Fletching Hall as Ruby's home; it was close to where they lived. He hoped one day she might change her mind. However, as the years rolled on, and he realised nothing would change, he was afraid Devon would discover the truth. Not that he had kept her from Ruby, but her own mother rejected her.

When the owner of the Fletchling Hall decided to sell the estate, forcing the residents to move on, Ben had no problem submitting plans on behalf of the developers. There was no reason for Ruby to remain living in the area. And then it happened. After all these years of not seeing her daughter, it was that unannounced visit from Devon, when she'd followed Tabitha to her apartment, which finally changed Ruby's mind.

When Devon found out the truth, she confronted her mother. Ruby admitted that, at first, she couldn't bear to look at her young daughter, reminding her of the life she once had before the car accident robbed her of being a proper mother. She felt Devon would be better off without her. She didn't want her being held back by a disabled mother.

'I didn't mean to come between you and your father. I wish I hadn't,' Cassie continued.

Devon shook her head. 'But that's the thing – you didn't. We weren't getting on long before you turned up on our doorstep with the radio.' Devon was thinking of her dad working all hours on his business, with little interest in anything else, including his own daughter.

'When you arrived, things changed. *He* changed. Then you left and he's not the same person. He stopped going to work. Dad hangs around the house all day strumming on his guitar, singing crazy, sad songs.' Devon rolled her eyes.

'Really?' Cassie suppressed a smile. It sounded so Kurt Cobain.

'Oh, yes. It's quite pathetic. I told him to call you, but he's a stubborn—'

'Devon…'

Devon sighed down the phone. 'I was going to say, *idiot*. He said it was his fault you left. He shouldn't have said what he said. What did he say, by the way…?'

Cassie remembered those cutting remarks about interfering

and coming between him and his daughter. The trouble was he had a point.

'Can't you come over and make things right?'

'Oh, Devon. I wish things were that simple.' She heard Devon's exasperated groan down the phone. 'Why do adults always say that?'

Cassie changed the subject. It was getting late and she had to go. 'Look, tomorrow I'm visiting the hall. There's someone I'd like Evelyn to meet. I read the diary you filled in with the rest of Evelyn's story.'

'You did?'

'Uh-huh. Will you come tomorrow to visit Evelyn?' Cassie wanted her to be there. She deserved to learn how her story ends.

'I'll be there. I visit Evelyn most days. I've got the keys to Gatekeepers Cottage.'

'You got the keys – how?'

'It was Olivia, she gave them to me.' Devon added, 'I only spent one night there. Jodie stayed over too. Dad thought I was at her house. It was cool, but…' she trailed off.

'You missed home.'

'Yeah. It's my birthday and Evelyn is organising something. I'm not sure what. She asked for the keys to Gatekeepers Cottage, but not to tell Phyllis. I don't know what she's planning. Will you come? It's this week.'

Cassie cast her gaze around the cosy single room she was booked into. They were staying in Sussex and then popping into London for a short break at the end of their trip to see the sights before flying home to Canada. Even though she'd be around, she didn't want to bump into—

'If you're worried about running into my dad – don't be. He

won't be coming to my birthday at the hall.'

'Oh.' That made up Cassie's mind. 'All right. I will.'

'Cool.' Devon paused. 'So, what's so special about tomorrow?'

Cassie didn't know whether it was being tired from the long-haul flight, but she'd lost track of the conversation.

'You said that you are visiting the hall tomorrow and there's someone you'd like Evelyn to meet.'

'Oh, yes.'

'Who is it?'

'Ah,' Cassie grinned. 'You'll see.'

'Shall I tell Dad to come too?'

Cassie shook her head, *please don't.* 'No, thank you, Devon. This is a family thing.'

'A family thing? As in *your* family?'

'Yes.'

'You've brought your family over from Canada?' Devon sounded excited. 'I'd love to meet them. They could come to my party too.'

Cassie paused at the end of the phone.

'Oh, please say yes. Wouldn't they like to see where you lived when you worked here?'

'I suppose so, but I don't see what that's has to do with—?'

'When Evelyn asked for the keys, I guessed she is planning to throw me a sixteenth birthday party at the cottage.'

'Really?' Cassie recalled the diary and Evelyn's sixteenth birthday she had spent at Gatekeepers cottage. Cassie had a thought. Maybe Dad would like to see the cottage where he lived with Evelyn and her parents, before he was taken away? 'Now I come to think of it that would be a brilliant idea.'

Devon was already saying, 'Cool… cool.'

Cassie frowned. 'The thing is there are quite a few of us.'

'Doesn't matter. There's always the garden.'

'All right, I'll have a word with the others. I've got a niece and two nephews who I'm sure won't say no to a birthday party.'

'Great. I will be at the hall tomorrow visiting my mum and Evelyn, so I'll see you there.'

Cassie smiled. She was looking forward to seeing Devon. 'Just promise me you won't tell your dad I'm back.'

Devon crossed her fingers and said, 'I promise.'

57

Cassie had ordered a minivan to pick them up after breakfast. It arrived later than she expected; they were all waiting in the small lobby of the pub when the minivan turned up. Cassie frowned when she glanced at her watch. She frowned again when she walked out of the pub and discovered there was already a passenger.

She was about to march up to the vehicle when Emma caught her arm. 'The driver made a detour to the train station to pick him up.'

'What are you talking about?'

'I told the CBC that I found Scott and they agreed I could do an interview – on camera. A cameraman is coming too. That's him in the taxi.' Emma grinned. 'I'm going to be on television! I'm doing a documentary about rekindling lost love.'

Cassie looked at her sister. 'You don't know if Scott and Evelyn will want to do an interview for television.' Let alone rekindle their lost love, thought Cassie. Ben came to mind.

'Scott said he would enjoy doing an interview.'

'You've asked him already?'

'Of course.'

'What about Evelyn?'

'I'm sure he'll persuade her.'

'I don't believe it! You're using this to further your career.'

'Oh, Cassie, we're talking about *television*. I couldn't pass up an opportunity like this. Besides, if we get Dad on camera too…'

'Dad?'

'I've got to tell the viewers a bit of background, and then there's how you fit into it with finding the diary.'

Cassie looked at her in shock when the penny dropped. 'Oh, no. I'm not going on television. No way!'

'Oh, come on, Cassie. It's for a good cause.'

'What – furthering your career?'

'Yes and for Dad.'

'What do you mean?'

'If people hear about Rosie's story, they might want to read Daddy's book when it comes out. Who knows, it could be a best seller.'

Cassie hadn't thought about that, although they both knew she was really doing it to get into television broadcasting. Cassie didn't begrudge her that. Perhaps she was right: what harm could a little publicity do? If word got around about the little boy evacuated to Fletchling Hall, who knows where that might lead? Cassie was thinking about the possibility, however small, that a long-lost relative of theirs might surface. 'Ok.'

'Great, now who wants to sit next to the cameraman?'

Her eldest son's hand shot up. 'Do you think he'll let me hold his camera?'

'You can ask him, sweetheart.'

Although Don had offered to take the children out for the day while they visited the hall, Martin wanted Evelyn to meet his family. She was the closest thing he had to relatives in England. It meant a lot to him for them all to be there when he finally met her.

Cassie was getting into the minivan when she noticed the cameraman shift in his seat and point his camera out the back window. Cassie turned to her sister with a question.

She whispered, 'How did he get here so quickly?'

Cassie nodded. He wasn't on their flight.

'He's a British freelancer.'

'I see.' Cassie stared at him pointing the camera. 'What's he doing?'

Emma hesitated. 'I kind of had an idea…'

The expression on Emma's face said she was up to something. Cassie knitted her brow. 'What are you up to?'

The roar of an engine drowned out Emma's reply. Cassie glanced out the rear window and saw an old camouflage-green open-top jeep pull up behind the minivan. It looked like something out of a war movie. Emma's cameraman started filming.

'What is going on?' Cassie was staring at the army vehicle when she noticed Scott step out of the pub and stroll to the jeep. He was dressed in a Canadian army uniform. She looked at her sister. 'You have got to be kidding me!'

Emma grinned. 'From what you've told me, Evelyn will be sitting at her window. He can't arrive in a minivan now, can he? She'll know it's him if he arrives in a jeep.'

'Emma, he's in his eighties. He'll do himself an injury climbing in and out of that thing.'

She laughed. 'He'll be fine. I've only rented the vehicle for the morning, so we better crack on. Don't look at me like that. This will be fun.'

Cassie sighed. This was turning into a circus. She caught Scott smiling from ear-to-ear as he climbed into the jeep. At least someone was happy. Cassie wasn't. After that phone call last night, Ben was constantly on her mind. Coming back here was a mistake. Could she trust Devon not to tell him about her visit?

Cassie caught her father's smile as he stared at the jeep. That's when she decided she must put her own feelings aside for now. Today was about them, her dad finding someone from his other life in England, and two octogenarians meeting up for the first time in decades and possibly rekindling lost love. Cassie looked at her sister and hoped this would not backfire.

❖

Devon was sitting in the chair next to Evelyn reading her a book, with the radio on low in the background, when her voice was drowned out by a car roaring up the drive. She almost jumped out of her skin. 'What the hell is that?!'

Evelyn heard it too. She looked at Devon in surprise. It was a noise she hadn't heard in years. 'It sounds like…' Evelyn reached over and pulled the net curtains to one side. Coming up the driveway was a jeep. Evelyn shook her head. No, it can't be…

'Quickly, hand me my glasses.'

Devon picked them up off the side table.

Evelyn put them on as Devon approached the window and looked down the drive. Evelyn was watching too.

'What is it?'

Evelyn shook her head, still convinced her eyes were deceiving her. 'It's a World War Two jeep.'

Now she remembered why it seemed familiar. Devon recognised the vehicle from those old war movies Gramps liked to watch on the television on a Sunday afternoon. 'What's it doing here, do you think?'

Evelyn stared out the window as the vehicle came to a stop on the gravel driveway. She spotted the driver, a young man, get out of the jeep and open the door for the passenger. That's when Evelyn noticed the passenger was wearing a uniform. Evelyn slowly rose from the chair.

Devon, who was standing by her chair, noticed Evelyn getting up from her seat. 'Evelyn?'

When she didn't answer, Devon said, 'Is everything all right?'

Evelyn's hand reached for Devon.

Devon grasped her hand. 'Evelyn? What is it, what's wrong?'

Evelyn walked right up to the window.

With Evelyn's hand tightly clasping hers, Devon had no choice but to accompany her. She followed her gaze to the man down below, climbing out of the jeep. He was wearing a uniform. 'Who is he?'

'He came back!' That's all Evelyn said before she collapsed. Luckily Devon was holding her hand and guided her to the chair; otherwise, she would have landed in a heap on the floor.

Devon pressed the emergency button on the cord around Evelyn's neck, picked up the book and started flapping it in her face, trying to give her some air. 'Evelyn? Evelyn!'

There was no response.

❖

'She's had a turn. She will need to get checked over by the doctor on call. In the meantime, she won't be receiving visitors today.'

Emma whispered in Cassie's ear. 'That did not go down as I expected.'

Cassie rolled her eyes at her sister. 'You don't say.' She thought it was lucky Evelyn had just fainted and it wasn't something more serious, like a heart attack with the shock when she realised after all these years, Scott had returned. Cassie had received a text from Devon saying Evelyn was okay but kept repeating Scott's name.

Cassie was standing in the entrance foyer of Fletchling Hall. She was joined by her family, the cameraman, and the old man in uniform and his daughter. She was doing her best trying to melt into the background as Phyllis told them all that Evelyn needed to rest.

'Cassie, can I have a word?'

Cassie had been hiding behind her dad, avoiding eye contact with Phyllis. She'd been on her way out when she heard Phyllis call her name. Cassie sighed and turned to her sister. 'Why don't you guys go ahead? I'll phone for a taxi when I'm ready.'

Martin was on his way to the minivan when he realised Cassie was staying behind. 'I think I'll hang back too and wait for Cassie.'

Emma said, 'Suit yourself.' She looked at the cameraman. 'I think we will have to call it a day and come back tomorrow.' She cast a glance up at the hall. 'I've got another brilliant idea.'

Scott was about to climb in the jeep when he realised Cassie and Martin were staying behind. He said to his daughter. 'I will hang back too and make doubly sure Rosie, I mean Evelyn, is all right.'

'I'll stay too, then.'

'No, you return to the pub and have a bite to eat. I'll come back with Cassie and Martin.'

'Are you sure?'

He smiled affectionately at his daughter. 'I don't need a babysitter. I'll be fine.'

She gave him a kiss. 'See you at the pub.' She went over to the jeep and got in beside the driver.

Scott made his way up the steps into the hall. Cassie was nowhere to be seen, but Martin was sitting on one of two high-backed easy chairs placed by the windows either side of the front door. Scott walked over and lowered himself into the other chair.

He stared out the window. There were lovely views of the extensive grounds leading down to the little cottage at the end of the drive where his first love lived with her family when he came to Fletchling Hall. He recalled the first time he saw her; a little slip of a girl standing outside the cottage with arms folded, her face like thunder clearly not pleased at their arrival.

Scott remembered hanging out the rear of a truck, crammed full of Canadians, and waving at the cute girl. 'This takes me back.'

'Me too,' said Martin.

They both sat lost in their own private thoughts of times gone by and how their lives might have turned out differently. What if Scott had found Rosie again after the war? What if Martin had returned to his family in London or he'd been orphaned and Rosie's family adopted him?

Would they rewrite the past if they could? Without the road they had travelled in life, the children, grandchildren, and in Scott's case, his first great-grandchild, wouldn't exist. But that road had led them back here. What did it mean? Scott was thinking about a second chance at love. Was that possible at his age?

His wife had passed away some ten years ago. In all these

years, he'd never forgotten Rosie. He came back once, when the war was over, just as he'd promised. As soon as he was able, he returned to England, to Fletchling Hall, and drove up to the house. The place was empty, abandoned.

Villagers told him the family had fled to Scotland and never returned. It was a long shot. He'd taken a train to Fort William, knowing it was crazy, but going anyway in the vain hope of finding her. On the journey, he remembered picking up a newspaper a fellow passenger had discarded. Inside, he'd seen a small announcement.

He didn't have to read the article; the photograph was enough. It was Rosie, her arm linked with a man in uniform, standing outside a church. She was wearing a white wedding dress. Scott had no choice but to return to Canada and get on with his life. He'd left it too late. Wounded in the war, it had taken him months to recover. Until he was well, he didn't want to send word or try to contact her. That turned out his biggest regret.

Scott wished he hadn't let Emma talk him into wearing this uniform and arriving in the jeep. It gave Evelyn quite a turn. He felt the biggest fool. Martin told him what Cassie said about Evelyn sitting at the window every day waiting for a visitor, waiting for him. He hoped it was true but didn't know how to go through another day without seeing her to find out. Scott glanced at his companion. He was here searching for answers too.

Martin caught Scott looking at him and smiled. He was sitting there thinking about the personal quest he was on, travelling across Canada, writing a book. It wasn't to find his own family, but to connect with others like himself who were coming to terms with their past and the cruel, inevitable passage of time that meant the chances of finding their English families had most likely passed them by.

For him, this was an incredible moment. Evelyn was right here, a link to his past in England; a girl who belonged to a family who treated him as one of his own. He would not leave until he saw her. Martin glanced at Scott and guessed he was sitting here for that reason too. After all these years, he wasn't leaving either.

Scott stared around the hall, his memories taking him back to the place busy with young Canadian serviceman unloading gear and moving into the stately home, and a teenage girl confronting him in one of her brother's bedrooms. He would never forget the first time he spoke to her. He smiled at the memory. He couldn't wait to see her again.

Martin sat there recalling a little three-year-old boy running up those stairs, playing hide-and-seek, and having cuddles from a girl he assumed was his sister.

He smiled when he thought of the little St. Christopher, and the girl putting it around his neck, telling him it would bring him luck and keep him safe on his journey through life. He never knew for sure whether that was a recollection, a memory, or just a dream, a story he'd made up about his pendant. He'd always assumed it must have been given to him by his mother, but he couldn't remember. Now he knew the truth, he couldn't wait to see her again, and tell her how the St. Christopher had brought him luck, and kept him safe, just as she'd promised.

Cassie walked along the corridor and came out into the entrance hallway. She saw her dad and Scott sitting next to each other, staring forlornly at the floor. She stood there for a moment wondering what they were still doing here.

Her father spotted her. He rose from his seat. 'Cassie, is everything all right? I wondered where you'd got to.'

'Oh, Dad, you didn't have to wait for me.'

'Actually, I was still rather hoping to meet Evelyn.'

'Me too,' added Scott, rising from his chair.

Cassie wasn't surprised. 'Hold on, I've got an idea.' She got out her mobile phone and texted Devon. Phyllis had told them that Evelyn would not be entertaining visitors today. Cassie was going against that advice and asked Devon, who she assumed was still with her, how Evelyn was feeling.

While she was texting, Martin asked his daughter, 'So, where did you disappear to?'

'Phyllis wanted to see me. They fired me. That's why I left.'

'You? Fired? From a job?'

Cassie looked at her father askance.

'I don't believe it.'

'I'm afraid it's true, but they have cleared me of any wrong-doing.' Cassie didn't want to go into details right now. She had suspected Ben was the reason she lost her job, getting his own back for interfering with his family.

However, while Cassie was in Canada, it turned out Ben had spoken with Phyllis, the first chance he got, and told her he bitterly regretted coming to her over the passport-sized photo of Ruby. Although Cassie had taken it from her file, it was incidental to what was really going on. When Phyllis gave her the sack, she wasn't privy to the whole story; Devon didn't know her mother, Ruby, was here, living at Fletchling Hall. He'd blamed Cassie when Devon found out, but knew she was just being who she was; a kind, caring O.T. concerned for the welfare of her patient – and Ruby's child.

The phone rang so Cassie slipped out of the office leaving Phyllis to answer the call.

'So, what did she say?' Martin asked, eyeing his daughter and cutting across her thoughts.

'Phyllis has just offered me my old job back.'

'Wow, that's fantastic news, sweetheart – isn't it?'

Cassie looked at her dad who had no idea she was meant to be returning to Canada for good. She gazed around the expansive entrance and knew that as soon as she'd walked through those doors, she felt she'd come home.

When Phyllis offered her the job back, Cassie's immediate inclination was to accept. Then she remembered the baby and the promise she'd made to bring him or her up surrounded by family. She wouldn't go back on that promise. Besides, this was still just a temporary position. Even so, Cassie had not said an outright no.

'Cassie, are you okay?'

'Yes, I'm fine, Dad. I've got a lot on my mind.'

'Do you want to talk about it?'

Cassie would like nothing more than to tell him her news, but right now Devon had texted back, and Cassie had something to announce. 'We're going to see Evelyn!'

Cassie started up the stairs. She glanced over her shoulder. They were both standing there staring at her in stunned silence. 'Well, what are you waiting for?'

58

Emma was sipping a glass of punch, watching Evelyn and Scott being interviewed by the local news for the BBC. She turned to Cassie. 'What do you think?'

The large entrance hall was festooned with bunting. There was a massive British flag and a Canadian flag hung on the wall on opposite sides of the room. Trestle tables had been laid out with chintzy table clothes from a local café who had also prepared sweet and savoury party food. The food, lemonade and squash were all paid for on Emma's handy expense card. Someone had made up an enormous punch bowl.

They had positioned the tables against two walls, so there was plenty of room for people to help themselves to the buffet and even dance if they wanted to. Evelyn's radio had been brought downstairs and was playing music from a bygone era. Cassie didn't recognise any of the songs, but it sounded very 1940s, which was quite apt.

Cassie turned to her sister and smiled. 'I can't believe you organised all this. What a fabulous idea.'

They were standing at the foot of the stairs watching three women from the local café laying out the food. Over by the front door, where Evelyn and Scott were sitting in two easy chairs by the window, a camera crew was set up. Two more chairs had been positioned by the couple, one for the young woman interviewing and the other for their father.

Emma finished her glass of punch. 'The party was my producer's idea at the CBC. I wish I'd thought of it.'

'But it was your idea to suggest people come in fancy dress.' Cassie looked down at her brown dungarees, checked shirt and wellies. She was also wearing a headscarf. 'I'm a land girl, by the way, working on the farms, doing my bit for king and country as part of the Women's Land Army. In case you're wondering…'

Emma hired a uniform so she could come to the party as a member of the WAAF, the Women's Auxiliary Air Force. She wore the uniform in honour of Scott, who stayed in the military after the war, serving in the Canadian Air Force. She had even put her hair up in a bun and toned down her makeup. Cassie thought she looked amazing. 'You really look the part.'

'Thank you. So do you. The dabs of dirt on your face are a nice touch.'

'I used brown mascara to put some smears on my cheeks.' Cassie frowned. 'It might be a problem getting it off though.'

Emma laughed.

Cassie was relieved Ben wouldn't be here to see her looking like this. Not that it mattered. He wouldn't care what she looked like. Even so, she felt a bit of a mess, her hair kept falling out of the headscarf, and her new wellies she'd bought in the village kept squeaking every time she took a step. She looked at her sister in her spotless uniform and wished she'd come as a member of the WAAF instead.

Emma read her mind. 'You look fine. You know I couldn't

pull off those dungarees. I'd need your long legs and slender frame.'

Don walked up to them, carrying two glasses of punch. He was wearing a Royal Air Force uniform. The children were similarly dressed in outfits from that era, the two boys in knee-length short trousers, shirts and little waistcoats. Their daughter was in a simple, but pretty floral dress with a matching band in her hair. The children were also carrying a box with a gas mask inside. Jared even had one. He got his out and tried to put it on.

Cassie smiled at Jared. He wasn't that much younger than her father when he was evacuated. Martin was holding his hand as they walked towards them. They'd just come back from taking the children for a walk in the grounds.

Emma was watching them too. She voiced her thoughts, 'I know I've said it before, but I still can't believe Dad was so little when he was sent by train, all on his own, to stay with strangers. I couldn't imagine sending Jared away and not knowing who he was staying with, and how he would be treated.'

Cassie stood fingering the little St. Christopher around her neck. She glanced across the hall. Her eyes settled on Evelyn and Scott. They were being interviewed. 'Dad was lucky.' She saw him pick Jared up. He was just making his way across the room when one of the BBC crew spotted Martin and called him over to join the interview. Jared happily sat on Grandad's knee as he took a seat next to Evelyn.

Cassie gazed around the room. The party had taken almost a week to arrange, and in that time, Evelyn had got to know Martin and Scott. She'd also spent time with Emma and her husband, and Martin's grandchildren. Cassie saw Evelyn talking to Jared before the camera rolled again. She recalled Evelyn saying that Jared took her back; he was the spitting image of his grandfather at that age.

The local radio station had already interviewed them, and word soon spread on social media of the couple who first met in World War Two at Fletchling Hall. They were interviewed by the local paper too, along with the CBC who were paying for all this. Now it was the BBC for the national news.

Who would have thought the story of an English girl and a Canadian Serviceman, who fell in love seventy years ago, might capture the public's imagination; but they had. The expectation was they would fall in love all over again. That was everyone's hope – including Cassie. It would be the perfect happy ending to a story spanning many decades.

Thinking of stories spanning decades, Cassie tried to get Ben out of her mind. It was over, and with him went any chance of her happy ending.

She turned her attention to the happy couple. Their story had brought the most unexpected news. An anonymous benefactor had stepped forward to save the hall from developers. It meant the future of Fletchling hall, along with the residents, was secure. Evelyn wouldn't have to leave her home, the place where they first met. It also meant they could, if they wanted to, spend the rest of their lives here together.

Cassie smiled. After all these years, wouldn't it be a lovely thought if they chose to live out their twilight years in the place where their love story began?

Emma took another glass of punch from Don, and turned to Cassie. 'So, who do you think stepped in to save Fletchling Hall? Any ideas about who the anonymous benefactor could be?'

Cassie grinned. Her sister was at it again, sniffing out another story. 'Honestly, I wish I knew, but I have no idea.' Emma's disappointment soon gave way to excitement. 'Oh look, people are arriving!'

Cassie turned to see the first arrivals step into the hall. She imagined Emma was pleased they had arrived in fancy dress. Even the women laying out the party food had dressed as forties housewives. 'It's Phyllis and her husband, and Jill and her daughter,' Cassie exclaimed. For a moment she didn't recognise them; she was so used to seeing Phyllis wearing a no-nonsense black skirt and white shirt at work, and Jill in her plain health care assistant uniform.

Phyllis was also dressed as a housewife from that era, whereas her husband chose to come as a sergeant major in the British Army. He made them laugh when Emma's eldest, John, ran up to him and asked if he was carrying a gun. Phyllis' husband saluted before showing John the fake gun and popping his helmet on the boy's head.

Jill was dressed in a WAAF uniform, like Emma, but her daughter was in work overalls, the kind women wore who worked in munition factories in the war.

'Oh, this is such fun,' said Emma.

Cassie thought so too. It was lovely to see people joining in the spirit of the party. Olivia and Randall were already here, standing over to one side, both with a glass of punch that Don had brought over to them as soon as they walked down the stairs. He'd quickly retreated, realising three was a crowd.

Olivia was also dressed as a land girl. Cassie felt she pulled it off much better, although Olivia disagreed. Randall had come in an Australian army uniform from that era, Khaki in colour with a matching beret. Cassie was impressed he got hold of his outfit at such short notice. She noticed the two of them deep in conversation. She caught Randall brushing a wisp of hair out of Olivia's eyes. It was inevitable those two would get together, she mused.

Her eyes drifted to Bertie dressed in a blue ill-fitting 1940s pin-striped suit. He'd picked up a paper party plate and was following the women as they laid out the buffet, helping himself to the food. Iris, wearing an evening gown, was sitting on the other side of the door in an easy chair, having a doze.

The health care assistants, who worked nights looking after Ruby, had also arrived, bringing Ruby along. Apart from the major holiday occasions like Easter, Christmas and the New Year, Ruby rarely got together with the other residents. Cassie could tell she was excited to be here. Not to be left out, Ruby was dressed in an outfit befitting the occasion. It was a uniform worn by women who were code breakers at Bletchley Park. Devon had told her mum all about the other resident she visited, and the work Evelyn used to do in the war.

Cassie glanced around the room. That accounted for everyone who lived and worked at the hall. She felt something brush her feet. Well, almost everyone. 'There you are.' Cassie got a loud *meow* in response. 'Where have you been hiding?'

Emma spotted Tabitha too. 'Hello, sweetie.' She had been introduced to the newest member of staff when they had first met Evelyn. Since Cassie left, vacating Gatekeepers Cottage where Tabitha used to sleep, she had made Evelyn's apartment home. The cat spent a lot of time snoozing on Evelyn's lap in between doing her rounds.

Emma wasn't the only one who spotted Tabitha. Eliza came running up to her mum. 'Can I stroke the cat, Mummy?'

Emma looked at Cassie. 'Is that okay?'

Cassie thought, why are you asking me?

Emma read her mind. She looked down at the cat circling Cassie's legs. Tabitha even jumped up, her two front paws clawing Cassie's trouser-leg, angling to be picked up.

Cassie picked her up. The cat lifted her head and rubbed up against Cassie's chin, purring loudly.

'Someone missed you,' observed Emma.

Cassie's thoughts turned to Ben. Despite Devon's efforts at convincing Cassie that her dad missed her dreadfully while she was gone, his reaction when he saw her at Devon's birthday party a few days ago said otherwise.

Cassie gave Tabitha a kiss on the top of the head and placed the little fluff-ball into Eliza's outstretched arms. Tabitha happily let Eliza cradle her like a baby. 'Can I have a kitten, Mummy?'

Emma turned to her sister, wide-eyed. 'Now, look what you and Tabitha have done. I will never hear the end of it – will I?'

'Oh, please, please, Mummy,' said Eliza as she sat down crossed-legged on the floor and stroked the cat on her lap. She got a loud, continuous purr in return.

Don overheard his daughter as he came over again with a glass of punch for Cassie. 'What's she after?'

Emma rolled her eyes. 'What do you think?'

They both cast their gaze down at Eliza with Tabitha.

Cassie caught Don looking adoringly at the cat. 'You know, I've always loved cats.'

Emma looked at her husband in surprise. 'I didn't know that.'

The expression on his face suggested he didn't mean to say that. 'We agreed no pets, so…' he trailed off.

Emma eyed her husband. 'I thought that's what you wanted?'

Don frowned. 'No, I thought that's what *you* wanted.'

They both stared at Tabitha.

Cassie glanced at the cat and smiled to herself; Tabitha couldn't have looked cuter if she tried. Something Phyllis said to Devon came to mind when the teenager first encountered Tabitha, *she has ways of making you talk.*

Tabitha was at it again, eliciting secrets, making people say things they didn't intend to. Cassie saw her sister and Don exchange a smile and guessed Eliza was going to get her kitten after all.

Cassie turned her attention to Evelyn and Scott. They had decided to marry. It was the shortest of courtships, but as they both said, at their age there was no time to waste. He couldn't get down on bended knee, but he had proposed to Evelyn, and she accepted.

Although they were celebrating the happy couple's engagement, this wasn't just a party for Evelyn and Scott. It was a reunion party too. Everyone who had a connection to the hall in the war years, whether directly or by descent was invited. It was a chance, like Evelyn and Scott, to meet again, get together and reminisce, find old friends and make new ones. Cassie couldn't wait to see who else might turn up.

59

Cassie noticed Evelyn's attention drawn to the new arrivals. She said she didn't want the party to be all about her. There were other stories waiting to be told too. Cassie's eyes drifted to her father. He was holding a hardback book in his hand.

After he met Evelyn again, although she knew nothing of his birth family, her dad decided it was time to finish his book. He'd saved his story until last, hoping that he would find his relatives. It was not to be. But he had found Evelyn, someone who knew him from childhood. It was more than he could have hoped for. Martin finished his book in the fortnight they had been in England. With the social media frenzy surrounding Evelyn and Scott, the publishers rushed through publication. They were also after publishing Evelyn's old diary too; such was the interest in a first-hand account of a young radio interceptor in WW2.

Cassie smiled when she saw her Dad plugging his book in front of the cameras. Good for him, she thought as she glanced around the room. He had travelled up and down Canada writing stories about people, like himself, who were transported from England during and after the war.

Now she hoped he would get a chance to meet some other

children who had been evacuated to the hall when he was living here. It's what Evelyn hoped for too. Like his grandchildren, Martin was wearing a wooden box around his neck containing a gas mask. Cassie glanced at the new arrivals, looking for those carrying a box. On social media, and in the news, word had spread about the reunion party at Fletchling Hall. Those children evacuated here during the war were to be given a box on arrival. That's how they would recognise a fellow evacuee at the party. Museums and personal collectors had provided them. A volunteer was standing at the door, handing them out.

'Oh, there's one!' Martin's eldest grandson pointed to a man who looked around his granddad's age, taking a box containing a gas mask.

Martin was sitting with the camera crew at the back of the entrance hall, near the stairs. They all turned to look at the new arrival as Don walked over welcoming him with a glass of punch.

Cassie was pleased her Dad met some other evacuees. It was a shame he finished writing his book. She bet he would love to have written about their experiences too. He'd have to write another one, thought Cassie. In fact, that was highly likely. The publisher had offered him a three-book deal.

More guests were arriving. Emma whispered to Cassie, 'I honestly didn't know if anyone would come.'

'Ah, the power of social media,' commented Cassie.

'Are people that age on social media?' Emma remarked.

'Dad is. And remember, most of them have grandchildren, so they probably learn a thing or two from them.'

'Hi, Cassie,'

'Oh, hi Devon.' Cassie did a double take. 'What are you doing here?' She didn't mean to sound so abrupt.

'Don't worry, Cassie, Dad isn't here, if that's what you're worried about.'

Cassie breathed a sigh of relief. She didn't want her personal issues, meaning Ben, turning up and spoiling Evelyn and her dad's party, like he did at Devon's birthday.

It was Evelyn's idea to host a little get-together for Devon at Gatekeepers Cottage. Cassie had been there, along with the other residents and staff at the hall, including Ruby. Jodie and her brother, James, were there. Scott came too. Then Ben turned up unannounced. He'd taken one look at her and fled. Cassie didn't want to think about that. Instead, she turned her thoughts to Evelyn.

Cassie recalled the expression on her face when Devon was opening her presents in the lounge; it must have taken Evelyn back to when she was sixteen, spending her birthday at the little cottage at the end of the drive. Evelyn bought Devon a book on Morse code, a blank leather-bound diary, and presented her with the beautiful pearls her mother gave her on her sixteenth birthday. Cassie could tell Devon had been overwhelmed.

In return, Devon had a few surprises of her own. She'd bought each of the residents a gift. When Devon stayed the night at the cottage, she'd found the memory books Cassie was working on. With Phyllis' permission she visited Bertie and Iris, continuing their memory books. She'd found a company online who printed the books, along with photos that Iris and Bertie provided, making them into a proper hardback book for their families as a keepsake.

What Devon gave to Ruby and Evelyn was a printed and bound memory book of her own life up to her sixteenth birthday. She had enlisted help from her dad and Gramps, who provided photos and memories for her book. It was something she could show Ruby, and she knew Evelyn, who looked at Devon as the grandchild she'd never had, was just as interested in her story.

Cassie had no idea Devon continued with the memory books. It brought a tear to her eye when she realised what Devon had done for the residents of the hall.

Devon had invited Cassie's family to her birthday. Although Cassie wanted them to see Gatekeepers Cottage, the last place Martin lived before he left the family for good, her father rightly said it was Devon's birthday; it was not the time for reminiscing about the past but looking to a young girl's future, turning sixteen. He didn't want her day to be about him. Cassie had gone to her sixteenth alone. Her father and the others visited the cottage separately, Martin spending some considerable time there with Evelyn and Scott.

Cassie smiled at Devon; if it wasn't for her none of this, her father and Scott meeting Evelyn again, would have been possible. She was the one who joined the dots and discovered Evelyn was hiding a secret – she was Rosie, the girl who wrote the diary. Devon had filled in the blanks in the diary, in Evelyn's life, and together with the St. Christopher it led them all back here, to a reunion party that would be a blast.

Cassie apologised. 'Sorry, I didn't mean to sound so abrupt, Devon. I'm so glad you made it.'

'Oh, I wouldn't miss Evelyn's party.'

Cassie knew she wouldn't. She looked Devon up and down. 'Hey, I love your outfit.'

'I'm a code-breaker from Bletchley, like my mum.'

'You look . . .'

'Different – I know. Everyone keeps telling me.' Devon

rolled her eyes. 'I saw Jodie before I left, and for a moment she didn't recognise me.'

Cassie wasn't surprised. It was the first time she hadn't seen her wearing black from head-to-toe. Her hair, which she dyed black, with a purple streak, was back to her natural blonde, and she was almost make-up free. With the heavy mascara, thick eyeliner, and pale foundation gone, she looked not only fresh-faced and younger, but the resemblance to the photo of her mother before the accident was uncanny.

Cassie glanced at the boy she recalled seeing at her birthday party. James was standing beside Devon, holding her hand. Jodie's brother looked adoringly at his girlfriend. By the looks of things, Cassie wasn't the only one who approved of the transformation.

'Where's Evelyn?' Devon asked.

'There they are.' Cassie pointed. Evelyn and Scott had moved away from the door into the back of the room at the suggestion of the camera crew when more people started arriving.

'Who's that being interviewed with Evelyn and Scott?'

'Remember the evacuee in the diary? Rosie called him Ted.'

Devon's eyes went wide. 'Really? That's him? I can't believe he's here.' She turned to Cassie. 'How did you find him?'

'It wasn't difficult.' Cassie showed Devon the pendant. 'He's my father.'

Devon's mouth dropped open. 'No way!'

'Yes, and thanks to you figuring out Evelyn's little ruse, keeping it to herself the whole time I was reading the diary that she is Rosie, he got to meet her again. I must introduce you when he's finished his interview.'

Cassie's sister stepped forward. 'I'm Emma.'

'Oh, wow. You're the reporter from CBC. I'd love to work in radio. Have you got any advice? Do you know that I repaired Evelyn's old wireless? It was the actual one that Evelyn used when she was a radio interceptor.'

'Really? Do tell…' said Emma, walking with Devon and James to get some food while they chatted.

Cassie rolled her eyes at her sister, sniffing out another interesting story. Don had taken the two older children over to a trestle table to get some party food. Cassie stood there sipping the punch and gazing around the crowded room. It wasn't just evacuees, but their wives, husbands, children and grandchildren who came too. Throwing open the doors of Fletchling Hall meant they all got a chance to see where their relatives stayed during the war.

Cassie was standing there watching more family groups arriving when she noticed a small group being barred entry by the volunteer on the door. She frowned. That wasn't right. They were supposed to be handing out gas masks and welcoming people, not turning them away.

Cassie put her drink down and made her way over. She saw the family – two men and a woman her dad's generation with an elderly lady – making their way towards a taxi. They caught the driver just in time. He was about to leave.

Cassie stood at the door and turned to the volunteer, a lady from the village. 'Why did you turn them away?'

'It's a reunion party. I was about to hand them one of them these, but they said they weren't evacuees here. When I asked what connection they had with the hall, none of them could say for sure. I don't know what they were doing here – do you?'

Cassie shook her head. She was about to return to the party, and her lovely glass of punch, when one of the men turned around as he got in the taxi and Cassie saw his face. Her eyes went wide. She ran down the steps. 'Wait!'

❖

At the other end of the entrance hall, Martin was just finishing his interview, and plugging his book, when he glanced toward the door. He spotted Cassie staring at him, with a look on her face he couldn't quite fathom. She was standing there beside two men and a woman around his generation. His gaze shifted to elderly lady standing between them leaning heavily on two walking sticks.

Martin lowered his book and rose from the chair.

The cameraman said in a hushed voice to his colleague, 'What's going on? The interview isn't finished.'

'I have no idea,' she replied.

His colleague, a seasoned reporter, caught the expression on Martin's face. She turned to Evelyn and Scott. 'We are going to leave you now. On behalf of the BBC we wish you the very best. Congratulations on your upcoming nuptials – and enjoy the party!' She whispered to the cameraman, 'Come on, let's follow Martin.'

'Why?'

She whispered back, 'Something is about to happen…'

The camera followed Martin at a discreet distance as he carried his grandchild across the crowded room towards the elderly lady.

The reporter, her voiced hushed, spoke to the camera, 'As you already know, Martin was evacuated here as a young child when he was not that much older than his grandchild, Jared. He was transported to Canada when Fletchling hall was requisitioned by the Government and Evelyn's family was forced to leave. Although he always assumed he was an orphan, it has since come to light that for many children that may not have been the case. He's been looking for his English family ever since.'

The moment the reporter set eyes on the two men standing with the elderly woman, she couldn't fail to see the family resemblance. She motioned for the camera to be turned on them.

Across the room, Martin's oldest grandson was busy scoffing some party food from a paper plate as he watched the cameraman following Grandpa across the room. He looked up at his Dad who was choosing some food, and said, 'Why is the cameraman filming that lady with the walking sticks?'

Don looked across to where his son was pointing. Martin was talking to the elderly lady. Behind them, Cassie was wiping her face, smudging makeup over her cheeks. Don stared at her. Was she crying? He turned to Emma who was also filling her plate with party food. 'What do you think that's about?'

Emma turned and saw people dancing in the centre of the room. The jitterbug was playing on the radio. 'It's the jitterbug.'

'I'm not talking about *that*. What's up with your sister?' He pointed over to where the group were standing, and the cameraman still filming for the evening news.

Emma and Cassie's eyes locked across the room. Cassie motioned with her head at the woman with the walking sticks.

Emma dropped her party plate.

Don looked at his wife. 'What's going on?' He searched her face. 'Are you…crying?'

'Mummy, are you all right?'

Emma, speechless, was staring at the group by the door.

Don turned and looked at the elderly lady, still wondering

what was going on. Then he saw her kiss little Jared and get out a handkerchief to wipe tears from her eyes. That's when the penny dropped. 'Sweet Jesus!' exclaimed Don.

Emma wiped her eyes dry with a tissue and grasped her two other children by the hand. 'Come on.'

'Where are we going?' they asked.

Emma smiled at her husband. 'We're going to meet my English grandmother.'

60

Cassie stepped outside for some fresh air. She stood on the stone steps and wiped her face with a tissue. She didn't even want to look in a mirror right now and imagined her face was a mess. Of all the times to be pregnant, with her hormones all over the place, she was sensitive enough as it was without what had just happened. Cassie glanced over her shoulder. She saw the children being introduced to their great-grandmother and their great-aunt and uncles – her father's two brothers and sister. There would be a lot of catching up to do. It would be an emotional journey for them all.

She still couldn't believe they were here. That was down to Martin's eldest brother. He had listened to the radio broadcast about Evelyn and Scott on the BBC and seen the chatter on social media. Like most people, he enjoyed hearing the heartfelt story of two young souls from the war years brought together by a cat called Tabitha and a long-forgotten diary languishing undisturbed for decades in the bowels of Fletching Hall.

What piqued his interest was learning about the pendant with the letter *E* etched on the back which had been given to a little boy, an evacuee from London, who lived in their household for a brief time before he was taken away. Evelyn never knew what became of him until now. They were due to be reunited, along with all the other evacuees who had passed through the doors of Fletchling Hall. It was all over social media.

The boy with the pendant was nicknamed Ted, but his real name was Martin. That really caught his attention. He could have been anybody, but equally he might be their Martin, his little brother. The boy would have been around his brother's age.

Cassie reached for the little pendant. When her Dad's brother read about the reunion, he'd bundled his elderly mother and siblings into a taxi, and they'd set off from London. It was a long shot, but however slim the possibility that Rosie's Ted might be his long-lost brother, Marty, they had to come.

Their mother had searched for him for decades. They all had. She'd always said if only she knew what happened to him then she could rest in peace. He wondered if that's what kept her going, living to a ripe old age, not giving up hope that one day, God willing, they would meet again. It was what he and his siblings wanted too. Especially him.

It was only recently that he'd come across an article about transported children. He had paid little attention in the past. He always thought those children were orphans until stories emerged which dispelled that myth. All these years he was convinced his brother was still alive, but he suspected they had been looking in the wrong place. He guessed Martin had been sent abroad to commonwealth countries along with thousands of others after the war without their parents' knowledge or consent.

Cassie sighed. It was a heart-breaking story. There was a reason he would never stop searching. They had all been evacuated together, the four of them. Being the eldest, he promised his mother he would look after them, especially little Marty. He had been holding his youngest brother's hand at the railway station. It was mayhem, children everywhere. Then it happened. As they stood on the crowded platform, Marty's hand slipped out of his, and his brother was gone. He never saw him again – until today.

❖

Cassie was about to step back into the hall, after she'd composed herself, when she heard a motorbike coming up the drive. She turned around as it came to a stop in front of the hall.

'Cassie!'

'Ben?' She watched him take off his helmet and climb off the motorbike. 'What are you doing here?'

'I saw you on television, on the local news.'

Great, that's all she needed. She asked him again, 'What are you doing here?'

He didn't have time to answer before the door flew open behind her and people started spilling out. Cassie turned around. 'Is the party over?'

Emma took her sister by the hand. 'Of course not. We're having a firework display.'

'Really?' She didn't remember her sister organising that. 'Oh, it wasn't me,' she said, reading Cassie's mind. She glanced around. 'I'm not sure who organised it. Perhaps it was a local company or that mysterious benefactor who bought the place. Anyway, I love fireworks. Let's sit on the wall.'

Cassie looked about her. Ben had disappeared. She frowned. It was just like before, at Devon's party when he took off. Why did he keep doing that? It was as though there was something he wanted to say. She couldn't imagine what.

There was a low wall running along the front of the property with a flower border. She walked down the steps and took a seat with her sister on the cushions spread along the wall. She saw her father with his brothers and sister. They were helping their mum down the steps. They all came over to sit together.

Cassie was just settling in, smiling at her Canadian and English family all waiting for the fireworks to start, when Ben reappeared. She frowned at him when he came over. 'What do you want?'

They all budged up so he could sit down next to her. 'I want to apologise about what I said. I had no right to blame you over what happened with Devon and her mother. Did you get your job back?'

Cassie didn't comment. Phyllis had already told her Ben had withdrawn the complaint.

'I've been a complete fool.' He leaned in and whispered in her ear, 'I love you, Cassie.'

Cassie swallowed.

He looked at her. 'Haven't you got anything to say?'

Cassie had plenty to say, she just couldn't do it here, in front of all these people.

Ben was about to say something else when the fireworks started. They sat watching them go off, one after another until there was a brief lull. Ben stood up, took a step back, and knelt in front of her.

Cassie's face coloured. 'What are you doing?' Everyone sitting on the wall was watching.

'What I should have done years ago.' He smiled at Cassie. 'Will you…'

Behind him, in front of the rose garden, some letter-shaped

fireworks attached to a six-foot-high trellis suddenly went off spelling out the words *marry me*.

Anyone who hadn't spotted Ben certainly noticed him now. He was still on bended knee in front of a lady dressed like a land girl, wild red hair escaping her headscarf and her face smudged with makeup.

A hushed silence enveloped the crowd.

Cassie sat there staring at Ben.

He smiled, and quipped, 'You can't say no in the presence of all these people, and the camera crews. And your family and friends.'

Ben produced a ring. Everyone clapped – apart from Cassie.

Cassie's brother-in-law looked at Ben and whispered to Emma, 'Who is he?'

Emma whispered back, 'I have no idea.'

Cassie took one look at the ring, burst into tears and fled.

Don was whispering in her ear again. 'What's the matter with her?'

'She's pregnant, Don.'

'She is? Wow. Where's Lars – does he know?'

Emma heaved a sigh. She hadn't filled him in with the details. 'It's not his.'

'Then who…?' His eyes drifted to the man looking like a plonker still on bended knee. So did Emma. 'Ah, I'm guessing she hasn't told him yet,' Don observed.

They watched him stand up and take after Cassie, following her through the rose garden and out of sight.

As people made their way back into the hall, Martin came up to Emma. 'I saw what happened. Do you know what's going on? Is Cassie all right?'

Don was about to put his foot right in it. Emma elbowed him in the ribs. 'Ow!'

'Everything's fine, Dad, Really it is. I think she's got a lot—'

'On her mind. Yes, she told me earlier.' His gaze drifted toward the rose garden. 'I expect it's got something to do with Ben.'

Emma looked at her Dad. 'Who's Ben?'

'The guy who just proposed to her.'

'You know him?'

Although Ben was older, Martin recognised him immediately. 'It was a long time ago. When Cassie and I made the trip back to England, she met a boy. I think he was her first boyfriend. They dated for a little while. She was heartbroken when they split up.'

Emma nodded her head. She knew about the boy, she just didn't realise Cassie had met him again. Now it all made sense.

'I guess Lars is out of the picture then,' commented Martin.

'Yes. He's met someone else. They're getting a divorce.'

'Good riddance. I never liked that selfish bas—'

'Dad!'

'Oh, sorry.' He looked at the grandkids staring at him. Martin hoped, whatever was going on, his eldest daughter patched things up with Ben. He knew Ben was the love of her life. She deserved every happiness. Although he was delighted for Evelyn and Scott, he didn't want to see his daughter wait that long to find true love again.

He glanced at his English family, making their way back into the hall. His older brother was hanging back, waiting for him.

Emma said to her dad, 'It's probably a stupid question, but how do you feel, after all these years, that you found them?'

He shook his head. 'I guess at first I thought of the word *closure*, but that makes it sound so final, as though I'm closing a chapter on my life. That's not true. I'm starting a new chapter.'

She smiled affectionately at her dad. Trust him to use a book analogy to describe the moment.

He thought about it some more. 'This will sound daft, but you know when you mislay something, and for the life of you, you cannot think where you left it? It bugs the hell out of you. Then the relief you experience when you find it and you don't have to go through your day wondering where it could be.'

Emma stared at her father.

'I've gone through my entire life with that horrible sensation in my gut that something is missing, and I desperately needed to find it. Now all I feel is utter relief, and a sense of peace.' He looked at his brother and smiled. 'I'm going back inside.'

'What about Cassie?'

Martin glanced toward the rose garden. He thought of the little St. Christopher that Cassie still wore around her neck and smiled. 'Things will turn out just fine. Come on, it's getting chilly out here. Let's join them inside.'

As they all trooped back inside, Don turned to Emma. 'Do you want me to search for Cassie?'

Emma shook her head. Although he meant well, she didn't want her husband to barge in on them in the middle of Cassie telling Ben her news. She linked her arm in her husband's and laid her head on his shoulder. Emma had always envied her sister, going through life with their Dad's St. Christopher. But, in hindsight, she realised she didn't need it. Perhaps that's why Dad gave it to Cassie because he knew his youngest daughter already had someone to guide her on her journey through life; they had been as thick as thieves since they were at nursery school.

He'd been there for her what felt like her whole life. And

he'd still be there when she was Evelyn's age. Don had always been her lucky St. Christopher.

Before Emma closed the door behind her, she glanced outside and saw the sun starting to go down. She could tell it would be a beautiful sunset. Emma turned to her husband and they exchanged a smile. This trip had been just what they needed; a break from routine to spend some time as a family. It had brought them closer together as a couple. They walked hand-in-hand back into the hall. She gazed at Don and hoped Cassie found the same happiness. It was the only thing that truly mattered.

61

'Ben?' She found him sitting on the bench by the old-fashioned cast-iron lamp looking miserable. It was the place he brought her to, with views across open fields and rolling farmland, when they'd been out together on his motorbike. Unlike that day, when the heavens opened and it rained buckets, as dusk approached, there wasn't a cloud in the sky.

Cassie had been walking around the gardens, trying to avoid him, when she realised he was no longer following her. That's when she went to find him. She knew where he'd be; their special place in the grounds of Fletchling Hall. She'd decided it was time to tell him why they couldn't marry. It would not be just the two of them walking hand-in-hand into the sunset. He'd have to go back to nappies and sleepless nights, and the terrible twos; years of raising another child when he'd just got through all that.

Cassie sighed so loudly Ben heard her. 'Oh, it's you,' he said flatly when he saw her. He was sitting there, turning the ring over in his hand. She walked over and sat down on the bench beside him. There was a long silence. She turned to him. 'I'm sorry I ruined the moment.'

'All you had to do was say yes. I realise I treated you appallingly, but I really thought you would forgive me. You still want to be with me – don't you?'

'It's not that simple.'

Ben turned to look at her. 'You've gone back to your husband, haven't you?' Devon told me you'd returned. I assumed it was over between you.'

'It is – he's gone.'

'Then what is it?'

When Cassie didn't answer immediately, he dropped his eyes to the floor. 'Oh. It's me. Dammit. I knew it. When I learned you were back, I had to come to Devon's party at the cottage to see you. I couldn't stay away. But when I saw you, I was so scared you wouldn't forgive me that I fled.' He sighed. 'After the party, when she got home, Devon convinced me you'd have me back. She said you knew what really happened about Ruby, and why I didn't take her to see her mother.' He said in a small voice. 'I shouldn't have listened to Devon.'

'Ben it's not you. I… I love you.'

He raised his eyes. 'You do?'

She nodded her head.

He searched her face. 'Then what is it?'

She took a deep breath. 'There's not just me to consider.'

'Devon is fine with this.' He couldn't get the words out quick enough. 'In the past, she's been a right—' Ben stopped himself. 'She's been difficult. Whenever I introduced someone new, she came between us. Not that there's been a lot of relationships or anything serious,' he added. 'But she knows this time it's different. I can't live without you, Cassie. I'd be lost without you.'

Cassie recalled the messages on Facebook from Devon

pleading for her to come back; she was so worried about her dad. Devon wanted her to come back too.

She sighed. 'It's not Devon.'

'Then what? Please tell me. I want to sort it out.'

'You can't sort this one out, Ben.'

Ben turned around and glanced at the house. He had an idea what this was about. 'Look, I'm really sorry about getting you fired. Can't you forgive me? Phyllis said she'd hire you again on the spot if you returned. She did give you your job back – didn't she?'

'Yes.'

He brightened. 'See, everything worked out perf—'

'It's the baby,' Cassie blurted.

'The baby?' Ben shook his head, confused. 'I don't understand…' And then he did. 'You're expecting?' He couldn't have looked more shocked if he tried.

Cassie caught his expression. 'Not something you imagined would happen at my age – huh?'

'You mean that one night we spent together in Rye…?

Cassie nodded, recalling that unforgettable day trip to the charming Sussex town culminating in an evening meal together, and a room, at the Mermaid Inn. They didn't intend to stay the night. They were taking things slow. It wasn't what either of them planned. And neither was this; she was just as surprised as he was that, at her age, she got pregnant so quickly.

If they had stayed together, if she could turn back the clock and be like other young couples, starting a family would be the best news. But they weren't young anymore. They were in their forties. No matter how much Ben thought he loved her, would he feel the same way at two in the morning when they were woken up by a baby? Cassie had already convinced herself he'd walk away. She glanced at him. He was very quiet.

She stood up. 'I better be going. I don't want to miss the rest of the party.'

She felt a hand reach for hers, stopping her in her tracks. Ben said, 'Where do you think you're going?'

When she turned around, he was kneeling in front of her once more. 'Let's try this again.'

She stared at him. 'Didn't you listen to what I just said?'

'Cassie, will do me the honour of becoming my wife?'

Cassie sat down on the bench in front of him and looked at the ring in his outstretched hand. 'But a baby, Ben, at our age. It means it won't be just the two of us.'

'You said that already.' Ben let her in on a secret. 'All these years, I wished we'd stayed together and Devon was our child.' He frowned. 'I should never have split up with you.' He got up and sat down next to Cassie. 'I made a right mess of things – didn't I.'

Cassie took his hand in hers. 'But if our lives hadn't played out that way, you wouldn't have Devon. Your daughter is amazing – like her Daddy.'

Ben turned to face Cassie. 'I want this child, Cassie. Our child. Nothing would make me happier – sleepless nights and all.' He held up the ring. 'So, what do you say?' he said in earnest. 'I want us to be together, you, me, the baby.'

'And Devon,' Cassie added.

'Yes, and Devon.'

'And your father…'

Ben hesitated. He hadn't considered that. Although his father no longer had a chip on his shoulder about Cassie because she was Canadian, would she really want to start married life living under the same roof as her father-in-law?

Cassie nudged his arm. 'I'm only joking about your dad. I can just imagine another grandchild sitting with Grandpa in The Radio Shack fascinated by those old radios.'

Ben frowned. 'That's what I'm afraid of.'

Cassie knew what that frown was about. 'If you're worried about Devon, she will be okay.' She'd already told her about the baby. It had been her birthday gift to Devon, hoping that although it wasn't what she expected, and Cassie wasn't with her dad, Devon would want to be part of her brother or sister's life. Although Devon had to promise to keep it to herself until Cassie told Ben, she could tell it had made her even more resolved to get them back together. Cassie was relieved she had been so happy to hear the news. In some ways, she felt more nervous telling Devon than Ben.

'He never liked the modern property I built on the land in place of his bungalow that used to be there,' Ben continued.

Although Cassie was impressed with Ben's self-build, it wasn't really her cup of tea either, but she didn't want to hurt his feelings.

'I could sell the house and give him a share to buy his own property.'

'But you love that house – don't you?'

Ben shrugged. 'Is that what you think? To be honest, I built it to impress potential clients for my business.'

'Really?' Cassie looked at him in surprise. 'But your dad's got the workshop in the garden and he's lived there since Devon was small. That wouldn't be fair to ask him to leave.'

Cassie had an idea. 'Maybe, when Devon goes to college, you

and I could move out, find a little place of our own.' Out of nowhere, Gatekeepers Cottage came to mind. She did love that cottage. It made Cassie wonder who the mysterious benefactor was who saved the hall from the developers. Would they be prepared to sell the cottage?

Ben shook his head. 'Let's forget about the details right now. What's important is that you and I – and the baby – are together.'

Cassie looked at him. 'You really want this?'

'You bet I do.' He put an arm around her shoulders and pulled her close. 'So, do you want this ring – or what?'

'Well, that's romantic,' Cassie said, smiling.

'Don't tell me I have to propose again! How many times has a guy got to get down on his knees to prove to the woman he loves that he wants to marry—' Ben's question was answered by a kiss. When she drew back, he said, 'Was that a yes?'

She laughed. 'Oh, yes.'

'We forgot something.' He held up the ring. 'We seem to be going about all this the wrong way.'

Cassie smiled. It was the story of their lives, going about things the wrong way; meeting later in life, having a family. But who made up the rules when it came to what was the right time to meet your soul mate and live your life to the fullest? Evelyn and Scott were an inspiration for never giving up on love, on life.

Cassie took the ring, gave him her glass, and slipped the ring on her finger. She sat there admiring it. 'It's perfect, Ben.'

He looked at her expectantly.

She leaned in and whispered, 'Yes, Ben, I will marry you,' and kissed him again. Cassie added, 'Sorry about…' She pointed up at the house. 'You went to all that effort with the ring and the fireworks. That was you, wasn't it, the whole firework display?'

'Yes, it was. I really thought it would go according to plan. It was a tad humiliating.'

'Just a tad?'

They both laughed. Ben looked at the ring. 'Ah, well at least we'll have a great story to tell the kids.'

Did he just say kids, plural? Cassie beamed at him. What a lovely idea. They were already making memories to share with their children. Cassie fell silent.

'What are you thinking?'

'About Evelyn and Scott,' Cassie replied. It brought tears to her eyes that, after all these years, they had met again in the sunset of their lives. Cassie looked to the horizon. The sun was setting. 'I never noticed before how amazing sunsets can be.'

Ben suddenly produced an empty glass from nowhere and handed it to her.

'What's this?' Only then did she notice another glass and a bottle of something in an ice bucket by his feet. She looked at him in surprise. 'You planned this too – didn't you?'

He nodded. 'I thought that after I proposed, we'd come and sit on this bench under the old street lamp with a bottle of bubbly and toast our new life together.'

Cassie looked at the glass. 'You realise I can't drink now, right?'

'Yes, this hasn't gone exactly to plan either.'

Cassie took the empty glass. 'Now, all I need is some of that lovely punch.'

Ben grinned. 'I'll be right back.' Five minutes later, he reappeared with the punch bowl. It still had the ladle inside.

'Ben! I can't believe you took it.'

'Anything for you, my love.'

Cassie laughed.

'Here…' He took the glass out of her hand and ladled in some punch. Ben then poured himself some champagne.

Cassie sat there recalling the firework display and what her sister said about not knowing who organised it. That brought to mind the hall and the anonymous benefactor. She turned to Ben. 'Are you him?'

He looked at her. 'Him – who?'

'The anonymous benefactor who saved the hall?'

Ben almost choked on his champagne. 'Now, when I said anything for you my love, I'm afraid there are limits.'

Cassie stared at him. 'So, you know about the hall – that it has been saved from developers?'

'Yes, but I'm sworn to secrecy.'

'You're sworn to secrecy?' Cassie sat up. 'Who is it? Tell me…'

Ben shook his head. 'I really can't.'

'What?' Cassie fiddled with the ring, working it down her finger.

Ben noticed. 'You wouldn't!' he said, watching her, wide-eyed.

Cassie was only teasing, but she wanted to know. 'Who is it? I promise it will stay between you and me.'

Ben exhaled in relief when he realised Cassie wasn't being serious about giving him back the ring. 'Look, Devon swore me to secrecy.'

'Devon? Devon knows?'

'She's the one who told me.'

Now Cassie was really intrigued. 'How did Devon find out who—?'

'It's Evelyn.'

'Evelyn? She bought Fletchling Hall?'

'Not exactly, you see she didn't need to buy it?'

'I don't understand...?'

'You don't need to purchase something you already own.'

'Huh?'

'Evelyn hasn't told you the whole story. According to Devon, Evelyn vowed many years ago, when her family were forced to leave the family home, that one day she would return and buy Fletchling Hall back.'

Cassie gaped at him.

'So, that's what she did when she retired. Apparently, she moved in, hoping that one day Scott would return. The trouble was she couldn't afford to run the place, so she needed...'

'Other people to live there too.' Cassie started to laugh. 'Her Ladyship.' Now she understood. At first, Evelyn must have abhorred having other people living in her house.

Ben smiled. 'Yes, Devon told me what people called her behind her back. Little did they know.' His smile faltered. 'Sadly, as the years passed by and Scott didn't return...' he trailed off.

Cassie nodded, getting the picture. 'She decided to sell up and leave. But now he's back, I don't understand why Evelyn wants to keep it a secret.'

Ben had an idea. 'She doesn't want her friends to treat her differently if they found out she owns the place.'

'Her friends?'

'Yes, all the people at the hall. I'm sure Evelyn would have told you in time.'

Cassie smiled when something Evelyn once said came to mind. *When you know the end of your story, I'll tell you mine.*

'I know you're good friends,' Ben remarked.

'We are?'

'Yes, that's what Devon told me Evelyn said about you.'

Cassie counted Evelyn as a wonderful friend. She was so happy to discover the feeling was mutual.

Cassie shuffled along the bench until her leg touched his. She felt his arm around her shoulders. He pulled her close. She looked up at the sky. 'Isn't the sunset simply amazing? Do you think Evelyn and Scott ever sat on this bench and watched the sun go down?'

Ben shrugged. 'I don't know. We could ask them – if you like?'

'Not right now.' Cassie could hear music coming from the party up at the house. She smiled when she recognised the song. She turned to Ben. 'Do you hear that?'

He smiled in answer to her question. It was Vera Lynn on the radio singing *We'll Meet Again.* They sat holding hands listening to the song as they watched the sunset, both visualising tomorrow and the dawn of a new life – together.

Out of the corner of her eye, Cassie spotted Tabitha sitting on the patio beside the bench watching the sunset too. She smiled at her cat and squeezed Ben's hand. Whatever the future had in store, this was home.

Dear Reader

If you enjoyed We'll Meet Again I would be extremely grateful if you'd leave a brief review on Amazon.

For further details about the author and her novels visit the author's website:

www.elisedarcy.com

Please feel free to add your email to the mailing list for updates on forthcoming book releases in the author's e-newsletter.

Also by Elise Darcy

The Living Apart Together Series

Living Apart Together

It Takes 2 to Tango

Dear John

Love on the Rooftop

Standalone Novels

Lola & The Man

A Mallorcan Affair

The Villa in Sicily